Chris Bunch was part of the first troop commitment into Vietnam. Both Ranger and airborne-qualified, he served as a patrol commander and a combat correspondent for *Stars and Stripes*. Later, he edited outlaw motorcycle magazines and wrote for everything from the underground press to *Look* magazine, *Rolling Stone* and prime-time television. He is now a full-time novelist.

By Chris Bunch

THE SEER KING
THE DEMON KING
THE WARRIOR KING

THE EMPIRE STONE

CHRIS BUNCH

THE
WARRIOR
KING

An *Orbit* Book

First published in Great Britain by Orbit 1999
This edition published by Orbit 2000

Copyright © 1999 by Chris Bunch

The moral right of the author has been asserted.

A CIP catalogue record for this book
is available from the British Library.

ISBN 1 85723 951 2

Typeset in Galliard by M Rules
Printed and bound in Great Britain by
Mackays of Chatham plc

Orbit
A Division of
Little, Brown and Company (UK)
Brettenham House
Lancaster Place
London WC2E 7EN

The clean parts are for
Judine
And the rest is for
Terry

The G

The Outer Islands

Island of Damastes's e

Palmeras

HERMONASSA   Kaldi

TICAO   THE KINGDOM

N

The Cimabuan
district of Belya   •Megiddo   Cicogna

DARFUR
CIMABUE
•Atikim   Khurram

TAGIL   ISFAHAN

Cambiaso

KHOH   NOWRA
BALA
HISSAR   CHALT   UREY
GYANTSE   •Mehul   Renan
SHAKI   Sulem
The Border States Urshi Hi
EBISSA   KAIT   •Sa

The Wild Country   Smugglers
Route

Unknown

Latiane River

Paestum

AMUR

at Ocean

s
one
VARAN

NUMANTIA

A
tto
River
nida
WAKHUR
tara HAILU
rn
n

BONVALET

DUMYAT   ROVA

ds   NINGSIA

•Zante   OSSETIA   Unknown

DEVELOPING
FARMLAND

•Penda
Suebi   *Ocean*

THE SUMMONS

The unexpected ships arrived an hour before dusk. We'd seen them sailing toward my island prison for some hours and wondered—no one was allowed to sail in these waters without government permission. There were three of them, one a large merchantman, the other two fast pirate chasers, low sleek galleys.

My warders scurried to their fighting stations. They were frightened the emperor, now revealed to be still alive, might be trying to rescue me, the last of his bloody-handed tribunes who used sword and fire to take and hold the throne of Numantia.

But the emperor grew arrogant, thought himself greater than the death-goddess Saionji, and invaded the kingdom of Maisir to our south.

Our army was destroyed, Numantia invaded by the Maisirians, and I myself hurled Tenedos from his throne when he threatened to send a nightmare demon against first the invaders, then against his rebelling countrymen and our capital of Nicias.

Tenedos, like I, had been sent into island exile. No doubt Bairan, King of the Maisirians, hoped we'd be quietly garroted or have a convenient fall from a battlement when matters had calmed.

Indeed, Tenedos had been reported dead, and I'd been waiting for my own assassin, not caring, for all the world was a bloody shatter to me.

But then the world had spun about us all: Tenedos had faked his death, gotten to the mainland, and was now building his army, ready to take back his throne from Bairan's puppets who ruled in Nicias.

But as the ships approached the tiny port below my fortress prison, they made certain signals, and my jailers relaxed. The ships were from Nicias, sent by the Grand Council.

I, on the other hand, felt a whisper of fear, in spite of my supposed readiness to return to the Wheel, to be judged by Saionji and sent forth to a lesser life as punishment for the thousands I'd led to their deaths as First Tribune Damastes á Cimabue, Baron Damastes of Ghazi.

Not that I had escaped the gods' raking in this life. My wife, now deceased—Marán, Countess Agramónte—had divorced me after our mutual love, Amiel Kalvedon, was murdered by the Tovieti cultists; and later, in Maisir, Alegria, my beautiful Dalriada, died in the long retreat from the Maisirian capital of Jarrah.

I licked dry lips and then had the intelligence to laugh aloud—I'd spent all these times mewling for oblivion like a coward instead of a warrior, and now it portended, and I was terrified. I found resolve and determined to die well, die proudly.

I returned to my spacious quarters, only a cell because of the barred windows overlooking the sea and the double doors with a guarded anteroom between them, and considered matters. I could either stand nobly and calmly at the moment of death as heroes were supposed to or else go down fighting. I remembered an execution in Maisir, when Captain Athelny Lasta, instead of dying quietly, killed the executioner and eight others before returning to the Wheel.

I thought of him and of the various trinkets I'd procured over the long times of imprisonment and laughed once more. For what purpose does a man build weapons if he's seeking a nice, immediate death?

I had a pilfered table knife I'd laboriously ground to an edge against the stones in my cell and a knob of iron such as I'd used to kill the Landgrave Malebranche, far away and long ago in Kallio. I also had that most important of all weapons—four gold coins and three silver ones I'd managed to acquire from making careful wagers with the guards, first with coppers, then escalating my bets. I put these items in various convenient places about my person, then waited.

Two guards summoned me to the warden, Jelap. He was a decent sort, a bumbling old domina who'd spent fifty years under the colors. This was his last assignment before retirement. I often wondered what he thought of this assignment—four hundred guards and an enormous stone fortress with but one prisoner.

There were three men waiting in his office, all wearing a strange uniform, a rather bilious shade of gray with red facings I realized must be that of the Peace Guardians, the largest military force King Bairan had allowed Numantia. They were mockingly organized into corps as my army had been, though each corps numbered only about 150 men, led by the traitorous Tribune Herne, its ranks filled with thugs so in love with force they didn't mind using it on their own countrymen.

The three were Shamb Catalca and Pydnas Bosham and Huda. It said all there was to say about the Guardians that their ranks, the equivalent of our captain and legate, were the same as the Maisirian Army. These three looked as if they would find a back-alley thieves' den more comfortable than an officer's mess.

I expected anything from a murderous attack to a beating to sneering contempt. What I received was formal respect, which I found a bit amusing. All three were behaving as they thought noblemen should, very much on their best, if unfamiliar, manners.

"We have orders," Catalca said formally, "to convey you to Nicias, to the Grand Council, where the Lords Scopas and Barthou would be pleased to receive you."

Pleased? I was hard-pressed not to show surprise. I glanced at Domina Jelap to see if I could read a clue in his face, saw nothing but stiff propriety, and, just possibly, distaste at being a Numantian officer now forced to deal with turncoats.

I could be as circumspect as they. I bowed. "Having no choice in the matter, but appreciating the manner in which your orders are presented, I shall be ready to leave within the hour."

"Good," Catalca said. "For we're under orders to make the greatest haste. This matter is of grave import."

"May I ask what the lords desire of me?"

The uglier of the two junior officers growled. Catalca glanced at him, and he was silent.

"We were not taken into their lordships' confidence," he said.

"Then let me return to my cell and collect my belongings."

"Very well. Pydna Huda will accompany you."

"There is no need for that," Domina Jelap said. "If we've guarded Tribune Damastes for over two years—"

"The prisoner has no rank," Catalca said harshly. "His titles were stripped from him long ago."

"I stand corrected," Jelap said. "We merely used the old formalities."

"Those days are real dead," Bosham said, repressing a sneer. "Best forgotten about entirely."

Jelap inclined his head. "While the prisoner is securing his property," he said, "might I at least offer you a bit of a meal and . . . ," he eyed the three carefully, " . . . some very strong mulled wine? It's been a grim day; more grim, I fancy, out there on the water."

"Now that's an excellent suggestion," Catalca said. He nodded to my two guards. "Bring him back here when he's got whatever he needs. Mind you, prisoner, your goods'll be well searched, so don't attempt any tricks."

"I have no tricks to attempt," I said, looking bland, and went out.

It took only a few minutes to gather my belongings. They said they planned to search me thoroughly, but by now I'd gained a few prisoner's tricks. The knife was in the sole of my boot, the small slug of iron in plain sight as one handle of my threadbare case. I considered that case and the worn cloak that lay over it and remembered when I had estates, castles, mansions, libraries, enough clothes to outfit a regiment. Life itself proves the Wheel's existence, with its own constant turning.

As we went back to Jelap's office, one warder, a Sergeant Perak, stopped me. The other went on a few steps, then stopped, out of earshot. Perak had always been a bit sympathetic and would give me forbidden news from Numantia. •

"Be careful, sir. One of the boat's crew said th' emperor's taken two provinces away from the scum Councilors already. Those three pig-futterers're scared of you, as I suspect th' Maisirian worshipers they serve are as well. Scared men do desperate things."

"Thank you, Sergeant. I'm always careful." An odd question came: "When I leave, what'll happen to this fortress? And you and the other soldiers?"

"Not to worry," he said, with a twisted grin. "These're rough times, and a prison that can't be gotten out of's always useful. Somebody else'll be here before long." He glanced up and down the corridor, made sure the other warder was out of hearing. "With any luck, it'll be those bum-kissers Barthou and Scopas."

"Careful, Sergeant. They rule Numantia."

"The hells they do," he said vehemently. "Only with the swords of the dogpiss Guardians and the Maisirians behind them. Things change fast, and where they sit can change faster'n most."

"So who do you want to rule? The emperor again?"

Perak hesitated. "There might be worse," he said. "Barthou and Scopas were part of the Rule of Ten fools, and from what I read in the broadsides these days, haven't learned anything since."

"The emperor almost destroyed Numantia," I told him.

"Maybe so," Perak said quietly. "But there's enough who'd like to see him try th' throne again, and this time make it right."

I didn't argue, and we went on to Jelap's office. They'd done less eating than drinking, and all three were a bit drink-hammered. Jelap must've been encouraging them by example, for his nose was a little red, and his speech the tiniest bit blurred.

"Are we ready?" Catalca said.

"At your command," I said.

"Then let's go," he said, draining his glass. "I know little of the ocean, but I do know it's best to be away from the land when night comes. Follow us, prisoner, and don't try to escape."

I almost laughed. Escape? From this rock in midocean? If possible, I would've done that a year or more ago. But I looked properly obedient and picked up my duffle. They made no effort to make the promised search.

As we went down the dock to the boat Sergeant Perak came close, and his hand snaked out and passed me something. It was a sheathed dagger. I slid it into my case, looked at him. His face was blank, thinking only of duty.

We got into the boat, and it began pulling away. I turned back for one last look at the prison I would never see again and witnessed something most odd.

The warders were drawn up, on the fortress battlements or along the path to the dock, Domina Jelap at their head. All were at rigid salute.

For whom?

Certainly not the Guardians.

I refused to believe it was for me, the last vestige of Tenedos's tyranny.

But I still got to my feet, braced myself against an oarsman, and returned their salute, clapping my hand against my shoulder.

Then I turned away to the waiting ship and what might lie ahead in Nicias.

CITY OF DECEIT

I kept trying to catch the future's drift as we sailed toward the Latane River and Nicias. I wasn't chained nor closely guarded, which I took as a good sign, although where I could've gone save overboard to my death I couldn't imagine. Catalca said if there was any attempt at rescue, he was under orders to kill me immediately.

I was given the first mate's quarters, which were fairly spacious. I spent happy hours just staring out the port or on deck, glorying in being able to look for leagues without seeing stone walls.

The ship's crew stayed well away from all of us and refused to be drawn into conversation.

The dagger Perak had given me was a nastily lethal item—a handspan long, about two inches wide at the hilt, both edges razor-sharp. Its hilt and pommel were the plainest of metal, the grip of a black hardwood. The weapon's purpose was clear. I devised a hiding place for it—a thin cord knotted around my loins, the sheath hanging in front of my cock. I'd seen how men are always uncomfortable searching around someone's genitals. I had to be a bit careful sitting down, for fear of being suddenly qualified for singing in upper registers instead of warfare, but I felt far better about everything, as a warrior always does when armed.

After four days we saw land, the low green jungled islets of the Delta, and I smelt the hot, tropic welcome of my homeland.

The coastal watch station at the end of the channel was unmanned, run-down, and the buoys marking the channel had gone unpainted. I saw few seagoing ships either coming up or going down channel, as well.

A day upriver we passed a manned heliograph station, and signals went back and forth, messaging our arrival to Nicias.

There was a scattering of fishing boats outside the channel, bringing up succulent green Delta crabs. One galley rowed alongside a boat and came back with a deck-ful, some of which were hoisted aboard to be steamed for our dinner.

The fishing boats were manned by young men, actually boys, a scattering of young women among them. Since I knew little of the Delta customs, I asked a seaman if this was customary, and if so, where did the menfolk work?

He stared at me as if I were a prime idiot, looked about to make sure he wasn't being seen talking to the disgraced prisoner, and said, "Their menfolk're fertilizer, in places like Maisir, Cambiaso, Kait . . . or'd you dis'member there was a war not so long ago?"

Chastened, I thanked him, went back to the rail. I noted the fishermen's expressions were hardly friendly, and one spat as we passed. I chanced being called another fool by asking Huda what price crabs brought these days?

"Hells if'n I know," he said. "You don't think Guardians *pay*, now, do you?" It was, indeed, a foolish question. A man with a sword only pays when he, or his officers, is honorable.

I saw Nicias when we were some distance away, by the glow in the night sky as if it were on fire. The city is lit by jets of natural gas seeping from underground deposits, and legend has it the day the City of Lights falls into darkness, Numantia's doom is at hand.

We anchored below the city that afternoon, so I guessed the Council had ordered me brought into Nicias under cover of darkness. Gods, what could they have to fear, I wondered. Wasn't I the cursed first tribune, hated almost as much as the emperor? Or had things changed?

We raised anchor when the dogwatch came on, and sailed on, landing at Nicias's docks near dawn. A mounted unit of Guardians was waiting, escorting four of the black, tiny-windowed ambulances Nicias's warders used to transport prisoners.

"You'll go in one," Catalca said, "and if anyone's waiting to lift you, they'll not know which one."

I marveled at the subtlety of his plan, wondered if he knew enough not to eat soup with a fork, and entered the indicated carriage.

I crouched at the tiny window as we clattered through the morning streets. The City of Lights had always bragged it never slept, but things had changed, for there were few abroad except the lamplighters extinguishing the gas jets, some few drunks, and early risers heading for their jobs. Even the drunks turned away when they saw the Guardians' uniforms—Herne's Harriers had exactly the reputation I thought.

Nicias was gray, tired, dirty, when once it'd been a flashing metropolis of light and color. The war . . . the occupation by Maisir . . . the looting of Numantia's treasuries by King Bairan . . . and above all the grinding knowledge of utter defeat had changed this capital I loved so well.

Entire blocks looked abandoned, and once-prosperous districts were now slums.

We passed brick barracks I remembered well, once the home of the Golden Helms, the useless parade-ground force I'd once commanded. They were shabby, lawns unmowed, the whitewash on the tree trunks peeling, falling away, stone walks cracking. There were lines strung from windows holding drying laundry, some of it women's dresses, then, a sign in front of the barracks, Maisir's yellow superimposed on Numantia's blue, a mailed fist over it, and a slogan: GUARD WELL THE PEACE.

I'd hardly expected Nicias to be as I left it, but the reality struck hard, and I turned away until the ambulance stopped. The door opened, and there were half a hundred Guardians, weapons ready. I got out, looked around.

"So this is to be my new prison?"

"It's not necessarily a prison," Catalca said. "Just a place where you'll be secure until the lords finish with you." He smiled, not pleasantly.

I smiled back, and was amused, not by Catalca, but by my new jail, one which I'd created for other purposes. It was the four-story tower with an interior keep I'd chosen for the Seer Tenedos's safety, back during the Tovieti rising, and I'd also taken shelter there with my bride-to-be Marán. Later it became the emperor's sorcerous retreat, where he called up the demons that encouraged him to begin the disastrous war with Maisir.

Again I noted the turning of a wheel . . .

I was escorted to my quarters on the top floor of the outer tower—the same ones the emperor had used. I was told there were three hundred Peace Guardians assigned to this tower, their sole duty to keep me imprisoned.

Here I was to wait until summoned.

Of course, Barthou and Scopas being who they were, I waited for two full weeks on this matter of "grave import." But this was all to the good, for I was able to suborn one of my jailers, a pompous fool named Dubats, one of those who knows everything and must prove it constantly, and got a rough idea of events in Numantia.

The emperor, after rising from the dead, still unexplained as mummery or horrid fact, had left Palmeras for Hermonassa State, which cast off the Grand Council's rule and vowed fealty to him. The two corps of Peace Guardians sent to deal with him changed sides and became the nucleus, such as it was, of his new army.

Tenedos, the warder told me, had moved south along the western coast of Numantia, gathering strength as he did. Ticao had been the second state to declare for him. Unsure of what I myself felt in a world of bad choices, I didn't know if I was proud or ashamed that my home state of Cimabue remained loyal to the puppet government, as had its coastal neighbor of Darkot. But Bala Hissar, Khoh, and Gyantse had gone for Tenedos, as had, on our eastern borders, Bonvalet and Varan.

The government still held the center of Numantia, as well as the vital Latane River, the primary navigational route north and south. Only Isfahan, directly south of the main province of Dara, wavered, and it'd been quickly pacified by Peace Guardians. Kallio, the other great state, which had risen first against the Rule of Ten, then continued its subversion against the emperor, naturally stood firm against him, as did Urey, which had been razed by first our own army in its retreat from Numantia, then, more savagely, by the oncoming Maisirians. The Ureyans wanted no more of war, on any side, in any shape.

The City of Lights had always been the first to overreact to any emergency, and so, the warder went on, they were planning barricades to hold back the emperor, plus which they worried that King Bairan would once more invade and this time destroy Numantia as he'd threatened, and of course demons would soon be sent by the arch-wizard Tenedos to turn Nicias into a wasteland.

This last was not unlikely, for Tenedos had planned on doing just that until I'd struck him down and destroyed the spell he was casting, before leading the last of the army's cavalry in a mad charge against Bairan's army as if I were a manifestation of Saionji herself.

But as yet, Dubats said, nothing much had really happened, other than rumors.

I asked about the Tovieti, the cult Tenedos and I had brought down once, only to see it arise in a different form, then vanish with our destruction. He'd heard nothing of the stranglers with the yellow cord, which was one bit of good news.

Knowing as much as anyone, there was nothing for me to do but wait . . . and spend hour after hour in muscle-wrenching exercise; for whatever was to come, I must be ready.

One other thing occupied my time. I'd originally found this tower for the emperor and made certain it was impossible for a Tovieti assassin to enter. Now I considered it from a very different perspective—how to get out. I'm afraid that I now thought little of my previous abilities, for I found three possible escape routes, two of which could also be used to enter the building. I'd gained new talents in Maisirian and Numantian prisons. It also helped that the Guardians' commander was an orderly, scheduled man, so the guards were fed, marched, trained, and checked with the regularity of a metronome.

But my scheming was purely to keep my mind occupied, for where would I go once I got beyond the tower's walls and guards? No one would shelter me, and I thought most would see my unfortunately quite memorable face and scream for the warders . . . or attack me with whatever weapons were at hand. If I had to die, I'd rather die by the clean ax blade or noose than be ripped apart by a mob.

Guards came early one morning, and once more I entered one of the ambulances and was taken to the Grand Palace, once the Rule of Ten's, then, massively refurbished, made modern and luxurious, the emperor's.

The carriage rattled across the moat into the central courtyard, then went to a rear entrance, and I was hustled inside to a small chamber, where once more I waited, four guards watching me nervously.

After a while, the door opened, and half a dozen other guards made sure I hadn't massacred my captors. Scopas came in next, even fatter than he'd been the last time I'd seen him, which was . . . and it took some thinking back . . . more than ten years earlier. Scopas had been one of the first members of the Rule of Ten to support Tenedos and was considered the shrewdest of those incompetents. After the emperor's coronation, he'd tried to weasel his way back into Tenedos's graces, but without success.

Later, when we were fighting in Maisir, he'd led a

revolt that failed, but managed to escape and hide before mounting a second, successful rising just before the defeat at Cambiaso.

Behind him came Barthou, formerly the Rule of Ten's Speaker, in spite of his position, never considered terribly astute.

I bowed courteously. Scopas did the same, while Barthou, puzzling on what the proper response should be, made none.

"Damaste á Cimabue," Scopas said, "we have brought you here to offer you life and a chance to rejoin Numantian society as a nobleman, with estates we shall grant you for a gracious living."

"All we want," Barthou put in, and I wondered if they'd rehearsed the put-and-take of their lines beforehand, "is for you to perform a task."

"I wish I could say I was at your service," I replied. "Technically, as your prisoner, I am. What do you wish me to do?"

"First," Scopas said, "I have a question. Have you been approached by the traitor named Tenedos?"

"How could he do that?" I asked, amused. "Remember, you've had me imprisoned, sealed off from the world."

"Magicians," Barthou said, looking from side to side as if for ears to magically protrude from the walls, "have ways of doing things mortals like us cannot know of."

"I'll answer your question with the obvious: No one has approached me to do anything," I said.

"We're aware you swore an oath to the one who was once our emperor," Scopas said. "And I'm also aware of your family motto, *We Hold True*."

I was slightly impressed—I didn't think the fat man was that aware. I nodded.

"Do you consider your oath still stands, considering the man called Tenedos still lives?"

I thought of various subtleties, decided I wasn't capable of them.

"I don't know," I said truthfully. "I was the one who struck Tenedos down, at Cambiaso, and possibly permitted the Maisirian victory. Doesn't that render the continuance of my oath rather meaningless?"

Both Barthou and Scopas reacted in some amazement. There were but two mortals who knew what'd happened in his tent before Cambiaso. I'd said nothing, out of shame, and evidently Tenedos had done the same.

"That's as may be," Barthou said. "The question stands—are you still willing to serve the emperor?"

I shook my head. "I serve no one now," I said. "As a prisoner, not even myself."

"Would you wish to change that?" Scopas asked.

"We must stop the interloper Tenedos," Barthou said, "and quickly. Or else the worst will happen."

"What's the worst?" I asked. "That Tenedos takes the throne once more . . . or that King Bairan comes back with his army, which I assume he would if the emperor returns?"

"You've answered your own question," Scopas said. "As to how we wish you to serve us, specifically: we are getting permission from King Bairan to increase the size of the Peace Guardians, to make the force large enough to stand against Tenedos."

"What's the matter with the traitor Herne, who now leads them? I understand everyone loves him for his political realism," I said harshly.

Both Grand Councilors looked unhappy.

"Guardian of the Peace Herne is not exactly a leader the

populace warms to," Scopas said. "We need someone better known, better thought of, both to gain the recruits we need so desperately and to serve as a beacon in battle."

This stopped me. I thought the people of Numantia thought me the worst of villains for having led them into slaughter. But if I assumed these two knew what they were talking about—quite an assumption from their past record—things might be different.

"You mean I'd be a figurehead," I said, "with Herne still in command."

"Of course," Barthou said. "What else could there be?"

"Since Herne is little more than raw ambition in the flesh, and completely unqualified to be a general of the armies . . . even a pissant one like the Peace Guardians . . . I'd be several species of a fool to serve under him. Particularly if his mistakes would be blamed on me, as you've indicated."

Barthou started to snap a retort, but Scopas held up his hand. "Let me try another approach, since you haven't rejected me completely," he said quietly. "Would you agree to take over the army . . . I mean the Peace Guardians . . . if Herne were set aside, in some sort of honorary position but out of the real line of command? You wouldn't be able to hold the rank of tribune, of course—there are political considerations that prevent that title from ever being revived. Perhaps we might use the rank of supreme *jedaz*, which should lessen any problems King Bairan might have with your return to the military."

"I know it's hardly civil to answer a question with another question, and I'm not doing that," I said. "But I need more information. An army . . . no matter what you call it . . . isn't led by one general, one tribune, or whatever Maisirian rank you like. Who else can you call on?"

"The liaison between us and the Guardians is Timgad," Scopas said.

I remembered him vaguely—a toady who'd been appointed to the Rule of Ten after the Tovieti riots began, a toady of Barthou's. He . . . and his position . . . didn't matter, for if I accepted their offer I'd no more listen to the Council than I would Herne.

"Lord Drumceat, even though he lacks experience, has a great deal of fire and enthusiasm," Scopas went on. "We plan to name him Rast."

Drumceat was the reactionary rural baron who'd taken over the death patrols created by my brother-in-law Praen, after the Tovieti slaughtered him. I'd once ordered him from my house.

"A man with great experience," Barthou put in, "is General, now Rast, Indore."

Experience . . . at being totally political. The Rule of Ten had tried to foist him on the army as supreme commander, and Tenedos had refused him. Hardly a plus.

"Another is Rast Taitu."

A decent man, relieved by Tenedos for refusing Tenedos's orders to attack at Dabormida. Something of a plus.

"Someone without experience, but, like Drumceat, with fire," Barthou said, "is Baron Lany."

He was the ex-head of warders in Nicias who'd replaced me as head of the provisional government in Kallio, after the emperor had sent me home in disgrace, who evidently did an excellent job. A plus.

"Probably our best officer," Scopas said, "is Guardian of the Peace Herne's adjutant, a real firebrand named Trerice. He never served in the army during the war but organized supply caravans to the borders. He prided himself on never losing a man or a bale of goods to bandits or anything else. Properly, he was rewarded. I guess he found peacetime boring, for he joined the Guardians and quickly rose in its ranks. Herne's been using him in the countryside, where he's been most effective in suppressing dissent. He's considered totally ruthless in following his orders, doing much the same task you performed for the emperor. I suppose you had the same reputation."

No, ruthless was not a distinction that I'd ever heard connected to my name, and I hoped it had never fit. I guessed this Trerice might be competent, since Herne wouldn't let him near Nicias and power.

"There are others, of course," Scopas went on. "Middle-rankers from the war, who've risen to the occasion. We're quite confident."

I refrained from sneering. If they were so confident, why'd they drag me out of jail? I could have given them the answer right then, but still liked the fact my neck ran directly from my body to my head.

"I see," I said. "Naturally, I'd like a day, perhaps two, to consider this."

Barthou looked unhappy, but Scopas nodded hastily. "Of course, of course. Take all the time you need. You'll forgive us if we don't herald your return for a while, nor permit you to reenter public life."

"No," I said. "I don't want to become an embarrassment." I started for the door. "So if you'll let me return to my . . . secluded quarters . . ."

Scopas oiled me out, and I went down the hall, surrounded by guards. I glanced back at the corridor's end and saw Scopas looking thoughtfully after me. Barthou came up beside him and said something. Scopas, still looking at me, answered, shaking his head.

I guessed my thinking wasn't as impervious as I'd hoped but wasn't that disappointed. Scopas had years and years of determining meaning from a flinch or a glance.

I'd already decided I wouldn't become a Peace Guardian under any circumstances. Not only was it morally abhorrent, but with lackluster buffoons for officers, my chances of defeating a brilliant sorcerer and sometimes-prescient general like Tenedos were nonexistent.

The question was, how could I turn them down and continue living?

The next question became—if I managed to survive this crisis, what came next?

I had no answers for either question.

I startled awake into a dream. The Emperor Laish Tenedos stood, arms crossed, in the center of my room. On either side of him were braziers, sending out scented smoke in many colors.

The emperor smiled, and I knew I was not dreaming at all.

I came out of bed, began to bow, naked as I was, then caught myself, confused.

Tenedos guffawed. "In spite of the oath you took," he said, "you do not have to make obeisance. I have not regained the throne." His smile vanished. "Not yet, but soon."

"How did you do this?" I managed.

"That perplexes me a bit," he said, reaching into invisibility and pulling up a camp chair. He reached once more to the side, came back with a crystal decanter and glass, and poured brandy. He replaced the carafe and sipped.

"This is a spell I devised," he said, "that began with the Seeing Bowl you and I used once, when you were in Kallio.

"With it, I've sent . . . messages . . . to certain men who served me in the past and whose service I now require. The few times I was able to connect with them, it was all very hazy, unclear, not like this.

"Perhaps it's because I worked great magic in the tower you're now in, and there's a . . . perhaps residue is the word.

"Or perhaps it's because you and I were closer than any of my other officers and officials.

"You see, Damastes? I am back, it was not a myth, not a double, and my powers are stronger than ever."

I managed to hide a shudder. The seer king's great secret was that he gathered his sorcerous strength from blood, from death, which was why he worshiped the death-goddess Saionji, when almost all other Numantians trembled at her name. I'd only realized this secret near the end, before Cambiaso; it was something I should've sensed years earlier.

So his powers were back, and more powerful? I wasn't sure if that meant he'd learned greater spells or, more frightening, if he'd made another pact with another demon, promising blood for power.

An even worse thought came: had Tenedos in fact died, rather than faking a death? Had he struck a bargain with Saionji herself and been able to return to this world in the same form, rather than being thrown onto the Wheel to be reborn in some other body in some distant land, perhaps an animal instead of a human?

Tenedos was looking at me closely.

"Might I ask your thoughts?" he inquired in a mocking tone.

I shook my head. "I'm not altogether awake, so they don't bear repeating."

Again, Tenedos laughed. "Damastes, my friend, you were always a terrible liar. But it matters not. Were you thinking about the past? About what you did to me at Cambiaso?"

I made no reply.

"You need not let it dwell on you," he said. "For that was in the past, and now is the time I call you to return to your duty as first tribune, commander of my armies, and assist me in regaining my rightful throne, my rightful possession of Numantia."

"In spite of what happened?" I said.

"I cannot say I love you for what you did. I was blind in my rage at being betrayed by Scopas, Barthou, the cowardly lice who populate Nicias, and was about to send them doom." He drank. "I was not thinking clearly at that time, for I never should have allowed myself to worry about them until I'd destroyed the Maisirians.

"You should have restrained me, but not in the manner you did. For Numantia's sake, as well as mine . . . and, considering your present situation, your own as well."

I thought for an instant of asking how one subdues a wizard in a terrible rage, a wizard who can call up demons able to destroy fortresses and armies.

"But, as I said," Tenedos continued, "that is in the past. During my exile, I had a chance to think of what I did, both right and wrong, and how I would change matters given the chance.

"I was given the chance, or, more correctly, I seized the moment. Now I am on the path of recovery, of return.

"I've amassed a great force of men, nearly one hundred thousand. But I lack officers to lead them into battle, men of experience, even though I have many with the desire, and blood that races to the sound of drums. King Bairan killed too many of our best.

"But I'm confident that I . . . that we . . . can win, and when I use the word we, I mean you, Damastes á Cimabue, my bravest soldier."

"What is your plan? How will things be different?" I temporized.

"First I must regain the throne, reunite Numantia behind me. Scopas, Barthou, their regime and especially the execrable Peace Guardians and the detestable Herne must be destroyed. There shall be no mercy, no surrender permitted. I made the mistake of being merciful once and allowing dissent. I will not make that error again."

"What about Maisir?" I asked. "Bairan will hardly stand by and allow you . . . Numantia . . . to return to its former glory."

"He will have no choice," Tenedos said. "Of course he'll call up his armies when he hears of my successes in the field and bring them north.

"By the time he crosses the borders, makes his way through Sulem Pass or the other route through Dumyat, it will be too late. Once here in Numantia, he'll be as we were in Maisir, campaigning in a foreign land, with everyone's hand turned against him.

"I'll meet him in the field when and where he least expects it. Then the Maisirians . . . and their murderous king, the bastard who put you under a spell and forced you to become a murderer and near-regicide . . . shall be utterly destroyed.

"Remember, we have a great advantage. You slew his greatest mage, the *azaz*, at Cambiaso. I was more powerful than he was then and am twice that now.

"So let Bairan come north with his War Magicians. This

time I know what I'm facing, and have begun to reassemble the Chare Brethren and ready my own battle wizardry.

"Before he reaches the border, I'll strike down all his sorcerers and leave him naked to my . . . *our* . . . hammer blows, material and spiritual!

"Once he and his army are destroyed, I won't make my other mistake of invading Maisir. No, I'll let them fall into utter chaos for a generation, perhaps two, while they're casting envious looks north at our peace, our contentment, our prosperity. Then they'll beg to be allowed into my hegemony."

Again my memory flickered, remembering how Tenedos had told me peace must never be allowed to reign in Numantia, for a nation not fighting for its life, for its soul, falls into decay and ruin. But what Tenedos said brought a more important question.

"Your Majesty," and I confess the words still came easily. "You just said something strange, something I don't understand. You said a generation or two must pass before the Maisirians want to serve *you*."

"Your mind is still as agile as always," Tenedos said. "This is another secret I'm on the verge of discovering, a way to extend our lives double or double again normal, perhaps even longer.

"This I find ironic, for as Saionji's greatest servant, perhaps she's going to permit me to remain free of the Wheel for a longer time as a reward, me and those I decide are worthy of this ultimate privilege."

I looked hard into those dangerously gleaming eyes I'd been held and commanded by for most of my life. I couldn't tell if he was telling the truth, was raving, or was trying to entice me, as if a promise of more years in this hardly pleasant life was much of a lure.

"I know you haven't forgotten the oath you took to me, even though some might say you broke it when you struck me down."

I'd spent many hours puzzling about how much grief that arrogant motto, *We Hold True*, must've brought my family over the generations.

"One thing, sir, I must settle now," I went on. "I refuse to admit I broke my oath when I prevented you from bringing chaos to Numantia. For isn't it the duty of an officer to keep his superior from breaking *his* oath? And you took one to your people, in front of me and the Great Gods Umar, Irisu, Saionji, to never treat your subjects with cruelty or disdain. Didn't you?"

The emperor's face reddened, and his fist clenched on his glass. I waited for it to shatter, but he forced calm, put a smile on his lips, and laughed sharply, falsely.

"I suppose," he said slowly, "that's why friends are so damnably uncomfortable. They keep reminding you of things that are . . . hard to accept. Very well, Damastes, my . . . my friend. We'll call the matter of oaths and their breaking even.

"Now I ask you once more. Will you revive your oath, your pride, Numantia's pride, and serve me again?

"Help us regain our rightful place in front of the gods, as the fairest, most favored nation on this world. Help me make Numantia even greater, so other worlds look on us with helpless envy.

"Help me destroy Numantia's enemies . . . before they unutterably destroy us!"

I felt his words shake me, shake my world, barely kept from falling to my knees.

"If I do, sir," I managed, "what about my present predicament?"

Tenedos smiled, the smile I'd seen often when he won a hard point, defeated a stubborn foe. Again he stretched his arm into nothingness, came back with what looked like a coin or an amulet.

"Here," he said, and cast it toward me. If I doubted I wasn't dreaming, the clink of the coin on the floor gave final proof. I reluctantly picked it up. It was warm, rapidly grew cold.

"Rub it, think of me, and I'll send magic to assist you in whatever escape you deem feasible," he ordered. "Once you're free, point it until it grows warm, and follow in that direction until you find me."

He stood. "Remember the good times," he said. "Remember what it was like, knowing we were the center of the world, and everyone listened to us? Obeyed us? Obeyed us gladly, for we were the shining light of the universe, tearing away the dull darkness of the past. Now it's time to return to those days. You and me, the way it was, the way it shall be.

"Welcome back, Damastes," he said softly. "Welcome back, my friend."

And I was alone, looking at the far wall of my chamber.

I stared long at the amulet, worked in strange figures not of this world's geometry, and carved with what I guessed were letters in an equally strange language.

So the Emperor Tenedos assumed I would return to his side, while the Grand Council dallied and I stalled them.

Slowly the thought came—I didn't want either of them, nor did I want to be a warrior any longer. Maybe after some time had passed I'd be willing to return to my calling, but not now. Not in this confusion.

"Remember the good times," the emperor had said. But I couldn't. I remembered battlefields strewn with bodies, cities aflame, demons rending warriors whose bravery was nothing against their fangs and talons. I remembered Amiel Kalvedon, dying with an arrow wound in her side, dying full of hope for the morrow, dying carrying my child. I remembered Alegria, wanting to make love in the frozen nightmare of the road north of Jarrah, then dying quietly, a trickle of blood runneling from her lips.

No, not good times, but gore-drenched nightmares.

All I wanted was to escape to somewhere completely peaceful, where no one would bother me and I would raise a hand against no one. I thought wistfully of the quiet, peaceful jungles of Cimabue, where I'd been but seldom since childhood, and now wished I'd never left.

Of course there was no way I would ever see them again, so I tried to put the thought from me.

At least, I consoled myself, there was a possibility I could escape the Council's vengeance if I told them no. Tenedos's magic would help. Then I'd only have to get away from the revenge of the world's most powerful wizard.

And did I really believe that Tenedos, the wizard who never forgot nor forgave an enemy, except so long as he needed him, would truly forget that blow I struck before Cambiaso? Did I believe if I helped him regain the throne, he wouldn't turn on me and wreak the most ghastly revenge for what I'd done at Cambiaso that a devils-haunted mind could devise?

Gloom fell, and I forced it away by going back to my dreams of Cimabue, the embracing jungle, gentle rain falling, a pool with mossy rocks growing out of it, being a boy curled under a leaf twice his size, a tiny fire glowing under my pot of rice and the fruit I'd gathered. I remembered the bark of a sambur, the cough of a distant tiger, and contentment in the moment, not fearing the morrow but looking forward to its promise.

I found my lips moving in a prayer, a prayer to small gods, to Vachan, the monkey god of Cimabue, and to Tanis, my family's private godling.

I must've slept, for the next thing I remember is Dubats calling to me and bright sunlight blazing in my windows. I had visitors.

"Send him . . . or her up," I called, feeling unwarrantedly cheerful.

My callers were Guardian of the Peace Herne and his aide, a bemuscled, scar-faced hearty named Salop.

I didn't know if the Councilors knew Herne loathed me for many reasons, the most recent my discovery of carriages of his private luxuries when we were fleeing Jarrah, while his soldiers were lucky if they had a frozen chunk of long-dead horsemeat every two days as they stumbled barefoot through the snow. I'd ordered these delicacies given out to the troops and told Herne if he disobeyed my order I'd have him stripped of his command and reduced to the ranks—a death sentence.

Both men were armed with sword and dagger and wore the gray-red of the Guardians, except properly tarted up with gold filigree here and there, as befitted men for whom position meant everything and honor nothing. Herne had a package which he put on a table.

"My man Catalca informed me you'd been brought to Nicias," Herne said coldly. "Our Grand Councilors are the fools they've always been to think they could use my Guardians and I wouldn't find out about it."

"I had no idea you weren't privy to their decision," I said.

"Don't expect me to be a fool," Herne said. "I knew they'd already discussed bringing you back and ordering the lapdog to lunge at his former master."

"One whose lips are firmly wrapped around a foreign king's cock has little reason to call another a lapdog," I snapped back.

Salop growled, started forward. Herne held out his hand.

"No," he said. "That isn't our way."

Salop grunted, stepped to the side, glaring.

"Yes," Herne went on, "not only bring you back, but let you steal my glory, let you take over my Guardians. Those arrogant shits!"

"Perhaps they sensed you couldn't lead a horse out of a burning building," I said, not giving a damn what Herne thought, able for the first time to kick back at those who'd put the boot into me for such a long time. "Not that I'm agreeing with your lunatic assumption that the Council plans to relieve you."

"And *you* will be able to destroy the emperor?" Herne said. He snorted. "The only thing that will bring that bastard down is for King Bairan to return and finish the task he left half-completed."

"Spoken like a true Numantian," I said sarcastically. "And then what? Do you think after he destroys Tenedos he'll obediently bounce back into Maisir as he did the last time, like a child's toy on a rubber string?"

"Of course not," Herne snapped. "This time, let him incorporate Numantia into his own realm, as he should've done before. I believe, Cimabuan, in the inexorable judgment of the gods. We were tried by Irisu and found wanting, and Bairan should've realized that and taken the gift so generously presented."

I stared at Herne in total loathing.

"I thought I'd enjoy baiting you," I said. "But there's no pleasure in badgering slime-worms. Go on. Get out. Even a prisoner is entitled to have some standards."

Herne rose. "No," he said quietly, his rage vanished. "For there are *matters to be dealt with.*"

I had an instant to notice the emphasis, realize it was a signal, when Salop jumped me, pinning my arms at my waist with his strength. Bigger, stronger, and younger than I was, he held me immobilized.

"A pity," Herne said, "you attacked me when I came on a friendly visit to discuss how we could mutually help the Council. Scopas and Barthou won't believe the story, but they won't have any choice, and the masses will eat anything we tell them to.

"We should have killed you after Cambiaso," he said, drawing his sword. For some reason, I had all the time in the world to consider its elaborately worked blade, its ivory grip, its golden, gem-encrusted guard, hilt, and pommel. With his free hand, he took the bundle from the table, opened it, and a shortsword clattered onto the floor.

"That," he said, "is what you attacked me with. I barely saved myself, and only because of my aide Shamb Salop's quick wits. I'll have to punish your warders most severely for allowing one of your accomplices to smuggle in the sword.

"I wish I could draw out your doom, former First Tribune, for your arrogance and how you shamed me in front of lesser beings," he said. "But my story must have some credibility, and someone missing eyes, nose, and cock might increase the difficulty of my explanation."

He drew his sword back, and I smashed my head back

into Salop's face. The cartilage of his nose crunched, and his teeth snapped. The man screeched, loosened his hold, and I sent my elbow back into his ribs, hearing them crack, sidestepping as Herne struck.

His lunge went home, keen blade driving into Salop's guts. The man gasped agony, grabbed the blade, eyes wide in disbelief, then fell, almost tearing the weapon from Herne's grasp.

I had no time to grab Salop's still-sheathed sword, nor to reach my own dagger. Herne's teeth were bared in a silent snarl.

"So you managed to kill my finest soldier," he hissed. "That shall make the story better."

He closed in in the careful steps of a skilled swordsman, and I was doomed.

I'd known soldiers who were known for battle rage, an uncaring frenzy that took them so they cared only about destroying their enemies, even if it came at the cost of their own life. In the final frenzy at Cambiaso I'd known that blood fever as well, in my complete despair, seeing my entire world shattered around me.

Now it came again, after the long months of confinement, fear, and hopelessness, a target I hated in front of me, a man who'd sold everything he should have held dear, from pride to honor to country, and I laughed in pure joy. Everything was easy, everything was mine.

Herne's expression of glee changed to fear, and he flailed his blade back and forth, forgetting his swordsman's training of calmness, direction, trying to create a steel web between us.

I had time, all the time in the world, stepped away from his slash, and struck hard with the back of my fist at his blade, which hung motionless before me.

The steel snapped in three parts, and they pinwheeled slowly up and around us, and Herne goggled at the stub of his sword.

He dropped it, fumbled for his dagger, but he was too late, far too late, and I had him by the throat, fingers digging into the sides of his neck, feeling the thrum of blood, fingers like the seizing talons of the eagle, and his face went red, his mouth opened and his tongue bulged and I was holding him, a man not much smaller than I, clear of the ground, shaking him like a trapped bear shakes a hound.

I felt a snap, and Herne's head lolled, and I smelt shit as his dead body voided. I dropped the limp corpse, stepped back.

The red thunder against my temples died, and I stared at the bodies of two men, one the highest-ranking soldier of Numantia.

Now I was indeed for it.

THREE

ESCAPE

I'd rather be cut down like a running boar than make a sambur's last noble stand. I stripped off Salop's uniform, tried to ignore the wet, dark stain around its middle as I pulled it on.

I checked both men's pouches, cursed when I found Herne's empty, but Salop's was full of gold and silver. The Guardian of the Peace must've been one of those pretenders who felt it's an underling's job to pay . . . or perhaps he was merely an inveterate freeloader.

I took my own coins, the dagger Perak had given me, and tucked that innocently deadly iron pig into a pocket.

I fastened Salop's weapons belt on, tore braid from Herne's uniform and tied Salop's boots together and strung them around my neck, and was ready to go. Then I caught myself and took Herne's gem-crusted dagger and, as a second thought, the stub of his sword, tucking them inside my tunic.

The last bit of corpse robbing was Herne's sword belt, which I stripped of its sheaths and looped around my neck. I considered the three possible escape routes, decided on the one I knew to be easiest and most likely to get me killed.

From the sun's position, I wouldn't have more than half an hour to wait, hoping Dubats wouldn't come to see if his commander needed anything. But Herne must've given orders to be left strictly alone, which made sense, not particularly wanting anyone to wander in while he was in the middle of murder.

Bugles sounded, marking retreat, when the guards would assemble in the inner keep, and the prison commander would deal with announcements, punishments, rewards, assign details, the night's duties would be told off, the watch would be inspected and changed, and the rest of the garrison would be dismissed to the dining rooms in the upper part of the keep. While they kept busy with the details of my captivity, I proceeded to begin ending it.

I crawled backward out of the window and started down the tower's face. The rock was rough-cut, with large cracks between each heavy boulder, and I picked my way down it, feeling fingers and toes bruise but paying no mind. A Man of the Hills like Yonge would have run up and down this craggy face one-handed, blind drunk, fondling a kidnapped damsel with the other hand and probably yodeling the Kaiti national anthem to boot.

I contented myself with not falling, which was one of the two worries I had. The other, more obvious, was that someone would look up at the tower, see this gray-clad fool about to fall, and sound the alarm. At least the sun was lowering, and I had the occasional shadow to hide me. I glanced down once and saw a boy on the Latane River's banks, gaping up. I prayed he was a nasty little urchin who was hoping to see me splatter on the stones below, rather than a good Irisu-blessed soul who'd trot to the guard post in front of the tower and ask what was going on up above.

Evidently he was as bloody-minded as I hoped, for I

heard no cries of alarm and put him out of my mind, con-centrating on putting one foot down, scrabbling for a crack, finding it, then lowering myself to another, con-vincing my fingers to let go of their death hold and find another one.

Three or four centuries passed, and I chanced looking down again. I was about thirty feet above the moat, and from here down the stone was smoothly polished, which was why I'd not worried before about anyone attacking us this way.

The dirty green water was most disinviting, and I hoped no ambitious sort had made the tower more secure by introducing a tribe of poisonous water snakes. It wasn't looking any easier, and so I crammed the belt into a notch to give me a last few feet of advantage, lowered myself to its end, took a deep breath, pushed away from the wall, and dropped.

I hit the water with a splash that must've sounded like a whale leaping and went under, not thinking about the foul water or its contents or residents. I pulled up into a ball, as I'd done as a boy, idiotically leaping into unknown rivers without checking for underwater crags, and then began rising to the surface.

I was about thirty feet from the lowered drawbridge, and two guards who must've heard the splash were stand-ing on it, gaping.

"Help!" I spluttered, hoping the green gunk around me was hiding my face. "Help . . . I fell . . . can't swim . . ." and swam closer, flailing my arms. One guard scurried closer, bent over, reached a hand, and I took it, and he pulled me up onto the wooden decking as if landing a fish. But this fish wasn't about to be gaffed, and I rolled, kick-ing, and sent him sprawling.

The other realized who I was, reached for his sword, and I came up with Perak's dagger, burying it to the hilt just below his rib cage. He gagged, died, and I spun and cut the throat of his partner before he could recover. I sheathed the dagger, tucked it inside my tunic. Salop's sword was in one hand, his longer knife in the other.

There were two more guards at the drawbridge's end, and they ran at me, grabbing for their swords. I feinted with my sword, put the dagger into the first's belly, and kneed him into his fellow. The man stumbled back, saw my threatening blade, made a noise like a parrot being strangled, and leapt into the moat.

Good enough, and I went past the guard post, hastily unbolted the sliding gate, went through, with still no hue and cry, had a moment to slide the bolts back in place and smash at the gate's hinges with the dagger's pommel, hopefully jamming it for a moment.

Then I was free, if for only a moment, free on the streets of Nicias! I saw the boy who'd been staring, felt like tossing him a coin for not helping, and ran past. He turned as I passed, still watching, still without a sound, and I wondered if he was a mute or just very, very slow.

This branch of the Latane was narrow, and there was an arching bridge for the city center a few hundred yards distant. I pelted for it, past a handful of somewhat astonished citizens strolling in the dusk. Then I caught myself and slowed to a saunter, no more than another Guardian among them, hoping they'd disregard I was helmetless and sopping wet, with a grotesque bloodstain on my gut and an unsheathed blade in each hand.

I heard shouts, the clatter of horses' hooves, and looked back. Three horsemen in the gray of the Guardians clattered onto the river walk after me. I didn't panic but kept my slow pace. I heard shouts of "Stop, you!" and "Stop him," and the horses' hooves broke into a hard gallop.

The horsemen were armed with lances, and they couched them as they closed. I don't know if they had orders to kill me or just didn't know how valuable I supposedly was to their Grand Council, but this was not the time to query the matter.

A man afoot against a horseman appears a one-sided fight, but that's not necessarily the case, unless the man panics and runs, in which case he gets spitted like a roasting fowl.

Three against one . . . I had two advantages: first, I wasn't facing properly trained cavalrymen—their legs stuck out at awkward angles on either side of their saddle, their lance butts weren't properly tucked in under their arms, and the points were weaving in circles, instead of being steadily aimed; second, there were three of them, all trying to kill me, all getting in each other's way.

When they were thirty feet away, I jumped to the side, as if about to leap into the river. The closest horseman pulled his reins left, into his fellow, and that man's horse skidded, almost went down, and the first had to rein away. The third was very close, and I ducked aside and batted his lance point down with my sword, into the cobbles of the river path. The point caught and vaulted the spearman out of his saddle high into the air. His lance snapped, and he fell, screaming, onto my waiting blade. The first was bringing his horse around in a caracole, but I ran inside his turning arc and drove my sword into his side, and he shrieked, fell from his mount.

The last man had his mount under control, and his lance point was leveled. I waited for him to kick his horse into the gallop and stood steady, waiting, breathing deeply, not afraid, letting my body find its own counter to his attack.

Very suddenly he whirled his horse and galloped back toward the tower, shouting incoherently in fear.

I ran the other way, remembering this time to sheath my blades. I went across the bridge, trying to think what to do next. To my right was a rich district including, I remembered with a bit of a wrench, where I'd lived with my late wife. Ahead and left led into one of the working districts of Nicias, and that was the way I chose.

Twice city warders saw me, saw the stains, and turned aside into shops, not wanting to know what bloody business I was about.

I came into a marketplace, a poor area where the stores had few fresh goods, and those at high prices, and the other shops around the square sold no more than the basic necessities of life. One had a sign: WE BUY USED CLOTHING, and I ducked into it.

The proprietor, a skinny bald man in dirty robes, took one look at my bloodied uniform and arms and held up both hands.

"I di'n't see you. Honest. Just take whatever you want . . . you never come in here, an' I'm just goin' out for air."

"Stay where you are," I ordered. "I mean you no harm."

"A' course you don't. Never intended f'r you t' think I thought y' did," he babbled.

"Turn your back."

"A'right, a'right. But don't take me in th' back, sir. I vow I'll never say a word t' nobody 'bout nothin', but please, don't hurt me. Got a wife an' three, no, four children, an' they don't deserve t' be left dest'tute," he yammered.

I heard him with but half an ear, quickly sorting

through piled clothing. I found dark brown baggy trousers, a near-matching woolen pullover whose previous owner might've bathed within this century, a hat that made me look a total, utter dunce, and, best of all, a sack with hand-sewn straps, such as a poor country peddler might carry. I stripped off my uniform, told the owner not to turn, so he couldn't tell what I'd taken, and dressed hastily. I tucked my most unmistakable feature, my long blond hair, under the cap. My weapons went into the sack, and I dropped two gold coins on the floor.

"Wait until you think a full turning of a glass has passed," I ordered. "Or expect the worst."

"Nossir, nossir, I won't turn, give you all the time you need, hours-anhours, an' thank 'ee for not takin' m' poor life, so m' wife an' child'n'll not be cast out t' starve . . ." and I was out of the store and walking away, thinking innocent thoughts.

I was halfway across the square, about to start down a narrow lane, when I heard the shouting from behind.

"Thief! Thief! Stop 'im! Robbed me of m' silver! Stop him!" It was, of course, the clothing merchant.

I cursed, wished I had cut him down, ran into the lane, went down one street, cut into an alley, then onto a broader avenue, this leading into a somewhat more prosperous district and, once again, tried to appear virtuous. A block ahead, I saw a knot of warders, moving toward me, eyeing each passerby carefully. Perhaps just a routine check . . . but perhaps not.

I looked for a shop, an arcade, an alley to duck into, saw none. High-rising apartments that'd once been wealthy, now somewhat run-down like the rest of Nicias were on either side of the street. Across the way, though, was an alcove, and there were three women in it.

Perhaps one lived inside and would take pity on me, even though I now wished I'd chosen clothes a little more prosperous looking. As I approached, I realized the three were whores, looking for the first customer of the night. One eyed me, said mechanically, "Say there, you look like you might like a friend." The other laughed, knowing a poor man like me couldn't afford even a simple street-walker, and the third stayed silent.

It was worth the chance.

"I could be," I said boldly. The one who'd spoken and the laugher had been in their trade for years, and the streets had marked them. The third was the youngest, in her late teens, and by far the cleanest, and, if she hadn't looked so miserable, the prettiest. She wore a blue dress, once long and flaring, with a close-fitting high neck that reminded me of a woman's lycee uniform. Its hem had been shortened radically and a bare midriff circle cut.

I smiled at her, and she looked startled, then forced a smile in return.

"Wouldn't mind havin' a friend like you," I said, using a country dialect I remembered well from my troops. "If y' have a place to go, not far, an' for the night."

The girl took a deep breath and stepped out of the alcove.

"Na like that, Lynton," the one who'd laughed said. "'Member what we taught you, an' when th' mot's not pelf-lookin', y' check th' color of his silver."

The girl, Lynton, stopped. "Can you pay?" she said, as coached.

I dug into the inner pocket of my tunic, fumbled out a few coppers, then, reluctantly, like a wanderer showing his all, two silver coins.

The two older streetwalkers looked surprised.

"Y'know," the first one said, "if y' like, y' can have two
... mayhap all three of us. If y've got another coin t' go
with th' others."

"Nah," I said, "Ah'm not th' lad for specials like that.
All I need's a bed, someone t' keep it warm, and p'raps a
bit of a meal."

"I have a place," Lynton said, a bit eagerly. "And we can
stop at a grocer's if you want." Unlike the others, she had
a bit of culture to her voice.

"I want," I said.

"Th' younger's lucky," the second woman muttered.
"Mebbe we'll be the same, Jaen willing."

I put my arm around Lynton; she stiffened involun-
tarily, then forced herself to relax and lean against me.
We walked on, toward the warders, who glanced at us,
then away, uninterested, as we passed. Whoever they
were looking for wasn't a poorly dressed man with a local
trollop.

We went down two blocks, and she stopped outside a
grocery. "This is the best one around," she said. "Or
would you like something not quite so dear?"

"This is fine," I said and purchased bread so fresh I
could smell the oven that baked it, some smoked sausage,
a couple of different kinds of cheese, fresh tomatoes and
cucumbers, and good olive oil, all the things that came
but seldom to my island prison.

"No wine?" the girl asked, startled.

"I don't drink," I told her, which was the simple truth,
spirits never having done anything but make me thick-
brained and foolish and, in the morning, a potential suicide
until I felt better.

I added soap and a toothbrush to my pile, paid, not letting either Lynton or the shopkeeper see my gold, and we

went on, turning, in a few blocks, into a rather imposing building, rather better kept than its neighbors. We went up three flights of stairs to a landing. There were only three doors off it, so the apartments inside would have belonged to rich tenants once. The girl tapped twice, then three times.

"There's thieves about," she explained. The door opened, and an older man, with white brushes of moustaches, opened it. He looked at me, his lips tightened, and he looked quickly away.

I was glad he did, for I recognized him. He was Domina Berda—I couldn't remember his first name—and had commanded one of the infantry regiments during the Tovieti rising, a tough regular who gave little mercy but, unlike too many of the soldiers, was scrupulously fair in who he hanged from lampposts and who he freed.

I stepped inside and was grateful the apartment, as large as I'd expected it to be, was sunk in gloom, making it even harder for me to be recognized. There was little furniture in the room, a couch, an end table, three lamps, a huge armoire holding only a few dishes, and a lovingly polished long banquet table that could've seated twenty. There were still a few pictures on the walls, but I noted the dark spaces where others had been taken down.

Sitting on the couch was a slender woman, Berda's wife, with great sad eyes and a worn face. She stared at me but said nothing.

Behind her, on the wall, hung Berda's old sword.

There was no explanation needed—I'd heard on the island that any soldier who survived the emperor's wars had been cast loose with no bonus or pension from the Council, left to survive as best he could. And what talents, beyond a willingness to endure and suffer, do most soldiers have, whether private or general? Little by little Domina Berda would have sold everything he owned as he slid further and further into poverty.

A great rage came, aimed at I didn't know who. Berda, for letting his daughter whore? His wife? The shit-heel Grand Council? The emperor? Or the gods themselves? I forced control.

Lynton had evidently been waiting for me to say something, and looked alarmed when I didn't.

"Come," she whispered. "In here's my room."

I followed her, and my rage vanished as I entered a little girl's playroom, still with its dolls on a shelf, a few yellowing, childish chalks and, incongruously, a full-size double bed, no doubt added when Lynton began selling herself.

She lit two candles against the growing dusk, took the parcels from me, and unwrapped them.

"I'll get a plate for you," she said, still in a whisper. "And something to drink?"

"Water," I managed, and stared down at the viands I'd thought would give me a fine meal. My appetite was gone. Lynton came back with a goblet, fine crystal, chipped at its base, and utensils.

"Sit down," she said. "Here, let me cut the sausage for you."

"No. Tell me something," I said, knowing the answer. "Those people out there are your parents, aren't they?"

She nodded.

"What will they be dining on?"

Lynton was surprised.

"We . . . they still have some bread left from last night. And Mam made soup two nights ago."

"Take them this," I indicated what lay before me. "And

here." I took a silver coin from my sack. "If your father drinks wine, have him buy a bottle for himself."

"But . . . you—"

"I suddenly remembered this is one of my family god's days," I said. "When I'm supposed to fast, and surely I've done enough already in this life to not want to anger her more."

Lynton hesitated.

"Go on, girl," I ordered, and she obeyed.

I lay on the bed, wondering what I would do next. She came back, looked at me, and smiled.

"We thank you," she said. "You're a good man."

I shook my head.

"No," I said, trying to keep anger from my voice. "I'm afraid there aren't any left, these days."

She sat on the bed, put a hand on my leg.

"Yes, there are," she said gently. She stood and slowly began unbuttoning her dress. "You'll like me," she said. "I swear you will. I'll do anything you want me to . . . and I'll like it. Anything."

The dress dropped about her ankles, and she stepped out of it. She wore only a thin slip under it, and hooked her fingers in its straps, let it fall away. Her naked body was unworn, fair, with small breasts and the merest curl of hair around her sex.

My cock stirred. It had been . . . how long, I couldn't remember, since I'd been with a woman. Since . . . great gods, since I'd made love to Alegria, the night she died, long ago and far away in the frozen *suebi* of Maisir. Strangely, I would have thought the memory would've dashed my ardor, but it didn't. Alegria, the greatest love of my life; Marán, my former wife; Amiel Kalvedon, who loved us both, all were now slipping into memory, and I realized enough time had passed, and their memories would have no more power to rule my life, for good or evil, than other remembrances.

I wanted to stand, take off my peasant's attire, and woo this girl, this nude woman who stood waiting.

Instead, I took her hand and sat her down beside me. Then I went to my sack, took out the promised two silver coins, added a third.

"I'm one of those," I said, "who likes things different."

Lynton tried to hide a look of fear. She licked her lips.

"I said anything, and anything I meant," she said.

"What I like," I said, "is to watch women sleep."

"*What?*"

"When I was a boy," I lied, "I used to look through a crack in the wall at a neighbor girl. She was older than I was, so of course she never knew I existed. Every night she'd prepare herself for bed, combing her hair, which was dark, like yours, and then lie down, naked, and look at something I couldn't see. Maybe it was a picture of someone she loved. I don't know. Then her eyes would close and she'd go to sleep."

"That's what you like?"

I nodded.

"You don't want to do anything . . . after I'm asleep?"

I shook my head.

"That's . . ." she stopped herself.

"Strange?"

"Yes."

"But that's what I like." I handed her the coins.

I got up, went to the nearby chair, sat down. She kept looking at me, waiting for me to take out a whip, no doubt, or something like that, then swung her legs up, and lay back.

"Do you want me to play with myself?"

"No."

Lynton lay there for a few moments.

"Whatever happened to that girl?"

"She ran away with a soldier," I said. "When I was only ten."

"Are you married?"

"Yes," I said. "With three children, and a fourth coming."

"But you still like . . ."

"Yes. With your eyes closed."

She was silent. I stayed motionless. Her eyes opened twice, looked at me, then closed once more. Her breathing grew regular, and still I waited. She began snoring. I covered her with a blanket, found what looked like a favorite doll, put it beside her.

I drank my water, curled on the floor, and, after a time of itemizing how many kinds of fools I was, slept.

I woke, as I'd always been able to, when I wished, about an hour before dawn. Lynton slept on, quite soundly, the doll now cuddled under the blanket.

I made myself one more sort of fool, and left all the gold from Salop's purse on the bed next to her, silently left the room, and went out into the slow drizzle of morning.

"And what's your business, might I ask?" the slender, almost emaciated man wearing a pair of seeing-glasses perched precariously on his nose asked.

"You buy gems?"

"So my sign indicates."

"I've got some to sell," I said. "From my uncle, who used to be a soldier, who died last week."

I took out the stub of Herne's sword and his bejeweled

dagger. It was a rotten story, but the best I'd been able to devise.

The man looked at them carefully, then at me, then back at the weapons.

"An officer, I take it?" he said dryly.

"No, sir. But he fought against Kallio, and he told me this used to be some lord's or other that he killed in a battle."

The man nodded, considered the weapons.

"If," he said carefully, "you are telling the truth, and of course I have no reason to doubt you, then these would be no doubt worth a great deal as collector's items. More if you'd happen to remember the name of the nobleman your uncle took them from."

I shook my head. "Been years since I heard the stories. My uncle died a month ago, and I thought I'd make the best price bringing them to the city to sell."

"That's correct, you'll find more buyers in the city than in the country," the man said. "The problem with selling them intact is that it will take longer to find the perfect customer, although there are three men I have in mind. There is a second option, which would be to remove the stones from their settings and melt down the gold and silver, which I would buy for its intrinsic value, no more."

"That's what I want."

"It's somewhat a pity to destroy works like these, even though they're somewhat gaudy for my tastes," the man went on, "but it also makes the gems exceedingly hard to identify."

I pretended puzzlement. "I don't follow you."

"Of course you don't. Now, if you'll excuse me for a minute, I'd like to summon my partner."

He smiled faintly, started for the back of the store.

"If your partner wears a gray uniform or looks like a warder," I said, "you'll not have the time to reap any reward."

The man smiled once more.

"I have even less use for the agents of the law than you, if that's imaginable," and he disappeared behind the curtain.

He was gone almost ten minutes, and I nearly bolted. I opened the door and leaned in the entryway, pretending casualness, scanning the street in both directions for alarums.

The man came back with a woman who was simply huge, not just fat, but enormous in every dimension.

"Interesting items you offer us," she said, and her voice matched her bulk. "Why'd you choose our shop?"

I told the truth: "It was the second one I came across. The first didn't have anything expensive in the window, so I didn't think it could afford my price."

"Do you have any of the Talent?" the woman asked.

I felt a chill. "I know nothing about magic."

The woman stroked her chins. "These gems are quite valuable," she said. "We'll be giving you a considerable amount of money, should we purchase them. How would you wish the transaction?"

"Gold, fairly small in denomination. Where I live, it's hard to change big coins," I said.

"Easy to carry, easy to dispose of," she went on. "Are you planning on spending them here in Nicias?"

"That's not a question I'll answer."

"You plan on traveling, then," she said, as if I had satisfied her curiosity. "But you won't tell me where."

I shook my head, and my hand touched the grip of the sword in my sack.

"We mean no harm," she said. "Unlike others in Nicias,

who seek hard a man with long, blond hair, a man with a handsome face and a strong build."

"Not me," I said, trying to sound careless, "for I've wronged no one."

"In these times," the woman said, "wrong is an extremely variable judgment."

"So I've seen."

"If I said there's a drawn bath upstairs, in our apartments, a bath intended for my own use, would you be interested?" the woman asked. "In a cabinet near it is a vial of dye, so a blond man might suddenly become black-haired. And a man with long hair might have a close-crop when he emerged from that chamber."

I eyed her carefully. "And what is your interest in my affairs?"

She shrugged. "We like to see our customers happy."

I found the situation suddenly amusing and laughed. "How much would this deduct from my price?"

"Nothing at all," she said. "I would propose to give you two hundred and seventy-five . . ." she picked up the dagger, looked at it more closely, " . . . no, three hundred and seven pieces of gold.

"That's somewhere between a quarter and a half what these jewels would fetch in the jeweler's market. I might add that if I were dishonest, which I'm not, and a fence, which I'm not, the going rate is ten percent of value."

"So I'd heard. I'll take your price."

"You haven't heard all of it," she went on. "Do you fear snakes?"

I looked at her in astonishment. "No more than the next sensible man, I suppose," I answered. "I'll slay a poisonous reptile, but the others I've found friend to man, those who feed on noxious insects and other reptiles."

"That's good," she said. "Now, I do need to know at least in which direction you plan to travel."

I was dizzied by this eerieness but obeyed her request, and then realized I'd not considered where I would flee to. North? I knew no one in the Delta, nor east toward the deserts. South, up the Latane, I might find some old comrades who'd shelter me. There really was but one choice for me.

"I travel to the west," I said.

"I thought so," she said. "The very far west, into the jungles."

I kept my expression blank.

"Very good indeed," she said. "Upstairs with you, and get rid of those disgusting garments. Wash yourself, and I'll be up directly to deal with your hair."

She saw my expression. "Don't worry. I doubt if you can show me anything my husband here, or my six sons, haven't already.

"I said go!" and her voice was as commanding as any drill warrant, and I obeyed.

Half an hour later, I was clean. Half an hour after that, I was shorn and black-haired. I stood, naked, and she handed me clothes. They were clean, often-mended, and the pants were those of an infantryman, the shirt homespun, the cowled cloak also that of a soldier.

"Put them on," she ordered. I did as she told me, and she turned to her husband. "Well?"

"Released after the peace," he said. "Wandered for a time, taking whatever job came along. Since he still has his sword and dangerous-looking knife, he's obviously a man who's willing to deal in death."

"Good," she approved. "That's a good thing for him to appear as. Such men are left alone on the roads, for they never carry silver, and taking whatever coppers they have isn't worth the bloodshed. He'll not be bothered much, if he keeps to himself, on his journey to Cimabue."

I jolted.

"How did you know that?" I blurted, not the most subtle admission I'd ever made.

She looked mysterious and changed the subject. "One more thing," she said, opening a small pouch, and taking something out. "Hold still now," and she pressed something against my left cheekbone, ran it down to my jawline, and she muttered as she did. It felt slimy, cold, then warmed against my skin.

"What—"

"A good soldier," her husband said, "generally has a scar or two. Interesting thing about people," he went on. "They'll note something about your features and forget the rest of your face. So you'll be seen as Scarface, and no one'll be able to tell the shape of your nose or color of your eyes."

"The device is one used by mummers," the woman went on. "It's slightly ensorcelled, so you can wash, eat, swim with it on, and not worry. The words to take it off, and remember them well, for I doubt you'll be able to come back here for a trot to the memory, are *'enem, enem, letek nisrap,'* said twice." I repeated them several times in my mind.

"You have them right?"

I nodded.

"There's bread, cheese, water downstairs, since you drink no wine," she said. "Eat quickly, for your new employer will be here shortly."

The thin man held out a heavy bag of coins, with a drawstring about it, which I just stared at, still shaken by the woman's knowledge.

"Here. Hang this around your neck. Your chest is big enough to conceal your wealth. Now hurry!"

The man smelled of sweat, even though his clothes and face were clean. He was scrabbily bearded and wore heavy boots, pants, and shirt, hardly ideal for Nicias's tropic climate.

"I'm Yakub," he said, grinning happily. "Come meet my children out back."

There were a dozen cages stacked on a handcart, each holding a large snake. Some coiled watchfully, some appeared to sleep, others slid from corner to corner of their cage, endlessly seeking freedom.

"Yakub," the woman explained, "offered you six, no, eight coppers, plus your passage, if you'd help him with his wares across the Latane. The ferry's ramps and such are treacherous, and Yakub needs a good strong man who fears nothing. I doubt if any warders will be too interested in closely examining such a cargo . . . or its owners.

"And it's best you be gone, for the next ferry that crosses the whole of the Delta will leave in two hours."

Yakub laughed, jumped up and down.

"Yes, yes, out of the city, and going once more, where we're free, away from everything stone and dirty." He giggled again, and I wondered if he was entirely right in the head. But no matter.

I bowed to the woman, then to her husband.

"Thank you," I said. "I don't know why you've helped me."

"It was not choice," she said, "but a command, but from whom you need not know. Although I would've given you aid regardless, with what the future will . . . must bring. Remember this, Damastes á Cimabue, and also remember that everything changes, and nothing is ever the same.

"There is no Wheel, contrary to what you believe, but only a Path that goes on and on, without turning back, and what we do on that Path determines its ending."

I gaped, and she held out her hand. I took it, and her blouse came open a bit at the neck, and I saw the deadly yellow strangling cord of the Tovieti!

THE WORN LAND

Pushing the snake cart through Nicias, I was an ideal laborer—a very strong back, and utterly no mind. I was dimly aware of the thronged streets, pushing through muttering priests, worried merchants, idling wastrels, but my brain was spinning, trying to figure out why the Tovieti had helped me. From the woman's words, it clearly wasn't an individual act of mercy, but a decision by someone of authority in the cult.

I didn't understand at all. First the Tovieti had been an anarchic sect, worshiping the crystal demon Thak, strangling anyone more fortunate than they with their yellow cords and stealing their goods. They'd been bloodily suppressed, I then thought destroyed, in the riots, before Tenedos took the throne, and the Seer had personally destroyed Thak.

Ten years later, they'd reemerged, but this time without a deity or leaders, or so the emperor's spymaster, Kutulu, had told me. They'd still promised to destroy all countries and bring down the rich and mighty, for only then could freedom and justice prevail. But this time, they worked without leaders, in small cells, saying perhaps one day a true leader would arise, but they did not need one until that day and that person came.

They'd tried to murder me twice, first at my Water Palace; the second time at my former wife's estates at Irrigon, killing Marán's brother, Countess Amiel Kalvedon, and our unborn child—and ending my marriage to Marán.

During the war with Maisir, I'd seen their signs occasionally—either a simple representation of their strangling cord, an upside-down U or, more often, a red circle that represented their martyrs with a nest of serpents rising from the pool of blood.

After Numantia fell to Maisir, and the emperor and I were sent to prison, I'd heard nothing more about them, nor had my warders heard of their continued existence. But clearly they were still active, and widespread as well, for how else could that huge woman have known who I was, my personal habits, and then a way to help me?

Wasn't I their greatest enemy, after Tenedos?

In the retreat from Maisir, high in the mountains of the Disputed Lands, a bearded old man had reminded me of the prophecy at my birth, that I was the boy who rode the tiger, and the tiger would turn on me, but my life would go on, longer than I would think. But the color of my life-thread would become bright yellow and be made of silk, like the Tovieti strangling cords.

The man had finished in mystery, saying, "Why shouldn't evil become good, if perceived good is evil?" That had been all he would say, other than his cynicism had satisfied both his duty and his sense of humor.

None of this made the slightest sense.

As the Tovieti woman had foreseen, the ferry docks at the Latane River were thronged with warders, and there were three of them stationed at the head of the gangway to our boat. The closer we got, the more Yakub muttered, cackled, laughed to himself, and, with a long feather, caressed his snakes through the cages. I began to have my suspicions about just how mad he was.

We reached the head of the line, and a warder snarled brusquely, "Names, place of landing, home?" glanced up from his tablet, saw a particularly curious cobra's head moving sinuously back and forth, about a foot from his, screeched like a eunuch, leapt back, and almost fell overboard. Quite satisfactory.

Enraged by his show of weakness, but still terrified, he snarled incoherently, and his fellow snapped, "Get these bastards aboard, and it'll be yer head if the cages come open," and didn't even glance at the tickets Yakub tried to give him.

Yakub tucked them into a pocket, murmured, "They'll do for next time," and told me to follow him with the cart. The ferry was crowded, but everyone made ample room for us.

"M' beauties'll like the center, the center," Yakub sang happily, "no movin', no swayin' to upset their little hearts, don't make 'em angry, make 'em want to sink their little bitey fangs into someone, don't want that, no indeed, don't want that 'tall," and we found a place for the cart tucked under the deckhouse's overhang on the main deck, looking aft at the paddles and the empty treadmills that ran them. The belts of the mill were cut from the hides of elephants, buffaloes, oxen, then sorcerously endowed with their strength, many times magnified, so no "real" power was needed.

The cart's wheels were on castors and came off easily. I lashed the cart securely to a stanchion. "Mild river, quiet river," he chattered, "but we'll take no chances, no, no, not and have the beauties slip out and play their games."

He tugged at my handiwork, nodded satisfaction. "We'll go inside and break our fasts, eh, soldier?"

I felt hunger, then saw four hard-faced Peace Guardians stalk into the mess.

"Uh . . . no," I said. "I did eat. Earlier. Not very hungry."

Yakub looked at me skeptically. "A soldier, not hungry? When the fodder's free?" Then he giggled. "Ah, ah, ah. You get sick, eh? From th' water?"

I tried to look embarrassed.

"Best thing," he went on, "a sailor taught me, is t' take a piece of raw pork, nice an' greasy, an' tie a string to it. Swaller it, run it up and down, then pull it back up, an' y'll heave ever'thing heavable an' be splendid. But when y' feel something round an' hairy, swaller fast, for it's yer arsehole." He almost fell over, he was laughing so hard.

"But never you mind," he said, "I'll see y' have some porridge or some. An' you can guard th' beauties, then."

He scurried away. I wasn't about to eat in front of the Guardians, not sure how good my disguise or the spell was, and didn't fancy the possibility of being caught munching on my own scar.

I put on the air of a "don't fool with me" near-outlaw, wrapped my sword belt first around the cage, then one leg, set my naked blade across my knees, and pulled up the cowl of my hood, pretending sleep but with my eyes open a crack.

Not far from the docks were steps down into the river, thronged with bathers in the midday sun. There was a rather pretty, naked woman, a few years younger than I, shepherding her flock of one little boy and his five equally nude sisters, none more than ten years old, around the shallows as they soaped and splashed. The woman had a golden chain about her waist, and I remembered years and years before, when I'd ridden the *Tauler* south to my first assignment, with the Seventeenth Lancers, when there'd been a young girl with such a chain bathing, who'd smiled invitingly. I wondered if this could be the same woman, grinned at my foolish romanticism, but wished it to be so, and that her brood marked her happiness and the more expensive chain her freedom from want.

Horns blatted from the captain's deck, and passengers thronged the rails as the paddle wheel churned. I watched the people, marveling at how differently they all dressed, not like warders or soldiers, and once more realized the war's effect. These weren't the same people who'd traveled in peacetime. There were trekking merchants as always, but most of these were accompanied by guards, and their ages were quite young or well into middle age, few the normal age of men who choose danger for a life.

Here were a gaggle of nautch dancers nattering on about the far cities of Numantia, but their silks were somewhat worn, and in the style of ten years gone. There were few families on holiday, either rich or poor. I saw Delta farmers, work-hardened faces and hands, muttering in low tones about this year's rice crop and how poor the markets were.

Boot heels rasped by my sandaled feet, and I saw gray, uniformed legs. There were two sets. My hand was on Perak's dagger. If I was discovered, I'd kill one, bowl the other aside, and be overboard before anyone could take action.

One voice said, "Nice friends to travel with, hmm?"

I hoped he wasn't expecting me to wake and respond

and was fortunate, for the other Guardian said, "Doesn't seem to bother *him*, now does it?" They laughed, moved on, and I began breathing once more.

In midriver, with no one watching, I took the amulet Tenedos had given me from its hiding place. I held it for a moment, considering, wondering, felt it grow warm, and hastily spun it over the side.

Let him seek me among the fishes.

The Peace Guardians disembarked at our second landing, and I told Yakub how much the porridge he'd brought had helped my stomach, and I thought I could manage a bit of solid food now.

Like most river craft, this ferry fed well, especially for travelers like ourselves who'd booked passage all the way across the Delta. I'd imagined I'd be enjoying one or another of the various roasts offered, or perhaps the smoked meats, but in fact I gloried in cascades of fresh fruit and vegetables, particularly legumes in the many variations Numantian cuisine offered. My body was telling me what it wanted, what it needed. Once my lust for green growing things was satiated, then I became interested in meat.

Yakub was somewhat appalled at my appetite, wondering what sort of a demon he'd roused. I didn't tell him an endless monotony of prison food, no matter how skillfully prepared, will make the most ascetic into a glutton, once he has the opportunity.

Yakub had spent his . . . or the Tovieti's . . . silver carefully, not paying for a compartment, but choosing to sleep on deck. This was hazardous, for thieves, generally members of the ferry's crew, stalked the decks after dark, and these ferries were infamous for robberies, rapes, even the odd murder if a deck passenger fought for his purse too hard.

Once someone approached us stealthily, heard the rasp of my sword being unsheathed, and turned away. Again I woke, hearing the sounds of a struggle, saw two men struggling, one old, one young, the young one with a knuckle bow. He didn't see me until I was on him, and I clubbed him down with the iron pig clenched in my fist. The old man stood frozen, and I tipped the would-be robber overside and went back into the shadows before the old one could recover.

I saw him the next day, going from man to man, peering into their faces, trying to identify his benefactor . . . or, possibly, to find a murderer to report to the ship's officers. But he, too, wouldn't approach my snakes, and the incident was ended.

Five days later, we reached the far banks of the Delta, put the wheels back on the cart, and disembarked in the small port of Kaldi. We stopped in a marketplace, bought a zebu and rope harness, and hitched the beast up. Outside the city, a highway ran north and south.

"Here is where we part, soldier," Yakub said. "I go north, to where the old emperor is building his army. He'll have magicians, and magicians need spells, and spells need snakes." He cackled. "And I have other things he needs."

I eyed his rags and the cart skeptically.

"Aye, aye, aye," he laughed. "Appears like there's nothing, doesn't it, doesn't it? Just as the cart can hide a traveler, so snakes, and where they shit, can hide . . . oh, many, many things.

"Many, many things," he repeated, his shoulders shaking, and I bade him, with sudden fondness, fare-thee-well.

I watched him become a dot on the dusty road, wondering what lay hidden in the sawdust in the snakes' cages. Gold? Diamonds? Secret information? I didn't know . . . but I did know one thing. Yakub, the Man of Snakes, was no crazier, and probably a great deal saner, than I.

I turned away from the highway and took a winding side lane that led west and southwest.

Toward Cimabue. Toward my home.

That night, over a low fire, roasting an unwary hare and potatoes I'd dug from a field in the coals below, I repeated the words to remove the scar. For an instant, I panicked, nothing at all coming to mind, then remembered, and the scar fell into my hand, and was tossed away.

Little as I liked it, the beard I'd decided to not shave would make as good a disguise.

It was a very long way, almost two hundred leagues. But I didn't walk the entire distance. Frequently there were caravans or just farmer's carts heading for the next village or going home from market. Once they realized my sword wouldn't be turned against them, they were glad for a warrior's presence.

But all too often they saw my blade and either galloped past or else, if they had armed men of their own, told me to move away into the fields or be killed. I obeyed sadly, for I could remember the times of peace under the emperor, when it was said a virgin could cross the kingdom with a bag of gold in each hand.

Of course that was horse apples—the poor lass would've been lucky to make it a league beyond her village before she would've been both poorer and more experienced. But it was still a boast very much of the past.

War hadn't touched these lands, at least not obviously, and the soil was still dark and rich, the irrigation canals spidering away from the rivers still bringing life to the land.

But their floodgates were rotten, the fields were all too often untilled, the canal banks sliding into the water, some of the waterways choked with weeds, as if the land was worn out and abandoned.

Fruit trees were just beginning to flower in this Time of Births, but their unplucked fruit from the previous season was rotting remnants on the ground or still dangling from the limbs.

Kites rose from the trees, their cry sounding raucously across emptiness.

The scatter of farms under cultivation were being worked by women, old men, children.

Where were the men, young, middle-aged?

The whisper ran across the land: "Gone to the army, gone to war, gone to the emperor, gone to Maisir, gone to the Wheel, never to return . . ."

The days passed, and the weather grew warmer, the fresh rains welcome. I traveled at my own pace, for the first time in my life not having to be somewhere at a certain time, whether to quell an uprising, take over a new command, deal with a recalcitrant baron, or to lead or train soldiers.

I saw no Peace Guardians, which didn't surprise me, knowing so small a unit must restrict itself to the cities and, possibly, harrying Tenedos's reforming army to the south. The scattering of warders in the small villages had little interest in anything beyond their own district, especially in regards to a well-armed man who kept to himself.

I stopped when I felt like it, sometimes helping with the planting or with heavy work a farmer's widow or children could not manage, and little by little remembered my boyhood skills helping my father's tenants with their plowing, herding, animal husbandry. I'd work an hour, or a day, and then move on, my pack full of the fresh food that'd been all the pay I wanted.

I also reminded myself of other skills, making a sling from tanned hides I found in a desolate village and practicing with it as I traveled, stalking sambur who gloried in the still-fallow, empty farmlands, snaring guinea fowl, chickens, or ducks gone wild for my meals.

I was alone and very content.

For the most part, my journey was undisturbed and uneventful. But there were some events that stayed with me . . .

The cart was overturned, its contents scattered, just beyond where the road had been cut through an embankment, perfect for an ambush.

Three men were sprawled in the road, and a woman's corpse lay half across the cart, a gaping wound in her chest, a look of horror on her face.

Five children, three boys and two girls, were tied together like ducks for the marketplace. The older ones' faces held hate, the younger ones' terror.

Eight men sat across the road from the wreckage, sharing a wineskin.

I approached, sword in hand.

A man stood, came toward me. He was big, bearded, and had a war hammer at his side.

"Greetin's," he said.

"Your doing?" I gestured at the shambles.

"'A course," he said. "Damn' fool of a shitdigger went and stood against us. Hells, we di'n't mean much damage. Mayhap sort through his goods, have a bit of sport wi' his woman, no more.

"'Stead, he kills two of us, and his wife afore we took him.

"Fool of a waste, it is," he said. "We'll take the young 'uns, see what the market is these times, 'though there's more'n enough spare babes already for the slavers.

"If'n that one was more'n nine, ten, maybe we'd keep her, train her. But we ain't got th' time nor me th' inclination. You innarested in buyin' any of 'em?"

I shook my head.

The big man looked me over carefully.

"You look like a fighter. Innarested in joinin' us? We do fair well, bein' about th' only band in the district."

"I've got my own work," I said flatly.

The man grunted.

"I'll warn you. A single man, these times, can have a hard way, with nobody t' watch whilst he sleeps, or when his back's turned."

"I'm not worried," I said. "I've got a demon guarding me."

The big man looked worried, and two of his men got to their feet, making strange signs.

"Thanks f'r th' warning," he said. "Pass on, then. Pass on quick."

I didn't answer but kept moving. That night, I camped fireless, far from the road, but never saw them again.

I tried to push the children's faces from my mind, but failed. What could I have done? There were eight of them, odds no sane warrior would dream of facing.

But I still had the taste of ashes in my mouth.

The farm had been prosperous, with three barns for livestock, a chicken run, a duck pond, a paddock, a long barracks for farmhands and a sturdy two-story house for the owners. Now the fields were desolate, the barns empty, and the buildings abandoned.

Scavengers had picked through the debris, taking what they wanted, befouling what they didn't. But they hadn't destroyed everything, and I unearthed a man's blouse that sort of fit, a pair of baggy pants that would do, and thought myself rich, now having a change in addition to the clothes on my back.

I found two cooking pots, one for an unlucky partridge I'd brought down with a stone earlier, the other for a thick wild vegetable soup I'd been planning as I walked, harvesting here and there as I went. There were spices in small jars the looters had scorned, so I'd eat well . . . and sleep dry, for thunder grumbled outside, and I'd be grateful for shelter this night.

I saw a gleam in the farmhouse's great room, wondered if the scavengers had missed a coin, and picked up a small cast metal flag of Numantia. I knew what it was, had seen a hundred or more of them.

Knowing myself a fool and what to expect, still I rubbed the flag, and two figures grew from nothingness. They were young men, actually boys, one perhaps nineteen, the other a couple of years younger, obviously his brother. They had close-shaven heads and wore the bare uniform of recruits in the Imperial Army.

They grinned shyly, and one said, "What do you think of us, Da? Ma? They wouldn't let us keep our hair, but they gave us these clothes in trade. Don't we look like soldiers?"

The other laughed. "He thinks *he* looks like a soldier. I don't. But they're trying to teach us how, and we're working hard, and we haven't gotten into any trouble."

The first turned serious. "They say we'll be going south soon, to the frontiers and then into Maisir, to help the emperor destroy their evil king. Pray for us."

The second nodded. "Please. But . . . don't worry. We'll come to no harm. We promise."

They both held their smiles, then vanished.

As I said, I'd seen the little cast flags before. Sorcerers by the dozens, little more than village mountebanks, really, haunted the army camps, in spite of the provosts' best attempts to chase them away. They'd pose a recruit, cast a spell, and trap the moment in a flag, or a toy dagger or small horse, with a bit of the recruit's spittle or blood. Naturally, the young soldier would pay well for this, and somehow it would get its way to the ones he loved.

I wondered where in Maisir these boys had died. Penda? On the *suebi*? Irthing? Jarrah? Sidor? Or in some nameless swamp, in a flurried skirmish that left two or three bodies sprawled in the mud or the snow?

And what of their Da and Ma? Why'd they leave everything? Had they word their sons were sore wounded in some hospital, left the land, and been snared in the web of war? No one but Irisu knew, Irisu and Saionji perhaps. I shivered, and the thunder rumbled more loudly.

But I took my pots and spices and left the farm, finding poor shelter in a grove of trees half a mile distant. I don't believe in ghosts, but that farmhouse was haunted.

* * *

One day I came on an odd sight. Nine or ten boys, perhaps fourteen to seventeen, all wearing the smock of farmers' lads, were straggling along the road, behind a man wearing the old, banned uniform of the Imperial Army. I puzzled at this imposter as he came closer, and he hailed me cheerfully.

Rather doubtfully I returned the greeting, and introduced myself using some name or other I made up on the moment.

"I'm Color-Sergeant Tagagne, once Third Imperial Guards Corps, now serving the emperor directly," he boomed.

"And how might that be?"

"Wait a moment, and I'll tell you." He turned to the boys. "You men, fall out around me. We'll take a breather here before we go on."

The young men gratefully found a bit of shade under the roadside trees, close enough to hear our conversation.

"Color-Sergeant?" I said doubtfully. "But the emperor's army's been dissolved and its men sent home."

"By who? The shit-for-brains who call themselves the Grand Council? By that homicidal fuck behind them who sits the throne in Maisir? Since when does the emperor listen to lickspittles like them?"

I nodded agreement, and perhaps a bit of a smile came.

"You look to have been one who served the emperor," Tagagne said.

"I was."

"For how long?"

I could have told him the truth, that I was Laish Tenedos's first follower. "For a long time."

"In Maisir?"

I nodded once more.

"Ah, that was terrible, terrible," he sighed. "But by Saionji, we fought well."

I noted a couple of the farmboys shuddered at the death-goddess's name.

"We did," I said. "But they fought better."

"The hells they did," he said, a bit angry. "There were just more of them than we could kill. Otherwise, we'd be in Jarrah, wearing silk uniforms and each of us ruling a province."

"But we aren't."

"But we will be again," Tagagne said. "That's why these brave boys have taken the emperor's coin. We're heading for . . . for where I'm not supposed to say, and join the new army. We're getting ready to fight back, proud again under the Emperor Tenedos's banner," he said, "and drive those jerk-off Councilors out of Nicias, and the mongrels who call themselves Peace Guardians into the Latane.

"Those we don't hang from the nearest tree first."

A couple of the boys grinned tightly at that idea, and I smiled as well. "Those bastards could do with more than a bit of hanging, I'll agree."

"Then come help us," Tagagne said. "You don't appear crippled. Come back to the colors, lad, for there's still fighting to be done, and Numantia to be won back."

"No," I said. "I'm my own master now and want to keep it that way."

Tagagne shook his head. "I'll not wave a white feather at you nor curse a man who served in Maisir. But there's a hard wind abroad, and there'll be no man permitted to sit the fence or plow his own furrow 'til Numantia's ruled by its own.

"Come on, friend," he cajoled. "Forget the hard times and the lost comrades, and remember the good times, the comradeship, the pride of your uniform, and the glory of marching under the emperor's banners. These boys haven't known that, haven't had their share of glory yet, but they're for it, they're true Numantians all."

Honestly, in spite of the horror I knew war to be, I felt a bit of truth in Tagagne's words, and remembered the fierce joy of being Tenedos's warrior. But I also remembered . . . other things.

"No, Sergeant," I said. "But I'll think well of you for offering."

"I'll not press my cause," Tagagne said. "There'll be others who come to you, in other times, and maybe you'll remember my words, and then join us, join us in making Numantia free."

He didn't wait for a response but turned to his charges. "Come on now, you men, for we've a long road to go before night."

Obediently, they tramped off. I watched them over the hill. At its crest the last boy looked back and waved. I waved back, then went on my course.

No, Numantia was not free, and sooner or later there must be a fight.

But that must no longer matter to me.

The village, unlike some others, was neat, and smoke curled from some chimneys. Its fields were plowed, fat cows grazed in them, and I saw women tending a fishpond on its outskirts.

I'd just happened to spot the settlement, about a sixth of a league from the road, almost hidden behind a rise, and, tired of my own cooking, decided to ask for a night's shelter for a day's work.

The track to the village was somewhat overgrown, as if

few travelers came. Then I saw the village had been skill-fully fenced with bamboo stakes, and the path was closed off with a log spiked with bamboo spears.

"Halloo the village," I hailed, and two women trotted out of a building. One carried a bow and quiver, the other a spear.

"Stand where you are."

I obeyed, knowing what would come next—they'd see my sword and the remnants of my uniform, and order me away, fearing me as a marauder.

A third woman came from another hut as the two stood to either side of the log, weapons ready. She was a bit older than I, slender, and carried herself like a noblewoman.

"Who are you?" she demanded.

"A traveler," I said. "Call me . . . Nurri. I would like a meal and will work for it."

She stared hard, and I felt her gaze pierce as the emperor's had and knew her to be a seer of some power.

The other two women waited for her decision.

"He means no harm," she said. "Let him enter."

Without argument, they uncoiled ropes, dragged the log out of the way.

"Thank you . . ."

"I am Gunett," she said. "I have been chosen village elder."

"Thank you, Gunett. What jobs do you have?"

"We could do with some wood hewed," she said.

"Gladly."

"And after that . . . there might be other tasks."

She smiled mysteriously, and one woman giggled.

I enjoy a simple chore like cutting wood, although when you've been away from the woodpile for years, it's not quite as simple as it appears. But each time the ax comes down, you remember a bit of your old skills, and in time you're able to put the blade precisely where you want it, with exactly the right amount of force—and not cut off your foot.

There was a lot of wood, but what of it? I stripped to the waist, shut off my mind, and became mechanical. I prided myself that I seldom needed the maul to split a log, and, as time passed, remembered the knack of splitting a log with a single blow.

Near the end of the pile, I became aware I had an audience. Two girls in their late teens were watching. I now had a duty to perform well and sent the last piece of wood spinning high to land atop the pile of chopped wood.

I bowed, they laughed, and one tossed me a clean towel.

"I'm Steffi," she said, "and I was sent to tell you it's almost time to eat. My friend here is Mala." Steffi had long black hair tied in a queue, very red lips, and eyes matching her hair. She wore a homespun frock, decorated with sewn flowers and sandals and was very cute. Her friend, Mala, was a little heavy-set, but with a flashing smile and an easy blush.

I wiped sweat and asked if there was a place I might clean up. The two girls escorted me to a small cottage that was the village washhouse. Wine casks had been cut in two and filled with water, and there was a great cauldron of heated water over a low fire. I dipped hot water into a cask until it was warm enough, found lye soap, stripped and washed thoroughly standing outside, then climbed into the cask to soak for a time.

I wished I had clean clothing to change into, but both sets were filthy. I washed them both in a bucket, hung one to dry on my pack, and put the other set on, after thoroughly wringing it out.

I saw a mirror on one wall and considered myself, grimacing as I noted the roots of my blond hair had grown out, and I was beginning to look a bit strange. But there was nothing I could do about that.

There was a table nearby, with various potions and perfumes. I found a tiny razor, such as a woman might use to shave her privates if she fancied, stropped the blade on my belt, lathered myself and shaved, while I considered that table.

Everything appeared to be for women's use. Was this village without men?

It was not, as I discovered at the meal. But there were only six of them, and only one, something of a dullard if handsome, well-muscled, and friendly, was under forty. The long cookhall swarmed with children—I counted a dozen and a half, half boys, half girls, all less than ten years old.

There were twenty-six women in the village, Gunett told me, and some weren't at the meal, but standing watch outside.

"We've had bandits try our strength," she said. "And, Jacini and Panoan be blessed, we drove them off."

"I think," said one of the older men, a scholarly-looking sort who looked like a refugee from a lycee, whose name was Edirne, "we hurt them badly enough so they'll not return. Scoundrels prefer easy targets."

"But we'll take no chances," Gunett said, "and keep our guards posted.

"Good," I said. "It's cheaper to waste hours staring at nothing than lives."

"You talk . . . and dress . . . like a soldier."

"I was one, once," I admitted, and changed the subject. "If I may ask—there's few men here. Did the war account for this?"

"Just so," Edirne said.

"We were hit particularly hard," Gunett said, bitterness in her voice, "because many of us came away from the cities during the Tovieti years to find a safer, happier life for ourselves and our children. Knowing how easy it is to become isolated, we made sure we kept abreast of everything that was happening."

"Since we were loyal subjects of the emperor," Edirne said, "of course, when the call to the colors came, we responded vigorously, and enough of our men joined to provide half a company, so they were able to remain together."

I waited.

"Not one came back," a woman sitting down the long table said, almost in a whisper. "We don't know what happened, where they died, or even if they died. But Gunett has made castings and says she's almost sure none live." She dabbed at the corner of her eye, turned away for a moment.

I swallowed hard. A whole town's life, wiped out, probably at some nameless Maisirian crossroads . . .

"But we refused to let ourselves be destroyed," Gunett said. "We'll carry on and prosper, even if the gods turned away for a time.

"But this is hardly something to talk about over a meal," she said firmly. "Troubles, or talking about them, do not improve digestion."

I agreed, and we concentrated on the meal. It was a good one—hot, spiced hard-boiled eggs, some sort of river fish cooked in a fiery sauce, new potatoes with mint drenched in butter, and hard-smoked pork with a mustardy sauce.

Gunett sat on one side of me, and a small redheaded woman in her early twenties was on the other. Her name was Marminill, and she wore her hair cut short, and freckles sprinkled across her nose. She had green eyes, pert breasts, and wore a frilly shirt that had to come from a city and a short skirt that buttoned up the side.

She asked if I'd come from a city, and like a fool I said yes, Nicias. She then wanted to know what people were wearing, what they were talking about, what sort of music was being played in the capital.

I didn't think it would be appropriate to say what little I saw of Nicias was through the slit of a prisoner's carriage or running through the streets with a sword in my hand and am afraid I told some fairly outrageous lies, digging up what I remembered of styles from before the war. But she seemed content with my fabrications. The others talked of their work, of the planting and cultivation, and I listened happily, for this was the talk I'd grown up with in Cimabue, and the only talk of killing was whether or not the village should butcher a milk cow that was no longer producing.

We finished, and some of the younger women cleared our plates. Steffi and her friend Mala were among them, and as Steffi took my plate, she winked and grinned, as if we shared some secret.

Dessert was winter melons and a pomegranate tart.

"I preserved the fruit from last harvest," Gunett said with some pride, "with a spell I devised from remembering more experienced seers' work. I was only beginning my apprenticeship when we . . . when I . . . came here."

Both dishes were excellent.

"We have some brandy," she went on, "that we traded for during the war. We've got grapes planted from cuttings, but as yet, we haven't been able to produce wine. But if you'd care to try the brandy?"

"No, thank you," I said. "I don't drink at all."

"Good," Marminill said.

"You disapprove of spirits?" I asked.

"Not hardly," she said. "But it shortens the evening."

I didn't understand but didn't press the matter.

When we finished, Gunett said, "We may choose a somewhat communal life here, but we're not ones who sit around singing and tale telling after we eat."

"Especially," Edirne said with a yawn, "when those damned chickens start cackling at dawn for feed."

The villagers wandered away toward their huts, and Marminill and I walked to the edge of the village.

The country was quiet, the only sounds a yapping of a fox somewhere in a distant copse, then the low hunting cry of an owl.

"You did right," I said, "leaving the city."

"I wouldn't know," Marminill said. "For I was only five years old when my parents brought me here from Cicognara." She looked at the setting sun, then said, a little wistfully, "Probably you're right. But it'd be nice to know something about the rest of the world."

"These days," I said, hoping I didn't sound like a pompous fool, "I think it's better to have your own world and let the bigger one roll by. It's safer."

"Maybe," she said. "But sometimes that other world comes to you, whether you want it or not."

I started to reply, decided to stay silent.

"Do you want to know where you'll be sleeping?" she asked.

I got my pack and still-wet clothes from the washhouse, and she led me to a small hut on the edge of the village. There was a single window, with a lattice blind, and the door was closed with a double lattice that unrolled from above. There was little furniture, beyond a surprisingly large bed and two long wooden chests that served as low tables. Marminill lit a candle; then there was a somewhat uncomfortable silence. I stretched and felt shoulder muscles creak from their unaccustomed work. I rubbed my neck with one hand.

"Do you want me to do that?" Marminill said. I looked at her curiously. "I'm very good at relaxing muscles," she said.

She was very pretty in the candlelight and the dim light from the window.

"Please."

"Lie down, then," she ordered. "On your stomach."

I obeyed, and she straddled my back, and her hands began kneading me. It felt good, very good.

"Would you . . . take off your shirt?" she said, her voice lower, a bit throaty. She slid off me, and I stripped, lay back down. I heard the rustle of cloth, and she bestrode me once more. But this time, instead of cloth, I felt silken flesh, a bit of wetness, the tickle of hair, and her massage was more a series of caresses than a real rubdown. Her breathing . . . and mine . . . came faster.

"This isn't exactly relaxing my muscles," I said. "At least, not one of them."

"No?" she whispered. "Perhaps you might turn over, and we could see what the problem is."

She got off me, and I obeyed. She stood beside me, naked, and her nipples were firm. She unbuttoned my pants, and I lifted my hips and she slid me out of them. My cock stood hard.

"Oh my," she said. "You're very big. Maybe you could do something with that muscle to relax it?"

I took her in my arms, rolled her across my body, and slid my tongue into her mouth. Her tongue met mine, worked against it, and her arms were around me, close-cut fingernails pulling at me, and we kissed for a long time, our hands sliding over each others' bodies.

"Yes," she breathed. "Now. Do it to me now."

"Not yet," I said, and teased her nipples with my teeth, nibbled on her stomach, then ran my tongue in and out of her wet sex, stroked her hard clitoris with it.

"Please!" she demanded, legs far apart, lifting into the air. "Now, please now."

I moved over her, slid my cock all the way into her tightness with a single motion, and she gasped. I did it three more times, was about to withdraw and caress her, but my body betrayed me, and I jerked and felt myself spurt. An instant later, she came as well, legs pulling me into her.

The world swam, came back, and I was still in her, still firm.

"Sorry," I said. "It's been . . . too long."

"For me as well," Marminill whispered. "And not many times at that."

I was curious about how the village managed love, with the imbalance of sexes, but was a little too bashful to ask. Besides, her body was still warm and wet about me, and I began moving, slowly, and her legs went higher, clasping me just under my shoulders, and I took her ankles in each hand, held them far apart, and drove hard, and she gasped, then screamed, so loudly I thought I'd have the sentries on me.

* * *

I slept, and then awoke, feeling soft fingers caressing my balls, my cock, and stiffened once more. The candle was out, but the blind was still rolled up, although the night sky gave little illumination to the room. I fumbled down, felt warm buttocks, and legs parted to welcome me.

I got to my knees, moved half-asleep between her legs, and entered her. She moaned, wriggled against me, and I began slowly moving in her, coming almost out with each stroke.

Her moaning grew louder, and her buttocks rose, fell with me, and her head came back. I dropped across her, reached under her, took large, small-nippled breasts in both hands, my head buried in curling hair and realized the woman I was making love to was not Marminill, but someone else, and she was moving with me, and thought vanished and I spun into the earth and cried out as she jolted against me.

I took myself out of her, moved aside, and she quickly got up and went to the door.

"Thank you," she whispered, pulled the lattice aside, and was gone.

Shocked fully awake, I sat up, looked around the hut. There was no one else in it. I wondered what the hells was going on, where Marminill was, but there was no one to ask. I found a pitcher of water, drank deeply, used the small brass pot I'd seen to one side of the room, lay back down.

Very strange . . . but I felt no threat, no danger, plus I'd cut a lot of wood . . . and done other things, so my eyes closed, and I was asleep.

I came awake, feeling lips move around my cock, teeth teasing its head. Two candles were lit, and I saw long black hair covering my midsection, wondered who it was this time, but weak flesh refused to let me stop my lover, and so my hands went to her head, curled in her soft hair, caressed her as she moved a little faster, taking all of me in her, and I contorted, gushing into her mouth, then sagging back.

My breathing slowed, but the woman kept kissing me, tongue moving on my balls and groin before her head lifted.

It was Steffi, very naked. I managed, I hope, not to show my surprise.

"I've never done that," she said. "Just read about it in Gunett's books. I guess I did all right."

She smiled, licked her lips. "I'm not supposed to be here," she whispered.

I didn't need to offend any local customs, and thoughts of ceremonial castration for the sin of bedding a woman the village thought too young ran through my head.

"Why not?" I was whispering, too.

Steffi rested her head on my thigh, and gently began caressing my cock with a forefinger.

"Because it's not my time."

"I don't understand."

"Marminill and Kima . . . this is the time when they'll most likely conceive. Have a child of yours. That's why Gunett sent them to you."

"Oh." Of course. That was the other task Gunett had spoken of, and why the woman had giggled. It made sense. How else was the village to repopulate itself safely and quickly, except by using acceptable wanderers, so the next generation wouldn't be intermarrying pinheads?

"But I didn't care," Steffi said. "Edirne finishes in an instant, then wants to talk about it, and Jalak's too dumb to talk to. And," she said, her voice going low, "I wanted to fuck somebody new.

"I just wish I could have been first." She looked away. "Or maybe the only one." Steffi forced brightness. "But that's not the way it is for us, so I'll take whatever I can.

"I wanted Mala to come with me, but she thought you'd think that was too strange, and throw us both out."

I thought *everything* was a little strange, but didn't say anything.

"You were sleeping so well, I almost didn't want to wake you up."

"You managed to do a good job of it."

"Maybe too good a job," she said, running a finger down the base of my cock. "It's still not doing what it's supposed to. Oh wait. It *is* alive. Stand up now, like you're supposed to. Gunett's spell is working."

"She cast a spell on me?" I asked, a bit stupidly, but still having a bit of fear of magic being applied to me, especially that part of me.

"Of course," Steffi said. "We wanted to make sure you would work for your supper." She giggled. "Do you like me?"

"Of course."

"Then fuck me, please now. And do something special, something I'll remember when you're gone."

I considered, noted the chest.

"Come up here," I said. "First, I want to kiss you."

"Whatever you wish," and she slid on top of me, and we kissed for long moments, caressing each other. I kissed the length of her body, moved fingers and tongue in and out of her until she was writhing. I picked up her dress from the floor, put it on the chest, and laid Steffi atop it on her back, her buttocks just at the edge, feet on the floor. I knelt between them.

"Put your legs around my waist," and she obeyed. I moved my cock up and down along her sex, and she was panting, head rolling from side to side.

"Please!"

"Not yet," I said, teasing her once again with the head of my cock, moving it in a bare inch, then out, and she swore, words a soldier would use, trying to pull me into her. Again I stroked her, and her hands were clawing at the dress she lay atop, and this time I pushed my cock into her, and she gasped.

"Put your feet back down on the floor," and she did, and I moved steadily in her, feeling her clitoris against my pubic bone, kneading her breasts, and then her feet came off the floor and around my neck and I kept moving, moving, and she came, trying to keep from shouting aloud, but I was still hard, still moving, and again she clasped me into her.

We were lying together, still joined, back on the bed, and she was stroking my chest.

"Can I ask something?"

"I might answer."

"I don't think your name is Nurri."

"It's not."

"Will you tell me what it really is?"

I hesitated, then, "Damastes á Cimabue."

She shook her head. "I don't know it. Should I?"

I made a noncommittal noise.

"You're running away from something, aren't you?"

"What makes you think that?" I asked.

"You dyed your hair, and I don't think anybody who's blond would want to be dark-haired."

"Why not? You've got dark hair, and you're beautiful."

She smiled at me.

"Thank you. Jalak's the only other one who ever told me that."

"There are some very blind men in this village."

Steffi sighed. "No. They're just used to me, like we're all used to each other. I wish . . ." She shook her head. "Never mind. Damastes, if you're running from something, why don't you stay here? With us? Gunett would love that. I know we could keep you happy. And we need somebody strong like you. Not just in bed, or with an ax, but with a sword.

"In case the bandits come back . . . or any other bad people. You'd be like our king maybe, or anyway king to everybody except Gunett, and she's a wizard so that doesn't count, and she's a good woman, and you wouldn't mind doing what she tells you to."

It wouldn't be a bad life, and I wasn't thinking of the sex. What more is a man supposed to do, anyway, in the span before he goes back to the Wheel, except find someone to care for, who cares for him, and make that person's life as good as it can be? Better if he can help more than one person, whether it's a family . . . or a village.

Perhaps if I did this and stood strong for these people, Saionji might lessen the penalty for my sins when she judged me.

No, it wouldn't be a bad life at all, here in this village, its fertile fields and loving people.

But I shook my head, not knowing why I refused her.

"I'm sorry."

Steffi took a deep breath. "I had to ask. All right, Damastes. Then fuck me again. Fuck me everywhere."

"With such a ladylike invitation," I said, "how could I

refuse?" and pulled her on top of me, stiffening, hands moving down to her hips, and I jerked upward and she squealed and buried her head against my neck.

I don't know if it was Gunett's spell or what, but I slept no more that night, making love to Steffi in every way I knew, she always ready, always willing, our bodies twisting, contorting on the bed, spirits entwined, and then we dressed and she kissed me chastely and I slipped away as the first villagers were coming from their huts in the golden hush of dawn.

Other things happened, and I met and dealt with others as I journeyed, some with words, some with a sword, but none were that memorable.

Then, one day, in the middle of the Time of Heat, I crossed a narrow, nameless river. I smelt cinnamon, jasmine, cloves and knew I was in Cimabue once more.

FIVE

SUMMONS OF
THE TIGER

Now my journey became even more leisurely, and I paused to wander a jungle glade, or to help a farmer thresh the first yield of rice from his paddies, or at a village inn and engage in spirited and pointless arguments about Cimabuan customs or history or religion over endless cups of tea.

I was a dry sponge, soaking up the ways and habits of my native land after so long an absence. But that was only part of the reason for my laggardly ways, and a small part at that.

For the closer I came to my family's estates, the greater the question became: so you go home, Damastes. Then what? What trade will you take up? There were other, darker, more obvious questions I didn't even want to consider as well.

But eventually, close to the end of the Time of Heat, I came on the dirt road that wound beside fields toward the compound I hadn't seen since my mother's funeral, when I was still the emperor's first tribune.

The land was still being worked, and the crops appeared plentiful, although there were just as many women, children, and dotards and as few young men working as in other places. Of course, with their native son heading the Numantian armies, patriotism during the war would've flamed high, and many must've marched out to join the colors.

I was still dwelling far too much in the past and forced myself to concentrate on the present and the future, for I had a life to lead and, since I was probably the most sought-after fugitive in the land, dangers to beware.

It was very hot, probably uncomfortably so for anyone not born in these tropic jungles. The air smelled of dust and burned slightly when it entered my lungs, but it was as welcome as mountain air is to others.

The main house was a sprawl in the middle of a great garden. The walls were freshly stained, and there were a few new rooms added to the main structure here and there, in the incoherent building style my father had made notorious. The gardens were well tended, which wasn't a surprise, since most of what we grew was intended for use as well as beauty, spices, some exotic fruits we didn't want zebu or sambur nibbling, and vegetables for our table.

I opened the gate silently, saw a man oiling the two hand-carved red vervain statues of Tanis. He straightened as I came up the path, and I recognized him, thinking in amazement that he hadn't aged in the years since I'd last seen him. He was Peto, and he'd ridden to war with my father when he was just a boy, to be Cadalso á Cimabue's body servant, and had stood by him well, even on the final bloody field at Tiepolo, when my father lost his leg.

Since then, he'd been our family's head steward, always there, a man respected not only for his advice, but for his greater wisdom of keeping his mouth shut when guidance wasn't wanted.

"Peto," I said, "you missed a patch, under Tanis's chin."

He came to his feet, and I saw the years had, indeed, cut at him, as they had all of us.

"Damastes," he said gravely. "I knew they could not kill or keep you."

Then there were tears in his eyes and in mine as well, and I was in his arms and truly home.

Appropriately, there was great outcry and joy at my return, and I was plied with every delicacy the estate had and given the finest guestrooms.

My youngest sister, Kassa, still lived in the house with her husband Mangasha, who'd been a sergeant in the Cimabuan state militia and was now overseer of the family accounts. She wept profusely and wanted to call for a holiday throughout our lands.

I saw Mangasha look a little wary as he stopped her.

"I'm a renegade, my crazy sister," I said. "Let's not advertise my presence until we're sure what comes next."

She called me a fool, no one in Cimabue would report me, but appeared to set the idea aside. She sent messengers for my other two sisters and their husbands, then asked what I needed, what I wanted.

"A towel," I said. "And clothes that don't stink of the road."

Or of blood and death, I thought, but didn't continue.

Surprisingly, some light linen pants and shirts from my last visit so long ago were found, and I took them, a towel, and soap to that jungle pool I'd dreamed of on those dusty days.

It was smaller than I remembered, but still cool, green, and welcoming. I tore off my clothes, tossed them into a pile for burning, dove and went deep, into the dimness, where time had a stop, and when I'd swim up I'd still be a boy, glad with the world before me.

But when I surfaced, all was as before, except for a servant waiting with an evaporative canvas bag filled with my favorite lime drink and a large glass. I drained one, then another, clambered out onto the rocks, soaped, swam, soaped, swam again, and finally, after one more scrub, thought I might be clean sometime this century.

I floated on my back, my head, chest, cock, and toes all that was above water, staring up at the sky more wondrously blue than anywhere else in Numantia, the current from the small waterfall that fed the pool turning me like a leaf, here, there. My mind wanted to drift away, but I refused it. The evening ahead required thought.

The dining room was lit with happiness candles, many-colored lights slightly ensorcelled so their flame and scents were as varicolored as the waxes they were cast from.

Everyone seemed happy, and tears were shed rather indiscriminately, and no one talked about the future or the past. Children clustered around, and it was obvious my clan was in no danger of extinction.

The meal was wonderful, and I thought wryly that sometimes the life of a running man isn't all bad, for I'd had some wonderful meals on the road and could have written about the festive dishes of the tropic Numantian north to go with my companion volumes on starving in Maisir and Numantian prison fare.

We had minced chicken rolled in wild greens; sour shrimp and pineapple soup; many-spiced vegetables; roast duck in honey, ginger, and wild plum sauce; green onion pancakes; spiced beans and aubergines; and, for dessert, steamed lotus with sour and sweet rice.

The others drank good vintage wine, and I had fresh orange juice.

Eventually the last dish was removed, the children rousted, a clean cloth laid across the table. I asked Mangasha to close the lattice doors and make certain no servants had their ears to them. The room was quiet, people looking at me curiously.

My plan was to seize the moment, and so I stood.

"I want to thank you for my welcome. It was everything and more that I dreamed of during those long months in that hell called Maisir and later in my island prison."

I looked at Traptain as I said "prison," and he shifted nervously. I'd never been able to warm to him, even though he was a charmer on the surface, a little heavy, always smiling, round-faced and cheery. Perhaps it was I'd seen that smile slip once, at my mother's funeral, when he realized he wouldn't be inheriting all the family lands.

"You are my friends, my loved ones, and I'm more than blessed by Irisu.

"However, we have a rather serious matter to talk about. I'm more than aware of the problems my presence will bring."

I was interrupted by a clamor of "no," "there's nothing," "let's not talk about bad times, bad things." I waited.

"We can't ignore what we'd like to go away," I continued. "Let's be honest about my situation. I'm being sought by the Grand Council in Nicias. I killed the leader of their wretched Peace Guardians before I escaped, and I know they'd like vengeance for that.

"Also, they're very worried that I'll return to serving the once-Emperor Tenedos."

I thought of telling them of his spectral visit, decided not to. Tenedos's reputation was already terrifying.

"I will tell you, in all confidence, that I was approached to return to his side. He's trying to reestablish his army, somewhere south of here along the coast, and then he'll move against Nicias and attempt to recover his throne.

"I'll tell you something no one else knows, and I ask it remain a secret."

Nods, agreeing murmurs, a somewhat indignant "we never talk about any family business" from a sister.

"Thank you again. I have decided I will not fight for anyone. I've seen enough bloodshed, enough of disaster. From now on, I'll live my own life, no more, and worry only about the people I care for, the people sitting around this table.

"I'm aware there is no peace in Numantia and won't be as long as Tenedos is alive. There's not only the Grand Council to worry about, but the Maisirian king as well."

"What should we do?" Daryal asked. He was a village subchief, Anadyr's husband, a small, balding man who always looked worried.

"I don't know, to be truthful," I said. "Try to stay out of harm's way. The rabbit must hide when tigers fight."

"Will we be able to?" Anadyr asked.

"I don't know that, either. Cimabue, at least as far as I know, has remained loyal to Nicias, at least so far. We're remote and don't have much anymore in the way of resources to lust after, either men for soldiers, iron for their swords, or food for their campaigns.

"Perhaps the armies, when they move against each

other, will stay clear of Cimabue, as they have thus far. We can pray to Vachan, to Irisu, to Tanis to keep our land at peace.

"Which brings me back to the problem.

"I don't want to do anything to disturb the balance and think it would be best if I lived somewhat apart from you and kept away from having any business with the family lands, as much as possible."

I saw a bit of relief flicker across Traptain's face. Kassa was on her feet.

"That's nonsense! We're not going to drive you away, brother!"

"No," I said. "I didn't think you would. But I don't see any problem in remaining here and being just a little bit invisible."

"How?" That was always-practical Anadyr.

"I know a place to sleep where very few know of," I said.

My sisters frowned, then Anadyr got it.

"That old building Father gave you when you were a boy?"

"Yes," I said. "It's still standing, and I require no more."

"You can't live in a shack like that!" Jeritza said. "That shames all of us! A great general, a tribune, our only brother—"

"Jeritza," I said gently, "those rooms are far more than I've had for most of my life as a soldier. The palaces the emperor granted saw me but little. I'm more familiar with mud for my bedstead and the sky for a roof. And don't worry about shame. Remember, no one is going to know I'm here."

"People talk," Traptain said cynically.

"Of course they do," I said, "and they're going to talk about me. But if we all cooperate, they'll do it in whispers and know this is information not to be spread abroad. Besides, they're Cimabuans, and since when doesn't someone from our state love to hold a secret close?"

That received some smiles and was certainly the truth. There was even a proverb among us—three can keep a secret, if two are dead.

"But what will you do to pass the days?" Kassa said.

"That's a good question," Daryal said. "For I know you won't be content to sit and twiddle . . . whatever you normally twiddle."

"A good question indeed," I said. "I'll know my trade when it comes to me."

That wasn't long in happening.

But first, literally, I set my house in order. My small bungalow had been given to me by my father, amid lamentations by my mother and sisters, and I was told to keep it like a barracks, and I did. It was one of the best things anyone's ever done, for here I discovered the joy of being alone and of being responsible.

I set to with a joy cleaning up the two-room building, whitewashing the walls, rethatching the roof, and reinforcing the heavy beam door.

The bungalow sat on the outskirts of the estate, with the jungle starting just behind it. I put in a comfortably firm bed—wide enough for two, for I remembered the farm girls who'd come after dark, giggling at being the first to teach the master's son the games Jaen wants us to play. I hung a map of Numantia on one wall, a sketch of the battlefield of Tiepolo on another, and took a handful of books at random from the family library.

I got my father's old sword from the main house, which was just the style he'd trained me to prefer and use skillfully: double-edged, with a simple guard and pommel, and sharkskin on the handle, so a bloodied hand wouldn't slip. I sharpened it with stone, steel, and then powder to a razor's edge. I hung it, in its sheath, within reach. I put hooks under the bed, on the far side, and hid Salop's sword there, and Perak's dagger was mounted next to the door. On the doorsill overhead I put that iron pig.

I did not intend to be surprised . . . nor taken alive . . . if anyone came on me.

I had the feeling I was waiting for something, and that it would come soon.

While I waited, I held to a schedule: waking at dawn, running for two or more leagues along jungle trails, swimming at the end of the run, having water and some fruit to break my fast. Then I studied my books, which I hated, never being one for dusty knowledge, but knowing my brain for another muscle that would wither if not used.

I'd eat at midday, very lightly, then go for either a run or a ride. When my father had been alive, we always had thoroughbreds, but no one now seemed much interested in horsemanship, and so our mounts were either intended for pulling carriages or wagons or indifferent saddle mounts. I thought of my two great horses, Lucan and Rabbit, that I'd left in Nicias when I left for Maisir, and hoped they'd found good masters and were comfortably out to pasture amid their mares, enjoying a peaceful old age.

After a ride, I'd work on one or another of the projects I'd had a somewhat scandalized Mangasha suggest, working around the estate either by myself or with two or three trusted servants. I did everything from rebuilding arbors to tearing berry bushes gone wild out of the gardens to replanting to draining and redigging a fouled fishpond.

I'd generally dine with one or another of the family, talk for a bit, then go early to bed.

Occasionally I would have visitors—one of the local sorcerers who was well trusted, who wanted to know all I could remember of Tenedos's great magical feats; a couple of the village lads I'd grown up with, who asked for tales of the outside world when I wanted to hear their stories of a calm farming life; and twice one of the maids came by to ask me if I wanted a walk in the moonlight, although we didn't do much walking.

There were other days spent hunting. I'd be out well before dawn, and generally, by midday, have made my stalk and harvested a sambur, a boar, once a small fruit bear who'd been raiding our crops. Sometimes I brought my prey back to the family kitchen, dressed and butchered it, and gave it to the head cook, other times I gave the carcass to the first peasant I came across who looked as if he could use a hearty meal. This wasn't altruism—the people I fed would not only be unlikely to yammer about my presence, but would give the alarm if any strangers came into our district.

Then I heard of the tiger.

It was a mankiller, fortunately not on our estates, but about three leagues distant. It had taken a farmer, out late seeking a strayed calf, then two women gathering wood in the fringes of the forest, where tigers always like to nap, then, most outrageously, a little girl in broad daylight who toddled behind her parents' hut.

Half the peasants of that village wanted to hunt the beast down; the other half knew it was a demon, not a creature of this world, and so unkillable. The braver half convinced the latter half, and so they formed a line, armed with their flails and scythes and swept the forest.

They found the tiger—or rather, it found them, coming out of nowhere and batting down one hunter, then the man next to him before they could lift their spears, then leaping over the beaters and vanishing.

Now it was certain—the creature was not of this world, and there was nothing for the villagers to do but huddle in their huts and pray to their own gods and Jacini of the Earth to bring them relief.

I heard of the killings two days after the abortive hunt and felt my heart beat a little faster, remembering I was the boy who rode the tiger, and who would be, or perhaps already had been, savaged.

Perhaps it was time for me to chance the gods once more.

I took spears, bow, arrow, and two trustworthy servants and made my way to the village.

I paid little attention to their yammerings about demons but demanded to be given directions to the scene of the last killings.

The villagers refused to enter the forest and face death, but I felt no danger that day of alternately blazing sun and spattering rain. I found the place and the remnants of the two men's bodies. There wasn't much left—the tiger had returned to feed and then, content, left the rest for scavengers. I had a servant wrap a hand and a leg to return to the village for funeral ceremonies and examined the ground. I found where the tiger had lain waiting and how he'd come in a tawny streak of death.

The pugmarks in the soft ground were those of a young animal, probably male, but one print was markedly larger than the others, as I'd expected. I went back to the village, bought a bullock, and staked him in that clearing. For three nights, his terrified bawling kept everyone awake; then on the fourth the tiger came.

I was waiting in a tree-hide about ten feet above the bullock and drove an iron-weighted spear down into the tiger's shoulderblades as he reared for the kill in bright moonlight.

He screamed once, rolled, claws reaching for me, then died. I sent a second spear into his guts, waited until I was sure he wasn't faking, came down out of the tree. I looked at his corpse, saw the swollen paw, oozing pus from the porcupine he'd unwisely swatted, whose quills made it impossible for him to hunt normal prey.

The bullock was still alive, to his and my surprise. I went to the edge of the forest and called to the village, telling them the terror was over. They swarmed out, torches flaring, shouting praise to my name, offering what little money they had.

I refused, of course, told them to take the tiger's skin, and as a favor, to allow the bullock to live until he died and honor him in the name of their dead.

In spite of the lateness of the hour, they brought out their best for a feast. I ate heartily of savory lentil stew, pretended to taste the wine they made from rice, watched their jubilant dancing to the tap of a drum and the whistle of wooden flutes.

I grew sleepy, thanked them for their hospitality, and returned to the hut they'd given me, which had belonged to one of the men the tiger had slain.

After a time a young girl, whom I'd seen eyeing me at the feast, tapped on the door frame and asked if I wished company.

After we'd loved, and she was sleeping, head pillowed

on my arm, I thought of the last few days and how utterly content I'd been. Perhaps this was the tiger's last gift, showing me protection of the weak from their enemies is satisfaction enough.

I thought further on Cimabue and how one of our greatest burdens is man-eating cats and occasionally a mountain bear, mostly because the poor tribes, far back in the jungles, think the way to honor their animal gods is to give them their weak, sick, and elderly. Animals develop a taste for this easy meat and then become adept at hunting the hearty and firm.

These cats, sometimes tigers, more frequently leopards, create havoc in Cimabue. It's easy to believe they are demons, for some of them have slain as many as seven or eight hundred men, women, and children, desolating whole districts.

Ridding my land of them was a task, I thought, becoming sleepy, that might well suit a murderous fugitive, once first tribune, and put an arm around the girl. She made a purring sound, came closer, and then I slept.

Full of plans, I trotted happily back to the estates.

A servant was waiting about a mile from the compound and told me Mangasha had stationed him, and another dozen, one at every approach, so I wouldn't miss the warning.

A man and a woman, escorted by armed horsemen, were waiting for me.

SIX

A SERPENT AND A SEER

Did you see them yourself?" I asked.

"I did," the man stammered. He was trying to keep from shaking. Soldiers, those who led them, and those they sought could produce nothing good.

"What . . . or rather, how did they say they wanted me to Mangasha?"

"I don't understand."

"Did they order him as if the knowledge was their due? Or did they sound as if they were asking for a friend they came to visit?"

"I don't know, sir. I don't know how to tell things like that."

I grunted in mild exasperation. "Very well. Where are they?"

"The soldiers are in front of the main house," he said. "The other two and one big man, who acts like he's their guard, are inside."

I strung my bow, stuck three arrows through my sword belt, and bade my two servants to follow me at a distance.

We went around the back of the estate, to a low rise where a great tree stood. I slipped behind it, slowly peered around its trunk. Damn. No one was making great events out of little. About half a troop of cavalry was there. I couldn't identify their uniform, but it was brown and would conceal them well. Yonge's skirmishers had worn brown, but that formation was long dissolved.

I noted something else. The soldiers had small tents pitched, and their horses on a picket line, as if they were bivouacking. They also had only one sentry posted, and he was sitting on a bench outside the gate, very much at ease. Not exactly the way troops in enemy territory behaved.

A door banged, and four people came out of the house. The first was Mangasha, the second a big man who looked vaguely familiar.

A third I knew too well—Kutulu, the Serpent Who Never Slept, the emperor's spymaster!

But he'd been sent away in disgrace before the Maisirian war began, to one of the outer states, like Chalt or Bala Hissar. And at least one of those had declared for Tenedos. Whose side was Kutulu on? How had he found my home? Why did he want me?

Then the fourth person came out, and I stepped boldly out from behind the tree and strode toward the house.

She was a stocky, middle-aged woman, also wearing brown, as she had throughout her service with me. It was Devra Sinait, the seer who'd saved my life in Polycittara and who'd left my employ when I went to Maisir.

Mangasha saw me, looked alarmed. Evidently Kutulu had told him nothing.

Kutulu was the next to see me, and I saw a smile come. The small, wiry man with the utterly ordinary features bounded forward, hand outstretched.

"Damastes, my friend!"

He had me by the shoulders and actually hugged me, which was more emotion than the Sleepless Snake had shown in the ten years or more I'd known him.

"You do not know," he said, "how glad I am to see you."

"And I you," I said honestly.

"You remember Elfric?" Kutulu said. "He's now my bodyguard."

The big man knuckled his forehead, and I nodded. "Yes. Be welcome."

I turned to Sinait.

"Seer, you honor me," I said.

"You look like you did the last time I saw you," she said.

"I thought only men were supposed to pay deceitful compliments," I said, and hugged her close.

"Mangasha, these are friends," I said. "Move their soldiers into one of the barracks we keep for the harvesting crews, give them anything they want or need and send to the village for more cooks. Tonight shall be the celebration you wished to give me, which should now include these people, the best of the best."

He looked skeptical, then nodded once and started away.

"You are still too trusting," Kutulu said. "You have no idea what brings us here."

"If it were just you, you'd be right to caution me," I said, grinning. "And I might've come out of cover with an arrow nocked. But Sinait, at least, I don't think means me any harm."

"Be careful," the woman said. "That also is not proven. But I hope you're correct."

"A question," I said. "Whose wiles found me?"

"Actually," Kutulu said, "both of ours. I knew, from

your file in imperial records what district in Cimabue you came from. When one of my agents . . . yes, I still have sources in many places, including the service of the Grand Councilors, reported you'd been brought to the mainland for secret meetings, then killed that abominable traitor Herne and escaped . . . well, there weren't that many places for you to go."

"I, also, knew your home," Sinait said. "Kutulu found me, perhaps six months ago. I was, well, I was where I was, remaining under cover since I foresaw anyone, especially a magician who'd been with you, might be of interest to both the former emperor and those two who rule in Nicias. Kutulu convinced me of what I should—what he said I *must*—do, and then, when he told me of your good fortune in escaping, I chanced a little magic, casting as I have before, and 'found' you where you could have been expected to be."

"I must ask one question," I said. "Is either of you in the service of the man who was once emperor?"

Even in this isolated spot, I hesitated to speak his name and somehow draw his attention.

"No," Kutulu said. "Not ever, not again. He came to me in a dream two months back and summoned me to him. But I refused his orders and determined I must . . . for what I owe Numantia, stand against him." His voice was determined, hard. "And that is why we need you," Kutulu began.

"Not now," I said. "First, give me a time for just enjoying your company. Later, after we dine, after we talk about old times, then you can tell me your business."

Again, we banqueted, but I'm afraid my family was a bit excluded from the conversation, although I tried to make sure we talked of matters they'd be interested in. But names would come up, and one or another of the three of us would ask what happened to him or her. All too often the answer was "dead in Maisir," or "I don't know," or "I think taken by the Peace Guardians," or just a simple shrug of ignorance. It would have been easy to turn the occasion into a wake, but soldiers must learn when not to mourn, even after a catastrophe as great as we'd lived through.

Eventually the three of us ended up in one of the house's sitting rooms, and the family made its excuses. Elfric stationed himself outside the door, and I made sure Sinait had a bottle of our best estate wine at hand. Kutulu, like myself, was sipping at fresh fruit juices one of our cooks had concocted.

I sat back and waited.

"We need you," Sinait began, "to help us destroy the former Emperor Laish Tenedos."

I'd expected something like that, but not quite that baldly put. I looked at Kutulu.

"He has about half a million men now, massed in Bala Hissar and Darkot," he said. "We have about one hundred and thirty thousand in Amur, living in the villages and cities.

"Some trained soldiers, some are Kallians who fought against us under Chardin Sher or in the guerrilla war afterward, and the rest are serving for excitement or because they hate tyrants or because the emperor did some wrong to them, or they imagine he did.

"The Grand Councilors—the Government, which I suppose is what we still have to call it—have recently increased their forces to about six hundred thousand men, either in Nicias or moving south on the Latane and forming up in Khurram, using the old Guards Training Depots as their bases, getting ready to attack either us or the emperor, whoever is closest and looks weakest."

"The odds aren't overwhelming me," I said.

"Of course not," Kutulu said. "Who do you think we have to lead our men? Who do we have to plan our strategy, our tactics? Who do you think we have to sit on a white horse with a sword in his hand and say the words that'll make them willing to die to destroy tyranny? Me?" He snorted. "The seer? She tries, but . . ."

"We need *you*, Damastes," Sinait said. "We need the man who was first tribune. You're the only one we think could rally all Numantia to stand against Tenedos, and also destroy those damned Peace Guardians and their masters, the puppets of Maisir."

"We're probably coming at this the wrong way," I said, "but let me ask this. Why must Tenedos be destroyed? Don't any of you remember the oath I swore? Kutulu, you made the same vow."

"No," Kutulu said. "Oddly enough, he never asked me to swear to him personally. Perhaps he thought the oaths I'd already taken, as a warder of Nicias, were enough, and my . . ." Kutulu bit his lip, " . . . overweening devotion to what I thought he promised, redemption for our country."

"What made you willing to renounce it?"

"I saw a change," Kutulu went on, "day by day, year by year, after you crowned him emperor. It was as if there were two Tenedoses: the one I first served, who would be the greatest ruler Numantia had ever known, then the one who fell in love with wielding power for its own sake, a capricious, even evil man. Little by little, the one I'd known faded away, leaving the new emperor, the one who brought everything down with his foolish invasion of Maisir.

"Or," Kutulu added, a bit forlornly, "perhaps I'm fooling myself. Perhaps there was only one Tenedos, and I put what I wanted to see, the king I wanted to have rule Numantia, in place of that reality. I don't know."

"I don't know, either," I said. "For I did the same thing."

"Damastes," Sinait broke in, "you're dissembling. I'm a seer, certainly not as great as Tenedos, but I made certain spells, and I have a good idea that, at the last, at Cambiaso, he was willing to put all on a single cast of the die.

"I also found . . . echoes, might be the only word that is suitable, of a great spell that was broken in the casting, a spell of monstrous evil.

"Damastes, I'm going to ask you . . . as a patriotic Numantian, to tell us what happened at Cambiaso. What happened before the battle?"

I stared at her. "How could you know I know anything?"

She stared, her gaze cutting into me, through me, forcing me back to the past.

I thought I'd never tell about Tenedos's power being rooted in blood, nor that terrible spell of his I broke before Cambiaso, the spell that would again rouse the demon who destroyed Chardin Sher, all his people, and the huge castle they held.

But I did, and by the time I was finished, it was past midnight. My voice was hoarse, not so much from the amount of talking, but from the raw emotion that'd gushed out.

"Good," Kutulu said firmly. "You did well."

"You did very well," Sinait agreed. "And I think I know what it cost you to do that to someone you'd sworn fealty to. But you didn't destroy Tenedos."

"No."

"Don't you have a duty to finish your task?"

Anger swept me, and I was on my feet.

"Duty . . . honor . . . oaths," I snarled. "Why in the hells is everyone so calm, so assured about what *my* gods-damned duties and vows are and how *I'm* supposed to honor them? I wish *I* was so certain about things!"

Sinait took a long breath. "You're right. I apologize."

"I don't," Kutulu said. "Damastes, don't you think almost the same thing happened to me? Don't you think my oath to Numantia tore at me when I realized the man I'd thought almost a god didn't care a rap for his country? All he wanted was power, power to rule not just Numantia, but everyone, the whole world and beyond, gods and demons? How could I serve someone like that, do the bloody things some people thought evil, for someone who wants to make himself a dark godling, perhaps a manifestation of Saionji herself? Or maybe take her throne for himself? Doesn't his evil automatically cancel anything I swore?"

I'd never seen passion in the man like this. I stared, and he ducked his head.

"You have the same problem I do, don't you? You have all these nice, logical reasons, but what you did still eats at your guts, as it does mine."

He nodded jerkily.

"All right," I said, and I was breathing heavily. "I swore an oath to Tenedos, and I swore an oath before that to Numantia. And my family's motto is *We Hold True*." I laughed bitterly. "Maybe I haven't done things all that well. Maybe Irisu is sitting up there somewhere laughing his ass off at my pretensions. So be it.

"I am not part of this great game anymore. Put one

oath on one side, the other on the other. Let them balance each other out, and leave me the hell alone.

"There're three armies in Numantia about to strike at one another, to rip the country apart again to see who sits the throne in Nicias, which'll most likely bring the Maisirians back to further rend and tear.

"I can't stop that from happening, and maybe I don't want to.

"But understand one thing most clearly. I am not playing. I am not going with you. Nor am I going to serve Tenedos again.

"Let all of you burn and tear and rip the country until it's nothing but ashes and corpses for all of me.

"I am not going to take part.

"I've killed enough, more than enough, sent how many million men to their deaths, been the cause of how many women, children being torn back to the Wheel?

"No more. I'm through."

I slammed out the door, pushing past Elfric. I heard Kutulu start to say something, then stop.

I burst out of the house into the waning moonlight, went blindly to my cottage, barred the door, and slumped on my bed.

Perhaps I wanted someone to come to me, argue with me, change my mind, give me a rudder.

But no one did.

In late morning, when I went again to the main house, Kutulu, Sinait, and their soldiers had gone.

SEVEN

DEATH FROM THE SHADOWS

The more I thought, the more firm my resolve became. The world could go spinning into whatever sewer it wished. I was done with great events and wished to be left alone.

But it might not be that simple. If two could find me, one, a far greater wizard, most likely could as well. I'd certainly talked enough about Cimabue to the emperor over the years.

Why he hadn't sought me thus far, I had no idea. Perhaps, I thought hopefully, he'd realized I would certainly never support his enemies. But I still spent some time, preparing for future troubles.

A few days after Kutulu and Sinait had left, a runner panted up to the main house. A district overseer, in Belya, which is a finger of Cimabue bordered by the state of Hermonassa on the north and east, and Ticao on the west, had somehow heard of the man-eater that'd been slain in Atikim by a nameless great hunter and sent a messenger to Atikim after that hunter. The witch there had used scrapings from the mat I'd slept on and certain other residues I delicately didn't inquire into and had divined I could be found within four days travel of Atikim.

This also gave me pause—first Sinait, then this witch had been able to scent me out, which suggested I was, in fact, trying to hide in an open plain.

The message was brief: Belya was cursed with a man-eating leopard, perhaps not even an animal but a demon. It had killed a dozen within two weeks, leaving the bodies uneaten as often as not, and the peasants had panicked, abandoning homes and farms to huddle in Belya's few towns. Could I, whoever I was, help?

I hadn't heard of this leopard, nor had Mangasha, but Daryal had, and what he'd heard made me wonder if this beast was, indeed, a demon. Over eight years, it had killed *at least* 850 people, and Daryal said most likely more, since Belya was a deeply jungled district, and records weren't carefully kept. That was about all he knew of Belya, other than it was studded with ancient stone temples built by the primitive tribesmen, which were still used by the hill people for worship. I'd never encountered these primitives, nor had anyone I knew, so naturally there were the wildest tales of their fierceness or gentleness, their ugliness or beauty, their friendliness or hostility. Supposedly, by worshiping these eldritch gods of nature, some of their more skilled magicians had learned how to change themselves into animals.

"Perhaps this leopard is one such were-creature," Daryal suggested.

"Perhaps," I said. I remembered the wedding dagger with hilt and pommel of silver that Yonge of the Hills had given me for a wedding present, how it had slain men and monsters, and how I could possibly use it now. But it was buried in the forgotten, rotting bones of the *azaz* I'd slain at Cambiaso.

This quest would give me a way to absent myself for a while, and perhaps the deep jungles would hide me from wizards.

I found the two men who'd gone hunting with me to Atikim and asked if they wished further sport. One turned pale and said his rice fields were particularly weed hung, and he was afraid to trust the work to his worthless wife and equally worthless sons, and . . . and I sent him away.

The other, a young man barely out of his teens named Perche, grinned and said why not. He'd as soon be devoured by a leopard as die of boredom or a broken back, pushing a plow.

I told him what we wanted to take and for him to assemble the items along with two good horses and better mules.

I then sought Mangasha and finally told him exactly what'd happened since I was taken from my island prison and what I'd been thinking. The seer Tenedos was a vindictive man, fully capable of obliterating an entire state like Cimabue if it displeased him, as he'd wanted to do to Nicias. If he came seeking me, either magically or in the flesh, he'd be most likely seeking vengeance for my having betrayed him.

Mangasha shivered.

"I guess I shouldn't have returned here," I said wryly.

"No," he said somberly. "A family must stand together, even more than a nation must. If you hadn't come back home and if we'd learned you didn't, that would have shamed us for all time.

"So stand by you we must, now and in the future. Maybe there's people in other parts of Numantia who can ignore the plight of a kin, but I don't think many in Cimabue could."

I turned aside for a moment, not wanting him to see me fight for control.

"Thank you."

"Buffalo shit," he said. "There's nothing to thank or remark on when someone's merely doing as he should. The question now, I'd guess, is what should we do to prepare ourselves for a visit from that gods-damned magician."

Mangasha was ever the sergeant, pragmatic, letting his superiors get him into the pig wallow, and then he'd find a way out for everyone, including the bastards who got him into it in the first place.

"I'll be leaving within a few hours," I said. "I want you to quietly assemble the family and tell them what we've decided." I took a deep breath. "All of them except Traptain . . . and Jeritza."

Mangasha eyed me. "You trust him as little as I do."

"Say, rather, I'm not sure of him, and these aren't times to put trust in anyone you're unsure of."

"Jeritza as well, because she's his wife," Mangasha said wryly.

I nodded. "A wife who doesn't stand with her husband isn't much."

"That'll be hard for me to do."

"Do the best you can," I said, then gave further instructions to put together a work crew of the most reliable men and women he knew. Have them find a spot, deep in the jungle, one that could be defended. Build platforms there, and put hard stores on them. Get one of the village witches to put a spell on it, so animals wouldn't raid the food-stuffs. If attacked, don't try to fight either soldiers or demons, but flee. The attack, if it came, would probably be magical and shouldn't last long, particularly once Tenedos realized I was absent. Hopefully, there wouldn't be much damage.

"I assume," Mangasha said, "if this happens, we can take Traptain and Jeritza with us."

"Of course. No one tries to negotiate with a demon when he's ripping at your throat."

"No," Mangasha agreed. "Not even someone like Traptain."

Further, I went on, I wanted him to post sentries on all the roads and tracks, so there'd be no surprise. If Tenedos attacked by magic, it'd likely be at night, so each hamlet must have watchmen out.

"Especially here, at the main compound."

"I'd already thought of that," Mangasha said. "There's been sentries posted every night since you've been back. And there's some other things I can do . . . not to fight back, for I'm not enough of a sloth-brain to think I can outfight or outthink our emperor that was, but to keep the worst from happening."

He sighed heavily. "These are not good times, are they, Damastes?"

"No," I said slowly. "No, they're not. But perhaps, if we do like the rabbits, and hide deep in our burrows, we'll be overlooked."

"Perhaps," Mangasha said, and there was doubt in his voice.

Two hours later, Perche and I rode away with the messenger after the Man-eater of Belya.

Belya's district supervisor, a harried man named Hokon, met me in the refugee-crowded village of Megiddo to give me what information he had about the leopard.

He showed me on the vague maps, the best he had, where the creature had last struck, or, rather, where he'd marked his new territory, and terrorized three villages so badly that their inhabitants had fled here, where they clamored for food, shelter, and most of all, a wizard to kill the demon.

"What do you believe the creature is?" he asked.

"I have no beliefs," I said. "I haven't seen this leopard yet, so don't know if it's mortal or not."

"And you're not worried if it is a demon?"

"Of course I'm worried," I said. "Do I look that much of a dunce?"

"No, no, of course not," he said, pulling at his wispy hair. "Forgive me, but these are not easy days. I don't know if you're political, but Hermonassa and Ticao have both declared for the Emperor Tenedos, Cimabue hasn't, and I'm being pressured from the governors of those other states to stand with them. I simply don't know what to do, what to do at all." He peered at me closely. "You look like someone I should recognize. Are you sure you've never had anything to do with the government?"

"Very sure," I lied. I'd not bothered to dye my hair again but had kept it short, since the easiest disguise is the best.

"Good, good," he said. "I wish to Irisu I'd chosen a simpler life. Now . . . forgive me, but I have other matters I must attend to. If you wish to speak to anyone who saw the leopard's attacks, my assistants can locate several."

I did, but the interviews produced little of value, for by now the villagers' stories had grown, the more they were repeated from inn to bazaar to teahouse, and the leopard was about the size of an elephant, with several sets of fangs, the ability to leap over banyan trees, tear huts apart to get at their shrieking occupants, and so forth.

I thought of purchasing another bullock or some such animal for bait, but we were several days' journey from the leopard's territory, and I didn't think much of dragging some terrified animal that distance. From what I'd been told, there were many animals that'd just been abandoned that I could use.

Early the next morning, we followed the narrow jungle trail that led into the jungle's heart. The track was easy to follow, littered with clothes, furniture, things the villagers had thought vital for their existence that had grown heavier as the miles and fear increased.

One day, on the trail, five small men came out of the brush and watched me approach. They were armed with very long spears and very light crossbows and wore loincloths and caps fashioned from the capeskins of monkeys. We could barely be understood, but I managed to tell them I sought the great man-eater. They looked frightened and chattered amongst themselves. The best linguist managed to say that they were sorry I was so cursed, for I seemed to be a cheerful sort, and they would speak well of me to their gods after I'd been slain. One wanted me to give him my sword now, for I'd have no use for it when I met the leopard-demon, but I reluctantly had to tell him no, I might need it in the encounter, for it'd belonged to my father, and besides, not even the gods knew everything to be for certain. I thanked them for their uplifting sentiments and support, distributed presents of salt and charms I'd bought in Megiddo, and bade them farewell.

The three villages the leopard had desolated formed a rough triangle on the slopes of a jungled valley. Through the center of the valley ran a river, and on its banks were the ruins of an ancient temple. One villager had said the leopard lived in these ruins, which proved he was a demon, for no honest creature would chance the wrath of the old gods.

First was to establish a safe shelter. The first village I went to had burnt after the villagers had left, and there were only two huts standing. I considered using the temple as my shelter, but my arrogance didn't run that deep. If there were any of the old gods hanging about, it'd be unlikely they'd be pleased by having their home profaned.

The second, and farther, village was intact, and its inhabitants had built a stockade around it. The gates were closed, and I wondered if some brave, or stubborn, sorts were still living there. There was no answer to my halloos, but the gate was barred when we tried it. Perche shinnied up the wall as deftly as he went up a coconut palm, peered over, and almost fell back.

He came down quickly, his face pale.

"They're . . . in there . . . dead . . ." he managed, then turned aside and threw up, shoulders convulsing.

I drew my sword, peered through a gap between gate and wall, saw nothing terrible. But I smelt rotting corpses. There was room enough to slide my sword through the gap and lever the bar out of the way. It thudded to the dusty ground within, and I pushed the gate open.

I'd seen more ghastly things than Perche had, but still my stomach recoiled. Sprawled inside the gate was a man, his guts ripped out and half-eaten, his face torn away. Next to him was the rusty scythe he'd tried to defend himself with. Ten feet away was a woman's body. She was un-scarred except for clawmarks across her throat. Closer to the scatter of huts inside the palisades were the bodies of two children, at least one of whom had been partially eaten, and a donkey, whose neck jutted away at an un-natural angle from the leopard's smashing blow.

"How . . . how did . . . what . . ." Perche managed.

My skin crawled. The answer was horrible, and I began to believe this leopard wasn't a natural being. The family must've lived distant from this village and hadn't known of the evacuation. Perhaps they'd heard the leopard at night, as he growled around their hut, and fled to the village. They found its gates open and the huts empty, but the crude fort promised safety, and so they hurried inside, and hastily barred the gate.

Then they heard the leopard's snarl . . .

Inside the stockade with them.

Perche fumbled a short spear from one of our mules' packs, peered about, expecting the leopard to appear from the dust, from nowhere.

I examined the bodies, ignoring the stench and my revolted stomach. The blood was black, clotted not long before. I pinched flesh, found it pliable. The death stiffness had passed, so, in this heat, it probably meant they'd been dead less than a full day.

"We must give them death ceremonies," Perche managed.

I was about to agree, then a rather disgusting notion came. I pondered it, and it made a deal of sense.

"No," I said.

"But . . ."

"We'll use them for bait. Instead of hunting the leopard, we'll let it come to us."

A ghastly thought, but if this monster had grown fond of the taste of human flesh and was so complacent he hadn't even bothered to carry the carcasses away to a hiding place, unlike most leopards, that seemed my best tactic. And leopards, man-eating or no, prefer their meat somewhat on the gamy side.

What was really worrisome, which I didn't tell Perche for fear of further terrifying him, is that the leopard must've slain the family in broad daylight, once more against the creature's normal habits. So the man-eater was beyond fear and stalked these hills as their master.

Perche swallowed hard, nodded jerkily. "If that's what you think best."

"First, though," I said, "we find something to put our backs against."

We turned the largest hut into a stable, so the leopard wouldn't be distracted from his nicely ripening meal. I made sure no real beast could smash in the door, and we blocked the windows with hay bales.

It was only a bit after midday, and so we ate. Or rather, I ate. Perche kept looking at the bodies, wrinkling his nose against the growing reek of their corruption.

I chose a hut close to the village's entrance and laid bow, arrow, javelin, and stabbing spear next to its doorway, unrolled a sleeping mat and positioned it near my weapons, keeping my sword close at hand.

There was nothing to do but wait for nightfall.

I passed the time looking through the abandoned huts, wondering at what people had chosen to leave behind. There were preserved foodstuffs I doubted anyone would grudge me for the evening meal. But even though I saw hand-carved chests that would've held the people's treasures, I refrained from looting any further.

With one exception. Hanging on the wall of a large hut whose well-kept furniture indicated it belonged to one of the village's more prosperous residents was a sword. It was very old-fashioned, such as I'd seen in museums, probably as much intended for ceremony as use. It had a curved, single-edged blade that was still fairly sharp and an ivory handle inset with gold. It was perfectly balanced, and the smith who'd forged it had known as much about fighting weapons as craftsmanship. But I took it because its hilt and pommel were of silver, and silver had been worked into the blade for its full length. I studied the engravings, warriors and demons fighting, the soldiers dressed as they would've in my grandfather's grandfather's time.

The shadows were growing long as the sun sank below the valley walls. I heard birdsongs, then the outraged squabble of monkeys, disturbed at their meal. I went to the gate, listened closely. Suddenly, there was complete silence.

Far distant, I thought I heard a soughing cough.

The leopard was out there.

I put Perche in the shed with the animals, told him to keep the door braced shut and not come out unless I summoned him . . . and make sure it was really me who called, although how he was supposed to make sure of that, if it was some shape-changing fiend, I didn't know.

I crept to my chosen hut and lay down just inside the doorway and waited. One thing soldiering forces is patience.

The moon rose, and its light crawled through the door toward me. Dust tickled my nose, but I didn't cough. A homeless flea from one of the hut's former residents bit me, and I didn't move.

It grew late, and still later. But I wasn't sleepy, nor restless, for the jungle beyond the village was still silent, listening to the killer in its greenery.

I don't know what brought me to full alertness—an almost unheard sound, a smell, something out of the ordinary.

I looked out at stillness, trying to determine where the leopard was lurking. There, close beside that hut? In the lengthening shadow of the wall, approaching the corpses? To my right, within the village?

There was a rustle from behind me, from *within* the hut, a soft thud onto the dirt floor, and a *rrrowl*. I spun, going for my sword, but late, too late, and a medium-sized, scrawny, abandoned tabby cat meowed plaintively.

Before either my heart stopped or I exploded in hysterical laughter, the night rumbled, and the leopard clawed over the walls.

There was nothing out there, nothing at all, but then darkness moved. If my eyes hadn't been flickering here, there, as I'd learned to see at nighttime, I might not have seen it, and the beast slid forward, toward the woman's body.

I was up, out of the hut, javelin in my hand, and I cast hard. The spear whipped through the air, buried itself a hands-breadth from the creature. A normal beast would have been gone, but this monster crouched forward toward me, jaws gaping, growling menace. It was big, far bigger than any leopard I'd ever hunted, and I stepped back into the hut, grabbed a short stabbing spear, and started toward it, braced for its leap.

I vow, in that instant, the stars flickered, as if something had moved across them, and then a voice rumbled across the valley, and I knew the voice:

"You should have chosen when I gave you the chance," and the leopard changed, rose to its haunches, grew until it was twelve feet tall, and became a man, but a man with the dripping fangs of a leopard, and its hands were taloned and flames flickered where its eyes should have been. It came toward me, in a strange walk, like a dog trained to cavort on its hind legs.

I feinted, and it batted at the spear tip, then a clawed arm lashed out. I ducked aside, and the other claw ripped at me, tearing across my chest, and pain seared. I dropped to my knees and rolled, came back to my feet, spear still in hand, and jabbed, one-handed, taking the monster just above the thigh, but no more than a superficial wound.

Again it slashed, and struck me full on with its pad, sending me stumbling back, spear flying. The leopard screamed, like a woman in anguish, but this wasn't its pain but mine, soon to come. It dropped to all four legs, was about to spring, and the door to the other hut opened, and Perche ran out, spear leveled like a battering ram. The leopard spun aside, came up with a slashing right into Perch's guts, and he screamed, went spinning away.

But his death gave me the moment, and my father's sword was in my hand. I cut at the leopard-man, and it screamed again, its own agony this time, struck, and I cut at its foreleg, cut it deeply, then jumped back like a fencing master on the mats as the monster's fangs sliced, didn't see the lashing paw that knocked my sword from my hand, spinning through the night.

I jumped back, into the doorway of the hut.

The leopard was on all fours again, tail whipping, its muscles tensed and it leapt. I ducked under its leap, had that ancient silver blade in hand, rolled onto my back, and drove upward with all my strength.

The blade caught the leopard above the stomach, stuck in its ribs and snapped. Again the beast screamed, and now the world, the jungle, the hells below screamed with it.

It crashed against the side of the hut in darkness. I had Perak's dagger and was on it, cutting, stabbing, flailing into that darkness, and each time I struck the leopard howled, and then I was cutting, cutting, and there was no sound but the thuds of my blows landing.

I sat, still, in darkness for a time, panting wildly, then found the lamp I'd set out, uncovered the slow match I'd hidden, and light flared.

The leopard lay motionless in the dust, and it looked as if a butcher had been at it with his cleaver. But I took no chances and hacked its head and paws off.

The Monster of Belya was truly dead.

Perche had also gone to the Wheel—the leopard's eviscerating slash had killed him instantly.

I took a moment to mourn, to curse, for yet another man who'd chosen to follow me was gone.

Then, working by moonlight, I smashed a hut down, dragged its timbers into a stack, then piled the bodies of the unknown peasants on it, Perche's body last.

I found lamps in the huts, drenched the pyre with their oil, tossed my smoking lamp into its midst, and flames exploded upward.

I waited until the fire was truly ablaze, said prayers to Irisu, Shahriya of the Fire, Jacini, Vachan, Tanis that these men, this woman, these children would be granted favor on the Wheel and rewarded with a fortunate rebirth.

For sacrifice, I pitched the body of the leopard into the flames, watched the fire roar for a while, then threw the broken pieces of the silver-worked sword next to it.

I collected my equipment, repacked the animals, and was ready to travel. Now there'd be nothing in the night to fear, the night that was properly alive with sound.

I'd brought unguents, and now I rubbed them on my

wounded chest, although I would visit a seer when I reached Megiddo, for wounds from a leopard's fetid claws always infect.

I was almost ready to leave when the tabby cat came out of the blackness, meowing. I took dried meat from my pack, shredded it, gave the cat water.

It ate and drank hungrily. After it finished, I tucked the animal into one of my saddlebags. It sniffed, purred, and went happily to sleep.

With a gold coin, there'd be someone in Megiddo more than willing to give it a home.

I swung into the saddle, bowed to the still-burning pyre, rode though the open gates into the dark jungle.

Was the leopard always a demon that Tenedos was able to possess?

Or was it merely a killing creature whose bloody past made it easy for him to take over?

I did not, do not know.

THE DANCING FIRES

Ismelled the burn half an hour's ride from the plantation. It was charcoal, drenched wood, seared cloth,
and another stink I remembered well. Many warriors
cannot bear to be in a kitchen where lamb is cooking,
because it smells exactly like man.

I dropped the lead to my pack animals and kicked my
horse into a gallop, rounded the last bend and saw what
I'd dreaded—Shahriya had been given my home compound. Fire had consumed everything, and not long ago,
for the ruins still smoked. A few tottering, blackened roofbeams still stood, but that was about all. Here and there
retainers dug through the rubble, looking for I know not
what.

"Magic," he said, and his face was ruined with tears. I
recognized him as Tutuila, one of the overseers of the rice
fields. "We had no warning, no warning at all."

"Who died?"

He stared, his mouth opened to frame words, and he
burst into tears again. I was out of the saddle, shaking
him.

"Come on, man! Who died?"

"Mangasha," he said. "My friend . . . the man I loved best of . . . and Peto's dying . . . they saved, saved us all," and he dissolved in tears.

I was slammed by an invisible fist, tottered, then forced steel down my spine.

"Take me to him," and Tutuila tottered toward the path leading to some stables the fire had missed.

Peto was terribly burnt, and it was only his iron will, plus spells and pain-numbing herbs a local witch was giving him, that kept him alive, alive and conscious.

He lay on oil-soaked muslin, on a bed of fresh-cut grass, but each movement sent pain tearing through him. Anadyr and Jeritza stood around him, holding bandages, cool drinks, but he was beyond that. Kassa sat nearby, eyes cold in shock, and she wore bandages on her hands and lower legs. Behind them were Jeritza and Anadyr's husbands, Daryal and Traptain.

I knelt, and he opened his eyes and recognized me.

"Damastes," he said. "I'm sorry I wasn't able to keep them away, that we didn't stop them from burning everything."

"What happened? Was it raiders?"

"No," he said in a rasping voice. "Magic. I was outside, snarling at a watchman who'd fallen asleep, and I saw flames coming, dancing like fireflies on the wind, coming in waves over the trees to the south."

To the south, where Tenedos was.

I knew that fire well. It had been created by the Maisirian War Magicians; then the spell had been taken for his own by Tenedos. The fires killed almost all they burnt and grew stronger as they did, just as Tenedos's strength grew with the men he destroyed.

"But they touched nothing, fed on nothing, but floated

free. I had time to scream a warning, and Mangasha came out, a torch in his hand.

"Somehow that drew the flames, and they clung to him, clung and then ate. I pushed him down, rolled him on the ground, but the flames wouldn't die, but attacked me.

"I was screaming with the pain," he said, "and I guess that gave time for the others to escape. Some of the fires swirled away and ate at the buildings."

Anadyr, my oldest sister, nodded.

"I was still in the fire's embrace but was able to stumble down, into the fishpond you and I dug, and hid, with only my lips above water."

A hand, burnt to a claw by the fire, came out, touched my sleeve.

"Do not think me a coward, Damastes, for not being able to fight them, for not saving Mangasha."

"You're not that," I said. "Not ever."

"I made myself stay alive, wait for you. Now I can let go, and go to the Wheel." Blistered lips pulled into a grimace of a smile. "I'll not be sorry to go, Damastes. Perhaps I'll serve your family again, in another time, another life.

"I would like that," he said softly. "I would like to see your father, Cadalso, when he was young and whole. And your mother. I don't remember anyone as pretty as she was, not even your sisters, when they were young."

His breath rasped in, out for a time. I squatted beside him, without moving, paying no more attention to the witch's ministrations, my sisters, or the farmers clustering behind me than he did.

"Maybe not," he said, "maybe you cannot go into the past, where it might have been better. That is what the priests say, that the Wheel moves ever forward. But the future might be better than this time, foul with strange demons and kings.

"Perhaps, when I return from the Wheel, there'll be peace. Peace and no kings. No kings. Now that is a dream worth dying on." His breath rattled, and he fought, thrashed, and was gone.

I stood, not seeing the ancient wood of the stables, the tropic brush behind, nor the ruins of the fire, but the flames themselves as they'd danced death.

I should have known, my mind drummed. I knew Tenedos would strike, I should have done more, I should have abandoned everything and had everyone move immediately into the jungle.

But why did he attack innocents? The answer came instantly—as the leopard-demon, he should have killed me, and this fire should have then obliterated my name from the earth. Total war, total revenge. That was his way, the way of someone half a demon, someone wedded to Saionji.

If Peto hadn't been outside, and shouted, there would have been no warning at all, and everyone would have died. I wondered what had made Tenedos's magic slip, so that his flames hadn't run through the darkness, finding and killing my sisters, but would never know the answer.

"When shall we build the pyres?" Anadyr asked.

"As soon as possible," I said. "For both Peto and Mangasha."

Then my stomach roiled at the idea of giving these two men I'd loved into another fire, and I remembered another custom, one used by the primitives of the forest.

"Clear the ruins of our compound," I ordered. "Dig deep holes, scent them with all the herbs and flowers

Mangasha and Peto loved best, and bury the bodies in them. Drive oxen across the burial grounds, and seed it with flowers, so the gardens will become beautiful again.

"Let the whole district know these gardens are a memorial for these two brave men, and let them be for everyone, for children, maidens and young men, but allow no warrior, wizard, or man with weapons to enter."

"And then what shall we do?" Jeritza asked. "You now head the family."

"No," I said. "For I'm leaving within the hour. Each of you will speak for the family, and all decisions will be reached by agreement. But there are things you must do, to keep the fire from returning. The fire or other killers. Pretend you are no longer my sisters, my brothers-by-marriage. Deny my name, my existence if necessary. The first thing you'll have to do is go into hiding. Traptain has property, many farms. He'll shelter you. The supplies Mangasha hid in the forest will help. Cut the rents we charge the farmers to work our land in half, and collect that in necessaries, not gold or silver. Avoid outsiders for a time, and plead ignorance of everything to strangers."

I'd seen Traptain's expression when I gave my orders and went to him, standing very close. His eyes widened in fear.

"You *will* do as I've ordered," I said, in a near whisper, "and not worry about the rents you'll be losing. If you do not treat my family, and my retainers, as if they were your own, you'll face my anger when I return. And if I die, I'll return and deal with you as a demon. I vow this in the name of Tanis, Vachan . . . and Saionji herself!"

He quailed at my anger and the death-goddess's name and nodded obediently. I would not have to worry about him.

"How long do you think we'll have to stay in hiding?" Daryal asked.

"Until the one who calls himself Laish Tenedos is dead."

"How will we know if . . . when he's gone? When it's safe to come out of hiding?" Jeritza asked.

"You'll know," I said.

"And you," Kassa said. "Where do you go?"

"South," I said. "South, to war."

NINE

MOVING SOUTH

I rode fast for the first three days, putting a state and a life behind. I broke out of Cimabue's jungle then, onto the rolling savannas of Tagil. The roads were winding dirt lanes at first, then became wider and in some places cobbled outside the towns as I swung easterly, toward the Latane River.

There were other travelers—traders, farmers heading for market, mostly older or very young people as I'd seen between Kaldi and Cimabue, riding together for protection.

But there were other men on the trails I'd not seen before. The first type was most unsettling: discharged soldiers, traveling in pairs or in small groups. Some were mounted, some afoot. Most wore some remnants of their uniforms, and quite a few were armless, legless, without an eye, or scarred. All were armed and had the hard gaze of men who'd seen too much death.

I chanced spending the night with five such men, although I kept my sword close at hand and my hidden dagger ready.

Where were they going? They weren't sure. Maybe toward Khurram, maybe south into Chalt. What were they looking for? Work, one said, and another's mouth twisted wryly.

"There's work enough if you're not particular," he said. "Any farmer'd be glad of a strong back. But that's what we left behind, when we enlisted."

"And we're not goin' back to it," another added.

"Why not?" I asked. "That's an honorable life."

"Fuck honor," a third said rudely. "I'll leave that for the nobles and generals that dumped us into the shitter in Maisir and hope they fuckin' choke on it."

"I'll ask," I said directly. "What are *you* seeking?"

He started to say something, stopped, and was silent for a time. He prodded at the low fire with a stick.

"Dunno," he said finally. "It's like war cut something in me, so there wasn't any home when I went back to where I'd come from. The people kept staring, real wary, as if I was some sort of uncaged beast, about to spring on them.

"Maybe I am. So I left. Met up with these other shit-brains on the road, and we're all looking for what we don't know together."

"You could go back under the colors," I suggested, then added, cynically, "there's enough of them to choose from, between the Peace Guardians, the former emperor, or those who don't want him to regain the throne."

"Fuck all of 'em twice," another man put in. "Man can get killed listening to generals. You look like you was an officer, anyway some sort of soldier. Didn't you learn that?"

I had to laugh. "Not well enough."

"We could always go to banditry," another said. "Live high for a year or so 'til they hunted us down and cut our guts out. You got any suggestions?"

I shook my head.

"So where are you bound?"

I told them.

"You was right. You didn't learn nothin'."

I slept carefully that night, but none of them tried anything. I would've been surprised if they had, for in spite of their weapons, rough dress, or rougher speech, I recognized them as the sort of soldiery I'd once been proud to lead.

I shared what was in my saddlebags for the morning meal, then reloaded my two pack animals and mounted.

"Again I'll make my offer," I said. "If you find there's nothing out here for you . . . come find me. I'll find a place for you."

"You never give us your name."

"Damastes," I said, looking at them carefully, needing to see the response. "Damastes á Cimabue."

Their eyes widened, and two jerked off their caps, and a third reflexively clapped one hand to his shoulder in remembered salute.

"Sorry, sir," one said. "We di'n't recognize you, and—"

"Fiddleshit," I said rudely. "Put your caps back on. Right now, I'm no more than a wanderer like you. But I know where I'm going, at least for now. Amur. To join the rebels."

The five exchanged looks, and the one I'd argued with the night before grinned ruefully.

"At least you made us an offer. More'n we've had lately. But no. We're not hurting that much."

"No," I agreed. "But Numantia is." I turned my horse. "Good luck to you all, no matter where you go."

I rode off and quickly outpaced them.

* * *

The other sort I encountered wasn't that different than the ex-soldiers, except few were armed with anything but cudgels and the stray hunting bow or spear. The closer I came to Amur, the more of them I encountered. Most were young, in their early to midteens, but a handful were my age or older.

Some were well dressed, some ragged. All of them had a single destination: the rebel army.

Rebels was the term used, although it wasn't a good one, but how else could you describe those who wanted neither the Grand Council and Maisir to rule nor the emperor? Some wanted to enlist for excitement or even that age-old draw of a full belly and new clothes. They didn't realize once fighting began, they'd likely be even more ragged and starved than now. But I said nothing.

Some wanted to enlist because they hated the emperor, either because of some wrong his minions had done or, as often, because one of their own had died or been mutilated in the stupidity of the Maisirian campaign.

But the oddest of all was a group of young men who galloped, on line, down a grassy hillside toward me one morning.

There were about half a hundred of them and they were quite spectacular, mounted on matching grays, and they wore a uniform I'd never seen before: green busbys, a similarly colored jacket with gold frogs and epaulettes, black pants stuffed into black boots. They were well armed, all with lance and saber, and the man riding behind their leader carried a guidon with a device I couldn't make out.

I had no idea who they were, nor why they'd decided to ride at me. If they intended harm, there was little I could do, but I loosened my sword in its sheath. I'd decided, as

I rode away from the ruins in Cimabue, I'd no more kneel to man or demon, nor would I permit myself to be taken captive.

Saionji could provide no more soul-deadening punishment after I returned to the Wheel than the degradation I'd twice known as a prisoner.

But the lances of the charging horsemen stayed vertical, nor did any of them draw steel. I noted with a bit of amusement most had enough of a task staying on their horses, as the field wasn't nearly as level as it looked.

"Turn!" the man in front shouted, and the horsemen swept in a semicircle until they faced away from me, and I wondered if they were going to ride back uphill as pell-mell as they came.

"And . . . HALT!" The formation, with much rearing of horses and shouts from their riders, did as ordered, wheeling until they faced me once more.

"Your pardon," the man called, "for using you for practice. But there've been few riders on this road today." He was in his mid-twenties, well built, medium height, dark complected, and wore a heavy moustache that framed his mouth to below his chin.

"No injury," I shouted back. "But, if you're interested, the commands are 'On line, charge,' then, when you wish to turn your formation, 'Wheel right or left,' in whichever direction you've decided. And you might want to find yourself a bugler or two. Saves the voice."

The man reacted, then kicked his horse toward me.

"You're a cavalryman?" he began, then gaped. "Sir! You're First Tribune á Cimabue. I thought you were dead, or a prisoner . . . no, I heard you'd made your escape. Forgot it for a moment, not being one with a quick memory."

"I'm Damastes á Cimabue," I said. "But not first tribune for anyone."

"Yessir! I saw you once before, sir, when I was very young, and you rode through our lands with your Red Lancers. You were on the way to Bala Hissar, I think. I never saw anything so magnificent. That's when I knew I was going to be a warrior."

"You have the advantage," I said, through his cheerful burble. I certainly didn't remember him, for when I was the emperor's fireman I was constantly on the move, and many were the noblemen who wanted to feast me and my men, whether out of patriotism or the hope that it would further endear them to the emperor.

"Oh. Oh yes. I'm Lasleigh, Baron Pilfern of Stowe. And these are my men. I raised the company, outfitted it, and we're on our way to enlist."

"With which side?" I wondered.

"Why, there's but one," he said, in astonishment. "The rebels, of course, although I wish they'd find a nobler name."

That surprised me a bit. Then I remembered the hatred the rural nobility had for the emperor, mainly for upsetting the nice, comfortable idiocy of the generations-old Rule of Ten and not letting them rule their lands as if there was no other authority in Numantia.

Nor would this Lasleigh have backed the Grand Council, since it was the puppet of the hated Maisirians.

"Good," I said. "For I have the same goal."

"Sir! Would you do me . . . do us . . . the honor of riding with us?"

"Why not?" I said with some amusement. "It will be good to be back among soldiers again."

Lasleigh looked embarrassed.

"I don't know if we're soldiers . . . at least not yet," he said in a low voice so his men wouldn't overhear. "But we're learning. Trying to teach ourselves. Maybe you could give us some help."

"Gladly," I said. "Teaching always cleans the rust away, and I suspect I'll need to be fairly sharp in the days to come."

Lasleigh stood in his stirrups. "Men! Raise a cheer for the First . . . for Damastes á Cimabue!"

The men bellowed lustily, and I had fifty traveling companions.

I rapidly realized this was good, for Lasleigh's eager questions forced me out of my broodings. I wondered if I'd been as prattling an idiot as he was when I was a fresh subaltern, decided not, for my father Cadalso had taught me enthusiasm is well and good . . . at the proper time and place.

But I attempted to answer his questions and those of his underlings. They were sure I'd be in command of the new army, which was probably correct. But I disavowed any ambition except to what I was assigned, for all too often the army—any army—says one thing and changes its mind the next moment.

I did have a question of my own that first day—why hadn't Lasleigh joined the Imperial Army, when every man was needed in Maisir? He was terribly embarrassed and said he was the eldest son, and his father refused to allow the bloodline to be endangered. I kept an even countenance, for this wasn't a unique idea, the old baronies' thinking the continuation of their own line came before anything, even their country.

"But he allowed my younger brother to join," Lasleigh said. "He was accepted by the Twentieth Heavy Cavalry."

Again my face showed nothing.

Lasleigh looked away, suddenly fascinated by a rather ordinary-looking bullock grazing in a paddy.

"He did well," Lasleigh said. "He went in, just before the emperor began the retreat from Jarrah, and joined his regiment after the army'd come back into Numantia. The last letter we had from him said he'd been promoted to captain, and that was in just a couple of months."

That wasn't all that remarkable—in those desperate days, a man who showed any leadership would be promoted faster than he could take the rank sashes from the bodies of his dead superiors.

"Then . . . then was Cambiaso." Lasleigh choked.

If Lasleigh's brother had ridden out with the Twentieth, just behind me and the Seventeenth Lancers, on the day of blood, the day when Saionji's laughter shook the land, and her sword blades were drenched with blood . . .

"I miss him," Lasleigh said after a moment. "He was always there, and it was more like having a friend, a real friend, than a brother."

I changed the subject. "Your father wouldn't let you serve. But now?"

"Now I am Baron Pilfern," Lasleigh said, "and there's no one to tell me nay. And I have a blood debt to settle with that man who was our emperor and wishes to drown us in gore again."

I could have said Lasleigh was standing in a very long line but didn't.

We came to a crossroads a couple of days later, where we should have turned due east to enter Amur, but Lasleigh said his course lay a day's travel farther south. There was something he must see.

"Cambiaso?" I guessed.

Lasleigh nodded.

I should have left him and rode on alone, for it's not good for a warrior to spend too much time considering his scars and defeats. But I did not, and we rode on south.

It was hot as we moved across the near-desert, and the creaking of our harness was loud around us. There was a sere wind whispering, and the occasional chirping of locusts.

We made camp beside a swampy creek. There was nothing to fear in this dead land, but for some reason we put out sentries.

The next morning, we rode on, and the rocky heights rose in front of us, the heights the Numantian Army held before making that last charge. I saw it again in my mind, saw the banners as the army roared down, even heard the screams of men fighting, dying.

But the present was as terrible as the past, for the battleground had never been shriven of its terrors. The bodies had been left where they fell on that dreadful day, and the wounded who couldn't drag themselves to succor had been left to die.

Numantia had an excuse—we were defeated, most of us down in our blood, the rest prisoners herded into staked compounds before being released to make their way to whatever home was left. But Maisir, as I'd seen, cared little for any man who couldn't continue to fight.

The bodies had been left to rot under the dry sun. Wild animals had done what they could over the years, and the wild grasses were growing to hide man's shame. But there were few beasts in this wilderness, and the grasses grew slowly.

Bones still littered the ground like driftwood I'd seen on a stormy beach on my island prison. Here and there were shattered spears, swords, bits and pieces of armor.

Lasleigh and his men were silent as they looked at this awful desolation, more terrible than any bard's tale of war's ruination.

Finally he said, "If . . . if I'd thought to bring a wizard, perhaps he could have divined my brother's resting place, and we could have had a proper ceremony."

"No," I said gently. "His spirit's gone to the Wheel, and if he was a good officer, as he must've been, wouldn't he want his bones to lie with his men?"

Lasleigh nodded solemn agreement. "Yes," he said. "He would. There's much I have to learn."

I didn't reply, but dropped the lead of my pack animals and let my mount canter forward slowly.

I've heard old soldiers say when they revisit a battlefield it's never as they remembered it. But this wasteland was just as I recalled. Here were the Maisirian front lines, here where we'd struck and broken through, riding hard toward that rise, a rise hidden on that day by banners and tents.

Here was where our charge had been broken, and we'd fought on, afoot, toward the king's tents on the rise. Demons had come at us, demons with the faces of brave Numantians slain in Maisir. But it was too late for horror, and we'd cut them down as we killed mortal soldiers.

I was out of the saddle, not noticing, walking forward, remembering, and the din of battle was all around, and my sword arm was slashing back, forth, killing, even though now, in this silence, it was really motionless at my side.

Here was where the Maisirian tents had been, and here was where the *azaz*, the chief wizard of Maisir, the man who'd put a spell on me and forced me to kill Karjan, had come from his tent. I'd drawn my dagger, the silver-mounted knife Yonge of the Hills had given me as a wedding present, and thrown it well, into the *azaz*'s guts and seen him go down, screaming.

The moment was very clear now. I was walking very slowly, moving as though I was ensorcelled, and I saw something, half-buried. I bent, picked it up, and saw without the slightest surprise that I was holding Yonge's dagger.

The blade was rusty, the silver tarnished, the multi-colored woods that mosaiced its handle chipped here and there.

This was completely impossible. Why had no one picked it up, as a memento or as a symbol of that dark moment when Maisir's greatest magician, King Bairan's closest adviser, had been killed?

Impossible.

Yet I held it in my hand.

I felt my lips curl into a strange smile.

I tucked the dagger into my belt. It could be polished, waxed, and a sheath made for it.

I still needed it.

There was still blood for it to drink.

It would be a worthy companion to my father's sword.

I turned, saw Lasleigh sitting his horse about twenty feet behind me. He flinched, arm coming up as if to block a blow, and I knew my expression was terrible.

I said nothing, but walked to where my horse waited.

We mounted and rode away from the nightmare of Cambiaso, no one speaking.

A day later, we crossed into Amur, and four days after that we found the rebel army.

TO BUILD AN ARMY

Kutulu and Sinait made much of my coming. I must become commander in chief, and all units must be informed immediately.

I said not yet. There were things I needed to know before I made a final decision.

First was our strength. They told me we now had, and this was changing daily, about half a million men wanting to fight, still scattered across Amur. This was very good, a fivefold increase in a time, so our cause was popular.

Next was the same question, for Tenedos. Kutulu had sent more than twenty agents into the heart of the enemy, and all but two were still reporting. But their information wasn't cheery—Numantians continued to flock to the imperial standard. Kutulu estimated, and said this was a very good, very close estimate, he now had nearly a million men and had moved those units in Bala Hissar into Darkot, for large-scale exercises.

An army, sensibly led, starts by training a soldier to march up and down and back and forth without questioning these or any other orders and to fear and follow his superiors. Then he's folded into a squad, a company, a regiment, and an army. At each stage, war games are held. The bigger the games, the closer the army is to battle readiness.

So Tenedos would not be holding in place much longer.

What about the government, the Grand Councilors? Their army had also increased slightly, to about three-quarters of a million strong, but hadn't moved beyond its previous positions: Nicias–the Latane–Khurram.

Another question—what of Maisir? Was King Bairan letting his worst enemy rebuild without taking any action? Kutulu made a face—he hadn't many agents that far south, and their reports took forever to reach him, and their reports were contradictory. Evidently Bairan had called up additional age groups, which was the way Maisir recruited, so he was increasing his troop strength. But no units were moving toward the Maisirian-Numantian border, although Kutulu had two fragmentary reports that King Bairan had sent a large expedition into Kait to quiet the always-restive bandits of the hill tribes. He had nothing at all about the expedition's size, progress, or capabilities.

"Interesting," I said. "We'll assume the Maisirians are still unready, but a definite threat." I turned to Sinait. "A question I should have asked, back in Cimabue: Tenedos is less a soldier than a wizard. What large spells is he preparing? What countermeasures have you readied?"

"I've studied every piece of magic he used against both Kallio and Maisir," she said, "and have devised counter-spells against most of them. The great demon he raised once and was prepared to summon is an unknown.

"The problem is that his power is far greater than mine. I could, for instance, attempt an oversight of his area, but I'm deathly afraid any normal sort of 'seeing' might be turned against us."

I remembered the demon Thak, seen in the "safe" Bowl, and how he'd ravened up at Tenedos and me before the seer was able to break the spell.

"I've summoned every magician I can find and am trying to teach them to work in unison, as the Maisirians did with their War Magicians. Their spells, I've heard, hit the emperor hard."

"They did," I agreed. "He said it was because there were so many of them, and their incantations swarmed around like bees. He'd break one, and another would take its place.

"But I've had a thought since then . . . remember, I know little to nothing about sorcery . . . is it possible Tenedos had problems not so much because of the *number* of spells sent, but because they each came from a different source? I know . . . you and Tenedos have taught me . . . a wizard tries mightily to find all he can about his enemy.

"But if there's ten . . . or a hundred . . . enemies, all anonymous, mightn't that not make a single wizard's task harder, even though Tenedos had the Chare Brethren?"

Sinait nodded slowly. "An interesting perception. Worth studying."

"If I'm right," I said, getting a bit excited, "mightn't it be possible to have ten or more people cast parts of a single spell . . . I don't know how you'd get continuity . . . to make it harder to break?"

"That *is* a worthwhile thought," she said. "I think so."

I took a deep breath, feeling I was standing on a peak, and my words would send me tumbling down into a new and completely unknown world.

"Very well," I said. "I'll take your high command. But send no messengers to broadcast the news. Instead, I want you, Seer, to have your magicians cast a spell to block Tenedos's 'sight.' Cast it slowly, subtly, so it builds.

"When you think it's dark, or thick enough, or whatever way you'd describe something like that, then summon the army. *All* the army."

"But that'll provide one great, easy target," Kutulu objected.

I knew very well the risk, but this was something that must be done.

"Yes, sir," Kutulu said after a momentary pause. "I'll not question your orders again."

"Yes, you will," I said. "For I'm mortal, which means I'm an easy fool and need to be reminded of that every now and again. That's what led the emperor into the mire—no one, or hardly anyone, ever asked if he was certain he was doing the right thing or told him he was full of shit. Not that he would have changed his mind or course if they had," I said, a touch of bitterness in my voice.

"So I'm yours," I said. "I'll make my staff appointments as time goes on. But the first two are these—Kutulu, you're to become my adjutant, although I don't want you to waste time worrying about supplies or soldiery. But I want you to have instant access to me with any news of Tenedos, Bairan, or the Grand Councilors."

"Yes, sir." Kutulu's face glowed, I swear, and he drew himself to attention and saluted, as if he were a soldier in uniform. I remembered his dream was to one day be named tribune, and he'd made the mistake of asking that boon of the emperor, which set Tenedos's hand against him, for the emperor believed spies could never be honored like soldiers.

I wouldn't make that mistake. A carved length of wood, or a sash, or a bit of metal . . . all have only the value the giver and the taker place on them. If they bonded a man to me, to my commands, I'd give him anything.

"You, Sinait, are to be Kutulu's equivalent for sorcery. Either of you can make necessary decisions, without having to wait on my approval.

"Just try not to do something that'll lose the war without giving me a couple of minutes' warning."

Sinait chuckled, and Kutulu tried a smile on for size, decided he liked it.

"Now, let's begin this probably hopeless task."

It took three weeks for my soldiers to reach my headquarters, a smallish town named Paestum, which I'd chosen because five major roads—at least major for a poor state like Amur—met there. Also, someone had built a huge inn on the outskirts in the grandiose and false notion that Paestum was about to become a great market town.

The abandoned inn was perfect for my headquarters. I wouldn't have to requisition anyone's dwelling or business and make yet another set of enemies nor be piously miserable in tents pitched in some field.

The soldiers marched, or rather straggled in, their bedding a blanket and piece of canvas to wrap themselves in rolled across their backs, carrying their cookware and, often as not, a chicken grabbed in some village they'd passed through. Few had any uniform, only half were armed, and that half with a huge array of weaponry from modern to antique to improvised. They bivouacked in fields around Paestum and thanked various gods the weather remained dry.

I'd had a high wooden stand built in the center of a bare heath, and on a certain day the soldiers were assembled around it, covering the low hills around me.

I clambered up its steps, hoping I wouldn't slip and begin my command with an ill-omened fall on my ass. I reached the platform, and a roar echoed around the hills. That was why I'd assembled my army, so my soldiers would see not a handful of fellows huddled in some byre, but a great host, and let these numbers give them strength, give them the courage of numbers.

I prayed to Isa of war and my monkey god Vachan for guidance and support while Sinait and three other magicians readied two spells. The first would amplify my voice, the second would subtly make anyone staring at me think they were closer than they were, able to make out the smallest change of expression on my face, yet not make me a giant.

"I am Damastes á Cimabue," I began. "Some know me, some of you've served with me.

"Now I call you once more to my standard. Numantia needs warriors like you more than ever before in its history.

"This time, the battle is for freedom, and for our very souls.

"The man who was once our emperor, the man many of us served willingly, the man *I* served for many years, is now our worst enemy.

"You all know how he's dedicated his service to a goddess I shall not name."

Murmurs came from the ranks, and a few brave or unwary soldiers muttered "Saionji."

"But by serving her, he has become a demon himself, serving only himself and death. He cares nothing for Numantia, nothing for you, his greatest servants, and will willingly sacrifice your lives, your souls, for one instant of the power he once held and the greater power he lusts for.

"The man who calls himself Laish Tenedos, the false

emperor, must be brought down, and we shall be the ones to do it!"

The masses cheered again, but a bit tentatively, and faces in the crowd peered about, as if expecting demons to come out of the skies or ground.

"You sound fearful," I said. "And you are right to be watchful, for Tenedos is a mighty foe.

"But he is doomed!

"He serves evil, and evil cannot triumph, at least not for long. Umar did not create this world for evil, although priests say he may have withdrawn in sorrow, after seeing the great wickedness his creations wreaked, leaving Irisu to rule.

"Irisu is a mighty god, as are his manifestations and the other gods who serve him, and whom we serve.

"He will triumph, just as we will triumph.

"Numantia must be rid of Tenedos. That will be a beginning. Once we stand together as one, and all Numantia, from Khoh to Dara to Kallio to farthest Ossetia is united, then our sun shall be brighter than it ever was.

"And this will be a new sun of peace, from border to border, and with no enemies beyond to endanger us.

"We are climbing a great mountain, and the first step is the hardest.

"The first step is the destruction of the mad half-demon who calls himself Laish Tenedos.

"The task will not be easy. We must work hard, train hard, harder than you dream possible.

"But I promise you, the warriors you will become can stand against anything, cold steel or fiery demon, and seize victory!

"Numantia had a great army once, greater than the world has ever known.

"But you shall be greater, for your cause is that of good!

"Look about! Remember the faces around you, for all of you will be ennobled by your task. This day is the beginning, the beginning of a new time. A time of peace, a time of prosperity, a time of greatness.

"Reach out, my brothers. Reach out for this time. Fight hard. Fight as one!"

I let my voice build into a great roar:

"For Numantia and our gods!"

The roar swept over me like a tempest, and I could feel the strength, the will in their cries.

Next I would have to change it from empty wind to harsh reality.

I thought I'd built an army before, when Mercia Petre, the emperor, and I had shaken the Rule of Ten's bloated, slothful organization into a new fighting formation. But even then we had something to build from.

Now I had nothing but half a million eager civilians, only a scatter of trained soldiers.

That eagerness could be a virtue, for my recruits would be willing to put up with far more ineptness and error than any conscript. But my grace period would only last for a time, and the mood of the volunteers could change, and they'd trickle away just as rapidly as they'd come to Paestum.

A civilian might think the hardest part was finding officers and warrants, but there's always enough men who love being able to shout their fellows around, even to their deaths, and wear baubles to proclaim that privilege. There'd be problems later, when we went into combat, and those with the pretty sashes and authority would find an army rewards its warriors for their willingness to die.

It's an old and true saw that the biggest blusterer is frequently the first to break and run or, worse, send others to a pointless, stupid death.

But there's no way of testing how men will behave in battle except battle itself, so I put that concern away for the time.

There was a scattering of men who'd served before, and I promoted them as high as I dared, and one level further, knowing many a sergeant wanted no rank higher and wouldn't be competent to hold it, either. I daily mourned the leaders I remembered, men whose bones were forgotten in the Maisirian *suebi*.

One gift from the past was Sendraka, once of Yonge's skirmishers, who, as a captain, had brought Marán and me from her estates to Nicias and I began my odyssey to Jarrah. I hadn't thought any skirmisher survived, since they were always the first to fight and gladly sacrificed by the emperor to build his blood spells. But there were a few. Sendraka had served through the Maisirian campaign, then been lanced in the upper thigh during the retreat through Urey. The scouts were seldom taken prisoners, since they were hated by the Maisirians, particularly by their out-riding cavalry, the Negaret. Sendraka had gone to ground and let the armies pass while he painfully recuperated. It had been a year before he could walk, a year and a half before he could mount, and by that time the war was long over.

I asked why he hadn't been promoted higher than captain of the upper half. "There wasn't much rank in the skirmishers, but a lot of death, the way the emperor misused us," he said. That's a problem in any elite formation. There's envy and dislike for them in the regular branches, and so rewards come but seldom.

"Besides," he said wryly, "I've never been one to keep my mouth shut if a man insists on playing the fool and then asking my opinion."

I grinned, told him that was now a recommended policy, promoted him to domina, and put him in charge of forming a corps of skirmishers. I didn't know how good he was in combat, but managing to elude the Negaret with a gaping hole in his leg suggested he might be properly devious.

I thought longingly of Yonge of the Hills, the sly fox I really needed, but there was no way to summon him from his murderously gained throne in Sayana.

Another officer came, Thanet, who'd been a young legate with my own formation, the Seventeenth Ureyan Lancers. He had been invalided home at the beginning of the war with a lung disorder and still broke into uncontrollable coughing from time to time.

Again, I asked the question—why do you wish to join my army?

"Because," he said evenly, "I'm three generations a warrior and think the emperor misled us into Maisir and, given the chance, would destroy us . . . and Numantia . . . once again." He half smiled. "I'll say this, but you'll think I'm browning you off, sir, even though it's the truth. I'd rather serve under a Seventeenth veteran than Isa himself."

Him, too, I made domina and set him to forming a new regiment of cavalry I privately vowed to rename after the Seventeenth if they proved worthy of the honor.

These, as I said, weren't the greatest of my problems.

Bigger problems were the ones that don't appear in the romances. It's possible to find a man who's a good horse trader. But what about one who can buy remounts for an army without either getting stung or deciding to tuck away a few gold coins for himself here and there? The same caution must apply to paymasters and quartermasters.

Or uniforms. I needed half as many seamstresses as I did soldiers, at least for a while. The solution here was to put anyone in Amur who could use a needle to work, and that included quite a few old men and children. For the moment, my army's uniform would be a simple sleeveless vest in green. As time went on, I'd try to provide complete garb, but the vest might help a man distinguish friend from foe in the frenzy of battle.

Or something that appears simpler—many men, more than are willing to admit it, are adequate cooks. From that group, find me one who can decide the victuals for half a million men and train others to cook them.

I'd wanted to set up central messes, which is far more efficient than the old system of squads messing by themselves, and also avoids a great plague I'd foolishly suggested to Tenedos—that the army become its own quartermaster and resupply itself on the march.

In Maisir, that'd meant every man was a looter, and each time he stole something from a Maisirian peasant, he made an enemy for Numantia out of someone who might've stayed guardedly neutral or even become an ally. Also, if all soldiers, not just officers, were given their meals, hopefully warm, morning and night, they'd be stronger and fight harder—and spend more time soldiering instead of scrounging.

But this wasn't possible, at least not yet, and so the old system continued.

We would be fighting in our own land, and there'd be inevitable thefts and crimes against our people. But I swore there'd be as few as possible, and those would be severely dealt with. Therefore, I sought me a bastard. I could have used Kutulu, but his ability to pry out the enemy's secrets was too important to waste him becoming a uniformed warder once again.

I finally found a man who'd been one of the magistrates dealing with the Tovieti after the rising was quelled, a harsh man who valued only the law and held no gods or men above it. He could oversee my provosts and the resulting courts-martial, and I could temper his austerity with mercy if I chose. In the meantime, the troops would curse him, and not me.

The largest problem was one I thankfully didn't have to worry about, because there was little I could do, and that was money. To put it simply—we had none. Or almost none. We paid our soldiers little, and that was in scrip we printed on the Paestum broadsheet's press, redeemable for gold within a year. If, a year from now, we were still fighting and hadn't been able to take any cities and loot their treasuries . . . well, if we were still in the field a year from now, that meant Tenedos had won, and we'd be dead.

The cavalry we sent out foraging also paid in scrip, and the farmers grumbled, as they have since the beginning of time. My response was short: sacrifice for your country and take the paper money, or we'll just requisition what we need.

Little by little and day by day, the army grew, amid dusty, square-bashing, shrieking warrants, galloping officers.

Sinait and Kutulu came up with a clever device. She ensorcelled a scrap of polished copper that'd been immersed in the mercury pool of a Seeing Bowl; then a spy slipped through the lines and hid it for two days outside Tenedos's headquarters.

The copper had been spell-commanded to reflect only one man.

Sinait swore there was no possible danger in using the copper after it'd been retrieved, but I was hesitant.

Sinait said the words, and the bowl came to life, and I jerked, seeing Tenedos walk toward me, deep in conversation with a robed man. I frowned, then remembered the other. It was Gojjam, a sometime member of the Chare Brethren, then the emperor's direct agent.

"I've found a man," Kutulu said, "who has the talent of reading lips, and he says Tenedos is instructing Gojjam on particulars about his new Corps of Wizards, evidently something like the Chare Brethren or the Maisirian War Magicians, which Gojjam is to head.

"I have the conversation transcribed, if you wish to see it, but I can assure you there's nothing you need notice, save the existence of this corps."

I nodded absently, paying less attention to his words than in looking at Tenedos. Gods, but he'd aged. His hair was beginning to thin, and he looked soft, as if he hadn't taken exercise in a while. Once he looked up, gaze crossing the copper, and I flinched. His eyes, too, had changed. Always hypnotic, now they had the glare of a driven soul, completely fixed on a single purpose, and that purpose beyond the ken of humans.

If anything, he was more frightening than before.

I asked if there was more to be gleaned from the copper and was told there wasn't. I ordered it destroyed, for I wanted nothing that'd been in contact with Tenedos to be close to me or my officers.

I returned to my quarters, very thoughtful, considering how the years had worn at the demon king.

Then I caught sight of myself in a pier glass and smiled

wryly. I, too, looked far older than my years, older and a trace haggard. But I refused to admit the hard look in my eyes was anything other than determination and fatigue.

A number of already-skilled craftsmen came to the army, no doubt wanting to be given sword and buckler. But they were too valuable for that, which I'm sure irked some of them, even though becoming such a specialist vastly increased the chances of surviving the war.

One such was an armorer, and I took shameful advantage of my rank and gave him Yonge's tarnished and worn dagger and asked him, as a favor, what could be done with it.

A few days later, the man returned. The knife was as new, even its varied woods replaced where chipped, its silver workings like mirrors, its blade gleaming, sharper than when it'd been first given me. Along with it came a tooled leather sheath, whose details matched the engravings on the knife's blade.

I tried to pay him, but he refused, so I rewarded him in a the traditional way the army has, without his ever knowing it, by making sure his superior promoted him as rapidly as possible.

In idle moments, I got into the habit of taking the knife out and polishing it with a bit of leather, thinking about the work it had done in the past.

And dreaming of the work it'd be given in the future.

Half a time later, I was on a square, watching Domina Thanet attempt to teach a line of budding cavalrymen walk-trot-charge, trying to be complimentary at how far these peasants and merchants' sons had come, since none fell off the plowhorses, carriage pullers, and merchants' pets we were trying to convince ourselves would be war mounts. Seer Sinait rode up, brown robes rucked in her belt, excitement coloring her face.

I handed her my waterbag and told her to drink. It was hot out, and heat stroke wouldn't significantly improve her ability to communicate. She drank deeply, lowered the bag, and stared at the horsemen.

"Something very odd just happened," she said. "We've been approached by the Grand Councilors."

"Scopas and Barthou are *here*? In Paestum?" I was equally incredulous.

"No," she said. "They're not that brave, nor that confident we'd honor a flag of truce, and honestly I don't know if we should if we got a chance to grab those scoundrels. They sent an emissary, a Rast Timgad. I note they're using Maisirian ranks still, although he doesn't look like much of a soldier." She was babbling a bit as her mind worked at the problem of what this meant.

"*That* ass—" I caught myself in time.

"That asshole, indeed," Sinait finished. "Although I've not had the displeasure of meeting him, I know full well what a lickspittle he is from Kutulu. He's also accompanied by the new head of the Peace Guardians, a dangerous-looking man named Trerice, who says his rank is supreme *jedaz*."

Trerice had been Herne's subordinate, and supreme *jedaz* was the Maisirian rank Barthou had offered me.

Sinait managed a trace of a smile.

"They want to meet with the head of the rebels. Tsk. I never realized we forgot to appoint somebody to the position."

"Kutulu declined to see them," she went on. "He said he works better in the shadows. So would you care to be our leader?"

"No, but I'd like to see what they're offering, if you accompany me," I said.

"I would be honored."

"Grant a minute for me to give my blessings to these sweaty sorts," I said, "and we'll see what these Grand Councilors want."

What they wanted, of course, was to see what we wanted.

Timgad was as corpse-looking as I'd remembered, ridiculous in uniform.

Trerice was every bit as dangerous as Sinait suggested. He wore the gray-red of the Peace Guardians, but where the late Herne had added lace and jewels to meet his ideas of how a properly dressed commander should appear, Trerice wore no glitter except for his rank sash. He wore both his sword and curving long dagger on the same side, and both sheaths were well-used plain leather. His face was hard, bones close to the surface, and his reddish beard was close-trimmed. His eyes were cold and held mine.

He stayed behind Timgad and kept silent while the Councilors' emissary sounded us out.

"You truly haven't chosen anyone to take the throne once you've destroyed Tenedos?" Timgad said in disbelief.

"First of all," Sinait said briskly, "whoever has said that anyone here has any interest in ruling Numantia?"

"How could you not?" Timgad stammered, then recovered. "This . . . perhaps this news simplifies my mission."

"In what way?" I asked.

"Well," he said, his voice growing cozy, "if no one with your rebels has an interest in ruling, it would seem to be logical we should combine forces."

"In other words, we do your scut work," I said, "and

Barthou and Scopas rule on? Or, rather, they continue to rule at the pleasure of King Bairan."

"Temporarily, yes, although the noble mission of bringing order to our country is hardly something I would describe as scut work. And I am safe in adding that the present arrangements with Maisir will not last forever."

"Let me give you a direct answer," I said, letting my voice rise, although I felt no real anger—these idiots were behaving in character. "Absolutely no! I won't allow a single soldier of mine to sacrifice his life for a regime as morally empty as yours or for roundheel traitors like Barthou and Scopas."

"But," Timgad said, trying to keep calm, "we *must* have plans to preserve order, Numantian society, after Tenedos is destroyed."

"That won't be done quite as easily as you seem to think," I said. "I seem to recall a fable about a man who sold the skin of a lion before he hunted him, and the beast was the victor that day. As I said, once the present danger is taken care of, then we'll worry about what comes next."

Timgad was about to wallow further into his morass, but Trerice held up a hand.

"Very well," he said smoothly. "But is there any reason we can't ally ourselves, the legitimate armed forces of Numantia, with your soldiers, such as they are?"

I wanted that as much as I wanted a second navel, but the inexorable numbers kept floating through my mind: Tenedos had at least a million men, I had perhaps 600,000 now. The Peace Guardians would add another 750,000, enough to give us advantage.

"Such as they are?" I parried. "I'd rather have my

honest peasants, who I know will stand and fight, than those treasonous thugs you command."

"We can manage without the insults," Trerice hissed.

"Yes," I agreed. "We can. I withdraw what I said. How would you plan to dispose these forces?"

"The most logical," he said, "would be to use your men to fill in my blank files—"

"No," I said. "My army . . . our army . . . will fight as coherent units, under their own leaders. That is not a debatable issue."

Timgad began to say something, but Trerice glanced at him, and he was silent.

"What about command?" Trerice asked. "My Peace Guardians will hardly be willing to serve under whoever you've made into officers. We do have, as you must know, legitimate, trained leaders."

"As requested, I'm refraining from giving my opinion of most of the ones I remember," I said. "However, let me make a suggestion: Bring your forces south toward Paestum, keeping on the west bank of the Latane. I'll hold a line here against the river."

"What advantage is there in that?"

Trerice might be dangerous, but he was not a strategician.

"Because Tenedos must destroy me . . . destroy my army . . . before he can move on Nicias," I said patiently. "He will not, cannot, allow a threat in being to exist behind his lines. Besides, you boast your men are well led and well trained, so it's more logical for them to move rather than me, since they'll be able to keep proper formations and assemble for combat more readily than my regiments."

Trerice hesitated, and I wondered how well trained his Peace Guardians really were.

"So Tenedos moves—from, where is he now, still in Bala Hissar?—against your lines," Trerice thought aloud. "If we can conceal ourselves during the approach, that would make it an easy matter for us to attack his flanks once he closes with you."

"I'll remind you," I said, not showing my surprise at how out of date his intelligence about Tenedos's whereabouts was, "the once-emperor is a master sorcerer. Unless the Grand Council has suddenly developed a wizard or group of wizards as powerful, it'll be unlikely you'd be able to hide for long."

"*We* have magicians-in-training," Sinait added, "and will have spells ready to partially confuse any seer, we hope. But being able to completely blind our movements, as you seem to think you can do, no. I can't be that sanguine about the level of our sorcery. Can you?"

"Perhaps," Trerice said. "Or perhaps not. The emperor isn't a general and isn't familiar with being actually in command of an army. He did, after all, have you, Damastes, throughout his career."

I wanted to shake him for being a fool—who with the Council forces *did* have as much experience as Tenedos? Indore, a political general? Taitu, who hadn't commanded men for many years? Trerice himself?

"Perhaps," he went on, "I am being too optimistic. It seems that I . . . or, rather, it seems Timgad and I . . . can present a good case to the Grand Councilors to accept your proposal, since that way no leader will be stepping on anyone else's command toes."

Timgad was suddenly all smiles. "Excellent, really excellent, Supreme Jedaz. This was a truly productive meeting. And I'm delighted that we'll be able to stand together against the common foe.

"Now, we must return to Nicias. If there are no difficulties, we'll send messengers back to confirm our decision and begin preparations for the great confrontation."

"Yes," Trerice said, coldly. "Yes, we'll do that. But, before we leave, I'd like a moment alone with you, General Damastes?"

Sinait and Timgad excused themselves, and the thin smile fell from Trerice's lips.

"I suppose I should be grateful to you for enabling me to take command of the Peace Guardians."

"You needn't bother," I said, my voice equally chill. "I had my own reasons to kill Herne, besides those of the moment."

He nodded once. "You should be aware that I'm not a fool, so I hardly accept your pious claims of being uninterested in power."

"Accept what you please."

"I think in prison your self-estimate became overweeningly large, for there is no way you'll be able to take the throne when Tenedos is destroyed. King Bairan will certainly not allow it."

"But he'll let *you* rule Numantia, after Barthou and Scopas have convenient little accidents?" I said. "I can smell your ambition all the way across this tent."

"Why not? I'm certainly more capable than either of those two. For instance, if I'd had the opportunity, I wouldn't have allowed either you or the emperor to live. Dead men claim no thrones."

I was amused. Men who brag to their enemies may be dangerous in an alley, but as foes they're hardly in the league of a Tenedos or Bairan.

"I take that," I said, "as my warning if we defeat the once-emperor."

"You should," Trerice said. He waited for a moment, no doubt expecting me to produce an equally bombastic vow.

I said nothing.

He looked a bit discomfited, picked up his riding gloves from a table, and without another word, marched out.

I didn't categorize him as a total fool—no one, even a boaster, who makes threats should ever be completely ignored.

But I had larger problems.

Such as the emperor, three-quarters of a million Peace Guardians who weren't my idea of the perfect allies, and a battle that could be no more than a time or two away.

ELEVEN

MEETING AT MIDNIGHT

I paid little attention to my own security, thinking the only important enemy I had was Tenedos, who seemed strangely unaware of where I was. Against him, I relied on whatever devices Sinait and her magicians had incanted and got on with my business.

I kept a single sentry at the door to my quarters on the top floor of the inn, but that was only to filter out the idiots who besieged me with the smallest problem.

One night I came back to the inn more than a little dissatisfied after a night exercise that'd started badly and gotten worse. My guard wasn't at his post, and I thought he was using the jakes or the guard commander had forgotten to make the posting. I shrugged and went into my rooms, one long almost-hall with a huge table I had maps, plans, and papers strewn on, a bathing chamber, and a small alcove to one side with my bed.

The room was dark, and I left the door open to give me light until I lit one of the lamps. I was halfway across the room when the door clicked shut, and I was in blackness.

One panel of a dark lantern came open, pinning me in its beam. My sword was halfway out, when a quiet voice came:

"Do not move, á Cimabue, or you shall surely die."

I let my blade drop back. A man came out of darkness, uncovering a slow match, and he lit two lamps on the table.

"Please unbuckle your sword belt and let it fall," the voice ordered, and I obeyed.

"You may turn now," the voice said. "We have no intention of killing you. At the moment."

I saw six men, or so I presumed, in the room. Two wore green uniform vests, all the others but one were in motley civilian garb, the last wore a hooded traveling cloak. All but one were armed with swords or daggers.

I assumed the hooded one to be their leader, and the one who'd given me orders, but one of the men in green spoke again: "Sit down."

I hesitated, and the other uniformed man gestured at me with his weapon. It was a bit unusual, at least for a man to carry: a small single-handed crossbow, the stock just over a foot long, with no butt, its prod about an equal width. Boys in Cimabue used similar toys to shoot sparrows or rabbits with.

I eyed it skeptically.

"The bolt is poisoned," the speaker told me. "You would have no more than a dozen breaths after being struck."

I sat, and the others followed, except for the hooded figure.

"You have the advantage, sir," I said.

"You may call me . . . call me Jakuns."

Clever—Jakuns was the roguish folk hero who had a thousand faces to aid his swindles of the rich and foolish.

"So what do you want with me?" I asked. "Obviously

nothing to my advantage, or you wouldn't have come in like assassins."

"That," Jakuns said, "is what we are. Sometimes."

He held out a hand, and a yellow silk cord coiled around it, as if it was alive.

Tovieti!

"Last time I encountered one of your believers," I said, "I was given assistance. I gather you're now back in your usual murderous form."

"Not necessarily," Jakuns said. "And, if you're curious, that assistance wasn't an individual aberration. The wisest among us approved it."

"Why?"

"You don't need to know, specifically. But your continued survival was thought to be helpful to us. At the time."

"And now?"

"Now may be another matter . . . or it may not."

"Speak your case," I said.

"We have no liking for you, Damastes á Cimabue. But we like your former leader less. The once-Emperor Tenedos was and is a very dangerous man. He must not be allowed to resume the throne."

"I know that . . . but what are your reasons?"

"He shook this world once, almost twice," the hooded figure said, a woman's voice, low, forceful. "He would have again, but you stopped him."

"You know a great deal," I said.

"We have powerful magicians of our own, and they've found out a lot about what really happened at Cambiaso," the woman said. "But that's in the past. Tenedos must not be allowed to take the throne again, for he'll raise great demons for his own ends, demons he may not be able to control, that might run rampant on the earth."

"Demons," I said wryly, "that will also wreak havoc with your cult."

"With everyone," Jakuns said firmly. "Do you imagine Tenedos will be content with just regaining Numantia?"

I knew that answer.

"Then he'll move against Maisir again," Jakuns went on, "and if he's successful, against other countries neither you nor I know of. He'll drive on, ever seeking more power, more to conquer, for his thirst will always be unquenchable.

"With this world in his hands, then what? Will he attack the demon worlds? The gods, if they exist? Or perhaps there are other worlds inhabited by men in this universe. If he can glimpse them with his sorcery, he'll never be content until he devises a means to reach them . . . and grasp them in his talons as well."

Jakuns's rhetoric left me unmoved. I knew all this, so he was like a priest, sermonizing to his chanters, who already accept his beliefs.

"He must be stopped," Jakuns said, a bit redundantly, "and we are not sure you have the power to bring him down, even though you are the most qualified. Even with your new allies in Nicias."

"Your spies are excellent," I said.

"They are," the woman agreed.

"We came tonight," Jakuns said, "not to harm you, but to offer you our assistance. All Tovieti will turn against Tenedos, if you agree to our conditions, from the smallest child watching his scouts through the forest undergrowth to the sutler who can offer his soldiers poisoned drinks to our mighty wizards. A thousand thousands shall be his enemy, without his ever knowing it, until it is far too late."

"Interesting," I said. Suddenly everyone wanted to join me.

"You said 'all Tovieti will turn against Tenedos,'" I went on. "I was told, some time ago, after Thak's . . . dissolution and the failure of your uprising, you'd abandoned your single-mindedness and worked in separate groups with a common goal.

"Has this changed? Have you once more found a demon to follow?"

"Nothing has changed," the woman said. "All is as you said. But the destruction of Tenedos will bring everything together."

"Ah," I said. "Now, what about these conditions?"

"First," Jakuns said, "as proof of your commitment, you must give us Kutulu. He has slain far too many Tovieti for us to allow his continued existence, and he must be removed. Second—"

I held up a hand.

"You may stop right there," I said. "I can answer without needing to hear your other provisions. Kutulu is not only one of the most important leaders in my army, but a friend as well.

"Normally I'd apologize for what I'm about to say, lady, but not now.

"Fuck you! Fuck all of you as traitorous scum." I fairly spat the last words.

"We should kill you now!" Jakuns snarled, and the man lifted his little crossbow.

My hand was in my shirt, blurred out, and Perak's dagger flashed in the lamplight, turning once and burying itself in the crossbowman's hand, pinning it to his chair's arm. I'd never been able to throw a knife before, in spite of the best efforts of snarling warrants, but boredom and countless hours practicing with Perak and other guards had taught me well.

The man shrieked, dropped his weapon and a thin stream of blood sprayed. My hand swooped, and I had my sword out and, a moment later, Yonge's silver-mounted dagger in my off hand.

"Yes," I mocked, feeling the hard rage of the past times of taking punishment with seldom a chance to strike back pound at me. "You can *try* to kill me."

Jakuns had a long dagger in hand, and I saw a sword flicker to my right. I was about to jump-lunge, impale Jakuns, and then deal with the others when the woman's voice snapped:

"Stop!"

The four became statues, and only the man with his bleeding hand continued moaning.

The woman stepped forward and knocked her hood back.

She was very young, no more than seventeen or eighteen, perhaps five and three-quarters feet tall, and simply beautiful. She had an intelligent face that reminded me a bit of a cat's, and I somehow noted that her eyes were jewel-green.

"No one will kill you," she said. Perhaps the Tovieti had no leaders, but I noted the four men instantly sheathed their weaponry.

"Do you remember me, Damastes á Cimabue?"

She was familiar, but no name, no circumstance came.

"I am Cymea Amboina," she said.

I'm afraid my control slipped. She came from deadly sorcerous blood, the daughter of the wizard Landgrave Amboina, who'd led the second rising in Polycittara and been killed by Sinait's magic; the sister of Jalon Amboina, an even more powerful magician a soldier's arrows had slain when I was trying to arrest him for being a leader of that conspiracy.

"My father died because of you," she said. "And you killed my brother. But we are in another time now. That is of the past."

I remembered Amiel, dying with a Tovieti arrow between her ribs, dying carrying my child. She read my face.

"In turn, we . . . or rather some men who thought they were Tovieti, although I won't disclaim them to an outsider . . . killed someone you loved. Does that make things even?"

"Does blood *ever* equalize anything?" I said, almost snarling.

She inclined her head, understanding.

"No," she said. "But the question now is whether we can combine against the most dangerous man who ever lived."

I forced my Cimabuan temper down and considered her words. But there was only one decision.

"No," I said. "For I can't have anyone serving me who serves another master, and I certainly cannot have anyone in my command who cannot be trusted.

"If Tenedos can't be brought down without you gods-damned, and I mean that quite literally, Tovieti . . . perhaps this world deserves him!"

She stared at me, then nodded jerkily.

"You're a fool, Damastes á Cimabue. But a noble fool."

She walked to where the man writhed, pulled Perak's knife from his hand, and cast it into a corner. Then she touched the wound twice, and the blood ceased to runnel, and the man stopped moaning. She, like the rest of her family, was a sorcerer.

"Do not pursue us," she said. "Or men will die. Your watchman can be found in the next room. We drugged the wine he had with his evening meal. Let him sleep until tomorrow, and he will wake unharmed."

She jerked her head, and the men obediently went to the door.

"A fool," she said, and this time her voice softened. "I hope you haven't doomed all Numantia."

She went out, and the door closed.

I should have cried the alarm, gone after them with my sword, but I didn't.

Cymea Amboina had escaped the dungeons of Polycittara during the rising and vanished. No wonder no one had been able to find her, not in the heart of the Tovieti. And now she was . . . was I didn't know what, since Jakuns had said the Tovieti still had no leaders.

But when she ordered, they obeyed.

I did not know what to think, other than a certainty I'd made the right decision in refusing them.

A week later, Kutulu's agents reported:

Laish Tenedos and his million were on the march through Nowra toward us.

TWELVE

THE DRIVEN WEDGE

It took half a time for Tenedos's army to reach Paestum, crossing Nowra, Chalt, and then Tagil, marching toward us as if we were a lodestone, although I found it wryly amusing that Tenedos diverted the march to avoid Cambiaso.

He was tracked first by Kutulu's spies, then Sinait's magic, and seemed to have no spells cast, attempting to deceive us as to his goal. He wanted us to know he was coming, and his reputation to bring terror as he closed.

Half a time before his arrival, the Peace Guardians arrived with Trerice at their head. Their force was divided into three wings, as the Imperial Army had been. The right wing was commanded by Drumceat, the center by their best general, Taitu, the left by Indore. Of course, they used the Maisirian ranks of *rast*, which I gritted my teeth and used in the service of temporary amity.

There was a scatter of civilian dignitaries with them, not as many as there should have been, but I supposed few wished to face the wrath of their former emperor. I was surprised to see Barthou, but wily Scopas must have convinced him one of the Councilors had to be with the army, or they'd lose heart.

As agreed, the Guardians formed a blocking line from Paestum north-northwest, linking with my soldiers holding a line running from Paestum due south. The village was just behind the center of our lines, since it would be foolish to give the enemy the cover of the town to fight from.

The Guardians were outraged by being handed shovels, being ordered to dig trenches. They weren't used to physical work, most having joined up to avoid their rightful callings as stone carriers and ditchdiggers.

I was slightly impressed with Trerice, who was far out of his depth commanding a force of such size but drove himself hard, in the saddle from dawn to dark, then held conferences with his aides until well after midnight. If his men had been adequately trained, he might have been accused of chivvying them into a frenzy, but these were Peace Guardians, not soldiers, and needed all the commanding they could take.

They tried to intimidate my men, boasting, bullying, calling the handful of taverns theirs. But just because my men weren't fully trained as warriors didn't mean some didn't know how to use a broken wine bottle as well as the best. I had my commanders name their finest goons for provosts, and set them to keeping the peace, turning a blind eye to the Guardian who got his ear thickened or arm broken in the process.

There were three burglaries and two rapes. The burglars I had brought to trial and, once guilt was proven, stripped of their uniforms and flogged through the camp.

The rapists were also court-martialed, but I gave them a harder doom than the whip. I had their regiments assembled around my high platform, plus a thousand witnesses

from my rebels. The platform was strengthened and modified for another purpose.

I'd said I appointed an official bastard, but this first time
I wanted to show I, too, could be merciless. The two con-
demned Guardians were a study in contrasts, one tall, lean;
the second squat, beetling as if he was related to the near-
men of the Gyantse jungled mountains.

"Look at them," I shouted, my voice once more ampli-
fied by magic. "These are men who swore to protect the
women of Numantia, first as Guardians, now as soldiers.

"Instead, they broke their oath.

"Now, they'll pay the price. And I'll not punish real
soldiers by making you listen to their last yammerings
when there's more important business at hand."

I nodded to their guards. Ropes were dropped from
new overhead beams, tightened around their necks. The
tall one gibbered in terror, the other man seemed barely to
know what was happening.

"Swing them off," I ordered, and soldiers put boots
into their backs and kicked them off the platform.

They dropped a few feet, the ropes came taut, and the
sound of their necks snapping was very loud. My stomach
lurched, but I paid it no mind.

"Take heed," I shouted, my voice harsh. "Anyone who
harms a man, a woman, a child like these swine . . . justice
will be real, will be quick, will be deadly.

"I want every man to tell his fellow what happened here
today and remember it well. That's all. Officers, take
charge of your formations and dismiss them."

Trerice was outraged, saying I'd implied his Peace
Guardians were no better than criminals. I told him I said
no such thing, and if he, or his men, had trouble looking at
themselves in a mirror, perhaps they'd better get to a priest

to be cleansed, although I didn't think there were more than a dozen with the army, and none at all with the Guardians.

"Soldier harder," I said, trying to keep malicious glee from my voice, "and your men won't have the time to hear imaginary incriminations."

Trerice gave me a black look, stalked out without saluting.

The next night Kutulu said there were rumblings in the Guardians' camps that their *jedaz* would make a far better leader of the armies, and "somebody should do something about that traitorous bastard from Cimabue, or else, when King Bairan comes back, we'll all pay for following him."

He said I'd have to start being more careful about my person. I grumbled, but knew he was right.

I'd considered making Lasleigh Baron Pilfern and his fifty men into a semblance of my Red Lancers. Certainly they were smartly turned out, and checking with Domina Thanet, I found Lasleigh and his men were doing well enough for Thanet to keep them together as a company.

But I needed cavalry more than bodyguards and so asked Kutulu for a handful of unobtrusive skulkers and swore if I became aware of their presence I'd send them back to window peeping.

Tenedos marched closer, and our training grew harder and harder.

One night, about halfway through the second watch, I'd just finished reassuring Barthou, who was getting very nervous, that he didn't need to return to Nicias to confer with Scopas, and, a bit amused, decided I'd give myself a treat, go to my quarters, and not think about this gods-damned army that was my life for at least six hours.

I'd barely kicked my boots off, poured a glass of a berry

juice, made a bit tart with lemon and chilled by ice from the distant mountains, when someone tapped at my door.

I swore if it was anything short of the return of Umar I'd have the tapper flayed alive and his skin used for a map case, went to the door, and growled.

"A man insists on seeing you," the timid voice of the sentry came.

"Tell him . . . never mind."

An officer who brags that his door is always open can't whine if his boast is believed.

However, remembering my callers of not long ago, I unsheathed Yonge's dagger and held it in my left hand as I opened the door.

Standing there was a monster of a man. I'm tall, half a head above six feet, but my eyes were at his chin. He was not only behemoth in height, but bulk as well, and his face could have given a raft of orphans nightmares. It had been hard and threatening from his youth, and was now twisted with two scars, one across his forehead that met another that twisted his lip and cheek into a terrible snarl of a grin. He was missing almost all of his right arm and wore hard-worn leather. A well-used sword hung from a baldric, and a knife was sheathed in one of his knee boots.

"Son of a bitch!" I swore.

"Good eve, sir," he said. "Can't salute like I'm s'posed to."

I had Svalbard in my arms, and almost broke into tears. I'd seen him last at Cambiaso, as we made that final desperate charge on foot through monsters to try to kill King Bairan. He'd killed a Maisirian who was about to finish me, then someone chopped away his arm, and he'd gone down, gouting blood. He'd served with me since the beginning with the seer king, always there, always quiet, always deadly.

He was stiff, uncomfortable, clearly not used to emotion, and I let him go. He turned his head aside and rubbed a sleeve across his face, no doubt to clear away some dust, which gave me the chance to do the same.

"I was somewhere else," he said. "A long ways away, doin' somethin' else, when I heard you were back. Thought you might need me."

"Hells, yes! Come in!"

I half-dragged him into my room, called for the guard.

"Chase down to the kitchens," I ordered, "and fetch brandy."

"Rather have a good honest beer," Svalbard said. "Unless that tipple's for you and you've changed."

"Not like that I haven't," I said. "Beer. Several tankards."

"But I'm supposed to be guarding you, sir," the sentry said, "and—"

"Do you think, with this juggernaut, I'm likely to come to harm? Get gone!"

I closed the door.

"You haven't changed much," he said. "Hair's gettin' gray, and thinnin' some. But you don't have too much of a paunch."

I grinned.

"Didn't anyone ever tell you not to talk to your commanding general like that?"

"Tried," he said. "But I never paid much attention to words that don't matter."

"How'd you get away at Cambiaso?" I asked, pointing him to a chair. He sat, uncomfortably.

"Nobody gave a shit about somebody bleeding to

death, without nothin' to loot on their body," he said. "I got somebody to tie off my arm, got to the river, found a witch, healed up."

"Then?"

"Since there wasn't any army left, other'n those mother-futtering Guardians, I found work with a sword. Doing this and that, here and there."

I didn't think I'd get any more of an explanation, and maybe I shouldn't want one.

"I need a bodyguard," I said, as abrupt as he.

"So I heard, coming through the camp. Happy to do the job, 'specially if it might involve dealing with Guardians."

"It might," I said. "But before you say you'll do the job, I owe you a story. Of what happened to Karjan."

He grunted, ill at ease, but I told him how I'd been be-spelled by the Maisirian *azaz*, and Bairan had insisted I kill my most faithful servant as a test of that spell. I couldn't look at him as I told the story but paced back and forth. The beer came halfway through the tale, but when I'd finished, his first tankard remained untouched.

He thought about things.

"Seems to me," he said, "we ought to hunt Bairan down and see how he likes having all his bones broken, one at a time and the jagged edges ground together for about a week."

I nodded, not capable of talking. Karjan's murder still tore at me.

"You told me the tale," he questioned, "to see if I'd change what I said?"

"I did."

"Don't see what that's got to do with anything today," Svalbard said. "Besides, I sort of guessed something like that'd happened, when you wouldn't talk about Karjan ever after you came back." He shrugged. "There's sufficient evil in the world to pull us all down, time to time."

He picked up the tankard, extended it in a toast.

"I'll only have the one," he said. "Then time to be getting about my duties, finding a place to sleep and all."

"There won't be any problem with that," I said. "Or not much, anyway. Remember, you were a legate? I'm promoting you to captain, making you my official aide, which means you'll have a servant of your own."

"For what?" the big man growled. "To take care of what I'm wearing, which is all I own? But I'll not refuse the promotion, not bein' stupid like Karjan was. I've noted the higher the rank, the better the strumpet." He drained the tankard, saluted, and went out.

Illogically, considering Svalbard, big and tough as he was, was still only one man, I was no longer worried about my safety.

I floated like an eagle, high above the rolling, dry land. Below was a road that wound west, and it swarmed with an army on the march, like ants, destroying everything in its path. In front of the columns were small farms, some with wheat ready to cut, some with vegetables watered from wells or tiny canals. Stone fences marked fields, some with cattle grazing, and each had its own house surrounded by a few trees carefully tended in this near-desert land, with outbuildings and gardens.

Then came the outriders, the scouts, afoot and on horseback. Behind them, the lead battalions under banners, the banners of the old Imperial Army, and behind *them* the wagons and shambles of the supply train and the camp followers.

In this army's wake was . . . nothing. Bare, burnt ground, crops snatched or trampled into the dust, houses burnt or torn apart for firewood, the scattered corpses of butchered animals and not infrequently their owners, the water despoiled, the trees cut down.

A wasteland, such as all armies, all wars bring.

I'd spent most of my life in this sort of desolation, not infrequently being its cause, but I'd never been lifted to this height, so I could see all its frightfulness.

But that wasn't why I'd insisted Sinait cast a Seeing Spell, in spite of her warnings. I wanted to see, to feel Tenedos's army, to size up my enemy, as a fistfighter goes to bouts sizing up a prospective opponent.

The cavalry screen didn't impress me—putting a man on horseback doesn't make him a real soldier, and these men looked more interested in galloping here and there and waving banners than looking for ambushes or roads that'd prove impassable.

The forward infantry units coming behind the cavalry moved well, however, their elements holding together, going smoothly up- and downhill, holding a steady march.

Farther back in the column, formations were more ragged, and they moved like inchworms, the men in front moving faster downhill, slower uphill, so the rear of the units were either milling about in the dust or running to keep up.

Not that my own army was perfect—but we would have the advantage, unless things went awry, of fighting from prepared positions when Tenedos arrived.

One thing I did admire—Tenedos had time and the magical resources to completely outfit his army. They wore black trousers and red caps or busbys, their jackets in various colors and combinations to mark the regiments.

I was still too far above the army to really "feel" what it was like and willed myself to move closer.

I heard Sinait murmur a warning.

At that instant, something struck "me" and sent "me" tumbling, as a falcon smashes a pigeon spinning toward the distant ground. I flailed like such a bird, seeing the sky above "me," but saw nothing that could have struck me, but I was falling, and I sensed that unseen force coming in once more, and then there was a clatter as the mercury-filled bowl clanged to the floor, and I was back in my headquarters at the inn.

I didn't feel any fear, but my hands were shaking as if I had the ague, my breath rasped hard as if I'd been running, and something was pressing down from the sky outside.

"That was foolish," Sinait said sharply.

I started to snap, remembered my instructions that she was to always speak her mind to me unless we were in the presence of underlings. Sinait poured water, and I drained it, momentarily wishing I had a taste for spirits and the momentary lift they gave.

"Tenedos sensed you as you were drawn toward his soldiers," she explained. "Or else he created a draw, such as a cataract can create a whirlpool, sucking any wizard into his grasp. An interesting counterspell, one that I think I can cast as well." She smiled tightly. "Perhaps not strong enough to trap Tenedos, but any of his Corps of Wizards who are curious might find their souls sucked out of their bodies."

I was curious, since that had almost happened to me.

"What happens to the soul then? The body?" I asked.

"The body becomes a husk," Sinait explained. "I've not had it happen in my presence, thank Irisu, but I'm told it can breathe on for a time. But without food or water, it perishes like an ignored plant.

"The soul? Who knows? I've heard a master magician can keep that soul and use it as his errand boy. I've also heard that the soul drifts for a time, then, when the body dies, Saionji takes it back to the Wheel as if the person had died normally.

"Still other tales say that is where ghosts come from. If you believe in ghosts, which I do."

"I've never been sure whether they exist, or whether they're demons," I said. "But that theory can't be right, for there's far more ghosts, or tales of ghosts, than of people being doomed by using Seeing Spells."

"Who's to say that's the only way a soul can be cast adrift?" Sinait said. "And you've done an excellent job of changing the subject while your body recovers."

I had. My hands were no longer trembling, and my breathing came normally.

But I still felt that presence outside the inn, hanging in the sky outside.

This was the second time he . . . or his magicians . . . had tried to kill me.

It was coming my turn, I hoped.

The enemy's arrival was presaged with spells—uneasiness, fear, a general malaise. But these were common to all military magic, hardly worthy of a master like Tenedos and quickly dispelled by Sinait and her wizards, and, for me, always that sense of being watched.

I wondered what master spell or spells would be in the offing, for Tenedos would hardly chance everything on mere arms.

Unlike Sinait, I was fairly sure he wouldn't call up that terrible demon that'd destroyed Chardin Sher. This war hadn't produced enough blood sacrifice for Tenedos to have the power yet, and I'd done a thorough enough job of destroying his wizardry at Cambiaso for the spell's ingredients to be easily reassembled.

Finally, and this was conclusive evidence, this first battle, even if Tenedos improbably managed a complete victory, wouldn't be the end of the war. There was still Nicias to take and hold, and the inevitable reaction from Maisir.

Still, Tenedos managed to surprise us badly. And I was one of the contributors to that surprise.

His army split outside Paestum, about a quarter of its forces marching on south to oppose my soldiers, the remainder lining up against Trerice's Guardians.

Tradition in a battle against a fortified enemy is for the attacking force to arrange its men in the chosen attack order, rest and feed them, then mount the assault, generally before or at dawn, to ensure enough daylight to finish the battle.

It was halfway through the afternoon before Tenedos's forces were on line, so I knew nothing would happen before the morrow.

I'd set my headquarters just outside Paestum and summoned my commanders for a final conference.

Tenedos attacked immediately.

Trerice was reporting on his dispositions when drums snarled and trumpets blared. An aide galloped up, reported that Tenedos's left flank was marching out, in an attempt to flank the Guardians.

Trerice vaulted into his saddle before I could give him orders. I swore, grabbed an officer, told him to ride after Trerice and tell him to be wary—the maneuver might be genuine but most likely was a feint. He should bend his right back—refusing the flank—as a precaution, but no more, and stand fast until the real attack was clearly begun.

I don't know what happened to that officer—he never returned, so I don't know if Trerice received my orders or if he got and chose to ignore them.

Tenedos cast his first spell then, and sounds shrilled from nowhere. They began intolerably high, so men shouted in pain, clasped their hands to their ears in the vain hope of shutting off the agony. Other sounds boomed beneath those first screeches, sounds so low we felt them in our bones, through the ground, instead of with our ears.

Horses were rearing, screaming.

I saw Sinait in the center of a dozen magicians, some with wands, some just waving their hands. I could do nothing here, so rode forward, fighting to keep my own mount.

As I cleared Paestum and reached a low hill, Tenedos's armies marched forward, and as they closed, arrows hissed toward us.

A second spell came then, and men screamed, clawed at themselves as if attacked by bees. I felt a sharp pain in my cheek, pulled a tiny dart from it, realized these darts were the attackers. I shouted for a galloper to go back to Sinait and report the spell, then the dart vanished in my hands, and I called the man back. Sinait had already broken that conjuration.

But the sounds kept slamming, high, low, and I had to fight dizziness. Two men ran toward me, eyes wide in terror, and I blocked them with my horse, sword in hand. They stopped short, realized the known was more dangerous than magic, and shambled back to their positions.

That took my eyes off the developing battle for an instant. When I turned back, I cursed, seeing Trerice's line sweep out from its left, toward the feint, against my orders. He left a hole between my men and the Peace Guardians, and that was just what Tenedos had wanted.

Tenedos sent the center of his line into that gap. I snapped orders, to Trerice, to the officer commanding my right flank, to Rast Indore, to close the hole. I ordered reinforcements over from my left to bolster the center.

Then there was nothing to do but wait. I dearly wanted to grab a lance and charge into the middle of the fighting but couldn't allow myself the luxury.

Time crawled as Tenedos's elements reached our lines and the free-for-all began, a swirling madness. Units were sucked into the maelstrom, and other formations came after them.

I sent a galloper for Sinait and her magicians, and they were on their way.

Far across the dusty melee of the center, I saw Trerice's lines, pulling back, *away* from the battle to form a C-shaped formation, keeping their own flanks safe, but leaving the gap open.

Tenedos sent his second line in to exploit the advantage, and I hit his flanks hard. But his commanders refused the bait, pushing forward.

I ordered Sinait to come up with a spell, any sort of spell, and her teams tried, casting incantations of terror, dust storms, stinging insects.

But Tenedos and his Corps of Wizards shattered most of those aborning, and his men scented victory.

I came back to myself, realizing the shadows were long and the sun had dropped below the horizon, and my army and that of the Guardians had been split apart.

I galloped back to my headquarters, ordered my commanders to me. I sent the cavalry to fill the gap in the lines, ordering them to light torches for the men still on the battlefield to fall back on.

Svalbard brought me a clay pot, and I saw, in the dimness,

water beading. I realized my voice was no more than a croak, and I hadn't drunk anything for hours. I drained the pot, told him to bring more, collected my thoughts as my officers rode in.

I had Sinait cast a Spell of Silence around the haggard men to make sure Gojjam or his wizards weren't eavesdropping, and, remembering Sinait's lip reader, held a hand in front of my mouth when I spoke, explaining the reason I looked like a country gossip.

There were three choices: to hold our positions, expecting an attack by Tenedos at daybreak; to prepare an attack at dawn to link up with the Peace Guardians; or to fall back toward the Latane River, two days' march distant.

"I came to fight," Domina Thanet said. "Not to defend. I think we should try to get through to those gods-damned Guardians, worthless though they are, for we're outnumbered, and they've got to realize the emperor, sorry, ex-emperor, will want their hides worse than ours."

Svalbard rumbled wordless assent.

"I agree," another officer said. "In part. But not with pulling the Guardians' butt out of the blaze. Fiddle 'em, as they say. Let's hold here, and let Tenedos come to us."

"No," a third said. "We need the Guardians, even for nothing else but to take an arrow intended for a better man."

I looked around, counting heads as the argument continued. I'd guess it was about half for one side, half for the other. I was pleased that no one suggested retreat.

"Very well, then," I said. "We'll attack, for I can't stand sitting and waiting either." I gave orders to move troops from my left flank across the army to my right flank, risky but necessary; and to prepare for an attack at dawn to link with the Guardians. The problem was, Tenedos would be a complete fool not to sense the obvious.

I asked Sinait if she could prepare an illusion that my center was in chaos, with troops moving back and forth, appearing about to fall apart. She shook her head—she hadn't the skill. I didn't think she or anyone other than possibly Tenedos or the Maisirian War Magicians would have been able to create an impenetrable fantasy of that size and decided to attempt the deception naturally. I sent more aides, suddenly realizing I'd almost stripped my headquarters bare of aides, to the commanders of the center, ordering their men to light torches, and move around erratically. I had no real hope they'd understand what I was trying, but anything was better than just waiting.

As the last rider galloped away, a grim-faced Kutulu slipped into the tent. My hand was on my sword when I saw him, for he was dressed in an imperial uniform.

"I've been through Tenedos's lines into the Guardians' camp," he said, without preamble. "Things are in worse shape than I'd imagined."

"They generally are," I said. I began to pour him a glass of wine, but he shook his head and filled a goblet from my water pitcher.

"Indore was killed in the attack," he said. "Trerice has taken over his wing as well as overall command of the army."

"What are his plans?"

"I don't think, at least from what I saw, that he has any," Kutulu said. "Probably form a line where he is now, and pray. They're swarming about full of panic and damned little sense."

"I know you're not a tactician," I said, "though I suspect you're better than most of the officers I have. Do you think he can hold long enough for me to break through and relieve him?"

Kutulu scratched a stubbly chin. "Maybe. But not if it takes too long. The Guardians were all a-mumble about how can anyone fight against magic, particularly the emperor's, and I don't think—"

A wind roared outside, and the tent swayed. I knew it for magic and we ran out.

Smoke and fire flared from the imperial lines, and then an enormous man grew from nothing. It was Tenedos, wearing battle armor, carrying a wand in one hand.

"Soldiers of Numantia," his voice boomed. "We have met in battle this day, and I have taken the field. You fought bravely, but you must not fight any longer.

"I summon you, as my lawful subjects, to surrender. You must not fight on, or I shall be forced to send the most awful demons to rend you.

"Throw down your weapons. If anyone, enlisted or officer, tries to stop you, strike them down. Then come across the lines to me. I promise, as your emperor, there shall be no punishment, not for rebels, not for Peace Guardians.

"Surrender now, and find an honorable place in my army. There has been enough damage done, and there is a great battle coming, when I shall need every man, when we must strike against those traitors in Nicias who call themselves Councilors and daily bow to the Maisirians.

"Come, my people. Come back to your emperor. I summon you to fulfill your duty as brave Numantians!

"Come now, or face the most terrible punishment I can devise!"

He held out his wand, and I heard, along the lines, the moan of despair.

Then the illusion blurred for just an instant, reformed, and Tenedos folded his arms. He blurred a second time, then spoke once more, and if the cadences of his speech were different than they should have been, no one except myself and possibly Kutulu noticed.

"Come now," he said once more. "For you know what I have to offer. Death. A miserable death for all of you, just as I destroyed your brothers and fathers in Maisir. Join my army, so that I may utterly ruin Numantia and bring it down in flames, despair and—"

Very suddenly, the figure vanished.

"Irisu dancing on his hat," I swore. "I didn't know Sinait could do something like that."

Kutulu shook his head without answering.

"Turn the provosts out," I ordered. "Get them down to the lines, and turn back anyone trying to surrender. Be merciless . . . we can't afford to lose any more men."

He saluted, disappeared.

"Come on, Svalbard," I ordered, going back into my tent. "We're for the right flank and see how big a mess we've got to deal with."

Sinait came in, slumped down in a chair, breathing as though she'd run for miles. She looked up.

"Well?" she asked.

"Gods-damned awesome," I said.

"I surprised me, too," she said, with a bit of a smile. "But do you think it'll work?"

"It can't hurt. But there is something else you can do . . . put spells out against fear, concern, and cast anything you can that'll calm the troops.

"Tenedos has the advantage, and I've got to try to turn it back before dawn."

*　*　*

The rest of the night was endless, all screaming and scrambling. By false dawn, I'd done all I could and had two waves ready to attack, and I'd stripped the lines for reinforcements. I don't know how many men obeyed Tenedos's orders, perhaps 10,000, perhaps 50,000. In the desperation, no one was holding roll call.

Tenedos struck first, driving his soldiers as a maul drives a wedge, first widening the line between the Peace Guardians and my rebels, then mounting a small attack against the Guardians, enough to push them back to the east and north, farther away from us, and hitting us with his main force.

We tried to hold, to counterattack, but no use, and were slowly, inexorably driven back. There were too many experienced soldiers with Tenedos, no matter if their march to battle hadn't been perfect, and my men, willing to fight and die though they were, simply weren't good enough to stand against the emperor.

We fell back for a day, formed up, and they hit us again. We didn't break—quite—but once more we retreated.

Scouts reported—which I knew well—the Latane River was less than a day's march distant.

If we couldn't drive Tenedos back, it appeared the rebellion was doomed.

THIRTEEN

TRAPPED

I decided on a stratagem—I would feint with my left flank, hit hard with the right, and knock Tenedos's army back enough to let us slip away to the north, toward Nicias, and later we could reunite with the Guardians and go on the offensive.

But it didn't work.

All went well until the day before the attack. I'd put one of the best of my new dominas, a former regimental guide with the Khurram Light Infantry named Chuvash, in charge of the right wing. I was with him, making sure there'd be no errors but mine, and sent a galloper with our exact attack time to the commander of the left, an adequate ex-captain named Lecq. The man disappeared, just as my messenger to Trerice had. Unfortunately, I didn't find this out until later and so proceeded as if everything was in order.

I'd asked Sinait and her magicians to raise a summer storm to mask our movements. The storm began on schedule, three hours before dawn, with fierce rattlings of thunder, wind whippings, but not much rain to keep from muddying the tracks we needed.

But the storm kept building, getting stronger, and torrents of rain drenched us. I swore, thinking Sinait had let her spell get out of control, and then my skirmishers reported Tenedos's army was attacking!

He'd somehow learned of our plans and moved first. My front ranks, still going into line formations, were slammed back. I sent orders to Lecq to pull back, refusing battle, toward the Latane, and concentrated on this catastrophe on the right.

But there was no salvation, and gray dawn came, wind still wailing and rain lashing, as if this were the beginnings of the Time of Storms, still fourteen or so days away. Tenedos kept hitting us in a series of jabbing fast strikes and withdrawals before I could get my stumbling, half-trained men to respond.

I sent a galloper for Domina Sendraka, another to the nearest regiment for two companies of infantry.

He arrived within the hour.

"You're going to think," I said, "you're under the orders of the emperor again. I want you to take as many of your skirmishers as you can summon, and put a screen between our forces and Tenedos's."

Sendraka didn't answer but waited.

"You'll be reinforced with two companies of infantry, unknown quantities to me. You're to hold Tenedos as long as you can. Notice I didn't say to the last man. An hour would be good, two hours would be better.

"Now this is my absolute order. You are not to get yourself killed, nor do I want a decimation of your forces."

"That's a difference from the emperor, a bit of one, anyway," Sendraka said.

"This frigging war's just begun," I said. "And I'm going to need you. So keep them off guard, then fall back."

"On what?"

"On the Latane," I said grimly.

"Shit," Sendraka said. A wide river at our back, a stronger, so far unbeatable force attacking—that would be our last stand.

I waited until Tenedos pulled his men back from their latest jab, then ordered withdrawal. I had my officers sweeping the line, trying to keep the situation from becoming a rout. Here and there, there were breaks, but no unit larger than a couple of squads, and the officers were able to stop them. Even those men didn't drop their arms and blindly panic but fell back doggedly, slowly.

Sendraka gave me an hour . . . then two . . . then a third, and we were disengaged and retreating toward the Latane. I rode back with Svalbard and a handful of cavalrymen to the battlefield, and saw, from the crest of a hill, Tenedos's army, pulling back to their previous positions and seemingly preparing camp.

There were knots of my men here and there, still holding defensive positions—a copse, a hilltop, the ruined huts of a crossroads, none in contact. We rode forward, puzzled.

I found Sendraka, thankfully still alive, in a farmer's barn. He was exhausted, filthy, but unwounded.

"What happened?"

"Damned if I know," he said. "Tenedos sent flankers around us, then about two regiments of infantry down our throats, and I thought it was time to follow your main orders and get out."

"But they stopped halfway to us, and a whole slew of men on horseback rode forward, under banners. I think . . . I'm not sure, for it was some distance . . . Tenedos was among them.

"They talked, then the officers shouted orders, and gods

damn me if they didn't turn around and go back the way they came.

"I don't understand it at all," he said, a bit plaintively, as if disappointed he hadn't been slaughtered.

"Nor I," I said. "But I've learned never to guess a magician. Get your men moving. Back to the Latane."

That night passed, and the next day, with no contact at all. It was as if we'd become invisible to Tenedos.

I sent Sendraka's skirmishers back out, and Kutulu's spies went with them, then through the enemy positions, and back with an answer, of sorts, by nightfall.

Tenedos's position was lightly held. He'd sent his main forces after the Peace Guardians and Nicias.

This was insane. No general splits his forces or attacks a second objective until the first falls.

But we were still doomed.

He would, the proclamation shouted through his camps the next day, destroy the traitorous Damastes and his rebels without losing a single one of his own.

Within a few days we would be wiped out to the last man by magic, and all Numantia would cower and wonder at the power of Laish Tenedos, once- and soon-to-be-again emperor.

I set my headquarters in a farmhouse, and my own quarters behind it, in a half-ruined byre that hadn't been abandoned by the oxen that long—or else I was even further away from my last bath than I thought. I hung canvas along one side and set hay bales for a chair and a table. I spread maps, trying to decide what I could do besides wait for Tenedos's killing stroke, like the meek beasts did who'd lived here before.

I wasn't willing to believe Tenedos's magic could unutterably destroy us, although I'd seen more than enough of its might over the years, so I wasn't willing to abandon our positions and flee like so many refugees south or north along the river, although I'd made what preparations I could for a partial evacuation.

But I must accept that he could do massive damage with his wizardry, then send in warriors to mop up with cold steel.

No solution came, let alone a good one, and so, long after midnight, after I'd ordered Svalbard to his blankets, I decided to get a breath of air, a drink of water from the bag that hung outside the shed.

I ducked under the musty canvas, had time for a long breath of air that smelt strongly of the nearby river, a smell I should have welcomed, but now would have gladly exchanged for the harshness of the desert and its winds, if the change would give me room to maneuver.

It was very still and very dark. Svalbard's great frame was stretched beside the guttering fire, and two other soldiers slept in their cloaks nearby. But someone besides myself was still awake. A cloaked figure sat on a log near Svalbard.

"Good morrow," I said.

"Most unlikely, Cimabuan," the voice grated. "You would have been more truthful if you'd muttered something about what a shitass day it's promising to be."

It was Yonge.

"What the hells are you doing here?" I managed, trying to keep surprise out of my voice, knowing the bastard would have waited where he was for three days just to startle me as he had.

"Perhaps," he said, "I'm thirsty for more Numantian

wine. Or your women. Or perhaps I wish to study honor once again."

"My apologies," I said. "King Yonge, you are always welcome."

"King it is no more," he said. "Shall we see what you've got in that cowshed for me to drink?"

"Nothing," I said. "But that'll soon be changed."

I kicked Svalbard, and he jerked to a sitting position, sword half-drawn.

"Be still, you boob," I said. "Look at what managed to slip past you. If it'd been an assassin, you'd be looking for a new master."

Svalbard peered at Yonge, then grunted and got up.

"I'll not apologize for letting *him* come up on me," he said. "Men are one thing, demons from the Hills another."

"A demon, yet," Yonge said. "Perhaps a promotion from what you usually thought of me?"

"Svalbard," I ordered, "stop jesting with this barbarian and chase down a bottle of our best, whatever it'll be. And you, Yonge, inside with you."

He followed me into the shed, and I found two other lamps and lit them.

"No one will be able to say I came to take advantage of your successes," Yonge said, slumping down into my chair.

"Why the hells aren't you in Kait, being king like you're supposed to?" I said. "And by the way, thanks for taking care of Achim Fergana for me . . . for Numantia."

"No debt incurred," Yonge said, waving his hand. "He was also my enemy. And we can stop this *king* nonsense. I'm no longer sitting the throne. Being royalty was ceasing to amuse me, and I had help in making my decision to abdicate."

"You were overthrown by someone even more devious than you?"

"Not more devious, but Saionji and Irisu fight with the big regiments. I wasn't overthrown at all, but chased out of Kait."

"By who?"

"King Bairan," Yonge said grimly. "He took Sayana and put it to the torch three weeks ago."

I felt a harsh glee, remembering how the Men of the Hills had ravaged us when we fled the city. It may have been the capital of Yonge's country, but I'd hardly mourn it being torn brick from brick, and the bricks torn apart for straw. I was trying to find a somewhat more polite response, when Svalbard came in, carrying two bottles in his big paw.

"Here," he said. "If you've come from the Hills, likely you'll be needing both."

Yonge took one, shook his head.

"Only this," he said, sounding regretful. "For we'll be fighting at dawn, and I'll need at least a few of my wits."

Svalbard snorted, went out. Yonge busied himself with uncorking the brandy, and pouring a full glass. He drank about half straight off, then sat once more.

"I know you'll not sorrow over Sayana being razed," he said. "But here's something to bring real tears. King Bairan entered Kait two months ago and has been systematically destroying every city and village in my country as he moves north like a pest of locusts. My *jasks* determined with their spells that Bairan's decided Kait shall nevermore raid across his borders.

"The slack-wit! All that'll happen is we retreat into the mountains where he dare not go, wait until he leaves, then rebuild. This has happened before in the Hills, and will happen again, as long as men know how to forge steel and lust after the herd of fat cattle across a border . . . or the herder's wife.

"We'll rebuild using our loot from his . . . and your . . . kingdoms. But not for a while."

"Go back to why I'm going to be mourning," I said.

"Bairan used this expedition as a smoke screen to close on Numantia," Yonge said impatiently. "Something even a balding ape from the jungles should have figured out. He's about finished resting his army and bringing it back to full strength after taking Sayana and will march for the Sulem Pass and Urey within the week!"

I wondered for an instant why Sinait or Kutulu hadn't discovered this, then chided myself. All our resources had been necessarily aimed in one direction, at Tenedos, with little attention paid elsewhere.

"He'll cross into Urey," Yonge went on, "consolidate carefully, then send his army on north, right for you and that shitgob Tenedos.

"If you and those drooling idiots called Peace Guardians . . . yes, don't look surprised, I may be a barbarian from the Hills but I, at least, keep my ears open, so I know what you've been up to. If you and those walking assholes couldn't pull out that burr who once called himself an emperor . . . well, then, Maisir will do it for you.

"Bairan'll no doubt set a price for his services higher than he did the last time he took a holiday in Numantia.

"Not that it'll matter to you, Cimabuan, for I'm sure Tenedos will destroy you within a day or two, long before Maisir begins moving."

I told him Tenedos had promised to destroy us by magic alone, and Yonge's eyes widened.

"That I hadn't heard," he said softly. "Perhaps, then, there is a chance."

I raised an eyebrow. Against the most powerful magician history had ever known?

"The gods, such as they are, don't like someone who tries to set himself on their level," Yonge said. "This emperor has not only forgotten honor, but modesty and common sense as well. Just because he could bring up a monster to take out one princeling and his flunkies doesn't mean he has the powers to destroy an entire army.

"There may be a slight chance we won't die on the morrow."

"Not much of one."

"No," Yonge agreed, pouring more brandy. "Not much of one. I have a question. When you agreed to march at the head of these raggedy-ass farmers, did you have the sense to create something like my skirmishers to keep the clotpoles from stumbling into perpetual ambush?"

"I did."

"What bumblefoot did you put in charge of it? Someone I know?"

"One of your captains. Sendraka. I made him a domina."

"Hmmph. Not that bad a man . . . for someone from the flatlands. I shall join him. What would be your orders?"

"First, a question. What really brought you here? As you said, it certainly couldn't have been for the accolades."

Yonge swirled the last of the brandy in his glass.

"Perhaps I was bored in Kait. I'd thought about giving up the throne for half a year now and going back to raiding. It's very dull and stupid when everyone bows to you, and all you have to worry about is who's conspiring against you, and all you have to wait for is the knife in the back from the man who wants to succeed you. Everything else is lies, nonsense, and gilt.

"Why did I leave my nice safe refuge, not two hours distant from the ruins of Sayana, cut around those stupid Maisirians, who are even worse at keeping guard than you Numantians, and come overland to this swamp?"

"A better question: Why not?"

He drank off the brandy. "Enough sentimentality. What are your orders?"

"My plan is to hope we can withstand whatever sorcery he brings. Then I'll use what's left of my best to hold the line while the rest of the army tries to get across the Latane," I said. "I've sent men north and south for every boat they can find. I've got enough now, back at the river, for perhaps a tenth of my army in a single passage.

"We need time. I'd like you to take a hundred . . . less if you think five score's unwieldy . . . of the skirmishers, slip through the lines, and try to close on the emperor's camp. I'll send a wizard with you. When he senses Tenedos has begun his spell, hit their camp.

"Try to be enough of a nuisance to shake them a little. Maybe my magicians can seize that moment and break Tenedos's spell, and it'll be more days before he can re-send it. During that time, most of my men can shuttle across the Latane, and I can hold Tenedos here long enough for them to make good an escape into Kallio to reform."

"Attack their camp with a hundred men?" Yonge said. "That sounds like an excellent way to get killed."

"It is," I said. "But why would a Man of the Hills be interested in an easy task?"

"I like this but little," Yonge grumbled. "But I had to come see what you were about. Especially since you yourself have evidently decided to stay on this side of the river for a noble last stand. Perhaps I'll live to join and fight in it, which might be amusing, more likely not. Very well, Cimabuan. Give me instructions on where I can find Sendraka and the rest of my thieves, and I'll see what can be done. When do you wish us to move?"

"As soon as you're ready," I said.

Yonge gazed at me long, shook his head, and went out, into the ending night. He didn't need to say anything. He and I both knew there was no chance I'd ever see him again, at least not in this life.

The morning was hot, still, and humid, as if a great storm was in the offing. A storm *was* coming, but not one brought by Elyot or Jacini. Tenedos's spell was building.

Sometime around noon, a skirmisher came with Yonge's compliments—which I doubted had been actually voiced—and told me the Kaitian and fifty other men, together with Sendraka, had gone through the forward positions. He said Yonge had told him to tell me he didn't need any more stumblebums to give everything away.

I had Sinait and her magicians assembled, ready to cast a counterspell.

Chuvash, in spite of his growls that he wanted to fight, not run, had been put in charge of the evacuation and ordered to be on the last boat to put out. If he escaped alive, there would be at least one good officer on the far side of the Latane to rally around.

If I'd had twenty or thirty thousand cavalry, reliable cavalry, I would have chanced all on a pathetic hope and led a flanking attack on Tenedos's lines myself and let his magical wards be damned. But I didn't. Nor could I have left the army, for there was no one at all who could command this disaster-in-the-making.

What I expected was Tenedos would cast his spell, Sinait and her underlings would unsuccessfully try to break it, but at least slow it down; Yonge, whom I'd no sooner welcomed than sent to die would do just that, but confuse Tenedos a little and further slow him; Chuvash's boats would shuttle back and forth as quickly as they could; Tenedos would either come back with greater magic or attack with conventional arms, and my rear guard and I would go down, possibly giving a quarter, maybe a bit more, of my rebels time to flee across the Latane and go to ground in Kallio or wherever.

Sooner or later a more capable leader than I would arise, in a year or a century, from the people or even from the Tovieti, and try to free Numantia from whoever's lash it would be under.

But for me, there would be no capture, no surrender. I just regretted not being able to personally send Tenedos, and his unutterable evil, to Saionji and the Wheel.

But men are the dice the gods gamble with, no more.

At midday, the sun was blistering hot, and I felt the first crawlings up my spine and sensed the spell that would destroy us was now cast.

I was in the forward positions, Tenedos's front about five miles distant. A heat haze shimmered over the dry grass and desiccated small groves, grew heavier, and I could feel the heat as it came in waves. I had a few seconds to realize this was the spell; then the grasslands burst into flame, not here and there as a wildfire does in the Time of Heat, but all at once. There was no wind, but the flames swept toward us.

An aide came from Sinait and said she was trying to fight the spell, but without success.

My line was wavering, and I had no choice but order them to fall back toward the river. The fire roared closer, then flickered, like a taper being blown on, almost going out, and I guessed that was Yonge's futile but noble death. The flames roared higher, and I mourned the passing of yet another friend but was too busy, riding back and forth across the battleground-that-wasn't, and somehow my men didn't break but retreated like seasoned campaigners, covering for each other as they went.

From a hilltop, I saw Tenedos's army start across the blackened ground behind the fire that was his shock troops.

We couldn't find a place to fight from, for who could stand against fire? We moved back again, and again, and then I was on the final hillcrest, the long slope before me that ran down through trees to the Latane, about two-thirds of a league across at this point. There were boats on the narrow beaches and the river, shuttling men to the far shore.

"We'll hold here," I shouted, and there were men rallying around. One was the company of Lasleigh, Baron Pilfern, still forty strong. Pilfern rode back and forth in front of them, calling commands, and I noted his voice was calm, sure, and his men were as ready to die here, in this hells-owned spot governed by dark magic, as anyone.

There were other strong points, one Thanet's cavalry, another under Lecq's banner, others that were merely knots of men who would run no farther and found ground worthy of their deaths.

Kutulu was beside my horse. He wore a mailed coat a bit too large and a conical steel helmet that slipped from time to time. But he had a long, curving dagger in each gloved hand, and the gloves, I knew, were weighted with lead.

"I never thought I'd die as a soldier," he shouted, and his voice was light, merry, as if he was making a joke.

I looked down the line of soldiers. This was as good a place to die as any other.

I must've spoken aloud, because Svalbard, sitting on his horse just behind me, growled, "The only good death is someone else's." His sword was ready.

The fire grew closer, and my eyebrows were hard, dry, and my nose full of the stink of burning.

Then came screams—from behind us!

I whirled and saw Tenedos's real spell.

Thak, the Tovieti demon, had once hidden in the Latane River before he attacked Tenedos and me, and perhaps the seer remembered, for the Latane was coming alive, brown water rising here, there, in swirls and eddies. The swirls firmed, grew taller, took shape, grew fangs and claws, ever-changing in their horror, and came across the water toward my boats.

Soldiers screamed, threw spears, shot arrows, without effect. Panicked, some dove overboard, flailing at the current that swept them into the monsters' clutches.

I could dimly hear the screams of terror as boats were sent spinning, overturned, men torn by these demons' talons, and the swift-flowing water was reddened by blood. The nightmares swept through the boats, tearing them apart, seizing the men in their jaws, and then they turned, moving slowly as if wading, not part of the Latane itself, coming toward the knotted, trapped army along the sandbars and beaches.

The fire before me roared higher, and I knew Tenedos's

magic was feeding off these deaths, as it had always fed on blood.

The demons were closer, if demons they were, and not simply created by magic from the water itself, as lesser magicians can create and animate tiny figurines from the living dirt.

Die well, my mind mocked, but how can you die well if your only enemy is water and fire?

I thought frantically of trying to charge through the fire, into the heart of the real enemy, but my men would see that as flight. There was nothing to do but accept death, embrace it quickly for an easy return to the Wheel, yet I couldn't go without doing anything.

Blind in rage, I screamed at the heavens, and I swear my scream was answered by a rumbling, and for an instant I thought the third god, Jacini of the Earth, had been suborned and was allowing Tenedos to cast a final spell and engulf us in an earthquake.

But the rumbling came from above, and from nowhere clouds whipped across the sky, driven by tempest winds far greater than anything I'd seen, yet there was nothing but the roar of the fire and terror as the water monsters ravened toward the shore.

The wind swept down on us, straight down, but its passage had barely touched us when it changed direction, and blew hard, down the bluff to the river, and as it reached the water it grew stronger, a full gale, sending the water demons wavering, spray whipping from their extremities as I'd seen storm surf whip against the rocks of my island prison.

The wind screamed louder, and the clouds opened, and sheets of rain, torrential, poured down, and the fire steamed, smoked, bellowing its own pain.

Sinait's counterspell was great, and I marveled at the power I'd not known she had. The rain grew greater, and I heard a horrible scream, echoing across the world, and saw the river monstrosities swirl, like so many inverted whirlpools, and vanish, and as they did, the fire behind me snapped out, like a candle pinched at bedtime.

The rain poured down over the blackened landscape, and I prepared for a counterattack through the ashes against Tenedos's line. But there was no need. The rain broke for an instant, and I saw, distantly, Tenedos's soldiery stumbling back, shambling as if they'd been shattered by cavalry.

I didn't know what was going on, was completely lost. I looked back at the river and saw the greatest marvel of all.

Through the drifting clouds of wind-driven rain I saw boats coming upriver. I don't know how many there were, many hundreds, thousands, of every sort, from tiny fishing punts to river trader's launches to yachts to dinghies rowed by boys and girls, oceangoing pinnaces and even one of the great *Tauler*-type river ferries, all heading for the blood-stained sands my army was stranded on.

Numantia had come to rescue us.

Or that was what I thought.

The first order of business was to get out of immediate danger.

I sent all my gallopers, including Svalbard and Kutulu the horse hater on a riderless mount grazing nearby, to sweep the line, telling my soldiers that we'd live the day, and for them to withdraw to the river in good order, taking their weapons and wounded.

I sat on the hilltop, alone, and prayed to Irisu, Vachan, Tanis, and the war god Isa, giving thanks.

A scattering of men, perhaps forty, stumbled out of the fire-torn mistlands in front of me, and I put my hand on my sword, thinking they were some of Tenedos's, separated in the tumult, either trying to surrender or lost.

Then I recognized them by their tattered brown shirts. Skirmishers. Better, I saw at their head Yonge, and he was half-carrying Sendraka.

I rode to meet them, dismounted, and helped lift Sendraka, who'd been clubbed down from behind and was still dazed, into my saddle, and we started toward the river.

"So you decided to live," I said to Yonge.

"I did. It's a bad day for dying, at least for me," he said. "And did I not do well with my impossible task?"

"You did," I said. "The spell lifted for a few seconds when you hit them, long enough for Sinait's counterspell to work."

"You idiot," he said. "You pretend to command men, and you think that is what happened?"

"I *don't* know, gods dammit," I said, perhaps a little angry. "I've been sitting on this fucking hill all day being fucking noble, not out having fun with people like you."

"Fun it was," and Yonge became serious. "I just wish I was a better bowman."

"You did well enough," a half-conscious Sendraka muttered. "I just hope that was Tenedos's spell arm you hit. Keep the son of a bitch's magic bottled up for a while."

"Wait a minute," I said. "You *shot* Tenedos?"

"With my little bow and arrow," Yonge said, "like a boy potting a sparrow. Bastard was waving his arms about with all these drones in robes behind him, and this was after we'd decided any gods-damned fool can die charging an army.

"So we crept through the rear of the Emperor of Pigs' forces, through his supply tents, through his doxie runs. You told us to make a difference, and we took your orders to heart.

"The fire was raging and something else was happening, for Tenedos kept pouring water or some kind of clear shit from bowl to bowl, and there were fumes coiling up and around, which is what spoiled my aim, but at least I caught him fair in the upper arm, and heard him screech like a goosed beldame and . . . and don't you have a drink, Cimabuan, for the man who almost slew an emperor?"

That was the first surprise.

The second was at the docks, a quarter-hour later. Sinait was waiting. I began to thank her for smashing Tenedos's magic, but she stopped me.

"No, Damastes," she said. "Tenedos swept our feeble spells aside as if they'd been mumbled by a village witch. We were truly beaten, but then something came from nowhere, those truly great incantations of wind and water. I felt a struggle between them and Tenedos, and then his spells snapped, broken as if they'd never been cast."

That would have been when Yonge wounded Tenedos.

So where *had* our savior come from?

There could be only one answer.

The boats hadn't landed yet but held a dozen yards off-shore. Other craft were rescuing swimmers and recovering overturned boats.

The big ferry was close inshore, and as I walked to the water, it pulled closer, and its gangplank slid out and dropped down into the shallows.

A dozen men and women, a few ceremonially robed, some dressed as soldiers, others as commonfolk, came down it.

All wore the yellow silk strangling cord of the Tovieti draped loosely around their necks.

At their head was Cymea Amboina.

"I greet you, Damastes á Cimabue," her voice rang across the water, over the moans of the wounded. "And now do you believe we Tovieti fight for you and for Numantia?

"It was our spell that took the dog-emperor by surprise," she went on as she came closer, lowering her voice. "And that startlement was more than half the reason for its success.

"It was cast with the will of all the brothers and sisters we could reach, asking them to grant us their will, as a priest calls for the faithful to send up prayers to whatever god he serves, and its power took him by surprise.

"I doubt if he'd be surprised that way a second time," she said, then suddenly grinned. "And didn't I sound just then like a bearded old poop who ought to have been hammering the ground with a staff or something? Sorry, but people expect certain things from wizards."

I smiled back; then, looking about at the carnage, my smile faded.

"We thank you, Cymea, and the rest of your people, for the spell. But what about those boats?"

"An underground order needs to know many ways of getting from somewhere to somewhere else, preferably quickly," she explained. "We knew you were trapped here in Amur more than a week ago, and had our faithful beg, hire, or order any boat they could, from Nicias to the Delta, to come south."

"Your arrival was in the best traditions of the romances," Sinait said.

Cymea looked at her coolly, trying to decide if the seer was being hostile, realized she wasn't, and laughed.

"I wish I could say it was deliberate, but there was thick fog on the river for two days, which the captain of this ship said is natural for this changing of the season."

"Talk later," I said. "Let's get the army across before Tenedos comes up with more mischief."

"Across the river?" Kutulu asked. "And then what?"

"Then we plan for the next attack. This battle is lost," I said. "But the war has just begun."

FOURTEEN

REGROUPING

We fell back into Kallio, away from the river and Tenedos's magic. He made no attempt to follow, although Sinait said that he cast frequent Seeing Spells to watch us and, with a note of pride, that she and her magicians were becoming increasingly adept at blunting his efforts.

Not that the situation was improving—agents came downriver to confirm Yonge's information. King Bairan was moving north, through Sulem Pass. The Men of the Hills watched sullenly from their peaks but did little to hold him back.

He crossed the border into Numantia, brushed aside the few border guards who tried to stand against him, and seized Renan, Urey's once-beautiful capital.

But he came no farther. The Time of Rains was approaching, and no sensible general would campaign during these monsoons or the Time of Storms to follow.

From them, at least, we'd likely be safe until spring and the Time of Births. But neither Kutulu nor Sinait took the Maisirians for granted, and I received constant updates from the south, as they thoroughly looted Urey.

Tenedos moved north, toward Nicias, harrying Trerice and the Council's army. I kept cavalry vedettes and agents on the far side of the Latane, watching him. They were resupplied and supported by the Tovieti boatmen.

He then made a terrible error. Rather than maintain his generous and logical policy of welcoming anyone who wanted to surrender, he evidently lost his temper after a probing attack he mounted was driven back by the Guardians.

He had a dozen prisoners hung on Y-shaped racks in front of the lines, then killed them most horribly. It was as if invisible ants ate at their flesh, and they twisted, screaming, and died slowly.

His magic terrified the Council's army, as intended, but it also reduced the turncoats to nearly nothing. The Guardians finally realized Tenedos intended destruction, and their deaths would build his power, his magic.

That gave them a bit of resolve, and they retreated slowly, fighting each step of the way, toward Nicias, until they reached the Latane Delta. Here they held, and Tenedos's tactics grew hesitant, as they had during the Maisirian campaign around Penda. Perhaps Tenedos was overly concerned with my rebels and the Maisirians. Or perhaps he wasn't sure what he should do next.

Sinait tried several times with Seeing Bowls to reach either Trerice or the government in Nicias, but we were firmly blocked by Tenedos, Gojjam, and their Corps of Wizards, and the agents Kutulu sent never returned.

I finally decided we'd fled far enough into Kallio, set winter quarters and took stock. My situation was a bit grim. I'd lost about 200,000 men, killed, wounded, sick, or, mostly, by desertion. As always, the bravest units, those who stood most firmly against Tenedos, had been the hardest hit.

I gave out medals and promotions lavishly, trying to keep my warriors keen. One honor I was especially pleased to make—naming Domina Thanet's cavalry regiment the Seventeenth Ureyan Lancers, as I'd vowed to do if their performance was worthy, and they'd done well against Tenedos.

There were a few pluses: I was heavily reinforced by the Tovieti, who came in singly and in groups. Cymea and her deputies insisted at first they serve in their own units. I was hardly foolish enough to permit this, still having little trust in them; I used the excuse that entire units of green recruits were dangerous for everyone and scattered them throughout the army.

She was skeptical but reluctantly agreed. Cymea may have been young, but she was quick and analytical. I hoped she, and the rest of the Tovieti, would stay on my side until Tenedos was destroyed but had no confidence they wouldn't turn against me as soon as they thought victory might be at hand.

The army viewed them with healthy skepticism. All knew the murderous reputation the stranglers had, and some had lost friends or relatives to them. But the Tovieti gave no reason for concern. They kept to themselves, observed no bloody rituals that I heard, and tried to fit in with the other soldiers.

My concerns about what the Tovieti would do if victory threatened were wryly amusing—I, too, was making a nice carpet of the lion's skin while he yet snarled in the jungle.

Cymea Amboina had three deputies: the man who still called himself Jakuns, whose abilities I respected; a sour, heavy man named Himchai I'd not been able to assess; and Jabish, who was a fanatic, so dedicated to her cult she'd bring it to its doom by insisting every decision had to be made in its favor.

But I would have cheerfully enlisted monsters from the deepest pits if they'd sworn even momentary fealty.

Another source of recruits was the native Kallians, many of whom had fought in the rebellions against the empire. They loathed Tenedos as much as they had when I'd been the military governor in Polycittara under the emperor's brother, so they joined my tattered colors by the thousand because we were the most dedicated, not caring a bit about my own past or that we were in the worst shape of any of the four armies in Numantia.

Even better, they opened their hidden larders, arsenals, and treasuries, so the process of rebuilding my army went more quickly than I could have dreamed.

It was interesting that my two biggest enemies, the Kallians and the Tovieti, were now my firmest supporters.

The question was, what should I do next?

I started my plans with estimates of what everyone *else* must or should do:

> The Grand Council must keep Nicias to control Numantia, and the key to Nicias was the Delta, which so far Tenedos hadn't attacked;
> Laish Tenedos must take Nicias as soon as the Time of Storms stopped, before King Bairan could move north and take him in the rear;
> King Bairan must destroy Tenedos before the former emperor could unify the country against the Maisirians.

Which left me . . .

Dangling in the middle, with a somewhat shattered army, unable to march against Tenedos both because of the upcoming stormy season and because I couldn't have the Maisirians threatening my lines of communication, such as they were, back into Kallio.

Dangling . . .

An idea of sorts came, but one that I would have to personally lead. That was impossible, since I could hardly abandon this mishmash of a soldiery.

Then the weather broke, the Time of Heat ending and the Time of Rains beginning, and the monsoons swept over us, and I and my army were locked in place until at least the Time of Dews.

Quite suddenly, a solution to my forced inaction came, in the shape of a man I thought fled to unknown lands.

It was Cyrillos Linerges, the only one of Tenedos's tribunes besides myself and Yonge who'd survived the battles in Maisir. In the time of the Rule of Ten, he'd been an army sergeant, then a wandering peddler who'd ended with a dozen stores scattered across Numantia. Linerges was calm, not at all inspiring physically, but brave beyond all comprehension and a tactician who seldom lost a battle.

After I'd welcomed him like a lost brother, he smiled slightly, and said, "I thought you might be able to use a little assistance."

"Hells, yes," I said fervently. "You're now . . . shit, I haven't figured out what titles should be, but what about first tribune? Or don't you think we should revive that title yet?"

He shrugged. "Titles don't mean much in the end, now, do they?"

"No," I said. "Not in a prison cell, nor . . . nor wherever you were. Somewhere outside Numantia, I heard. I hope it was incredibly romantic."

"I let some friends spread that tale," he said. "Actually,

I thought I'd be safest with my wife, Gulana's, family, figuring no one would ever come after me."

"I thought the same," I said bitterly, "and went back to Cimabue. I was wrong."

"I wasn't . . . for a time," Linerges said. "Gulana's people sheltered me, and I learned how to farm. Terribly hard work, in case you haven't tried it. Can't recommend it as a career. But I didn't think it would be entirely bright to open another store or even go out with a pack train.

"But I didn't mind farming. I thought I'd had my time in the sun and had no more desire to soldier, but the times don't seem to leave you alone, do they?"

"No," I said. "Nor does Tenedos. He came after me to serve again, then, when I chose not, he attacked my family."

"He didn't get bastardly with me," Linerges said. "Perhaps I'm not as important to him as you were . . are, evidently. Or maybe I did a better job of going to ground. I heard rumors he was looking for me and wanted me to serve him once more. I made no response, since I wasn't intending to serve anyone except my family and myself. But the more time passed, the more I realized I couldn't remain outside the swell of affairs, and doesn't *that* sound pompous?"

"Why, if I may ask, didn't you return to the emperor's service?"

Linerges sighed and scratched his nose. "I don't like to jump to conclusions. But the emperor's performance in Maisir was appalling. I think—hells, I know—he violated the oath he took when you crowned him emperor. But there were other vows he broke, ones that none of us speak aloud.

"You know what I mean, don't you?"

I did. Vows to humanity, to the army, to his soldiers, to his citizens. But I did no more than nod.

"So if I couldn't stand aside, and I couldn't bring myself to serve Tenedos, and certainly no one but a bully could be a Guardian . . . well, you were the last, sorry option."

"And I've never been so glad to have a new recruit," I said. "You know, Yonge's come back, too."

"I saw him when I rode in, and he called me several dozen species of fool for coming back. And he asked if I still thought I was immortal."

"Do you?"

"Of course." Linerges didn't smile. He'd told me this before, and I was never able to determine if this was his idea of a capital jest or if he was sincere.

"Then, O Immoral, I mean Immortal One, it's time for you to get your stubby ass to work. I'm turning this whole gods-rotted mess over to you for a time. Try to keep them in line and don't screw things up too badly."

"While you do what?"

"I'm going out to play in the rain. Me, Yonge, and maybe a couple of hundred other mad fools."

Sinait and Kutulu thought I was, indeed, a lunatic after I told them what I had in mind. But I remembered going out in the rain, long ago in Kait, when we first sought the demon Thak, and how no one thought any soldiers would be about in the dismal storms.

"We cannot afford to lose you," Sinait said.

"Yes, you can. You have Linerges now."

"Linerges," Kutulu said, "is like me, or rather like me if I were a soldier instead of a warder. No one will follow him. Not like you."

"Batshit," I said irritably. "You might as well make me king right now, then."

Sinait and Kutulu looked at each other.

"Well?" I snapped. "Why the mysterious looks?"

"Never mind," Sinait said. "You're set in your course."

"He is," Kutulu said. "And if he is, then I'm going with him."

I started to growl that the army could hardly do without its primary collector of intelligence, then caught a bit of a grin on his face. If I could do it, so could be.

"Very well," I said. "You, and . . . six, no, ten of your men. Your best spies."

"I already know who I'll take," he said. "And you're right. It might be fun."

"If I'd been the first to volunteer," Sinait asked, "would you have taken me instead of him?"

"No," I said. "You *must* stay. You're the most powerful wizard we have."

"I knew you'd say that," she said. "I just wonder how many other people who shouldn't go, will, however."

Yonge was the next to insist, which I'd expected. I guess he was a little surprised I didn't argue. By this time, I knew better. He'd simply agree he shouldn't go and then meet us three days later on the trail.

I wanted fifty skirmishers who could ride, but Sendraka couldn't be one of them—he, too, was needed with the army. Yonge said he'd have them, tough, furtive, and dishonest—his best.

I took two companies of light infantry, not wanting separate volunteers, but men who'd trained and fought together, and had them mounted on mules. They were led by Captains Alcium and Turfan. That gave me 150 men.

The others were volunteers, men like Svalbard, who could never stand garrison life if there was a chance of getting killed.

Lasleigh, Baron Pilfern, said he must go, whatever the task, wherever it was, because he had to wash away the sour taste of the retreat. He still had forty of his originals, and ten more Kallians he was training.

I'd need some light cavalry for scouting. As much as I longed to take Domina Thanet and the best of his men, I couldn't stand losing what few good cavalrymen I had on this enterprise, so I'd take Lasleigh and train them as we rode.

That gave me 230 men, and I made sure each was well shod, clad for the weather, and armed. They had the best horses and mules in the army. Each man would carry twenty-five pounds of foodstuffs for us, twenty-five for our horses or mules.

Svalbard came to me with the 231st man, a new arrival, another of my bodyguards who'd survived the bloodbath at Cambiaso. This was Curti, the best archer I'd ever seen, whom I'd seen go down with an arrow in his leg.

He apologized for not coming sooner, but he'd been living in Chalt, and it took time to work his way around Tenedos's army and get across the Latane. I welcomed him, of course, and told him to serve alongside Svalbard. With two such warriors at my back, I had no reason to fear anyone.

All of the force was given the Spell of Understanding to enable them to understand other tongues than their own, and I set seamstresses to work.

Two nights before we left the army, Cymea Amboina came to my tent after the evening meal.

"I've heard you're planning an adventure," she said.

"An adventure? I've heard that's really a disaster happening a thousand leagues away."

She inclined her head, acknowledging my humor but not laughing.

"You're not taking any of us with you?"

"Us meaning Tovieti?"

"Yes."

"No," I said. "And I meant no offense by not doing that." I was speaking truth—I simply hadn't thought of them.

"There are still Tovieti in Urey," she said. "One of us could be of use in contacting them."

I jolted. "How did you know we were going to Urey?"

"Remember," she said. "I'm not unfamiliar with magic." She grinned. "And one of your tailors happens to be with us and showed me his work."

"I hope you've told no one," I said. "Those who even know about my planned sortie imagine we're going north, after Tenedos."

"I've told my three advisers," Cymea said. "All keep secrets well."

"Your people do that," I agreed. "Yes. I'm going south."

"Toward the Maisirians."

I made no reply.

"Could I ask what you intend?"

"No. You may not," I said, not sharply. "I wish no one even speculating about that. I don't think there's a sorcerer about who can read minds, but I'd rather not take the chance."

"It's good to be cautious," Cymea said. "Which is why you're taking not only a Tovieti, but a wizard as well."

"You propose?" I said, already knowing the answer.

"Myself. I've as much power as anyone else here, except Sinait possibly, perhaps more."

I could have said something damned foolish, such as she was too young, or a woman, or something equally idiotic. But there were soldiers in the ranks far younger than she was, and while we had no women as warriors, there were many hangers-on, sutlers, "companions," and such, and many of them knew which end of a dagger or sword should be put to work.

"I would think your people might object to possibly losing you," was all I did say.

"As I've heard you say, no one is indispensable. I choose to go, and my brothers and sisters found no good cause to object. Do you?"

"Why should I?"

"You seemed to hesitate," she said.

"No," which was a lie. I still feared and hated the Tovieti, and its evident leader more than most. Cymea was looking at me very directly. I tried to turn her attention.

"So you were able to winkle out my intent that easily. I'm impressed, and wouldn't want to be the friend or lover who tries to hide anything from you," I went on, trying to make a small joke.

"Friends? Lovers? How odd," she said thoughtfully. "I don't think I've thought a lot about either, not for a long time. I guess the order's been all I need. Just as the army's everything you need."

"It wasn't always like that," I said, saw her expression harden.

"I thought we agreed to forget," she said, voice cold.

"I'm sorry," I said hastily. "I didn't mean that the way it came out. I just meant . . . one time I had something of a life beyond carrying a sword around."

It was my turn to be overtaken by my thoughts. Cymea started to say something, then stopped. I wasn't really aware of her.

"Maybe," I said, musing aloud, "maybe I'm wrong. Maybe I never did have a real life. Maybe the whole time it was nothing but soldiering, and what I thought was my private life was just a spare moment here and there." I dragged myself back. "Sorry. Talking about yourself is always a bore. My apologies."

"None needed," she said. "So I'm to be ready when?"

"Two days hence, at the beginning of the last watch."

I shouted for Svalbard and ordered him to help Cymea get ready. She left the tent, looked back through the flap for an instant, then went on.

I poured a glass of now-cold tea, sat, deep in thought. How odd. What life *had* I really had, even before? Certainly I was married to Marán, had palaces, went to dances and feasts. But what part of my life could I say I truly owned? When the emperor called, I came running, and served well and hard, as my family had before me, regardless of holidays, days of birth, or personal importance.

Those palaces, perhaps even my now-dead wife, all these were the rewards of duty well done, not a real life, such as most men build as the years pass. I was given riches easily, and they were taken away by the emperor, by the gods, just as easily. I had no children, now no family at all.

All I had was Numantia.

For an instant, I felt childishly sorry for myself, then pushed the absurd mood away.

That was as it was supposed to be, wasn't it?

My family motto, *We Hold True*, meant we held to something, we served something, emperor and country.

What more was there?
What more could there, should there be?

The day after, in driving rain and predawn blackness, we slipped out of camp and rode south.

Toward the armies of King Bairan.

FIFTEEN

RAIDING

I kept away from the Latane River, marching almost due south on a caravan route that ran from Polycittara to a ferry landing across the Latane from Renan. It was slow going—the rains seemed heavier this season, but perhaps it was only because I was out in them, still brooding a bit over my defeat.

The mucky track, its paving not maintained for years, slowed our horses, and there was no need to exhaust them—or ourselves—before we came on the Maisirians.

At first, there were few travelers abroad, and most fled into the surrounding country as they saw the column, having learned soldiers seldom bring good with them. We were scrupulous about paying for supplies and fodder in the villages and farms we passed, even though we paid in scrip, which would only be good if we won the war.

I was a bit sorry there were so many of us, because we mostly were forced to sleep outside, only occasionally finding an unoccupied barn to crowd into.

When we came to a village, generally one of the elders would suggest my officers would be gladly quartered in the people's houses. The men could use a field to pitch their scraps of canvas in. It might have been tempting, but I remembered a certain banquet on the long retreat from Jarrah and how sodden warriors had watched as their leaders ate dishes the common men hadn't seen for weeks, from gold and silver plate.

When we crossed into Urey, there were more and more people about, refugees fleeing the Maisirians to the south. They'd been moving long enough for the old and feeble to fall by the wayside and to discard the odd bits and pieces people take in hasty flight.

These people didn't run when they saw us—they were too worn, too tired, and bandits had probably combed their ranks and taken the best, living and material.

Muddy faces looked up when we came on them, showed a moment of fear, then dully looked back at the endless mud they traveled through. Once or twice we were cheered, although no one could tell whether we were rebels, Guardians, or Tenedos's army.

I wondered what I would do if I were ever in their position. Was it better to flee with what little you could carry into the unknown or stay where you were and hope the invaders wouldn't be too harsh? It was a choice I hoped I'd never have to make.

Then we came on ruins, recent ones from this invasion, older ones from the last time. Ironically, in this battered, forlorn land, we were able to get out of the weather more often, sometimes taking over an entire abandoned village or one of the great barns the farmers had built for their vanished cattle.

The highway turned west until we were in sight of the river, then ran south beside it, generally no more than half a league away.

One night, we saw a ruined pavilion on the river. It was

huge, and I wondered who'd dreamt half the people of Renan would need a single dance hall. The outbuildings were collapsing or burned, and the main hall had sagged into collapse as the years pulled at it.

Some walls had collapsed, but the roof still stood on its sturdy supports. I was afraid to bring the horses inside, because the flooring was musty, rotten, barely strong enough to support a man, but there were sheds enough around the main building for most, and we tied our canvas between them and gave overhead cover to the others.

I was glad for the shelter, because it'd been raining steadily all day and now, near dark, the storm was building, wind whipping, rain tearing.

There'd been fireplaces here and there along the walls, for cooking and warmth, and there was plenty of wood scattered around. I wasn't worried about the smell of smoke attracting attention. We were still days beyond Renan, Cymea's magic said there was no danger, and the pavilion was half a league away from the road.

It was chill, and we crowded around the fires making our supper. At least we weren't starving or thirsty. We'd bought and had slaughtered five beeves two days earlier, and everyone had meat in his pack. We'd passed a field of potatoes the refugees hadn't completely dug up, and a handful of men shoveled productively for a few minutes.

Beef, potatoes, herbs the more talented carried, garlic, water, other vegetables not entirely desiccated, a splash of the wine we'd gotten two villages ago, and there was a tasty stew.

I allowed an extra tumbler of wine for each man who wished it, and we lined up before the pots, officers last, filled our tin plates, and found a place to sit.

Cymea asked if I wished company. I did—in spite of the meal, my mood was a bit gloomy in this moment to dead peace and dreams. My soldiers were also quieter than the circumstances warranted, mostly eating in silence.

We finished our meal, I went to the river, washed the plates in sand, rinsed them and came back.

"A pity we can't chance some singing," I said. "Cheery things up a trifle."

"There are ways," Cymea said. "I could set wards out, so no one could hear us."

"Excellent," I said.

She opened her saddlebags, took out herbs, lit a brazier, and whispered a spell.

"There. No one can hear the loudest bellower now. Nothing will carry beyond the sentry line."

I was about to call for the men I knew had the widest and bawdiest repertory, when another idea came.

"We always depend on our own," I said. "Sorcerer, can you bring up the past? If it doesn't attract attention from any other wizard."

"Perhaps," she said cautiously. "What sort of past do you want?"

"This arena's. I wonder what it was like, before it failed, back in peacetime."

"A long time ago, I sense," she said. "Perhaps before I was born. But your idea's interesting. And I shouldn't worry about any Maisirian wizard seeing my efforts. This isn't very high-grade magic."

Again, she rummaged through her bag. "We'll try this . . . some hawthorn . . . that . . . lavender . . . shepherd's purse . . . rosemary . . . maybe this . . . that for certain." She got up, found a dried flower in a corner, a scrap of paper that had been a handbill, some dust from a corner.

Again the brazier flamed, and I smelt the sweetness of the lavender as the herbs burnt. The men had noticed what she was doing and were watching curiously. I warned them what Cymea was attempting. A few edged away, people who felt magic brought nothing but grief, but most pressed more closely.

She sprinkled the trash on the fire, and whispered:

"You were once
Return again
Turn back
Turn back

Time is not
The rain is not
The storm is not

Life come back
Return again

Remember, dust
What you were
What you saw
What you were

Time, turn back."

Very slowly, like a mist rising from nowhere, the floor repaired itself, became highly polished. The walls were erect, brightly papered, the gapped roof solid, and colored tapers gleamed in chandeliers. We heard music, dimly at first, then louder.

The pavilion became peopled with wraiths, and the

styles and fashions were those of twenty years earlier, when the Rule of Ten held Numantia, and I was a young legate.

Men and women, richly dressed, filled the room, some dancing, some chatting, some leaning against the drinking bars along the walls. I saw a captain in the uniform of the Seventeenth Ureyan Lancers, my first regiment, tried to recognize him, failed as he bowed to a woman and led her out onto the floor.

"Are those ghosts?" I asked Cymea.

"No," she answered. "Or anyway, not ghosts if you mean do they have will, could they, for instance, come over and buy you a drink? They're but real images of the past that I've called up."

I hoped that it was more, that these men and women's spirits, even though most of them must've gone back to the Wheel years ago, were able to feel a bit of merriment, pleasure, far distant in their new selves.

Magic it was, but I mean more than just wizardry, for the spectacle held 200-odd dirty soldiers bound, watching another time, before war, before hatred, enjoy itself.

Then the spell was broken . . . just a bit . . . as a soldier I recognized as one of the army's prized clowns got up, bowed to another private, and they swung onto the dance floor, dancing not well but enthusiastically. Laughter grew, and I was smiling, too. The illusion may have been spoiled, but I didn't miss the loss—if my men were cheery enough to joke, that was a good sign.

Svalbard rose, went onto the floor, and began dancing by himself. His eyes were half-closed, and his thoughts were I know not where. The huge man moved gracefully, as if he'd been a professional dancer at one time, in elaborate arabesques.

I wondered where he'd learned to dance so well, realized he'd probably never tell me.

I looked at Cymea, and she was smiling, also in her own world. She noticed my attention and leaned closer.

"You know," she whispered. "I never learned how to dance."

"Really?"

"I suppose my father thought there were other things more important," she said. "I suppose there were," and there was a tinge of bitterness in her voice.

"Perhaps," I said, "when the war is over, you would allow me to help you learn?"

She blinked, then smiled, and her smile was the dawning sun.

"Perhaps," she said.

A thought came . . . what if I would ask her now? Here? Absurd. Commanders did not involve themselves with their underlings, particularly if that underling happened to be a murderous woman whose fellows had . . . had done what they did.

Who would think ill of me if I did?

Would Cymea refuse?

My mind was whirling like a boy at his first fete.

I don't know what I would have done, but suddenly the officer of the guard burst in. He goggled at what was going on, saw his commanding officer, hurried to him.

Cymea gestured three times, and the illusion was gone, and there was silence except for the whine of the wind and drip of the rain, and the ruined pavilion was lit only by a scattering of candles.

The officer crossed to me.

"Riders," he said. "A patrol coming up the road toward us."

"Turn to," I ordered, and the magic was forgotten as men pulled on battle harness and readied their weapons.

A second man came into the room.

"They've turned away," he reported. "Gone back to the main road."

We relaxed again, but Cymea made no move to re-create her fantasy.

I went out into the darkness, made my toilet, sluiced water on my face from a cistern, brushed my teeth, then came back and laid out my canvas strip with a blanket inside.

Cymea had spread her blankets not far away, and in a few minutes she came back, her face shiny and wet.

"It's cold out there," she said.

"It felt good," I said.

She pulled her boots off and slid into her bedroll. None of us undressed any further than that. She loosened her sword in its sheath beside her, lay back.

One by one, the candles were blown out, and silence grew through the grunts and low murmur of voices.

"That was nice," I said. "Thank you."

"Thank *you* for thinking of it," she answered. "Good night."

I slept well until I was roused, as I ordered, two hours before dawn, and my dreams weren't of war or death.

We took advantage of the still-pouring rain, stripped off our uniforms, such as they were, washed, and put on the new garb my sewers had labored at in secret. We now wore pants and tunics of a light brown like many of the Maisirian units, and I'd had Maisirian banners for our guidon bearers made from memory.

I'd wondered if I should restrict my 231 men to one

side of the pavilion, and the 232nd, Cymea, to the other, but she solved the problem for me by nonchalantly stripping off with the others and pretending she didn't see the interested looks she got.

It worked well—her casualness shamed even the most lascivious into silence, although I'm sure many thought of her slender, small-breasted body at night. Perhaps I was one of them.

Re-uniformed, we ate hastily, mounted, and rode on. In our new garb we'd be subject to instant execution as spies or partisans, but no one cared. The Maisirians were careless about taking prisoners, with a captive's best hope being sold into slavery. Knowing this, our army had become equally brutal.

In our retreat, Kutulu had acquired a set of large-scale maps of the Latane River, from Nicias to Renan, so I wasn't navigating blindly as we rode carefully south.

A day later, we saw the first Maisirians. They noted our banners, waved or ignored us, and kept about their business, which was either unauthorized looting or authorized procurement for their commissaries, which is a difference it takes the keenest to determine.

A few were the dark-armored Negaret, frontier guardians, nomads. I'd ridden with one tribe of them when I first went to Maisir as the emperor's false peace envoy. They were near-bandits, brave when it suited them, cowardly when survival dictated, and in spite of their sometimes-barbaric ways, I'd loved the time and sometimes thought wistfully of leading such a life myself, without anything to hold me to one place, losing myself in their rather mindless ways of hunting, riding, and sport.

I wasn't worried about being ambushed—no one in his

right mind would imagine this small a body of Numantian soldiers close to the Maisirian lines. Plus I had Kutulu's men in front, screening, then cavalry vedettes at every vantage point. Cymea's magic scanned for unpleasant surprises, and she had a continuing skein of spells around us, so one of the Maisirian War Magicians could "look" at us and hopefully find nothing of his concern.

The next day, only a dozen leagues outside Renan, two of Kutulu's men said they'd found the Maisirians' camp. I rode forward with them, over rolling foothills, taking only Svalbard and Cymea.

The main scout, Kutulu's prized bodyguard Elfric, led us on a sheep track that wound up a commanding bluff. We tethered our horses below the crest, went on foot to the top.

Spread below, across a wide valley with a river running through it were the Maisirians. I counted at least twenty individual camps separated by farmland and assumed King Bairan had told them off by divisions. There were at least a million men, their tents and crude huts stretched as far as I could see.

We lay on our bellies in the muck while I considered what I'd do next. It was cold, and then rain began pattering. Fortunately, none of us could get any wetter, so it was just another bit of misery.

Cymea crawled up beside me. "I've an idea," she whispered. I asked about it, also in a low tone, which was absurd, since the nearest Maisirian was far distant, half a league or more. But fear brings its own logic.

She said she thought she could cast a spell like the Seeing Bowl. I said that spell was far too dangerous, and I'd have to assume Bairan's magicians would be overwatching the camp. Cymea said she thought she had a new way of casting, using a puddle of water and the rain, that would be far subtler and harder to discover.

Reluctantly, I told her to go ahead.

She used no brazier, no fire, but ran her fingers across the tiny pool again and again, as if writing invisibly. She muttered her spell in a monotone, over and over. I was starting to yawn in boredom, in spite of my unease.

The water seethed, turned translucent, then we were high above the Maisirian camp. I had Svalbard hold his cloak over the map, which I oriented to the picture.

"Can we get closer?"

"We can do anything you need," she said. "Closer, or showing you bits of the camp . . . whatever you wish."

I took writing implements from my bags, and as Cymea sent her "eye" skittering around the valley, made rapid notes. Here was their front line, here the secondary, here were their reserves, there mess tents and quartermasters, supply dumps here, here. I tried not to stare too long into the puddle—its swoops and dips were unsettling to the stomach, and I lost any desire I'd had to return from the Wheel as a bird.

I noted something interesting. The Maisirians had burned or torn apart most of the valley's buildings, and the few standing had likely been commandeered for officers' lodgings or unit headquarters. But to the rear of the camp was a great estate, whose fields of autumn wheat stood tall; vineyards with the vines dry and sere but unscathed; fruit trees not violated; and the estate's buildings white, rich, and palatial.

"Can you close on that?" I asked. "It looks like something important."

"Very carefully. It also looks like it might have wards set."

The estate grew larger in the pool. Cymea sent her "eye" spreading over it.

"Still clear," she said. "I'll come back more slowly."

Guards posted . . . smart-looking . . . but they weren't that alert, as if there wasn't any particular reason to be watchful right now. There was only a handful of horses here and there and not that many men about. The main house had a dozen chimneys, but only two were smoking.

"Vacant?" I wondered. "Who lives there now?"

I looked at the map, and it showed the estate, but with no legend to give a clue.

"I sense something," Cymea said, after about an hour. "Something coming."

"Move away from the mansion," I ordered. "And get ready to kill the illusion."

She gathered a handful of mud, whispered into her fist.

"I sense something coming toward that big house," she said. "I'll use the rain to turn the view toward it."

The image swung, and we were looking west. If it'd been clear, we should have been able to see the outskirts of Renan.

There was motion, and without orders Cymea closed on it. I had an instant to see a regiment of Maisirian cavalry in dress uniform, with carriages and banners behind, then mud splashed into the pool and all vanished.

"Somebody," Cymea said hastily, breath coming fast, "had a counterspell out, and I felt suspicion, as if our presence had been sensed."

What . . . or rather who . . . those cavalrymen guarded came in a flash. The king was coming. Bairan would've taken over a mansion in Renan for his usual quarters, no more interested in sharing the mud with his common foot soldiers than any other Maisirian lord, especially in the winter, and he used this estate as his headquarters when he visited his army.

A notion came, was discarded as absurd.

I'd seen enough. Now I was ready to remind Bairan that Numantians did more than flee or make obeisance.

The first order was to find a haven, close enough to the Maisirian camp so we could chivvy them easily, far enough away so we wouldn't be discovered.

I'd gone over the map, looking for a nicely dense forest we could bury ourselves in, something with great thickets no casual enemy scout would bother pushing through. Two places suggested themselves, but one was a bit far away from the Maisirian camps, the other too close to the river and Renan.

I found an interesting dot on the map and sent Kutulu and Elfric to investigate it.

They came back with good news. The dot was a ruined castle, built on a crag that jutted up from the valley floor. A winding dirt road led from the nearest village, almost a league distant, to the gate. They had ridden around the castle, seen a twisting path at the rear that would serve as an escape route if we were discovered.

Still better, they'd stopped a farmer and asked him about the place. Shaking in terror, sure these Maisirians were about to rip him apart, he quavered answers. The castle hadn't been lived in for . . . for as long as he and his father and *his* father had been alive. Longer, for no one knew who'd lived there or how long ago. All everyone knew was the castle was demon haunted. How did they know this? Had any of them investigated? No one, not even the most foolhardy village boy, dared approach it, by day or night. Then how did they know it was haunted?

The farmer looked perplexed, Kutulu told me, sounding amused, then said "everybody just knew."

Very, very good. If "everybody knew" the castle was haunted, no one would think whatever lights we showed were anything but supernatural, and the Maisirians, even more superstitious than our most craven peasant, would stay well clear.

I asked Kutulu if they'd taken a look inside.

Kutulu looked suddenly uncomfortable, and Elfric wouldn't meet my eyes. No, they hadn't. Why not? Well, they wanted to get the word back as quickly as possible.

"'Sides," Elfric rumbled. "There *is* some'at strange about those walls."

I dismissed him, poured Kutulu a bit of a sweet yellow wine from Dara that I'd discovered he fancied. He sipped at it once, twice, which was as much as draining a flagon for the spymaster.

"Getting superstitious?" I asked.

Kutulu grimaced. "No. Or at any rate, I don't think so. But . . ."

"But what?"

"Never mind. I'll go back tomorrow morning and go through the damned place top to bottom." For some reason, he sounded a bit angry.

"Never mind," I said. "We don't have that much time. We'll move this afternoon and be inside it by nightfall."

I gave orders to break camp, then called Cymea, told her about the two men's discomfort.

"*Kutulu?*" she said in disbelief. "Afraid of something?"

"I don't know if afraid's the right word . . . but something about that place bothers him."

"Perhaps," she said thoughtfully, "we might walk carefully when we approach. And you, I, your great thug, and a scattering of other muscle-bound sorts might reconnoiter before we wander inside with our slippers in our hand looking for the guest bedroom?"

I thought that an excellent idea, and so Curti, Svalbard, myself, Kutulu, and Lasleigh's cavalry rode out within the hour, the rest of the force not far behind.

The castle was only two hours' ride distant, and by midafternoon we'd skirted the village and were at the base of the road leading up to it.

One look, and I understood Elfric and Kutulu's hesitation. The castle, if that was what it should be called, *was* weird. At first, I thought it had been a single very high round tower whose upperworks had been smashed by time, the elements, or a conqueror, but as we rode closer, I realized the tower was not that ruined, that it had been conceived as a low, squat cylinder. It was as strange a building as I'd ever seen.

There had been no moat, but the gaping main entrance was on a second floor. A stone ramp and rollers lay overturned to one side, which we could hitch horses to and drag back in place. We tethered our mounts, and Curti and I went hand-over-hand up the rough stones to the portal. I tossed a knotted rope down, and the others swarmed up, and we went inside.

Our footsteps echoed on the ancient stone, and as we entered the courtyard, a scatter of pigeons scrawked alarm, and my sword was in my hand as the birds fluttered away through the open roof.

I was sheepish, until I noted that everyone except Cymea also had drawn steel. She had a wand in hand, and her eyes were wide, as if she'd sensed something.

I drew a question mark in the air, she shook her head, and we continued. Ramps in the walls, not stairs, led upward, and as we went, things grew stranger and stranger.

We came across stone tables, benches, badly worn, some tapestries whose detail I couldn't make out that turned to dust when I touched them. Cymea found a bit of a scroll, said a spell over it, and was able to unroll it. The words, if words they were, were in no language I'd seen, nor did they look as if man's logic had any part in their construct, one "letter" being a handspan tall, and next to it others not as large as Cymea's fingernail. She, too, shook her head in ignorance.

There was room enough for many men, the rooms being set into the thick outer walls. They were small and somehow wrong in their proportions, ceilings low enough to make me duck my head, but they were very wide, perhaps thirty feet by twenty.

The top floor was broken away and open to the heavens, looking down on the valley below, but its flooring was sturdy enough yet for guards to make their rounds.

We went back down to the courtyard and found a ring-bolted hatch to one side.

"Is it safe?"

"I . . . think so," Cymea said. "But be wary."

Svalbard and I lifted hard, stumbled back as the hatch came up as if it were counterbalanced. There was a ramp leading down.

A terrible smell rolled up, and we gagged.

"I do not like this," I said.

"I still feel no immediate threat," Cymea said. "But we can abandon this building and sleep around the walls. Or find another hiding place entirely."

"No," I decided. "This place is otherwise perfect. Let's see what's below."

We took bits of ensorcelled wood from our packs, struck sparks, and they grew into full-size tapers, fire sputtering from their tip.

We went down into darkness.

There was a center room, with corridors spidering out. At intervals, there were barred doors, a small spy hole in each one.

"Dungeon," Svalbard guessed. It made sense. Curti lifted the balk on one, opened it, held high his torch.

There were bones on the inside, as if a prisoner had been abandoned when the castle was vacated. But these bones, moldered by the centuries, had belonged to nothing human.

My skin crawled, but we went on. All of the corridors dead-ended against the outer walls but one, and at that one was a doorway, this with four stone balks barring it, and a strange symbol carved into the stone.

I remembered another demon, who'd lived in the depths below another ancient castle, and how Tenedos's spell had brought it ravening forth. I didn't need Cymea's warning to leave that door blocked and was glad to go up into the dying light.

Lasleigh was standing in the courtyard entrance, so the rest of my troops had arrived.

I drew Cymea to one side. "Well?"

"I do not greatly like this place," she said. "Something terrible happened a very long time ago, and there's a great sadness. I feel no echo of man here, as if this tower's builders were not human."

"Demons?"

"I've never heard of demons requiring housing," she said, trying to make light.

"So we should leave?"

"It's your option. But I still don't feel threatened. But I've never been anywhere that felt so dead, as if it'd died a thousand thousand years ago and still kept on dying." She shook her head. "I know, that doesn't make sense."

I was most reluctant, but the day was growing late. One night could not hurt.

I supervised moving the ramp into place, and it slid easily, as if it were as light as pumice, but very strong. I watched the horses and mules carefully as we led them inside, for I've a belief animals can sense things, even the supernatural, better than man. But none of the beasts appeared nervous, and they seemed quite happy to be out of the dank.

I assembled the men, told them to take rooms by four-man fighting sections. I had guards told off and sent those who wished to wash back down the road about a third of a league to a creek. Other men I detailed to find dry wood for our cooking fires.

We cooked and ate, and then I called them together again.

"None of you have been told what you volunteered for, but it doesn't take the brains of a recruit to know we're here after some Maisirian hide. I want to hit the bastards here, there, and everywhere. Piss them off, make them afraid, then get the hells out of here.

"I want them to be like a man who's stumbling through a forest, bitten by bugs, slashed by berry bushes, stumbling over vines, half-mad, not thinking right.

"When the weather changes, they'll be marching north, toward us, toward Nicias, like that man in the forest. When they reach us in Kallio, we'll have set them up for the kill.

"Any of you ever see an owl that grabs a nice rabbit just

at dawn and goes to a perch to enjoy his feast? Then a bunch of crows see him and start picking at him, picking here, there, until he's in a frenzy. Pretty soon he says the hells with this gods-damned rabbit and takes off for the deep forest, while the crows dine well."

There was some laughter.

"We're crows, and the Maisirians are the owl. We want their ass . . . I mean, their rabbit."

I waited until the laughter faded.

"But remember something else. Every now and then, a crow gets too bold, and the owl rips his throat out."

Silence dropped like a weighted curtain.

"You understand me well," I said. "Don't fuck up and become that crow. Or make *me* into that crow. We're here to help some other sorry bastard die for his country, not us.

"Now, go to your rooms. Tomorrow is make and mend. Get your weapons cleaned, check your mounts, get some sleep, and be ready to move when ordered.

"When we go out, I want us to get more gods-damned rabbits than you've ever seen!"

I set a heavy watch, less because I was worried about intruders than this castle itself.

Kutulu had the room next to me, Cymea next to him. Svalbard and Curti insisted on sleeping outside my room, in spite of my telling them to find a room of their own because there was nothing to worry about.

I spent an hour going over the map, forming my plan for the morrow. I thought it good and found myself most sleepy. I still felt uncomfortable, but not endangered, more as if I was spending the night in the home of someone I disliked, but who was neither my friend nor my enemy . . . yet.

I wrapped myself in my blankets on the stone floor, cold but not as cold as the mud we'd been sleeping in, blew out the candles, and went to sleep instantly.

I dreamed, and my dream was strange.

I was not a god, not a demon, nor human either. I had great powers and could manipulate the nature of matter itself. I was beyond good, beyond evil, and so offended greater powers, greater beings.

I was exiled, with those many beings who were connected to me, not quite family, but more than friends, to a far-distant world, where everything was hideous, strange, green.

I built this tower and continued my studies, cast my spells. I needed servitors, and so created, or perhaps brought from another place, smaller beings, pale, hideous to look at, pathetic in being locked into one shape for their brief existence.

Time passed, and once more I lusted for power. I reached out to the old realms, conspired, used all for my own ends, even those around me.

I was struck down from behind, by someone I trusted. As I lay dying I realized I'd used all my powers for nothing, trying to grasp at something that didn't matter, and given up what did, and then I died.

I was laid to rest in the bowels of this tower, and the others like me escaped or were taken back to whatever we had come from, while those horrible beings who'd served us fled into the wilds.

I was dead, but still lay dying for aeons, alone on this alien world, and I came awake, guts wrenching in sorrow.

I sat, shaken for a time, then dressed, strapped on my sword, and went out. Curti was half-dozing against a wall, and his eyes snapped open.

"Stay here," I said, trying to sound calm. "I'm just going out for air."

I went up to the roof. It was chill and overcast, but at least the rain had stopped.

The sentries saluted. I returned their salutes but didn't speak, gazing out at the blackness of the lands around, only a tiny light here and there at this late hour, then noticed someone else, huddled against one wall.

It was Cymea. I tried to greet her cheerily, not wanting anyone, this close to battle, to notice my illogical upset, then saw that she'd been crying.

"What's the matter?"

"Nothing. Never mind. I'm being silly."

I waited.

"I just had a stupid, stupid dream."

"So did I."

"About this place?"

"Yes," I said.

"Tell me about it."

I've never believed dreams mean anything much, so've always been bored by those who insist on talking about them and their supposed significance. But I obeyed Cymea. As I spoke, I saw her nodding.

"You had the same dream?"

"Almost exactly," she said.

"This place," I said. "This was where the . . . hells, I don't know what he was . . . this was what he built?"

"I think so."

"So how old is it?"

"How old *could* it be?" she responded. "Older, I think."

I shuddered, then another thought came, even worse.

"Those little creatures he . . . it . . . created or called up. Were those supposed to be us? Is *that* where we came from?"

"I don't know," Cymea said. "I hope not."

"Abandoned flunkies for a degenerate god," I said, finding it almost funny. "So there's no Umar the Creator, no Irisu the Preserver, no Saionji?"

"Don't be sure of that," she said. "Maybe our wizard, our demon . . . if he even existed . . . was one of those we call gods."

"I think I know a way we could find out," I said.

"You mean open that crypt? No, Damastes. I think that might drive me mad."

"Good. As the saying goes, I'm mad, but I'm hardly crazy."

We stood in silence for a time, letting the cold night wind blow across our faces, and slowly the sadness ebbed.

"Maybe," Cymea said, "that dream was worse, harder for me than it was for you."

"Why?"

"Because I'm from a magician's loins," she said, bitterly. "I can feel what that creature thought. I know what price sorcerous power exacts. And what people are willing to do to gain it."

"You mean," I said, choosing my words very carefully, "the way your father, Landgrave Amboina, conspired against Tenedos?"

Her lips twisted. "You think conspiracy is the worst sin magicians contemplate, when they're clawing for omnipotence? Damastes, you are a *very* naive man."

She whirled, almost ran to the ramp, and disappeared.

No, I could have replied, I know there are far worse, at least in my eyes. Tenedos was willing to betray whatever ideals he'd had at one time, his country, and his people to satisfy the blood-drinking demon he thought his servant, the one he actually served.

Somehow I didn't think that was what Cymea meant. I

wondered if she'd ever tell me, then wondered if I really wanted to know.

We carefully reconnoitered the Maisirian positions. First Cymea used sorcery, then I sent out skirmishers, with orders to avoid contact at all costs, and little by little, I filled in details on my map.

As Amboina had promised, there were Tovieti in the district, farmers, shopkeepers, some caravan masters, and their drovers. Cymea summoned them, refusing to tell me how, but daily men and women slipped up the road to the tower, and she and Kutulu talked to them, slowly building a complete picture of everything in and around Renan.

Then it was time to strike.

I planned the first attack to hit the hardest. The Maisirians didn't know there were enemies within a thousand leagues—their patrols were pillagers, not scouts; their convoys from Renan were guarded by a handful of soldiers; and the camps' security was as slack as any peacetime cantonment.

We would strike with magic and fire. Cymea took twigs, soaked them in a mineral solution, and chanted a spell over them. Then she built small fires around the tower's courtyard, set soldiers around them with the twigs, and had warrants standing by with glasses. She chanted a spell loudly, then, at periodic intervals, from three minutes to a full hour, the warrants shouted orders, and the soldiers passed the twigs through the flames for an instant.

She had two other spells half-prepared, and we then rode down the road and toward the Maisirians, taking a circuitous course to the river, then south along it, until we were just beyond the loose perimeter around Renan.

Cymea felt a warning spell, so we withdrew to a copse and settled in for the night. I could see the lights of Renan in the distance, remembered it as once, an ancient, beautiful city out of time, full of magic and romance.

But our army had retreated through Renan after the Maisirian campaign, the Maisirians following, laying waste to all Urey. I wondered what splendor was left, Renan occupied once more by the loathed invaders.

At the beginning of the last watch, we were roused, saddled our horses, and led them to a farm pond for watering and grain from our saddlebags, while we shivered in the cold mist, near rain, chewing disconsolately on sour bread and dried meat. We still wore our mock-Maisirian uniform, but all of us had a red scrap of cloth around our necks, so we'd not be slaughtering each other in the coming confusion.

We went forward slowly, at the walk, along a winding course, a small pass through a cluster of hillocks. Here I told off one company of infantry. I was pleased they'd been angry at being cut out of the forthcoming action, rather than delighted at not going into danger.

I'd noted a distinctive rocky formation the day before, just after the pass widened into the valley, and when we reached it, I shouted for my buglers to send the troops out on line. That roused the Maisirians, but they had no more than a few minutes before we hit their vedettes and sent them fleeing or lying still in the mire.

Cymea cast her first spell, rocking in the saddle, and the sky behind us turned red, but not red with a false dawn, red with death fires and flame. Swirling through the mist, which blew in curtains around us, were ghost figures of horsemen, monsters, giants, striding forward as the bugles sang for the trot.

We went through their front lines, no more than shallow trenches for the most part, and were among them.

Our ears twinged as sound screeched, like pipes but shriller, setting my teeth on edge. Cymea had studied and learned some of Tenedos's best spells. Then there were tents ahead, and we were slashing at tent ropes, canvas anyone who stumbled out, gaping for an instant before we sent them back to the Wheel.

Chosen men tossed away the ensorcelled twigs as they rode, and after we passed some flamed up, far larger than the bits of wood warranted. The fire licked at the Maisirian canvas, and wet as they were, the tentage took fire. Other twigs would flame up later, adding to the chaos.

The sound changed, became lower, the screaming of terrified men and women. It built, and now it was echoed by human throats as the Maisirians broke.

A man wearing a gaudy uniform ran out of the darkness, an officer, but armed with an infantryman's pike. I slashed it in two, cut him down, rode on as he fell. A man was mounting a horse, waving a sword wildly, and I killed him from behind and his horse stampeded as blood gouted, the dead weight of his rider slumping over the animal's neck.

There was a group of soldiers, a *calstor* shouting at them, and he went down with Curti's arrow in his bowels, and the soldiers fled, no warrant left to stiffen them to battle.

We cut through the camp to my real goal, one of the supply dumps that held I know not what under long rows of tarpaulins, and we smashed the wooden fence around it, and more fire twigs were scattered. There was a fence and my horse leapt it. Another balked, three men were thrown in the milling confusion, and others pulled them up behind, and we rode on, into open country.

We cut left, circling back the way we came, slicing through another camp, and fires were roaring up around the valley, not our arsonous flames, but the lamps of head-quarters as officers came awake.

Again bugles brayed, and we slowed to a walk, the mule-mounted infantry caught up with the cavalrymen, and we hit the Maisirians as they stumbled into their battle lines, still not sure who was attacking, where the enemy was coming from.

We ravened on, destroying as we went.

I counted ten turnings of the glass, then commanded the retreat to be sounded, and we slashed back the way we'd come.

We'd tarried too long, or so it must have appeared to the Maisirians, and there were mounted men coming after us, far more than my hundred and a half. We fled, gallop-ing hard, trying to look as if we ourselves had grown clumsy in fear, and the Maisirians came after us, and Cymea's second spell, intended to give the enemy confi-dence, was sent out.

We thundered through the low pass beyond the lines as if demons were after us, then reined around.

Our ambush element rose up on either side of the track as the Maisirians rode past, and arrows spat and lances thudded into the bunched-up mass of horsemen.

We charged into the melee, as the ambush's rear el-ement closed the gate on the pursuing cavalry, and it was a nasty, swirling bit of various hells; then the Maisirians were able to break out to freedom, back to their lines.

"To horse," I shouted, then heard somebody call, "We've got a prisoner! An officer!"

"Toss him across a mule and come on!" I shouted. "The rest of their damned army's coming fast."

We galloped away, Cymea now at the rear, casting spells of confusion, spells to suggest we'd turned off at this ford or into that thicket. Twice we stopped after crossing water, and she made other incantations to muddle our pursuers.

But the skirmishers I sent to the hilltops we passed didn't see any pursuit, and I remembered how the Maisirians could either be the most dangerous or the most foolish of enemies.

Cymea rode up beside me, breathless, cheeks red with the wind and the driving rain.

"So that's war?"

"That's war," I said. "When you're on the winning side. It's a whore's get when you're the one being ambushed."

"Either way," she said, "I didn't like it much."

I'd misread her expression for pleasure. Oddly enough, I liked her better for hating what we'd done.

"You're not supposed to," I said. "Just so long as you're good at it."

She nodded understanding, dropped back to add more bafflement.

The prisoner's eyes opened, and he sat up. He rubbed his ribs and grunted.

"Bad enough knocking the wind out of me, you had to keep me foozled across that fucking jackass," he grumbled.

I handed him a cup of wine. He drained it, glowered at me.

"I should have known it was you. You bastard."

He looked at Yonge.

"And *you*. What a shit-heel *pair* of bastards."

"How'd you ever get so gods-damned sloppy as to fall into that one?" Yonge demanded. "If you'd ridden like that on the border, I would have killed you ten years ago."

"If I'd ridden like that back on the border, I would have deserved to die," he agreed. "Now give me some more wine, Bandit Who Once Was a King, and try to stop gloating."

He tried to stand, but his legs gave way. I caught him, helped him up.

"I thank you, Damastes of Numantia, Shum á Cimabue," he said. "I wish I'd let them kill you back when we chased you across our border instead of playing the gentleman. Shit! Now you're more of a Negaret than I am, it appears."

It was Jedaz Faquet Bakr, leader of that Negaret tribe who'd met me at the Maisirian border and escorted me to Oswy. We'd ridden together, hunting, fishing, across the barren *suebi*, and I'd often thought enviously of his life.

"It's only fair we took you," I said. "Since you always insist on riding at the front."

This was true, and of course it made sense that the half-horse, half-men Negaret had been first to pursue us, Bakr and his men the first of the first.

"A little far forward this time."

"A little far forward," I agreed.

"I've been fighting fools for so long I've gotten careless about someone who has brains enough to trap his back trail." He sighed. "If you're of a mind to kill me, I wouldn't object that much. Perhaps I'm getting old and foolish, too old to lead my people."

"Yak shit," I retorted. "You're just a prisoner. Stop feeling sorry for yourself. When we leave, I'll cheerfully turn you loose, not even requiring parole, for I know you'd not honor it."

"What about you, Yonge?" Bakr said. Back then, Yonge had disappeared just before we came on the Negaret. I'd known the Man of the Hills had been a smuggler and bandit, but never that he knew Bakr, evidently well.

Yonge picked up the flask of wine from the courtyard floor, drank deeply, then refilled Bakr's flagon.

"You were a hard foe," he grudged. "But never murderous. I don't remember you ever killing any of my wounded unless they couldn't ride, nor was your name connected with evil.

"I welcome you, Negaret, as guest to our camp. Now drink your gods-damned wine. It's cold out here."

We sent out daily raids, but none as large as the first. One or two men would lurk on a trail and waylay a messenger; five men would ambush a supply convoy beyond Renan and fire its contents after looting what they had time to take; twenty men would rise from the brush and volley arrows into a patrol, then vanish.

My Kallians were particularly good at this, for this was the very war they'd waged against me.

Others, Tovieti, crept into the camp and killed when they could, with dagger or silken cord.

I was bringing terror to the Maisirians. We had only four killed and seven wounded in half a time and caused a hundred times more casualties among the enemy. I knew I had only a brief time before Bairan, his army, and his wizards moved on a large scale against us and I'd have to flee.

Each time we hit them with more than a few men, Bairan and his entourage would ride out from Renan, spend a day or less, no doubt tearing commanders apart and promoting, possibly even having those who'd failed killed, a rather self-defeating Maisirian custom.

Kutulu, Yonge, and I spent some time talking to Bakr, happily loosening his tongue with wine. Like the rest of the

Negaret, patriotism only applied when he was winning, so he wasn't reluctant to talk freely about what had happened since Bairan had come back from Numantia after humbling us.

"*Very* full of himself," Bakr said. "For the first time, I heard tales that our king was thinking beyond our borders. Why should we wait to be attacked by our old enemies on the south and east? Perhaps we should do what we did to you Numantians, except strike first.

"That, I must say, didn't meet with much approval at court, I heard. We've always held to our lasts, and expected others to do the same.

"So Bairan shut up. For a while. But I think he'd gotten the taste of being a conquering hero firm in his mouth, although all of us know Numantia was really beaten by Jedaz Winter and Jedaz Suebi, eh?

"That's his right," Bakr went on. "He's the king; kings think like that. Or, maybe *don't* think like that, for surely there's no logic or gain from such fantasies.

"He decided he was going to turn us Negaret into crack cavalry, and tried sending out some *jedaz* to various *lanx*es to train us, make us more like regular soldiers.

"Two, I heard, came to odd accidents. You remember the tale I once told you about the king's *shum* who slipped when walking by the river at night? At least one of those *jedaz* was given a liberal coating of tar and sent back to Jarrah without his pants. It was good that it was the hot season.

"Next the king decided he was going to destroy the Men in the Hills, in the Disputed Lands, which we all thought was stupid, because if that happened all the little city-piddlers would come to the frontiers for free land, and what would happen to us Negaret then?

"But," Bakr said, putting one finger beside his nose, "that was but a ruse, and for a moment I respected this Bairan, even though he wasn't a Negaret."

"Burning my frigging city wasn't much of a ruse," Yonge growled.

"Eh," Bakr said. "Cities are stones. You can always pile new ones on top of each other, can't you?"

Yonge was forced to grin and refilled Bakr's glass. I realized both he and the Negaret were a little drunk, and determined to seize the moment.

"Who's the new *azaz*?"

Bakr looked frightened for an instant, then covered his expression.

"I do not know, Damastes, and would never dream of asking. Perhaps there isn't one, for when we marched south I saw no particular pig of a wizard kissing the king's bum, but rather he was surrounded by a host of those mumbling men who wish they could become demons."

I found that interesting and had another question, after Yonge and Bakr had reminisced with a few tales of war and pillage.

"Something else, Jedaz Bakr," I said, keeping my voice casual, "with the king here in Numantia, who governs Maisir? His *ligaba*, Baron Sala?"

"You are a fool, Damastes," he answered, "and unwise in the ways of kings. Ligaba Sala, I have heard, is a man of wisdom, deep thoughts, and careful deeds, although I've not had the pleasure of meeting him."

"I know Sala," I said, remembering the man with the drooping moustaches and the infinitely sad eyes, as if he'd witnessed all the evil Man and Saionji could wreak. "Both in Numantia and in Jarrah, and he is indeed wise, and I would almost consider him a friend. But I don't understand why you call me a fool."

"Then you are doubly one, for what king would leave a wise man in charge of anything when he's away, for he might return to find a new man sitting his throne, a man who was once his *ligaba*? Baron Sala is with the king here in Numantia and lives with him in Renan, where they have commandeered palaces, without letting us poor Negaret have more than our black tents." He hiccuped.

"You didn't answer my question," I said. "Who rules Maisir in Bairan's stead?"

"No one," Bakr said. "For we are such a huge country it takes time for anything to have an effect. The king would have given explicit orders to his flunkies, and those mindless little asslickers will still be putting them into effect when we finish defeating you and return home."

"Bairan has no successor?"

"None he's recognized, and everyone would have heard if he did legitimize any of his bastards. Bairan prefers to keep everyone curious, so there can be no conspiracy and therefore no princeling to kill when he returns to Jarrah.

"I suppose he thinks that if Irisu is so stupid as to return him to the Wheel without a proper successor, then Maisir must have sinned and deserves the shambles it'll fall into.

"His father kept the same policy until he became very sick, then named Bairan's brother, who was too dumb to sit a throne, not unlike you, Numantian, for he went hunting one day with Bairan, and Bairan was the only one who rode back. I understand his brother had a magnificent funeral.

"His father died just after that, and we should all believe Bairan when he tells us it was a quiet, natural death." Bakr laughed.

"You see why you should not aspire to a throne, Damastes? Strange things happen."

The idea I'd had before, and set aside, came as a full-blown plan.

"Strange indeed," I said.

"I think he's mad," Cymea said. "Or suicidal. Don't you, Kutulu?"

The spymaster considered.

"No, not mad. But a dreamer. Damastes, what you envision cannot be done by a regiment or an army."

"No," I agreed. "Not with a regiment. But with three men, no more, I think I can break the Maisirians, send them scuttling home, and maybe live to tell the tale."

SIXTEEN

STALKING A KING

M y idea was quite simple—to enter the Maisirian
camp and make King Bairan come to me.
Then I'd murder him.

In the ensuing madness, I might even have a chance to
escape.

"Three men," Kutulu said. "Who?"

"Myself. Yonge, for he's the best scout we have. For a
third man, I'd like to have the archer, Curti, but he can't
move that well. I'll take Svalbard, for even one-armed he's
more dangerous than anyone I know with a full set of
limbs."

For an instant, I thought Kutulu wanted to volunteer,
but logic prevailed in his calm mind, and I was able to
avoid embarrassment. Instead, the problem came from
another quarter.

"You'll need a magician, to ward off casting spells from
their War Magicians," Cymea said.

"Not you," I said, instantly understanding her drift.
"And you're the only wizard I have here. The way I plan to
approach the king can't be done by more than three, and
two would be best."

"You'll be naked to their spells," Cymea said fiercely. "And die like a fool."

"Some say I've lived like one," I said. "No."

"Yes," Cymea said. "You've told me how you plan to get into the Maisirian camp. I'll go with you, then drop off before your attack. I'll be close enough," she said, her voice excited, "to ward off any castings that might reveal your presence."

There was merit to her words. A sorcerer *would* vastly increase the chance of success. It would be best if I took a combat-experienced magician instead of Svalbard, but I had none such with my raiders nor, with the exception of Sinait, with the army.

I thought of asking Cymea what would happen if the Maisirians found her, but we both knew the answer. It would be terrible, and the best she could hope was a swift death. Then I thought of a rather gruesome option.

"Very well," I said, which got a look of surprise from both Cymea and Kutulu. "You can go. But there'll be a fifth. Curti. And he'll have orders that neither of you is to be taken alive."

"I wouldn't allow that in any event," Cymea said. "But someone to guard my back when I'm mumbling nonsense and waving my hand around is a good idea. What are the chances of this succeeding?"

I thought honestly. "One in twenty . . . no, one in ten."

"Better than some we've faced," Kutulu said.

"Better than most *I've* seen," Cymea agreed.

Kutulu looked at me for a long time. He licked his lips, began to say something, then pressed them together and hurried out.

"That man likes . . . maybe loves you," Cymea said. "Not in a sexual sense."

I thought of telling her about Kutulu's former adulation for Tenedos, and how the once-emperor had betrayed that love, but didn't. Cymea started to leave, then turned back.

"I sense . . . I *feel* . . . something strange about your idea," she said. "This is more than just a maneuver, a tactic, to you."

"It is."

"You hate Bairan."

"I do."

"I think I need to know why," Cymea said. "Not from curiosity, but because your feelings must be masked by my magic, or they might be sensed too easily by the enemy."

I took a deep breath. So I was going to be forced to tell my story yet again.

"Sit down," I said.

It took far less time than I'd thought, for I didn't go into the details. Cymea was familiar with the type of spell the *azaz* had cast on me, although she'd never seen its casting. It wasn't as painful in the telling as before. Perhaps Karjan's murder was lying less heavily; perhaps the long process of becoming self-shriven was under way.

When I finished, I'd drained the tin pitcher of water beside me and almost wished for wine. I couldn't look at Cymea, so I don't know if she was staring.

"I sensed something, as I said," she said. "Nothing that terrible, though."

I looked up then and saw her face, pale with anger.

"What a monstrous bastard he is!" she said.

"Yes," I agreed. "And no. He's no more than a king, no more than anyone who has nobody to answer to, nothing over him, except the judgment of the gods when he dies, and who even knows if they exist?"

"They exist," she said. "I believe in them."

"I'm not sure I do. Not anymore."

She picked up her sword belt, started toward the door.

"You sensed something, eh?" I said, trying to end this on a lighter note. "The man who falls in love with you had best be faithful, for a cheat will evidently meet a swift doom by his own feelings."

She stopped, didn't turn.

"The man *I* choose will never look at another woman," she said, "because I'll keep him so happy he won't have the time or energy for anyone else!"

I tried to keep a straight face, failed, and am afraid a bit of a snicker came.

She started to stalk out, stopped once more, still didn't turn.

"Did that come out as arrogantly as I think?" she said.

"I'm afraid so."

"Oh hells," she said, then laughed. "So much for grand exits."

"I could never manage them either," I said, then I started laughing.

Strange merriment from two who were most likely going to die unpleasantly in the next few days.

My strategy was very simple: If we were able to kill King Bairan, what would his now-leaderless armies do? I'd seen how tightly they were controlled during the war, and how, if leadership was absent or removed, the Maisirian soldiery would flop about like so many headless chickens.

From what Bakr had told me, this invasion wasn't popular, only favored by the king. Without Bairan . . .

Cymea asked how, if we were successful, or if we were exposed, I intended to get out of the Maisirian camps.

I hadn't much of a plan, other than scouring the map for possible routes, so I told her, "My stealth and my terror will give me a plan at the proper time. I hope."

"You definitely need a sorcerer," she said firmly. "Or a caretaker. Look you. Why can't we get out the same way we go in?"

"I thought of that," I said. "But I've no way of knowing how long the stalk will take. The best we can do is try to get outside their lines to the assembly point I've set on the map. Hopefully there'll be horses there, and a couple of men waiting, and then we can ride away into Kallio." I stopped. "You know, when I came up with that plan, it sounded somewhat feasible. Now . . ." I didn't say anything more.

"I can enchant something, give it to Kutulu, and it'll respond to my signal," Cymea said. "I'll also need spittle and a bit of blood from everyone. And I've already set up amulets that'll guide us like compasses toward that assembly point."

"I thought magic was going to be supporting me, not taking this whole thing over," I said.

"At the proper time, the best always rise to the top. Like cream."

"Or pond scum," I added.

She made a face, hurried away, and I went back to my maps, thinking perhaps it was very well Cymea hated war so passionately. She was beginning to behave like that most fearsome of all soldiers, a born warrior.

We used the Seeing Bowl to scout the target area three times; I then forbade it as the attack date grew closer, for fear of alerting Bairan's magicians. I noted, close to the target itself, an overgrown topiary garden for a hiding place. Cymea also noted it, and said, thoughtfully, "I may be able to do something there that'll surprise you."

"Like what?"

"Now, if I told you, it wouldn't be a surprise, would it?"

Once before, at Sidor, I'd flummoxed the Maisirians by marching into their midst quite openly. I proposed to do much the same thing again, with only a slight variation.

One of Cymea's Tovieti had told us of an old road that led to Renan, abandoned for some twenty years and forgotten. Parts of this road had been used to make up the new, improved route, which was perfect for my intent.

Again, we'd attack at full strength, and at dusk we made ready to leave the castle. This would be the last time any of us would see it, no matter which way things went.

My plan was to attack the Maisirians, and the assassination team would use the confusion to infiltrate to the target. If we were successful in killing Bairan, or if we were forced to abort, a second feint would be made by my raiders as cover for us to get out.

Then the entire force was to withdraw through a given series of assembly points into Kallio.

I hoped that the five of us would be able to rejoin them somewhere along that route.

The Time of Rains had come to an end, and the Time of Change brought sharp, cold wind whistling.

"Well, Kutulu," I said, "you've always wanted to command soldiers . . . now you've got your chance."

"I can only hope I do well."

"If you don't, we'll all see you on the Wheel," I said.

"Then I'll do well for certain." He looked at his horse. "As I said once before, one of these days I'll find a profession that doesn't require the use of these monsters."

The five of us would ride at the head of the formation, and I'd command the initial attack. Curti and Cymea were dressed as Maisirian *shamb,* officers low-ranking enough to be ignored by their superiors, but still to be kowtowed to by any lower-ranking soldier, the rest as Maisirian *calstors,* warrants but not of any particular importance. The uniforms had been taken from Maisirian dead and altered to fit by Curti, who surprisingly had quite a talent with a needle, thread, and scissors.

The three who'd go after Bairan carried bows, short but powerful recurves used by the skirmishers and by jungle hunters, slung on our backs, short swords and daggers. In our pockets we carried the round iron pigs so useful as hurled weapons or clenched in the fist.

As I pulled myself into the saddle, Svalbard clapped Curti on the back.

"Here we go again," he said. "Death or glory, eh?"

"Something like that," Curti muttered, sounding uncharacteristically glum.

"Come on, man," Svalbard said. "Cheer up, I wager I'll pass you running when the shitting and shooting starts."

"I'll see you again," Curti said. "But not in this life, my friend."

He mounted, and Svalbard, without replying, did the same. We rode out from the castle for the last time.

I'd planned to leave the three prisoners we'd taken, two Maisirian officers plus Bakr, tied with ensorcelled ropes inside the castle, but Cymea had taken me aside and said, "If you really want them to live on, I'd not leave them bound inside these walls. That which is dead, but not dead, might be tempted."

I thought . . . hoped . . . she was being overly sensitive

but still had the three taken to the creek down from the castle and lashed to trees.

I ordered the column to halt as we passed and rode over to Bakr. The other two Maisirians were deathly pale, obviously certain I'd butcher them now rather than leaving them the slightest possibility of escape.

Bakr tugged at his bonds. "You're certain your witch, your *nevraid*, didn't make a mistake?"

"I hope not," I said. "But if she did, I'll visit this place when there's peace and make sacrifice to your bones."

"Don't try to be clever, Shum á Cimabue. But I wish to thank you for treating me honorably as a captive, even though you didn't provide me with a woman. I would have given you one."

"Didn't happen to have one around," I said cheerfully. "Dreadfully sorry."

"I'll forgive you," Bakr said. "But let me ask something. You talked about when peace comes. What will you do then?"

"I don't expect to live that long," I said, suddenly somber.

"Come, man! Be foolhardy! Assume you do make it. What then?"

I shook my head, no thought coming.

"Typical soldier," Bakr said. "Whyn't you cross the border, though Irisu alone knows what the borders will be like after the fighting stops, and I doubt if he's certain."

"What, and become a Negaret?"

"Of course," he said. "Call yourself by another name, and no one in Jarrah will give a rat's ass who you really are. Join my *lanx* for a year, maybe two, then I'll stand you for a *lanx* of your own the next time we gather for a *riet*. Then you'll be as free as I am, living your own life with no one to answer to but the gods and yourself in the mirror. Bring that wizard you've got as your woman if you want. She's pretty and seems not to mind living like an animal. Eh? Is that not an attractive proposal?"

I thought of several responses, but my horse stamped impatiently.

Without a response, I saluted him and rode back to the column and on toward the Maisirians.

I was glad Cymea hadn't heard the last part of his words, suspecting she'd rage at any fool thinking she'd do anything with anyone that wasn't her idea.

Then I wondered at myself, even thinking about her.

The old road was choked with brush, and it took a bit of pushing to force our way to it. Then the rutted way was open, and we rode up it, in a column of twos, as it wound around rolling hills.

About three leagues inside the Maisirian lines, we stopped.

Cymea dismounted, drew figures, and sprinkled herbs. "They have watchers out," she said when she finished, "but it's as if they're atop a hill, looking here and there, so far seeing nothing, I think, for I sensed no alarm. It's interesting that so far the Maisirians haven't done any of the great magic you told me they worked during the war.

"Maybe that *azaz* you told me about had the only real talent, or maybe he got rid of others who were equally gifted and used only hacks in his corps. But that's only a theory.

"I think a real problem with their magic is they aren't using local materials, but rather the herbs and such they brought from Maisir, so their spells aren't as effective as they would be with matter more easily able to call to its own, plus they're feeling a bit insecure in foreign lands. Great magic requires some arrogance, since you're forcing your will on stubborn matter or even more stubborn people or demons.

"Also, maybe they're doing it by rote, the way you told me their army usually does things."

A horse nickered, and Cymea grimaced.

"I'm babbling, aren't I? It's because I'm scared."

"Who isn't?" I said. "Let's go."

She smiled wryly, and I had the sudden, odd urge to kiss her.

She looked at me for a moment, as if expecting something, then remounted, and I told the point men to go cross-country until we cut the new road.

When we did, we rode brazenly down it, with two outriders in front, lances held high with scraps of cloth tied to them, like banners. We looked like a company of Negaret or light cavalry returning from a scout, or so I hoped.

We were challenged once by sentries, and I shouted some gobbledygook in Maisirian. That must've been enough, for no one shot at us or sounded an alarm.

We rode deep into the valley's center, our target a series of stables for remounts that looked, in the Seeing Bowl, lightly guarded.

Beyond the paddocks were tents, temporarily unoccupied as far as we could tell, and then the estate King Bairan had commandeered.

I was about to call for the trot, when the lead rider pulled up abruptly. If we hadn't been riding in extended order, we would have banged into each other like a line of stones a child pushes over with a finger.

Sometime in the past few hours, after the last scout had withdrawn through the lines, somebody'd built a sawhorsed barricade of logs across the road and topped it with thorny branches.

Why this unexpected roadblock? Did it mean they knew we were coming and had set an ambush? If so, it was badly laid—they should have let us ride unknowing into the killing zone before springing the trap.

"Four men," I ordered. "With ropes. Pull it away."

The barricade was quickly dragged back. No arrows sang about my head, and we remounted and rode on.

I signaled for the trot, and our horses moved eagerly, seemingly as anxious to end the suspense as any man.

The paddock was just ahead, and, as ordered, my men took out the first of the two packs they carried inside their jackets, out of the weather.

Cymea had used spells of contagion and similarity. Three or four of my raiders knew how to whittle out whistles from wood, and so details had been sent to scour the banks of the nearby river for lengths of willow for them. Each of these whistles was given a spell by Cymea. Then the whistles were cut into bits, and each fragment had been given a third spell that afternoon, so the second spell was invoked when water touched them.

These bits were hurled into the paddock, into the mire beneath the horses' hooves, and as they struck they began whistling, but not the cheery whistle they should've made, but a shrill dissonance, like the warning of ravens, but louder, harsher.

The horses reared in fear, pawed at the air, and pulled away from their picket lines. The shrilling grew louder, and the animals panicked, and ropes broke, and the horses stampeded wildly. This I hated doing, for sometimes I think I love horses better than men. But I threw my pouch with the others.

We went into the gallop, toward the tents, and again I shouted an order, and the second packs, these fire-twigs, were thrown.

"Kutulu! Take command!" I called, heard him shout acknowledgment, and I pulled out of the formation with my four, and we rode hard down the tent row, away from the clamor and madness as my raiders cut a swath through the Maisirians. The enemy was a bit more watchful than before but still seemed fuddled that we'd dared to invade the heart of their camp. Only two men ran in front of us, and they went down as we passed.

Ahead was the grand estate of King Bairan, and we galloped toward it. The estate was surrounded by stone walls, as white as the buildings within. We slid out of our saddles, grabbed our kit, and clapped our horses on the withers. They nickered reluctance, were struck again, and this time they trotted away.

Two hundred yards on either side of us, around curvings of the wall, were the main gates, and I heard the shouting of sentries as the guard was reinforced.

"Go," I ordered, and Cymea and Curti ran back into the maze of tents. I thought—perhaps hoped—she took time for a glance back before she vanished.

I used Svalbard's cupped hand as a ladder to get to the top of the wall. There was no glass or embedded knives—Urey had been a fairly peaceful land before the wolves came. I braced, gave Yonge a hand up. He eeled over and dropped to the ground. Svalbard braced a boot on the wall, came up with me, and we went over into the estate.

I took a moment to establish the manor's layout in my mind. On either side of me was the long main entrance road, a C-shaped curve from gate to gate whose midpoint was in front of the main building. Ahead was the still-uncut wheat that stretched for a third of a league, then what I thought were wells, then the topiary garden in front of the mansion. To my left, east, were fruit trees and then vine-yards. To the right, or west, were more wheat fields and then stables, with outbuildings to the side. There were long barracks for workers to the rear of the main building, then orchards and more fields until the rear wall of the grounds.

The sounds of battle were dying away as my raiders fell back through the lines.

Yonge crouched a few feet away, blackness against lesser dark. I came up beside him and scribed a question mark in the air.

"They've plowed the field around the wall," he whispered. "Maybe for planting, maybe to show footsteps. You lead; I'll clean the track."

I obeyed, moving slowly, crouched, toward the wheat field. Svalbard stepped where I did, Yonge to the rear in a duckwalk, smoothing our footsteps in the turned earth.

Half a dozen times we froze as riders holding lanterns high galloped into the estate, no doubt reporting on the raid. Then we reached the wheat, and Yonge took the lead, showing us how to move quickly through the rows, bend-ing back the shoots we'd touched, zigging so our track toward the mansion wouldn't be obvious to anyone look-ing down, either from a tree, rooftop, or magically.

We had to move quickly, before the dew came, for we'd then draw a most obvious line as we shook the moisture off the plants.

I hoped to be in position, across the fields and hiding somewhere in the garden, waiting King Bairan's arrival, within two hours.

We'd made it two-thirds of the way through the field when disaster came.

I hadn't dared sending Cymea's magic over the area for two days.

In that time, they'd begun to cut the wheat.

Now there was several hundred yards of open land, the scythed plants no more than knee high, between us and the gloom-ridden garden before the main building.

But it wasn't so gloomy that I couldn't see sentries pacing back and forth outside the garden.

I considered cutting through the wheat toward the entrance road and chancing a shot from there when Bairan came. But it would be too far a shot to chance, and Bairan would be in a carriage. All that would happen is we'd be killed without accomplishing anything.

Yonge and Svalbard waited, perhaps expecting I'd abort. Instead, I went to my knees, and began crawling, moving slowly, but ever aware of the swiftly passing night.

It was agonizing after a dozen yards, muscles not used to this strange exercise, hands bruised by the stubble, deadly after that. We crawled on, and I became aware the night was ebbing and the world was gray.

I crawled on, Yonge and Svalbard behind me, but now on my belly, moving one knee and hand up, then the other, then the first, over and over.

Overcast dawn came, and the wind whipped cold. I was soaked from the sodden ground and wanted to rest, but knew I mustn't.

My hand moved out, and something hissed.

I became stone, turned my head, and stared at the small green serpent. It was no more than a forearm in length, but I knew it for the deadly viper it was. Its tongue flickered in and out, perhaps in alarm, or perhaps that was its way of sensing its surroundings. There was no movement to my rear, and I was grateful for Yonge and Svalbard, who'd learned years ago to never question a patrol leader's movements, no matter how strange.

The snake's mouth opened farther, and its fangs gleamed white, but I never moved or breathed.

The serpent slid forward, across my arm, and my nerves screamed as it slipped down my side, then turned, and coiled away through the remains of the wheat.

My breath came out with a gasp, and I'd not realized I'd been holding it for what, an instant, a month, a year?

Very suddenly I was shaking, and then the shaking was gone and I was calm again.

I crawled on toward the garden.

Where was King Bairan? Surely he must've been told of the latest raid and was riding toward the valley, unless my pinpricks had become familiar and he no longer bothered to consult or rail at his generals.

I didn't know, and there wasn't anything I could do but crawl on.

We heard voices, sharp commands in Maisirian, other, lower tones I couldn't make out. I didn't know what was happening but pressed close to the ground, motionless.

I heard footsteps, looked up to the side, and saw two Maisirian soldiers, not ten feet distant, looming high like giants. They were chattering away about the night's raid and how one of them had almost gotten a clear chance at one of those bandits, had fired anyway, and perhaps he'd struck one, although he'd heard there were only one or two enemy casualties.

"They're like fucking ghosts," his companion said. "I don't think they're out there in front of us at all. I think they're hiding in secret caves here in the valley, and all our magic is looking in the wrong direction."

"Surely, caves," the other scorned. "That's why I see you volunteering for patrols outside the line every day, out where they aren't, where it's safe."

"I said that's what I *think*," the other growled. "And I'm no more a fool of a volunteer than you are."

"It isn't right for the king's own guards to get themselves killed on some shitty little patrol," the other agreed, but they'd passed on, and I could hear no more.

The other voices grew closer, and now I could tell they were speaking in the Ureyan dialect. They were close, very close, and then a bare foot came down on my hand. I looked up, almost came to my feet, staring into the shocked eyes of a boy no more than ten or eleven. He wore ragged clothes, a crudely cut canvas jacket against the chill, and held a scythe. He was one of the workers harvesting the wheat, guarded by the Maisirians.

My other hand slid to my dagger. I could have come up like the serpent who'd almost struck me, brought the boy down, and killed him without a murmur, without a struggle. Then we could have either pulled out or gone on, hoping his corpse wouldn't be found for a few hours.

But I didn't. I stared deep into his eyes, wished I had the powers of a wizard, and murmured, "We fight for Numantia." I hoped he'd discount the uniforms we wore.

He showed no sign of understanding.

"Go. Don't report us. Please. We are Numantian soldiers on a secret mission."

Again, nothing, then he edged around me, always facing me, waiting for death. I knew he was going to run, going to start screaming, but he didn't. He backed away a few steps, then turned and walked on.

I was lying on my side, looking after him, and saw Yonge and Svalbard staring, waiting for orders.

I motioned.

On toward the house.

Yonge bared his fangs at me, but obeyed, and we crawled on, muscles screaming, still waiting for the guards to begin shouting.

Then we reached the end of the badly harvested land. There were three artesian wells in front of us, and I heard the purl of the water, saw it bubble out of the brick pools, and felt the parch in my throat. I looked for the sentries, but there was no one. Either the guards were out with the harvesters, or the mansion's garden was only posted at night.

I came to a crouch, went forward like a rockape, hands almost brushing the ground, and was down again behind the brickwork. Yonge and Svalbard were beside me, and for an instant our guard slipped, cupped hands splashing water into our mouths, and I can seldom remember a sweeter drink.

But that was only for an instant, and then we slid into the garden, its paths winding through the tall bushes, once carefully sculpted, now abandoned. I could still recognize some of the topiary, dragons, lions, elephants; others were overgrown or fantastic beasts I didn't know. All were evergreens and gave good concealment.

We hid, and there was now nothing to do but wait, praying that boy wouldn't change his mind.

An hour passed, then another, and I knew Bairan wasn't coming and everything had been wasted, when guards began scurrying back and forth around the house, and officers shouted orders, and the men formed up and were marched back toward the estate's entrance, leaving two, no four, guards at rigid attention, and three or four officers pacing anxiously.

We slipped through the garden closer to the mansion. Bairan's carriage would come up the drive in front of us, and he would dismount and go up the steps into the building.

In that instant, we'd fire, and kill a king.

We readied bows, nocked arrows. As I'd been trained, I began breathing deeply, calming myself. I held out my hand, and it was rigid, still.

Horses' hooves made a drumroll, and cavalry trotted around the bend, then past us. Three carriages came next, one very ornate, drawn by six matching, beautiful bays, the other two not much more than ambulances.

The carriage stopped, fifty feet away, and our bows came up.

The door opened, and a cloaked figure started out.

Our bows were drawn, aimed, as King Bairan stepped out.

In that instant, just before loosing, one of the king's equerries jumped down from the carriage's driver's bench, between us and our target.

Svalbard growled, not realizing it, a lion cheated of his prey, and I looked for a chance to shoot, any chance, no matter how feeble, seeing once more that imposing figure, half a head taller than I, hawk face hard with power and arrogance, and gods be damned, there was no chance, no way, we'd lost our opportunity, and I dropped the bow and jumped out of my concealment, into plain view in front of the horses for an instant, then behind a bush at the mansion's steps, up them, and through the open, unattended doors, all eyes on the king and his courtiers prancing before him.

The hall was large, leading straight through the house, and chambers led off it. I saw a curtain, jerked it open, saw hanging cloaks, and was inside, pulling the curtain across, mind seething, lungs gasping as if I'd run for leagues. My dagger was in one hand, smallsword in the other.

Voices grew closer, and I knew one of them, that confident rumble, then others, agreeing, some lilting in fear, some soothing, and they were close, very close.

I tore the curtain open, and a man shrieked in terror, screaming like a woman, and King Bairan was standing no more than three feet away. He'd unclasped his cloak, and an aide was lifting it off his shoulders.

He saw me, and his mouth opened. I'm not sure, but I think he remembered me, knew me, and I leapt across the distance like a tiger, and Yonge's silver dagger buried itself to the hilt in his guts, and I drove it upward, turning the blade, feeling it tear and rip his heart open.

Bairan made a terrible noise, a gagging groan, and blood gouted from his mouth into my face, and I kneed him away, pulled the blade free. A fiercely bearded man wearing the emblems of a *rast* was pulling at his ornate sword, and he died, and I was running toward the door.

Standing beside it was Ligaba Khwaja Sala, once almost my friend, and I think he knew what I had to do, for he was the best Maisir had, their hope with their king dead, and my blade flickered through his throat under his moustaches, and he spun and fell, and I was out the door.

A sentry saw me, waved feebly with his pike, dropped it and fled.

"This way," I shouted, and Yonge and Svalbard ran toward me. All behind was screams, shouts, frenzy, and I paid no mind but ran for the side of the house, running for its rear, hoping to break away in the confusion, my mind drumming over and over, *he's dead, the king is dead, Karjan is revenged . . . I am revenged . . . the bastard is dead, the king is dead . . .*

Bugles hammered to my left, and the king's escort turned back, and, lances leveled, was in a ragged line, charging away from the drive after us. All of us knew better than to run from a horseman, and so we stopped, spread out, steel in hand, ready to take as many of them to the Wheel as we could.

This was the end, but it was a warrior's end, and who could die more easily than a soldier who'd slain his country's greatest enemy?

I felt the smile on my lips and felt a strange, singing joy I've known but seldom, as the first rider's lance drove toward me.

I brushed it aside with my sword, stepped forward, and sliced his horse's throat. The horse screamed, went to its knees, pitching the rider into a tree, and there was another rider beside me, and I drove my sword into his side, and he rolled out of the saddle, and now there was a whirl of horses and men, the cavalrymen taken aback at the temerity of three men attacking an entire squadron. But the surprise would last only a moment, and then we'd swiftly be returned to the Wheel. I had time to wonder how Saionji would judge me, would judge the killing of Bairan, but there were two men coming at me, swords flashing.

Then came the coughing roar of a lion. I flashed a glance to the side and saw the great beast as it leapt completely over me, onto the back of a horse, its claws ripping the rider away, but the beast was green, green as grass, and behind it an elephant, also green, trumpeted its challenge and rumbled forward, trunk coiled, then hammer-striking a cavalryman out of his saddle with it.

The horses, untrained around elephants, went momentarily mad, kicking, bucking, stampeding. There were soldiers afoot, but there were other beasts attacking them, tigers, strange winged snakes, claws, fangs, all of them green, and this was Cymea's promised surprise, her magic had animated the topiary bushes, as great a spell as any I'd seen cast by the greatest of wizards, the Seer King Tenedos.

Other beasts were roaring out of the garden, boars, enraged gaurs, and I shouted to Svalbard and Yonge, and we were running. Blood was trickling down Yonge's arm, and Svalbard was favoring a leg, but we ran hard, behind the mansion, cutting behind the stables and through the orchards. One farmworker saw us, thought about shouting alarm, dove into a pig wallow instead.

I heard distant shouting, which would be my raiders feinting again against the Maisirian positions, but only a feint, intended merely as a diversion to help our escape, and then the back wall was there.

We scrambled over it and ran for another mile, then slowed to a walk, sheathing our weapons, as we came on another camp, trying to look like no more than Maisirian soldiers heading for a post somewhere. We tried to look solemn, but were hard-pressed to not laugh, not caper like fools.

We'd done the impossible.

We'd killed the king of Maisir and his most trusted adviser.

Now all we had to do was the impossible once more and escape with our lives.

HUNTED

O ur intent was to loop south, then west and north, through their lines to the pickup point, where horses were to be waiting for us.

But this was impossible. The Maisirians were like wasps that have just had their hive banged on by a child's stick. They swarmed here and there, sometimes in regimental formation, sometimes squads, sometimes single men. I couldn't tell if they were looking for us or just stumbling around, confused and enraged by the loss of Bairan.

But they were everywhere, and one incoherent stumbler could be as fatal as an organized sweep.

We went south almost to the ends of the valley, then ran into a cavalry screen that stopped us cold. I decided to go to ground for a time. We refilled our canteens at a stream, waded up it to leave no sign to either tracker or magician. The stream wound past a knoll high enough for an over-look that would give warning of intruders, and its top was covered with brambles.

We forced ourselves into its midst, then waited. The elation drained away, and now there was nothing but fear. If we were discovered, we'd have to go down fighting, for the most creative torturers the Maisirians had would be turned loose on us.

The day ended, and a long, cold night crawled past. I hoped Cymea and Curti had better luck than we did and had gotten through to safety. I realized I was worrying more about her than if she were just another soldier. Very well, I thought, it's because she's a woman, and, yes, very beautiful, but that still wasn't enough explanation.

I turned away from those thoughts and took out my map. Nothing much came, except to stay where we were until the heat died. The word heat brought shivers . . . it was getting colder, and I sensed a storm coming.

Then dawn came. Yonge dug a tunnel, a mole tunnel, to the outside of the thicket, not for entry or exit, but for observation. Sometime about dank midday he finished his slow, silent digging, and everything was quiet except for the rattle of raindrops and the occasional dejected chirp of a wet bird.

I admired Svalbard, for he had the ability to sleep or become a silent stone for hours.

As for myself, I tried to think beyond this dripping clump of thorny brush. The memory of warm fires came, honey-sweetened mugs of spice drink, and that led naturally to food. We hadn't brought anything to eat, not wanting to burden ourselves, and no one had been vaguely hungry until now.

I remembered one meal in the greatest detail. It was years ago, and I'd been assigned by the Emperor Tenedos to a mission in Hailu, one that, strangely enough, didn't involve applying the empire's iron boot to someone. I'd been returning from consultations with a local official, on a dreary day like this one, without escort, without bodyguard, when night caught me on the road and I was sure

I'd be stuck, trying to pretend a tree was a proper roof, when I came on a tiny country inn.

The innkeeper wasn't the best-tempered sort, nor were his half-dozen children and slatternly wife. But the room was spotless, the linen was clean, and the meal, ah, that meal. It began with a clear soup, with two mushrooms, spices, and a few diced green onions. Then there was a country pâté; trout broiled and seasoned with a strange spice that was alternately bitter, then sweet; young lamb chops in a mustard sauce with the freshest of garden vegetables; a cool drink of various fruits, followed by—

Yonge hastily crawled backward out of the tunnel. He motioned us to him, whispered, "The whole fucking Maisirian army's on the march! Straight toward us!"

I was halfway down the tunnel, forcing my bulk through places Yonge would've slid through like a serpent, peered out.

The Man of the Hills wasn't exaggerating. On both sides of our knoll were long columns of infantry and cavalry, all moving steadily south. Back toward Maisir!

We'd won! Then I saw smoke clouds billowing across the horizon to the north.

The Maisirians *were* retreating, but taking vengeance as they did, burning everything, fields, houses, villages as they went. I knew there were sprawled bodies and screaming innocents below those distant flames.

Once again, Urey was being put to the sword, and I'd been the cause.

I'd been afraid this would happen if I was successful. But I'd seen no other choice—it was either Numantia or Urey.

This was the sort of high judgment kings make and possibly glory in their great vision and power, but it nauseated me. I didn't want to see any more of my handiwork and crawled back.

"We broke them," Yonge whispered fiercely, and Svalbard nodded, a broad smile on his face. I'm sure they thought there was something wrong with me, that I felt no second onrush of joy.

The Maisirians grew closer, and there were more of them. Svalbard put an ear to the ground, waved at me, and I did the same. The ground was rumbling faintly from the million marching men, their wagons and horses.

All we had to do was wait until they passed, then make our way into Kallio and reunite with my army.

I no longer dreamed of meals but relearned the stoicism of a soldier, to simply wait until something came, without fear, without hope, without, in fact, thought. We just sat, half-asleep, swords ready, boots touching so anyone hearing anything could alert the other two.

In midafternoon, Yonge kicked me. But I was already alert. I'd heard the sound a moment after he did. Someone was pushing his way slowly into our thicket, moving directly, like a pigeon in sight of its coop.

Svalbard moved to one side of the tiny clearing, Yonge to the other. The intruder would come out between them and be dead before he could sound the alarm.

The rustling came closer, then stopped. A voice came.

"This is Cymea. Don't kill me."

There's an old vulgarism—I didn't know whether to shit or go blind—and that perfectly described the three of us.

I finally managed: "Come ahead," and the bedraggled magician pushed her way through the last brambles and I had her in my arms. She looked startled, then gave me a one-handed hug. The other still held her ready sword.

Embarrassed, I let her go.

"They backtracked us after I cast that spell against the garden," she said, without preamble. "The king's magicians must've been very alert, if slow. We cut our way out the back of the tent we'd been hiding in, and there were five soldiers coming toward us.

"We ran, but Curti's leg slowed him. He told me to go on, that he'd hold them."

Now tears came, in a slow trickle.

"I refused, and he cursed me. Then I did as he told me. There wasn't time for me to cast a spell. Did I do right? Should I have stayed with him?"

Before I could answer, Svalbard rumbled, "You didn't do anything wrong. What would two deaths rather than one have gained?"

She dropped the sword, slumped on the ground. "That's what my mind says. But not the rest of me."

"He told me his doom before we left the castle," the big man said. "Perhaps he wanted death. Perhaps he'd had enough. I've seen it happen before. And he died saving somebody else, which isn't a bad way to go back to the Wheel."

Yonge said, correctly but a bit coldly, "A magician is harder to replace than any archer."

Cymea looked at me. For a brief moment I mourned Curti, who'd been with me since Kait, the best bowman I'd ever know, yet a man I'd always taken for granted, a friend but not a friend, and I should've told him how much he meant, always at my back, never someone I doubted for an instant. Slowly the best of the warriors were being taken away, and I could only hope Saionji judged them mercifully.

All these thoughts flashed, and I knew I couldn't hesitate.

"Cymea, there wasn't anything else to be done. Forget about it. Every time you fight, someone dies, and all you can do is keep going. We'll sacrifice for Curti when we're safe, and drink to him until we die."

I'd said—and meant—words like that before. This time, they felt hollow. But I couldn't think of anything better.

Cymea took a deep breath. "All right. What happened, happened," she said. "Your plan worked. The Maisirians are fleeing Urey. What do we do now?"

I told her what I'd planned.

"So we just wait?" she said.

"Yes," I said. "Once it's dark, then perhaps we'll chance moving. Or wait until the morrow."

"I don't suppose," Svalbard said, a bit of hope in his voice, "you've brought anything to eat?"

"No, unless you like dried herbs that might turn you into a mandrill."

"My belly isn't that pissed at me," he said.

"Then we just wait," Cymea said.

But we didn't . . . not for very long.

It was almost dusk when we heard the drum rattles. The sound swept an arc east northwest, and this time I went up the tunnel.

It was bad, very bad. About a third of a league distant, two lines of soldiers swept toward us, movement regulated by the drummers. They were sweeping slowly, methodically, and they could have but one prey. I craned out and saw, to the north, a single robed figure directing them.

I went back and reported.

"They've tracked me," Cymea said. "Hells!"

I was puzzled.

"A magician leaves, well, a scent, sort of," she explained. "Another magician can use his wiles to follow that trace. If

I'd had time, I could have swept my tracks clean, but I didn't have that luxury. Honestly, I didn't think I'd have to.

"And now I've led the Maisirians to you."

"The hells with blame," I said. "What can we do about it? Run?"

"If they're almost all around us," Yonge said, "aren't they like the peasants you hire to drive sambur into the trap? Don't they *want* us to move south, toward what looks like the only way out, where they've got to have a killing team waiting?"

"Probably," I said.

"I'd chance a seeing spell," Cymea said, a bit forlornly, "but that'd be like a lodestone to iron."

"What'll they have waiting for us, if we do run?" I asked.

"Magicians," Cymea said. "Soldiers."

"The only way to break a trap," Svalbard said, by rote, as we'd all learned, "is to do something unexpected. Bust an ambush by going straight into them."

"We're a little short of troops for that," Yonge said.

"If we could get rid of that magician," Cymea said. "Then, maybe . . ."

"At least we'd better get our gear on," I said, "and get out of this hidey-hole that's become a snare."

We worked our way to the fringes of the thicket. The sweepers were closer now, working methodically, and yes, I was reminded of beaters driving game.

I scanned the terrain around us, looking for an escape. The brook we'd waded up swept past the knoll, then on, curving north, bare brush on its banks, which were about four feet above the shallow water.

"There's a way out," I pointed. "But that gods-damned

sorcerer would surely sense us . . . Yonge, could you hit him with an arrow at this range?"

Yonge considered. "Not I. Not even, given the wind's against us, could this great lump beside me, even if he had both arms and an eye like mine."

Svalbard curled a lip, said nothing.

An idea came:

"Cymea, do you know a spell that'd draw that wizard to us?"

"Of course, but—"

"Could you reverse it?"

"Oh," she said, understanding. "Easily."

"And is there any reason you can't make an arrow fly like a bird?"

"Simple."

"Course she could," Svalbard said. "That's why they don't allow witches anywhere close to a shooting match."

Cymea scrabbled in her pack for the necessaries. Yonge spotted a rather bedraggled bird's feather in the brush, brought it to her as she scribbled on a bit of parchment, strange letters I didn't know. The parchment itself was odd, dark green in color, not cream or white. As she wrote, she was whispering, the same words over and over.

"Now, Damastes," she said, "give me one of your arrows." I obeyed, and she touched its fletching with the feather, chanting softly:

"Remember what you were
Before man
Before pain
Remember wind
Coursing under your wings
Turning

Floating
High-flying
Now you live
Elyot claims you
Give heed
Give speed
Take flight."

Perhaps it was my imagination in the fading light, but I swear the arrow stirred, as if coming alive. Cymea used a bit of string to tie the parchment around its shaft.

"Now, give your best aim at that wizard."

"Don't blame me," I said, "if the arrow comes out spinning like a whirligig. Just getting it away'll be a bit of a miracle."

"I deal in miracles," Cymea said sharply. "Now shoot!"

I closed my eyes, half to sense the wind, half to pray to Panoan, to Isa, to Tanis, then brought the bow to full draw.

I opened them, looking at that distant wizard, the man who sought our doom, considering him coldly, without anger, as my prey.

I wished Curti wasn't dead, for he might make this shot, which I could not. I remembered all he had taught me over the years about archery, how a master archer waits for the moment when the arrow is ready, when it shoots itself.

Perhaps his spirit came back from the Wheel or wherever it'd gone, or just his memory, for my fears dropped away, and I felt one with yew, with ash, with the string, and my fingers opened and the arrow sped away.

It curved high, sailing farther than I'd ever shot in my life, then dropped, as if traveling on a line strung between my bow and that distant, robed figure.

For a moment I lost its fall, then saw the magician fling his hands high, stagger, and go down.

I whispered thanks to Tanis, looked at Svalbard, whose eyes were wide in awe.

But I still think it was not me who made the shot, but Curti.

Soldiers shouted alarm, seeing their master dead on the ground, and the searchers' careful line broke apart. Men were running here and there, some to the dead wizard, others shouting orders, some firing arrows at who knew what.

"Now," I said. "Down the hill into that creek and away."

"No," Yonge said firmly. "That's your path. With her. Svalbard, you and I'll find another way."

"Don't be stupid!"

"I'm not, you gods-damned Numantian! You two are more important than we are, and that's the best route. Don't think I'm playing hero," he said. "Two are less visible than four. And I'm not a stumble-witted Numantian nor a spastic Maisirian."

"But—"

"Sit on your butt later," he said. "Now go, before they recover! Come on, Svalbard! Let's find another place to harry them from, and then we'll haul ass."

He was right, and Cymea and I went down the hill without being seen. We slipped into the creek and crept away, past the line of soldiers, and were gone, into the coming night.

And all the while my mind keened the death of two more of the best.

EIGHTEEN

THE RIVER

Renan was a city of flames and fear, light flickering across the tossing waters of the Latane River, smoke swirling in the cold wind. It'd been savaged once by the Maisirians during the war, its ancient beauty and charm violated, its canals polluted, its lakes churned muddy by soldiery.

Afterward, it had begun to rebuild, its fathers trying to recapture the charms of its winding lanes, leaning buildings, and gardens.

Now the fire had come again, and Renan was madness.

Cymea and I had tried to turn north or east, but the press of the retreating Maisirians had pulled us south with them. We'd been able to cross three or four of their columns, but only by moving west toward Urey's capital, directly away from the way we wanted to flee.

Soldiers scurried here, there, some intent on their own business of blood and loot, others staying with their columns. We moved with them, no one realizing who we were. Twice drunkards saw Cymea was a woman, thought she was part of my loot, tried to take her.

Once two men died, and two more writhed in their

blood; the second time only two went down. Cymea killed one, I cut the guts out of the other, and their fellows lost interest in rape.

I spoke fluent Maisirian, so was able to move through the pack, shouting occasional orders, just another arrogant *shamb* or *shalaka* without his troops.

We reached the high stone bridges that looped across the Latane from islet to islet into Renan, and here the press was terrible. It was just short of a panic, and I was afraid of being crushed if we pushed on. I managed to pull Cymea into a niche in one of the low parapets before the bridge, out of the eddy of wagons and men.

If it was madness on this side of the river, it was far worse on the other. I hesitated, wondering what we should do next.

Cymea was half-sitting on the low parapet, and looked over at the dark, chill Latane River, rolling past below.

"Look," she said, pointing.

I saw a boat, held by the current against the nearest piling. It was fat-bellied, a half-scale navigable version of the famous lake houseboats of Urey. I remembered Jacoba and the passionate affair we'd had on one. This boat was held against the stone by the current, almost broached, and the stone pilings had smashed the solid wooden railing in one spot. At least it wasn't taking water over the deck that I could see.

"We could jump down to it," she said. "And if there's still oars, push it free, and go downriver without worrying about the Maisirians."

"In this Time of Storms?" I said skeptically, almost having to shout over the chaos. "I'm no boatman."

"I am," she said. "When I was a fugitive from your . . . the army, I spent some time with a river family afloat."

A bearded, smelly soldier pushed against me.

"Hows 'bout sharin' th' cunt?" he suggested romantically, his breath a reek of garlic, stale wine, and filth. He still carried a quiver of arrows, but no bow, and his scabbard was empty.

I stamped my boot across his arch, he screeched, grabbed for it, which put his head low enough for my knee to slam up into his face, and he collapsed and was trampled into the mire by the pushing, fleeing men around us.

"Go!" and Cymea was on the parapet and dropped down to the tiny, muddy beach. She clambered onto the boat, and it rocked under her. I went over the wall in a roll, almost slid into the water, then she had me by the hand and I was on board.

I saw faces looking over, shouting things I couldn't make out, paid no mind.

"Here," Cymea shouted, pulling a long oarlike rudder from a clip at the stern and fitting it over a thole pin near the stern. "I'll steer . . . you push it off!"

I put my back against the cabin's walls, both boots against the piling the boat was jammed against, and pushed hard. The boat rocked, stayed trapped.

There were louder shouts from above, and a javelin thudded into the deck. I pushed again, and Cymea forced the rudder out into the current, and the river caught, spun us, and raced us under the bridge and we were away, turning like a leaf in a whirlpool.

"Help me!" and I hurried to the stern, and both of us levered the steering oar back and forth, and the boat's prow came around, riding high, and the Latane had us, rushing us away downstream, away from the burning city into the safety of the night and the river.

*　　*　　*

Cymea thought we should keep moving until dawn and stay in the middle of the river as best we could. She sent me forward, with a hooked pole she found, and told me to keep a sharp eye for any debris. Twice I fended off logs, once something that could've been a smashed boat, half-submerged, rolling over and over as it went. I shuddered at dying like that and kept a doubly close lookout.

Morning came gray and cold. Cymea still held firm at the rudder, but her face was as gray as the day. I offered to spell her, but she shook her head.

"After I show you how to do it. I'm going to try for that little island over there. You go back into the bow and help us come ashore."

She cleverly let the current take us almost to the island, spotted a small inlet, and steered us into it. Brush overhung this backwater, and I lifted it, and we slid into a tiny cove that might've been intended just for our craft. Cymea told me to uncoil the lines that were on the deck, and tie the small boat, fore and aft, to overhanging trees. She tugged at my knots, told me we'd hold firm.

"Now let's see what we salvaged," she said.

The boat wasn't big, no more than twenty-five feet, and the cabin's roof took up most of the deck. There were curtained portholes, and steps leading down from the cockpit to a glassed double hatchway. A broken mast protruded from the center of the cabin's roof.

I went down the steps and opened the cabin door. The cabin was tiny, but immaculately laid out. To the left of the stairs was a small kitchen, which Cymea told me later was to be called a galley, with spirit cooker and even a tiny oven, a washbasin with cunning metal and rubber pump, and cupboards. On the right was a table with charts in pigeonholes, a small settee, then a jakes with a chamber pot. The walls were rubber coated, and there was another pump with a hose on it for showering.

The cupboards were full of all sorts of preserved, smoked, and magically preserved food, most likely stocked for escape from Renan.

"It appears this boat has everything," Cymea said from behind me.

"All except one thing," I said. "Its owner was obviously Sleepless Sleth."

"Lift the stairs, fool."

I found the steps were hinged, and behind them was a bedroom, with a large single bed almost filling the space. I almost thumped my head on the deck above me, but it was big enough once you'd stepped down into the compartment. The bed was already made up with blankets and sheets, and pillows were stacked against the rear of the compartment.

"All right, it *does* have everything," I said, then yawned. I suddenly realized how long it'd been since I'd had more than an hour's doze . . . three days? Longer? Exhaustion slammed down.

"Do you want something to eat?"

Hunger came, and the fear and energy that'd kept my body at fever pitch disappeared. I blinked, vision blurring for an instant, sat hastily down on the settee.

"Irisu with a cane but I'm tired," I said.

"Dead," she agreed. "Can you make it until I do a pot of soup? We'll sleep better."

"Where are you getting all this energy?"

"I'm still young," Cymea said. "Remember what that was like?"

"If I had the energy, I'd chase you around the deck and throw you overboard for that."

"Save your strength and read me the instructions on the soup packet."

I did, and somehow, mutually yawning at each other, we managed to eat. I washed the dishes, then figured out how to drain the basin, refill it, and wash my face with the soap I found.

Cymea sat on the settee, trying to stay awake, owling at me.

"Your turn," I said. I checked the deck and the river, saw no one through the drifting mists and wind, went below, lifted the stairs, and collected blankets and two pillows.

Cymea finished scrubbing her teeth with a small brush, turned.

"What are you doing?"

"Making up a bed for myself."

"On that couch?"

"I've slept on smaller."

"Don't be foolish," she said. "There's room enough for half a dozen in there. Half a dozen having an orgy."

I was too tired to either be noble or argue, put the blankets back, and arranged the bed. I was about to pull my boots off when I became aware of how appallingly filthy I was. I went back out.

"What now?"

"I'm ashamed of myself." She lifted an eyebrow as I pumped water into the chamberpot, found a towel, took the soap, and opened the hatches to the deck.

"You're mad."

"Probably," I said. "But I'm going to be cleanly mad."

"Have fun," she said.

I went on deck, pulled my boots off, wincing at how badly I smelled, stripped off my clothes. I sluiced with river water, washed, rinsed, washed again, and made myself carefully wash my hair. It was terribly tangled, and I noted I was losing more every day. I was impossibly tired, but now I was too cold to nod off, so I rinsed my undergarments. I went down the steps, dried myself, and hung my dripping clothes here and there to dry.

I remember lifting the steps, and seeing that great warm bed spread in front of me, a lump that must've been Cymea, stumbled toward it, and the world ended.

I awoke without an ache, without a twinge, and feeling the world was marvelous. I wondered idly how much time had passed, pulled a curtain away from one of the cunning octagonal portholes, saw gray daylight, with misty rain blowing past, looking as it had when I collapsed.

I was alone in the compartment, looked for a towel to hide my nakedness, and found my clothes neatly piled at the foot of the bed. They were quite dry, and smelt of violets. I dressed, except for socks and boots, and made my way out into the main cabin. Cymea was curled up on the settee, reading a book she must've found in the shelves. Her close-cropped hair shone dark and lustrous, and I smelt a perfume, exotic sandalwood and musk.

"Good morrow," she said. "I thought you'd died."

"I did," I said, showing my teeth. "But a magician brought me back from the Wheel. How long did I sleep?"

"Well, I sort of woke up sometime in the night, then went back to sleep. Then I woke up again, not long after dawn, and saw that it was storming too badly for us to chance traveling, so I went back to sleep. Got up an hour ago, made some more soup. There's some left in that pot."

"Is soup all we've got on board?"

"No . . . but I'm not a very good cook, and all of the stored foods look like they'd take a lot of work."

"Nice to know you've got *some* faults," I said. "I assume magic dried my clothes?"

"In this weather nothing else could've." She looked about the compartment. "When I was a child, it was wonderful being on that riverboat. I guess I forgot how cold and damp a boat really is."

"Whyn't you cast some variance of the clothes spell and dry the room out?"

"Oh, for the sake of . . . I'm a ninny. I never thought of that."

"Tsk. That's the failing of youth . . . stupidity rules. So while you do that, I'm going to go out to bathe."

"Gods," Cymea said. "Aren't you overdoing it?"

"No," I said. "Any fool can be dirty and uncomfortable." I grabbed the soap and lowered the stairs. "Don't peek. I'm bashful."

"Pah! And by the way, I already made myself beautiful and clean, while you were playing Great Snoring Beast." Cymea was digging into her pouch for herbs and such, and I went on deck. More awake than before and dry, it was even colder than before, but I stiffened myself, stripped off, and jumped overboard, trying to suppress a yelp as I went into the cold, gray water. I surfaced, and saw a head peering out.

"Are you drowning?"

"No. Freezing. Get back inside."

I washed twice over, and most of the ground-in filth from the campaigning came away. I got back aboard, toweled and dressed, considered the river. It was almost half a league from shore to shore, with islands dotting the white-capped water. The wind had picked up, and the branches covering our hide whipped back and forth. I shivered and went below.

The compartment was warmer and no longer felt dank. Two tiny braziers were just smoking out.

"There are virtues to magicians," I grudged, and started digging through the supplies.

About an hour later I had hot-spiced rice, dried fish, various dried vegetables reconstituted, some dough I charitably called bread rising in the oven, and various condiments and jellies on the tiny table. I bowed to Cymea.

"Your repast, m'lady."

We ate hungrily, not talking much. Cymea was very easy to be around. I didn't feel I had to entertain her or talk if I felt like being silent, and evidently she felt the same. We finished, and I found a net bag, sluiced the dirty dishes in the river, dried and put them away.

I took out my battered map, compared it with the river charts.

"Cymea," I said, "I don't know anything about sailing, but it doesn't look like a good idea to be traveling until the storm breaks."

"It isn't," she agreed. "Maybe we could, if we had to, if we had a sail. But we'll just be drifting with the current now. And if something happens to the rudder . . . it's a long swim to shore.

"How far north do you want to travel?"

"Just looking at the map, now, I'd like to keep to the water until we get to the Kallian border. Then we can put ashore and do it the hard way from there."

"Agreed," Cymea said. "A boat's a lot softer on my sitter than a saddle. And we'll travel faster with the river, anyway. So that's our plan. Now what?"

"We could explore the island."

Cymea looked disappointed. "It's a mud wallow. I thought you were going to propose something sensible, like a nap."

"Hah! I don't need one," I said. "You young whippers use up all your energy, and us old fuds know how to husband our strength."

Cymea yawned, and reflexively I yawned with her. We both laughed.

"They say it's impossible to store up sleep," I said. "But I never believed it. Ever since I became a soldier I always thought there was a plot to keep me from getting enough of it."

"Try being a conspirator," she said. "Nobody ever meets anybody except after midnight."

The reminder of the Tovieti froze me for an instant, but I brushed that away. The past was dead, and all that counted was the present. Perhaps I showed the thought, for she turned away for an instant, then back.

"I'll send your own orders back to you," she said. "Don't speak."

She lifted the stairs, went into the bed compartment, and I heard creaks and such, then, after a while, "Very well."

I went in. Cymea was invisible under the blankets. I undressed, leaving my underclothes on, slid under the covers, careful to remain on my side of the bed.

"You once made a suggestion about one of the qualities the man I choose to love should have," she said, voice muffled.

"I remember . . . and remember getting my head bitten off for making it."

"You were being unseemly at the time, sir, and I was

concentrating on business. But I will now tell you what one of the virtues must be. He must have warm feet in bed."

"That's an excellent quality," I said. "But doesn't everyone have warm feet there?"

The response was a pair of icicles pressed against my calves. I yelped.

"Good gods, woman, did you soak those in the river while I was washing up?"

She giggled, slid them down until they were on mine.

"Warm like fresh-baked bread," she said. "That's good, very good. But my feet aren't really that cold."

"The hells they aren't! There were icebergs off that gods-damned prison island I was on that were warmer."

"Sorry, O General of the Armies. But there's something far colder."

She slid closer, and *very* cold, but very silken flesh pressed against my belly, my thighs. Reflexively, I pulled back. Cymea was completely naked.

"Jaen on a tightrope! Your butt's even more frozen!"

"Jaen, you said?"

"It was a slip," I said. "I meant Varum."

"I'll take the slip as it slipped." She giggled again. "And is that what you always wear to bed?"

"I'm trying to be a gentleman," I said. "Remember? And whatever happened to concentrating on business?"

"What sort of business should we be concentrating on?" she asked in a husky whisper.

I was about to move back and cuddle her icy buttocks, but my cock stirred, came awake, so I stayed where I was. She was still for a bit, then rolled over to face me, pulling down the blankets.

"You're willing to let a woman freeze?"

"I thought we were supposed to be taking a nap."

She looked at me carefully. "Damastes, you know how old I am?"

I nodded.

"And you're, what, thirty?"

"Almost thirty-eight."

"Does the difference bother you?"

I smiled wryly. "I don't know," I said. "I don't see why it should." I was speaking the truth, remembering Marán hadn't been much older when I met her, Alegria a couple of years older, and I'd bedded Steffi, in the village of women, without more than a moment of hesitation.

"Or am I being too forward?" Cymea reached out, curled chest hairs around her fingers.

"Of course not."

"Or perhaps you've never kissed a sorcerer?"

"That's certainly true."

"Well?"

Her lips parted under mine, and our tongues slid against each other, and I pulled her to me. I felt her nipples firm against me, and I slid my hand down, caressing her buttocks, running a finger between them. Cymea sighed, lifted her left leg over mine, came closer. I kissed her neck, teased the lobes of her ears with my teeth, ran my tongue in and out of her ear. Her breathing came a little faster.

I rolled her onto her back, half-lay across her, supporting myself on my elbows. Her eyes opened.

"I heard you were called Damastes the Handsome," she whispered. "You are, you know."

"And you're very beautiful, you know."

She smiled. "Nobody gets told that nearly often enough, do they?"

"Anybody who doesn't say that to you has a certain problem with his eyes."

She opened her lips, and I kissed her for a very long time, then nibbled at her neck, down across her chest until I found her breasts. I kissed them, teased her nipples between my teeth, while my hand stroked her stomach.

Her hand moved down my chest and pushed at my underclothes. I untied them, pushed them down to my ankles, kicked them away. Her fingers found my cock and, very gently, caressed its length, ran a finger around its tip.

"You're very big, Damastes."

"I'll be bigger when I'm inside you."

I kissed her stomach, ran my tongue in and out of her navel. Her legs opened, and I kissed down her smooth abdomen. She had only a tuft of hair around her sex. I kissed her lips, sliding my tongue back and forth, then moved between her legs.

She lifted one leg across my back as I ran my tongue up and down her sex.

"Am I wet?"

"Yes," I said, and slipped a finger into her. She gasped, lifted her hips to my moving tongue. I kept caressing her clitoris while I moved my finger slowly in circles inside her.

Cymea murmured wordlessly, her hands smoothing the back of my hair as I loved her.

"Does that feel good?"

"Yes . . . yes . . ."

"Shall I put another finger in you?"

"Please."

She moaned hard when I did, and I licked my left finger, slid it into her anus.

"Oh gods!"

I kept both fingers and my tongue moving, working inside her.

"Do you like that?"

She just gasped.

"Would you like something else inside you?"

"Yes, Damastes. Yes."

I touched her with the head of my cock, and she jerked, then I slid it in a bit, and she made a sound, halfway between a moan and a low shriek. I moved all the way into her, then almost out, and her legs went around the backs of my thighs.

"Come lie on me, please."

I moved once, twice in her, then took my cock out, and began caressing her sex with it.

"Oh, don't do that, don't, please, oh you fucker, you bastard, put it back in me."

"Put what back in you?"

"Put your cock, put that big thing in me, please, please . . ."

And I pushed it hard until I was buried in her, and lay down on her, on my elbows, moving rhythmically, slowly, long, hard movements, and her legs moved up and down on my thighs, her hands pulling at my back, her mouth open, head moving back and forth, face wet with our saliva, gasping, then her body began jerking hard against me, and she screamed and went limp, and I emptied myself in her, and fell across her body limply.

We lay like that for a time; then I came back and lifted most of my weight back onto my arms.

Her eyes opened, and she smiled a bit.

"You're the first man I've ever seduced. You feel good."

"You feel better."

"Oh yes. I do."

I turned her on her side, and, hardening, began moving in her slipperiness, and she sighed happily, pulled herself to me, and again we were a world to ourselves.

"Now what? Do you want to finish in my mouth?"

"No," I said. "Lie back."

She obeyed, and I slid into her, lifting her left leg up onto my right shoulder. Her hands were stroking, almost clawing at the sheets. After a while, I turned her on her side and continued moving slowly in her, my hands stroking her back, her breasts, her stomach.

Again I turned her, sliding a pillow under her upper thighs.

"Gods . . . this is good, so good. Don't stop, Damastes. Do anything you want."

I took the oil I'd found in the kitchen, dipped my finger into it, slid it into her very gently while I fucked her. I moved my finger in circles, felt myself in her, felt her ring relax.

"There, now," she moaned. "Fuck me there."

We made love all that day and deep into the night, neither of us satiated, sometimes fiercely, sometimes gently, while the river waves rocked the boat and the storm drove against the wooden walls around us.

But we never noticed, buried, lost in each other.

It was somewhere near dawn, and we lay together, bodies wet with sweat and love.

"I hope I don't have to be a very good boatman tomorrow . . . today," she said softly. "I'm going to be a little bit sore."

"I feel a little stiff myself," I said.

"Stop bragging and give me a few minutes to get over that last one." She kissed me. "You're a very good lover, you know."

"You make me into a good one," I said truthfully, for her imagination and desire ran as deep, perhaps deeper than mine.

"Did you mind?"

"Mind what?" I said, bewildered.

"That you weren't the first."

"Why in Jaen's name would I care about something like that?"

"I've heard it bothers men when they're not the first, especially with somebody who's not that old."

"Of course it doesn't bother me. Does it bother you that *I* was a virgin when I met you?" I asked.

"If I had the strength," Cymea said, "I'd knee you in the balls. Instead, pick me up. I want you to fuck me standing up."

"Yes, O wizard. What a terrible penalty."

We slept most of the next day, woke, bathed, ate, went back to bed, made love a couple more times, then slept.

When we awoke this time, the storm had passed, and the river was flat and cold, and the land around us was empty, smoke still coming from the ruined city to the south.

We used ropes to pull ourselves out of the inlet, and Cymea swung the boat into the current and we let the Latane carry us north toward Kallio.

The land around was rutted, desolate. We saw wandering bands of Maisirian soldiers, deserters now, unlikely to rejoin their formations on the long and dangerous march back through the Sulem Pass and Kait. Bringing down these bandits would be another burden for whoever won this now-civil war, the second in a generation. I'd determined to be the winner and wondered who'd rule after I managed to destroy Tenedos. I certainly didn't envy him . . . or them, because for all I knew it might be another Council, though I couldn't imagine who they might be.

It was a flat, calm day, and Cymea was teaching me how to steer. We'd seen two small fishing boats that morning, which cheered us—the river wasn't entirely depopulated. We were reaching the end of the wasteland, getting closer to the Kallian border.

We speculated how long it'd take for news of Bairan's death and the Maisirian retreat to reach Nicias, and Tenedos, who we assumed was still in winter camp above the Latane Delta, since the heliographs we were so proud of had been torn down in the years of unrest.

I was cutting didos with the wake, flat S-curves in the rippling gray surface under an overcast sky.

A wave, nearly fifteen feet high, rose from the calm waters at our stern, curled, and tossed me overboard like a wood chip. I hit the water flat, hard, and went under, and the current caught me, whirled me away and down, toward the bottom. I managed to swim out of it and kicked up, toward air, toward life.

I broke surface, saw our boat yaw as Cymea tried to turn it against the river, and swam hard. For a moment I thought I'd lost, that it was being carried downstream faster than I could swim, but then I was closing on it, breath rasping, arms starting to weaken, and Cymea tossed me a rope. She missed, threw again, and I had it, pulling myself hand-over-hand to the rail.

I'd exhausted myself and was barely able to pull myself aboard, Cymea grabbing me by my pants and tugging, and then I rolled onto the deck. There were long moments when I could only gasp for air, but finally my breathing slowed, and I staggered to my feet.

I looked up. "Nice try, you bastard!" I shouted.

Cymea was looking at me strangely.

"Now we know word's gotten to Tenedos," I said.

"Are you sure that was him?"

"No, I'm not. But that wave was certainly doing his business." I took off my shirt, wrung it out. "Accident or not, I'll add it to his account."

It was storming again, and once more Cymea had come up with a clever stratagem. A huge tree, over two hundred feet long and wider than our boat, ripped from the land by the winter storms, was speeding silently downriver. Cymea steered us to it, had me moor the boat to its branches.

I told her I didn't like it; what happened if the tree rolled?

"Then we drown in our sleep and I'll meet you on the Wheel," she said. "But nothing like that's going to happen."

I was about to protest further, when she added, "Plus I can cast a spell around us, and if that was Tenedos who knocked you overboard, he'll not be able to find us, just another bit of debris clinging to this log.

"Not to mention we'll travel a great deal faster tied to it than on our own. At least so long as it holds to the river center."

She was the one with water knowledge, not I, and so I went below and made dinner.

We finished eating, and she cleaned up, and we went to bed. Instead of making love, as we had done every night, she wanted to talk. About my former wife, about my former lovers. I'd had women do this before and had been uncomfortable. I never had much interest in their previous lives, but it didn't seem to bother them.

"I never had but one real lover," she said, after a spell. "And he was only for a month or two."

"A pity, for that means you don't have anything for juicy confessions," I joked, suppressing a yawn.

She made a sound in her throat, bitter, harsh.

"Very well," I said, "you do have juicy confessions. My apologies."

She was silent for a very long time, and I had sense enough to dread what would be coming next, for it wouldn't be anything funny.

"What do you know about my family? About the Amboinas?"

I thought back, to what Kutulu had discovered from a now-dead sage named Hami, long ago in Kallio. "A bit," I said cautiously.

"You know that our men were wizards, if they had the Talent. And sometimes our women as well."

"I knew that."

"If the men showed no signs of ability," Cymea went on, "they'd become members of the court, always helping the family advance. It was our ultimate aim to rule Kallio, and then all Numantia."

"Which Chardin Sher prevented."

"Until his death. Then my father saw, in two, perhaps three generations, our way would be clear to the throne, which is why he formed the conspiracy to bring down the emperor."

"Ah," I said. "I'd never considered that. I thought the conspiracy was just because he'd been a high-ranking member of Chardin Sher's retinue and hated us for destroying his lord."

Cymea laughed humorlessly. "My family cared little for anyone except another Amboina.

"But that's going too fast. Do you know what the Amboina women were fated for?"

I chose my words carefully. "I was told, by someone who should know, that they would become the wives of other sorcerers if they had no talents at magic themselves."

"Wives . . . or mistresses," Cymea said.

I'd heard that as well and remembered two of Amboina's daughters, from his first marriage, had supposedly died when the demon destroyed Chardin Sher, his magician Mikael Yanthlus, and the brooding castle atop the mountain.

"Yes," I said.

"My father had a great vision for the Amboinas, after his first wife died. He then married a village witch, a bit of a scandal, for she brought no dowry, no lands to the Amboinas. He married her for her power. A wizard and a witch . . . two children.

"My brother Jalon and myself.

"My father had a plan, which he told us about after my mother died, when I was ten and Jalon eighteen. I don't know what my mother thought of the idea, if she even knew about it.

"He proposed for us to . . . not marry, but bed each other. First, each of us would have greater powers, at least in the black region, for incest, forbidden sex magic. Then he hoped we'd have children. Our child, our children, would have powers beyond any magician alive, far beyond even the emperor. What I, or anyone else, felt of the matter was meaningless."

My stomach roiled.

"My brother," Cymea went on, "thought that was an excellent idea. He tried to . . . to carry the plan out three times. He almost succeeded once. I felt . . . feel defiled just thinking about it. He used to talk about that, whisper what he and I would do, the black joys we'd experience, when he was alone with me. My brother was dark, darker even than my father, and his dreams of what he would do with power, of the way he'd use people like they were dolls, were as disgusting as the evil books and grimoires he found those ideas in.

"That's why I wasn't able to hate you that much, Damastes, for being responsible for his death. Truthfully, if I consider the balance, we Tovieti did you far greater harm."

I didn't know what I should say, if anything.

"Well," Cymea said harshly, "did that disgust you? Now are you sorry you slept with me? Am I soiled as my family?" She sat up. "Or maybe do you think that's intriguing, and you're aroused? The only other person I told this to, my first lover, had to fuck me as soon as I was finished telling him about it. Is that the way men think, Damastes?"

"No," I said slowly. "I'm not aroused. And I don't know if other men would be, should be. I don't think so. All I was thinking was just how evil men can become when they're powerful, when they're wizards. I'm very glad I've nothing of the Talent, if that's what it brings." I sat up, took her gently by the shoulders.

"But I know one thing. What other people wanted, thought, has nothing to do with you, with what you are. Does it?"

Her shoulders quivered a little. "It shouldn't."

"The only thing that would worry me is what you said about the Amboinas caring for no one but themselves."

"Am I an Amboina anymore?" she asked. "Or am I just Cymea the Tovieti?"

"That's not a lot better from my perspective."

"It should be," she said. "At least the Tovieti give a shit about something, about human freedom."

"You don't free people by strangling them," I said. Nor, my thoughts went on, by killing them when they're pregnant.

Cymea was silent for a very long time.

"No," she said finally. "No, you don't. But I guess, when you're serving what you think is a greater good, you're willing to do just about anything."

I was suddenly angry.

"Fuck this greater good!" I snarled. "That means you can do anything, everything, as long as there's this gloss that, in the end, everything'll be just fine and lovely. To hells it is! We're in the middle of what that kind of thinking produces, a fucking wasteland that used to be the prettiest part of Numantia!"

Somehow Cymea must've understood I wasn't angry at her. "I know," she said dully. "I know."

It was still in that room, and I could hear the wind against the portholes, the river washing the planks beside me.

"But it doesn't *have* to be that way, does it?" she asked.

"It had better not," I said, anger gone. "If it is, then everything I'm doing . . . you're doing . . . is like pissing into the wind."

"Lie back down," she asked. "Let me put my head on your shoulder."

I did, and she came close.

"Tell me what Urey was like, before," she whispered. "What it'll be like again."

I forced my wind to wander.

"It was a magical place," I began. "Very old, a summering place for the kings of Numantia once. Cool, a pleasant breeze blowing down from the mountains and stirring the trees of the many parks in the city. The trees were of a type I'd never seen, sixty feet in circumference, with multicolored leaves big enough to use for umbrellas in the gentle rains that fell occasionally.

"In the center of the city, rather than a palace or a grim fortress, was a garden, where fountains rose and sang among pillars of black marble, worked with gold, and the water ran laughing down cascades into small pools.

"Canals stretched through the city, connecting—"

A gentle snore came, and her body was soft next to mine.

I stared up at the deck above me, thinking about what she'd told me and what I'd said and wondered what would come in six months, a year, two years.

I'd thought once before about that and decided that it was unlikely I'd survive to see anything resembling peace, which I found strangely comforting.

But suppose I did?

What then?

It seemed that we were in a time of our own, but that was not so, when I remembered how few days we'd been traveling.

The question that came, even though I didn't want to ask it: What of the armies?

Cymea cast Seeing Spells south, saw fragments of Bairan's army, grimly retreating in long, sullen lines toward Maisir.

She tried a spell north, to see what Tenedos was doing, but felt a building, malevolent pressure, and broke away.

"He's still there," she said. "We didn't get lucky and one of his demons ate him."

"That'd give even a demon terrible indigestion," I said. "What about Nicias?"

Again, she tried, said she could not be sure, but felt presences beyond Tenedos.

I guessed that both sides were holding their positions, the Grand Councilors in the capital, Tenedos somewhere outside, hopefully above the Latane Delta.

I assumed Tenedos had discovered Bairan's death, and the Maisirian retreat. But that would do no more than take some of the pressure off him, and make it easier to take care of first my rebels, being the hardest fighters, then the Grand Council.

Cymea wasn't able to call a Seeing Spell on my army, but she tried to send what she called a feeling to Sinait . . . we were alive, well, moving as fast as we could.

Or as fast as the river could take us.

"Look at this," Cymea said. She held a container that looked like something intended for flour. "I was going to teach myself how to bake and almost dropped this because it was so heavy. Look what was inside!"

She held three imperial gold coins in her hand.

"There's two dozen more just like it."

I tapped one of the coins on the tabletop, could tell by its ring it was genuine, then patted the cabin wall beside me.

"Boat," I said earnestly, "I think you're being too good to us."

I drove my hips upward, letting her body pull my semen out, my hands kneading her breasts, and she contorted back, cried out, then fell limply forward on me. I stroked her back, her hair, and after a while she murmured, "I'm back."

"That's nice."

"I've got a question."

"Mmmh?"

"What happens when we rejoin the army?" she asked.

"We'll have to fuck less publicly, and you'll have to learn to not shout so much when you're coming?"

"That wasn't what I meant! What'll your soldiers say when they find out we're sleeping together?"

"You won't lose your temper?"

"No," she said. "No matter what."

"They'll probably think it's great that their General Damastes is fucking a Tovieti. Subverting from within."

"That was a really rotten joke," she said. "But they really won't care?"

"No. Some of them probably think we were anyway, since soldiers normally think any two people who're reasonably good looking of different sexes are going to end up in bed together."

"That's not very fair to women," she said. "What are we, nothing but creatures of lust?"

"That's what soldiers hope, especially the young ones, because that's what *they* are. When I was a youth, thinking about *sand* could make me lustful. But that brings up a question for me. What are *your* people . . . the Tovieti . . . going to do?"

She thought for a while.

"Honestly?"

"Of course."

"I don't think they'll like it a lot. You—all of you who aren't Tovieti—are their enemies, and they've only signed a temporary truce."

"Odd," I said. "A time or so ago, you would've said 'we.'"

Again silence, then: "I would've, wouldn't I?"

"Again, my question—what are they going to do?"

"I don't know," she said. "Probably nothing but growl. I'm a wizard, so I'm allowed a great deal of license, even though I'm a Tovieti. I guess, so long as I don't become a turncoat, which I won't, nothing much should happen.

"Besides," she sighed, "as I heard Svalbard say once, back in that tower, 'fuck 'em if they can't take a joke.' And we surely have more important things to worry about. Like the emperor and those fools down in Nicias."

"Of course," I said. "First those fuckers, then we worry about other fucking."

"Speaking of which," she said, "since I'm not really sleepy, and since I've been a really good girl today and let you steer the boat for a while, and I brought the oil in, which is right beside you, what do you think about doing it everywhere, the way we did the first time we made love?"

"I think that could be arranged," I said.

She rolled on her side, then onto her back.

"Then come up here and let me taste you."

I obeyed, getting to my knees, and a thought came: I think I'm very close to falling in love with this woman.

The land on either side of the river was unburned, unlooted, and every now and then a brave soul had chanced rebuilding within sight of the Latane. I identified where I thought we were by various bends in the river, although the great river changes its course often enough for no one except an experienced boat captain to be sure.

We landed not far from where we saw enough smoke to suggest a village, or at any rate a prosperous farm, and disembarked with our gear.

We'd debated on what to do with our boat. Logically, we should have tied it up where we landed and sold it to someone in that village.

But there was something wrong with that idea.

So, when we had everything we needed ashore, I pushed it back out, and let the current take it.

It spun twice, then was carried to the center of the stream, moving steadily, as if an invisible pilot were at the rudder.

"I hope it goes downstream and finds two other lovers who're in trouble and helps them," Cymea said, leaning against me.

I put my arm around her.

"That's not very good, coming from a pragmatic sorcerer."

"Right now I'm just someone who's feeling sad, feeling like we had something very special, and now . . ." her voice trailed off, and she looked back at the boat.

"Would it help any if I said I love you?" I said softly.

"It would," she said. "It would a lot."

We came to a rather small farm that had two beautiful horses in a tiny paddock, one a gray, the other a bay, the bay reminding me of my own long-lost Lucan, who I hoped was having a peaceful retirement on some horse ranch beyond Nicias. Neither horse was fit for plowing nor even a carriage.

We talked to the farmer, who claimed they'd shown up in his field one day, and he was holding them for their proper owner or owners.

"Meantime," he grumbled, "they're eatin' me outa house an' everything."

We examined them carefully, found them to be in good shape. One had the earcroppings of a cavalry mount, which I ignored. Three of the boat's gold coins, two more for saddlery, and we rode on.

I named the bay Swift, Cymea called her horse Wanderer.

We rode due east, and even though it was the end of the Time of Storms, the new year beginning, and it was wet and cold often, it was a wondrous time.

The farmers we met were mostly cheery, this being the time of year they didn't have to labor from dawn to dusk and beyond in the fields, and they had food to spare and, not infrequently, a loft to let for the night.

There weren't many fresh vegetables, but this was hog-killing time, and so we had succulent pork chops with dried fruit, freshly smoked hams, roasts with berry or mustard sauces, breads and pies made with dried fruit.

But the land still showed the scars of war, with abandoned farms and acreage lying fallow, and we went for leagues without seeing anyone, riding as fast as we could without foundering either ourselves or the horses.

But for us this wasn't lonely, but the best nights, when we were alone.

Sometimes we slept in these abandoned houses, but more often, for they gave us a bit of a shiver, in their barns or haylofts.

*　　*　　*

We wove our way through a strange forest, the young trees planted in even rows like corn or wheat.

"Who grows trees just for the wood?" Cymea wondered.

"Lazy carpenters," I guessed, and Cymea stuck her tongue out.

I rode to one, leaned close to its trunk.

"I wasn't far wrong," I said. "This is some kind of hardwood, and the trunk's been guided with wire wraps to grow perfectly straight. Maybe in its normal state it's twisty, bent, and someone wants straight-grain lumber for something. Expensive furniture."

"I don't believe you're doing anything other than guessing," Cymea said. "We'll ask when we come to the owner's house."

But if there was one, it was well hidden, for we saw nothing by dusk but this endless plantation, with straight lanes cut at intervals.

"It appears we'll be sleeping out," she said.

"And there's nothing the matter with that," I said. "We've supplies in the saddlebags, you can make some sort of soup, and I'll prepare the most luxurious bed you've ever slept in."

"So where do we stop?"

"At the next creek."

Cymea took care of the horses, piled stones together for a fireplace, built a large fire as I'd asked her. I cut the limbs off two trees twenty feet apart, clambered up and topped them where they veed apart, hacked down the ones between, and muscled out the shallowly rooted stumps. One of the slender trees I'd cut went across the vee-notches of the two standing trees, and others were laid against it on one side. I laced branches between these trees, until we had a good, strong wall against the brisk wind.

On the inside of the single-sided shelter I carefully laid leafy boughs, layer on layer, until we had a high-piled bed. On top of that went our bedding.

In front of the bed, I made ready another fire, this one narrow, as long as our bed. I found dry wood, cut and piled it ready at hand.

"And there you have it," I announced. "We sleep in the windbreak, with a fire on the outside. When somebody gets cold, all that's necessary is to throw another log on the fire."

"*You* sleep on the outside," Cymea said, "so you're closer to the wood."

"We're not even going to draw straws, or twigs, rather?"

"Not a chance," Cymea said. "You cheat. And if you don't, I would. I'm a magician, remember?"

Dinner was half a loaf of bread we'd bought a day ago, heated by the fire and buttered, and a thick lentil soup, spiced with herbs picked along the trail. I'd learned a sorcerer's plant knowledge wasn't just for magical benefit.

We washed ourselves and our dishes at the creek, and I took coals from the cook fire before I banked it for the night, and started the fire in front of our bed.

A winter wind whispered, but we were very warm.

"Pretty impressive," Cymea said as we cuddled. "You do know all sorts of woodsy lore, don't you?"

"The product of a misspent youth," I said. "Less schooling, more woods running."

Neither of us was sleepy, the smell of the boughs we lay on like incense.

"Speaking of youth," I said. "All you've told me about yours was the bad parts. Was that all?"

"No," Cymea said. "Of course not. But are you sure you want to hear it?"

"As long as it's not an endless array of the lovers you had to make me jealous."

"Fool," she said, turning her head and kissing my chin. "Who can be jealous of the past?"

"Me."

"I meant," Cymea said, her voice very serious, "that if you want to hear about me, you're going to hear some things you won't like and about some people you'd probably rather see dead. And sometimes it isn't that pretty."

"I asked, didn't I?" I said after a moment. "Which means I'd best be prepared to listen. Start with what happened in Polycittara. Leave out your family, if you wish."

Cymea took a deep breath.

"Very well. And I think I do wish. So let's start with me in your prison cell. I was still stunned with what'd happened at Lanvirn, so I don't remember the first couple of days.

"But slowly I came back, and what I remember is the jailers. There were women in the cells, and the jailers were always going on about what they wanted to do with them. Or to the boys in the cells. And to me, even though I was a little girl.

"The worst of them was a bastard called Ygerne. I can still remember his name, see his face. He had the most appalling imagination. I still have trouble believing any mind can be that much of a sewer."

"He wasn't just a jailer," I interrupted. "He was a torturer. A warder from Nicias."

"That explains a great deal," she said. "I told him once he wouldn't dare do anything to me, or I'd report him to the prince regent.

"He thought that awfully funny and said after the emperor's brother pronounced sentence on me, which could only be one thing, no one would care what happened.

"I saw he was right, for now and again a warder would let himself into one of the cells and pleasure himself. Ygerne loved to watch that." She shuddered. "But I knew, before I'd submit to him, I'd have the strength to bite my tongue through and bleed to death, and, strangely enough, that gave me heart to stand firm.

"But then the castle was attacked, and we heard the sound of fighting, of dying. None of us knew what was going on, but all knew whatever it was, it couldn't be worse than what we were facing.

"The guards retreated into the cells, and some said they should hold us as hostages. Ygerne thought that was a great idea. But before any of the cells could be unlocked, a wave of men burst in, killing, cutting.

"Ygerne pled for mercy, but we shouted what a monster he was, and he was killed, as was every other guard, even a few that had been passing human."

"That wasn't a day when anybody showed mercy," I said.

"No. The cells were opened, both in the block I was in, which was for political prisoners, and in the other areas for common criminals.

"Two men shouted for silence, said they were Tovieti, and anyone who wished to join them would be taken care of.

"I'd never known any of the Tovieti, although I'm sure my father, and perhaps my brother, had. But I had nowhere to go, and so I said I'd go with them.

"When they found out who I was, they immediately detailed three men to get me out of the castle.

"I was hurried out through the courtyard, and everything was madness. I don't know where you were."

"In the far wing, getting ready to counterattack," I said.

"I didn't want to stay there. Men were doing things I didn't want to see." She shuddered. "There were women . . . sometimes girls younger than I was, being, being . . ."

"Never mind," I said. "I know what was done. So you fled down into the streets of Polycittara."

"And rode out that same night, just as the battle was at its fiercest. I wanted to stay in the city, wait for my father. Even if he was what he was, he was who he was. But they said no, that it appeared the emperor's dogs, sorry Damastes, that slipped out, were winning.

"They took me to a farm somewhere outside the city, and we hid for three days.

"I heard of my father's death then."

She sat up in her blankets.

"I've heard that sometimes, when people have a whole line of shocks hit them, they turn cold. True?"

"True," I said. "I think it's a gift from the gods, to keep us from completely falling apart."

"That's what happened to me," Cymea said. "I felt bad for the deaths, for the ending of the life I'd had, and worried, scared of the unknown.

"But I knew I was going to live, not only live, but become strong, and one day find vengeance.

"The Tovieti spirited me out of Kallio within the week, and I was passed from family to family. Something you . . . or Kutulu . . . no doubt already know is there are various levels in the sect. First are the believers, the storekeeper you buy from, the drover on the road, the farmer or the clerk, the quiet soldier in the ranks, people who accept the teachings, but practice them quietly, the ones the warders and the noblemen never know about. They're our strength, our spies, our shelter, and our treasury. Then there are what we call the Gray Men, the ones who, either by choice or circumstances, are the people of action."

"The stranglers," I said, feeling anger in my voice.

"Yes. Or the ones who sell the contraband the men with the silk cords bring. Cell leaders frequently don't have time for a double life, and so they become gray.

"The last group are what we call the Ones Who Are Sought, those the warders have found out, the ones who face prison or worse, the ones who can't show their face by day in any familiar place.

"I was one of them, passed from home to home, from believer to believer, until I came to Khurram.

"To my new home."

She looked at me and smiled, her smile just a bit on the wry side.

"You really won't like this. I was taken in by the head of a lycee, whose school taught the sons and daughters of the rich men of Khurram, many of them vintners and merchants."

I *didn't* like that—a subtle poisoner from within.

"No one ever caught on to what he was doing?"

"Citizen Yarkand was very subtle in his teachings," she said. "By the way, I'm giving away nothing in my tale that might expose my brothers or sisters. Yarkand is dead now, which is one reason I know something about boats."

"Don't worry about exposing anything," I said. "I vow, right now, that anything you've ever told me, good, bad, or criminal, will never be used by me nor told to anyone else without your permission. On whatever god you want me to swear."

"Your word's enough," she said.

"Thank you," I said. "But a question, if I may: What do the Tovieti teach their young?"

"The first is the Tovieti think there's almost no limit to what someone should know who wants to learn. So it's not like normal schooling, where the girls learn to read and sew and handle the accounts of a household, no more, and the boys get everything interesting.

"The Tovieti make no distinction between boys and girls. Anyone can learn anything. And another difference—no one's held back from progressing if the boy in the next seat's thick or unwilling. He'll be dropped back to learn with younger students or even taken out of school, while anyone who's still learning can go on and on.

"I was like a great sponge," she said, a bit dreamily, "for I quickly realized I knew very little, that all my father had allowed to be taught was magic, magic, magic."

"That's not exactly what I meant. Let me try my question another way," I said. "What do the Tovieti teach children about themselves?"

"That we are a secret order," Cymea said. "That many men's hands are turned against us, so we must never tell anyone about our sect or our secrets. We teach that this world is in monstrous disorder and that all governments must be brought down and the altars to the gods men now worship, destroyed.

"When all is ruined, when all is chaos, then whatever the new society should be will be clear, and we can build a truly free land, where no man is better or worse than his neighbor.

"When that day comes, then all evil shall fall away and the gods, who surely exist, will appear in a new form."

"Do *you* believe this Golden Age can come about through death and destruction or, for that matter, any other way?" I asked gently.

She was silent for quite a long time.

"I wish I could," she said, and her voice suggested I not pry further.

"Another question," I said, changing the subject slightly. "What are the children taught about the stranglers, the Gray Men, the Ones Who Are Sought?"

"They're considered the elite, most holy, sent against those who've offended our order as warriors. If things were different, they'd carry swords and wear armor like any soldier. But outnumbered as they are, as we are, all they can safely use are the yellow silk cords."

I thought what a crock of shit *that* was, remembering them as roving bands of thieves, caring nothing for politics and everything for loot.

"You believe that?"

"I did then, remembering what the emperor had done to my family. Now . . ."

"Never mind," I said. "So you came to the lycee of Citizen Yarkand."

"Yes," Cymea said. "I became part of his household, and he and his wife told everyone I was his niece, that my mother, his sister, and her husband had died of the flux.

"Yarkand was a very good man. I wish I'd gone to stay with him when I was younger, no more than a babe, and then I'd think of him as my real father and probably love humankind better than I do.

"He taught me a lot of things. Book knowledge, everything his school offered. What the Tovieti believe, and he didn't have to make his lessons subtle for me. But the most important thing I got from him was learning things don't have to be black, white, good, bad, and the world isn't always evil, and you don't have to kill someone who doesn't agree with you."

She looked a bit surprised.

"Strange," she said. "Maybe what he taught me, what I learned from a Tovieti, was what set the seed that makes me wonder now about the order that's been so good to me. Odd. Very odd."

She broke off.

"I do wish I had a glass of wine," she said. "It'd make the storytelling easier."

I extended the flagon of water beside us. She grimaced but drank.

"Yarkand knew I was an Amboina and that I came from a family of great wizards, so I also got secret lessons in my craft. Magicians are a roving lot, always moving, learning new spells, new incantations, challenging other sages, so there was always someone, sometimes Tovieti, sometimes not, who'd be put up by Yarkand in exchange for teaching me for a day or week.

"I was very happy," she said softly, "and knew it and also knew I'd never been so content at Lanvirn.

"Who knows what would've happened? Maybe I would've stayed in Khurram, been a competent wizard for my brothers and sister, probably a cell leader, for I've always been able to see things a bit more clearly, more quickly, than most.

"Who knows? But Yarkand grew sick, and no chirurgeon, no witch, no wizard, could help him. I was frantic, trying spells of my own, going to my teachers in magic, begging them to do something, anything.

"But nothing helped, and Yarkand died.

"This time, I wasn't calm, cold, but raged against everything, against the gods, for they'd taken this man I loved. Now I wanted the yellow silk cord, but not to kill men, for they had nothing to do with Yarkand's death. I wanted to kill the gods if I could.

"I knew how absurd that was, and that ended my rage or, anyway, buried it within.

"But I couldn't stay at the lycee, even though Yarkand's widow wanted me to.

"Next the Tovieti sent me to a roving family who had a small riverboat that traded up and down the Latane, selling mostly necessaries, stopping at any farm who flew the little flags we gave out. We also carried packages for our brothers and sisters, never asking what was in them, and had secret passengers, the Gray Men on the run from the warders.

"An old man, his wife, and their son, who would've been about your age, but who'd fallen onto a low dock when he was a boy, and never grew beyond ten or so. Everyone loved him, took care of him. They were my new family.

"That was when I gained real knowledge, knowledge of what people really do and say, not what books pretend. Also, using my notebooks, I practiced my spells, and discovered the Amboina blood ran clear in my veins, for I was able to advance far more quickly than a girl my age should have.

"The war was raging in Maisir, and we prayed for the emperor's destruction, believing with him down in the dirt, we might have a chance to bring about our better world."

She looked into the fire.

"It didn't happen that way, of course. I'm not sure why. Maybe Numantia lost too many good men, and some of those were Tovieti. Maybe when the Maisirians ravened through Urey and then came on to Nicias, something went out of our sect, some of our pride and confidence was shattered. I don't know.

"We hid in a backwater when we saw soldiers, either Numantian or Maisirian. Then there was peace, and so long as we avoided the Peace Guardians, life went back to normal.

"When I was fifteen, I had that love affair I told you about. He was twenty-two."

"Oh," I said.

"Exactly," Cymea said. "Worse, his family was wealthy, considered among the lords of the district we'd chosen to trade in for a time.

"But I didn't know, didn't think, but knew this was the love of my life, and we'd be together for always, somehow a rich man's son would be happy with a bargee's child, for that's all he knew of me, and somehow the Tovieti would understand, or perhaps he'd join us. Oh, I had all kinds of girlish dreams.

"And then I found out what he really was. Probably now I realize he was no more than a spoiled brat saying anything I wanted to hear so he could fuck me, no worse than a lot of boy-men I've seen."

Her voice had held rising anger, and she broke off. She took a couple of deep breaths, then grinned.

"Don't I just sound like a wise woman of vast experience?

"Anyway. He took a nasty way of ending our affair, and I thought he was a monster then and couldn't stand the hurt, and again I fled. But this time I knew where I was going. I went to a witch, really a very powerful wizard who'd turned away from the world to live a quieter life in a Delta backwater. We used to buy special things for her when we were in any kind of a city, and she cast spells for us in return.

"She'd been a Tovieti, left the order ten years before. I studied with her for a year, learned a lot, and began helping the poor people around me with potions or, as often as not, just advice I thought obvious. There's a lot like me, not cell leaders, not holding any kind of official position, but still leaders of our movement. I learned we avoided creating such hierarchy after the disastrous rising, when Thak still ruled us, and the survivors blamed our leaders for that arrogance.

"Anyway, some of these respected Tovieti came to me last year and said I was wasting myself in that swamp, that the order needed me, momentous events were about to happen, that the emperor we thought was dead had returned and was trying to recover his throne.

"The only task a Tovieti should have was stopping him, seeing that he was dead.

"I listened and obeyed and went with them, working as a wizard, and as adviser, when I thought I saw something that wasn't being done right or wasn't noticed. I usually remembered how young I am and how older people generally aren't going to listen to someone my age, so I found the soft way, the calm way, was the only way for my ideas to be accepted.

"I guess I did well, for I was listened to and given a certain amount of respect. There were emergencies, when there was no time for subtlety, and I felt like an army officer, some kind of bully.

"But people still listened to and obeyed me. Sometimes I wonder why I didn't get arrogant, become overly full of myself. Maybe being cast down so utterly back then, from being a noble Amboina to a child in a cell facing rape and worse kept my head from swelling.

"Then an agent, hidden in the upper echelons of the Grand Council, said they were going to bring you back— and make you general of their armies. Somehow they'd discovered you'd changed your mind and weren't the emperor's puppet any longer.

"At first, we decided you must be killed as someone almost as dangerous as Tenedos, even though you'd turned away from him, and there were plans being made to deal with you.

"Then you escaped from the Councilors' prison, and killed Herne, another one high on our list of monsters.

"Some Tovieti elders in Nicias thought it might be interesting to help you, to keep you running loose to see what trouble you could stir up, since we had no use for either the Council or Tenedos."

"So I was no more than another die," I said, not terribly happy finally learning the reason I'd been helped when I was a fugitive in Nicias, "this one with beveled edges, so it'd bounce and roll every which way, to be cast into the game?"

"At first, that is exactly what we wanted you to be," Cymea said. "Then things changed once more, and some theorized that you might be the best, perhaps the only, weapon to destroy Tenedos. I was approached, since I'd had some dealings with you, even though it was long ago and for a very brief, very unpleasant time.

"They wanted me to go to you, with Jakuns and others, and see what would happen if we offered a measure of help.

"You, of course, told us to fuck off, as traitors. Some of the Tovieti thought that should doom you; others, like Jakuns and me, were impressed.

"When you were trapped on the Latane, it was obvious we had to support you and your army, because the Peace Guardians were nearly useless and sooner or later Maisir would come back into Numantia.

"I volunteered to lead the relief ships.

"Little did I know that things would change as they did."

She looked at me, waiting for a response. "Well?"

"Umm," I said. "That's a great deal to think about. But I, for one, am damned glad what happened, happened."

"So am I," Cymea said. "And I hope I haven't said anything wrong . . . I mean, wrong for whatever's going on between us."

"How could you?" I said, mostly being honest. "I said the truth shouldn't be able to ruin anything that shouldn't be ruined, didn't I?"

"No," Cymea said. "You said nothing like that at all."

"But I should have."

"Not necessarily," she said. "No one expects great oratory from a demoniac monster of a soldier."

"Demoniac monster, is it?"

Cymea yawned and nodded.

"Your doom is sealed," I growled, and pulled her down on the bed. "We demons are double-dicked, you know."

"Very good," she said. "For I'd really like to love you, for you to love me, so I can believe my brook-running mouth didn't ruin anything."

She might have wanted to say more, but my lips were on hers, my tongue curling around hers, and her arms came up and around me.

Once we were mewed up by a storm at an abandoned inn, and this was the most magical time. There were a few chickens who foolishly thought they could evade an experienced field soldier such as myself, and they went into a pot with some potatoes, not-too-ancient carrots, and spices we found in a grown-over garden behind the inn. The amateurs who'd looted the inn hadn't been thorough, and I found, hidden behind a board in one of the inn's cellars, three bottles of wine for Cymea.

There was a small cascade and a pool behind the inn, and I discovered, in the stables, a wine barrel that'd been cut in half, intended to be used as a horse trough. Cymea and I rolled it to the cascade, and she used rain gutters torn from the building to channel water into the cascade, while I built a great fire, heated cobblestones, and then dropped them into the barrel. When the water was steaming, we got in and soaked, jumping occasionally into the frigid pool. I made herbed tea for myself and spiced hot wine for Cymea.

I'm afraid things got a little silly, and by the time we remembered the chicken stew, the pot had boiled almost dry. But we added more water and had a very passable chicken soup.

I wished I could have wandered this country for the rest of my life with Cymea, without goals, without plans. But that could not be.

The farms became less plump, the farmers less friendly, and I knew we were drawing close to the army.

We found a widely rutted road many horsemen and wagons had used and followed it.

On a hilltop, I spotted the vast smokes of my winter camp, and we started toward it.

"Damastes," Cymea said, and I turned in the saddle. "I love you."

I smiled, and a nearby bush spoke:

"Neither of you move. State your business and keep your hands away from those swords." A bearded man with a ready crossbow came from his hiding place, and two other bowmen backed him.

We were home.

The army's headquarters was in a trading village, not unlike Paestum, and I hoped, as we rode through it, I'd be able to keep it safer than I'd managed for that town.

It felt as if we'd been gone forever, but not even a time had passed since we'd killed Bairan.

The few days with Cymea had been wonderful, but now they were gone, to be put aside with other memories of days not soaked in blood and death.

Kutulu had taken over a large inn, and we dismounted, were greeted with cheers, and went inside.

Kutulu was studying a map, Yonge by his side, and Svalbard lounged on a bench at the rear of the room.

The hillman eyed us.

"What took you so long? We've been here since yesterday."

NINETEEN

CLOSING

"March out!" I ordered, and drums thundered, bugles sounded, horses stamped, and officers and warrants shouted. At the head of the column, behind our banners, was Domina Thanet and his newly renamed Seventeenth Ureyan Lancers.

"Not bad," I told Linerges.

"I had them do a bit more than shine brass while you were out playing hero," Linerges agreed. "The bugles are almost keeping the same tempo, aren't they?"

"I wasn't referring to the music," I said, "but to the soldiery."

"Eh," Linerges said. "It got boring, sitting around doing our knitting, so we had to do something to take up the time. A little square-bashing fit the bill."

Linerges, Cymea, Sinait, Kutulu, and I, with our staffs, were atop a hill, and the army was moving past, almost in review, below.

"We'll see how they'll do when blood's the issue," Linerges continued. "I'm impressed by nothing until then." He looked forward, where Yonge and his skirmishers, behind the scouting cavalry, swept the line of march.

"It's almost a pity," he said, "that we haven't a month or so before we begin the campaign."

"We're halfway through the Time of Dews now," I said. "Tenedos has always liked to start campaigning early."

"Still," he said. "After your game playing with the Maisirians, I'd like to stay in one place and let all those fat-cheeked young recruits who can't wait to serve under the banner of Damastes the Fair flock in."

"They'll find us if they're serious," I said. "Armies mark the line of march rather thoroughly."

Time *was* what we needed, but time was what we didn't have. Time would give the ex-emperor space to build his spells and develop his strategies.

My own was simple—march north, along the east bank of the Latane, while Tenedos held the west bank. I hoped to link with the Council and their army somewhere around the Latane Delta, then cross over and hammer Tenedos into defeat. I made no strategy more deliberate than that, waiting to see what circumstances would offer.

I gigged Swift to where Kutulu sat uneasily on his horse.

"Any further developments?" I asked.

"Nothing," he said. "Two more agents came in early this morning. All they did was confirm the other reports."

Tenedos was rounding up villagers—old men, women, children, everyone—throughout the area he controlled. No one had any idea what his purpose was, but I knew it couldn't be good, remembering how his magic fed on blood. Until I knew what this meant, I kept this from my commanders, so they wouldn't begin worrying before the proper time.

I rode back to Linerges. "Shall we join the dance?"

*   *   *

We met no opposition until we reached the Latane and turned north, and then no more than a handful of Tenedos's long-range skirmishers, as much spies as soldiers. Some we killed, some we captured, some fled with the news we were on the march.

I didn't worry, for I knew, despite Sinait's best spells, Tenedos's magic would already have alerted him.

As we moved, we rebuilt the heliograph towers, so we had constant communication, when the weather allowed, with our rear in Kallio. That doesn't sound like much, but it was one small step to restore order, to remind Numantians they belonged to a single nation.

The weather was chill, and it showered occasionally, which kept the trail dust down, but I could feel the new life in the land, the Time of Births coming hard upon us, and hoped the new year would finally bring peace to Numantia.

Our peace.

"A question, m'lady?" Cymea and I were riding apart from the rest of the group. "Two questions, actually, somewhat idly put, to pass the leagues."

"You have but to ask, sirrah," she said, "and I'll possibly answer, perhaps even with the truth."

"How *did* Jakuns take the news that you and I have decided to keep company?"

"As any sensible person would, when a wizard tells him something he hates, and he would rather not chance her wrath and be changed into a hearth spider."

"Can you do that?"

"No, but you don't have to tell him that. Seriously? Not well. But perhaps he feels I'm seducing you into our ways, instead of the other way around."

"That leads me neatly into my second question. Why *did* you seduce me, as you said?"

She giggled. "I saw the bulge in your trousers."

"Seriously."

"If I must." Her smile vanished. "I could probably come up with three or four reasons, things I saw you do. But I'll give you two.

"The first was a very long time ago, after my brother had been . . . killed."

"I didn't mean to bring that time up."

"But it is. So be quiet and listen to me," Cymea said. "When I was securely bound, and your soldiers were taking us back to Polycittara, away from Lanvirn, you kept looking at me with a worried expression.

"At first, I thought you were afraid I'd attempt to escape; then I studied your face more carefully. Even though I hated crediting you with any humanity, I saw you were worried about me. About what you feared might happen to me once we reached the imperial dungeons."

"I was," I admitted. "But I never thought my face was that easy to read."

"Damastes, my love," she said. "Do not ever give up soldiering to become a traveling trickster."

"So much for masculine pride," I said. "What's the other reason?"

"That first night, when we came to attempt a truce of sorts, and you refused to give up Kutulu. There were six of us, and you still told us to get fucked as traitorous scum."

"Sometimes I don't use the kind of words a general's supposed to, I guess."

"Or maybe those are the words a general *is* supposed to use," she said. "At least a good one. Things like that make sure there's no possibility of being misunderstood."

"I'm blushing," I said. "So you thought I was brave?"

"Oh, not at all," Cymea said. "I . . . we already knew that. I was taken by your charming stupidity. In your position, I would have agreed to anything we wanted, then shouted for the guards as soon as we left, if that was your intent. Doing it that way increases the life span, you know."

"Your reasons get more and more appalling," I said. "I'm sorry I asked."

"Poor baby." She reached across, patted my gauntleted hand. "The truth is always a harsh mistress. But I do love you, you know."

"And I you."

The northern reaches of Kallio aren't as fertile as the rest of the state, and in some parts almost as barren as Tagil and Amur. A week on the march, and we were forced away from the Latane, tributaries and wide sloughs making it difficult to keep to the banks. We wound our way around the obstacles, through sandy soil and rolling hillocks. There was little on the map ahead of us except a dot of a village, not named, just on the river. I planned to stop there and consolidate my forces.

Tenedos should be not that many leagues distant on the other side. I hoped to be able to send couriers past his lines to Nicias, to tell Barthou and Scopas to have Trerice march south and join me.

I was riding at the head of the army, enjoying the clear, cool air, chatting with Cymea and Lasleigh.

"So," I said, "when all this is over, and we're victorious and covered with laurels, what will you do then? Go back and rebuild your estates, with whatever gold and honors a grateful government bestows?"

He shook his head solemnly. "I doubt if I'd be suited to slip back into country bumpkinry."

"Why not? That's what I intend."

Lasleigh stared in disbelief. "I'll only go back to my estates now and again," he said. "Probably I'll purchase a house in Nicias, for convenience."

"Convenience?"

"I think, once we've won, there's a place for me in government," he said solemnly.

"In what capacity?" I asked, amused. "Inspector of Wayward Girls?"

"You jest, sir. I'm one of those who's keeping himself pure until he marries," he said, serious as always. "I would like to assist in restoring the monarchy."

Both Cymea and I looked at him in considerable surprise.

"Why not?" he asked defensively. "This Grand Council isn't any different than what my father told me about the Rule of Ten. Who else could there be but a king?"

"A council," Cymea said evenly, "is what you make of it. If it's made up of representatives of the people . . . all the people, not just the nobility, then we would have a vastly different nation."

"Yes," Lasleigh said, his voice scornful, "yes, we would, wouldn't we?"

Cymea gazed at him coldly, let her horse drop back until she was beside Sinait, began a deliberately casual conversation with the wizard.

"A bit of advice," I said. "It's not wise to make an enemy out of a magician, even when she's on your side . . . for the moment."

Lasleigh began to reply, caught himself.

"Sorry, sir. You're right, sir."

"Go on about this monarchy," I said, mildly interested,

letting the miles pass under Swift's hooves without notice. "The last king died over two hundred years ago, and his son not long afterward. I looked at the records, a long time ago when I was first stationed in Nicias, and there's not even a pretender. Who should be king? Or queen?"

"I think we should have to have a nationwide examination . . . dammit, that's not the right word," Lasleigh said. "Some kind of selection process, and who'd be the judges I don't know. Once some possible candidates have been picked, properly noble, of course, then let the country choose its own king. The Wizard Cymea's got a point there—why shouldn't people have a voice in who governs them, at least at first? It could be you, sir."

"No, it couldn't," I said flatly. "I've got mangoes and coconuts to plant."

A snort came, and for a moment I thought it was his horse, then realized who'd made the sound.

"That'd be a waste, sir," he continued. "Especially after all you've done for Numantia."

"And *to* Numantia," I said, my mood bleak for an instant, then returning to normal. "Suggest someone else."

"I don't know," Lasleigh said, his eyes turned away. "I'm sure someone, someone with a proper record of bravery in this war, someone with the proper bloodlines, acceptable to everyone, someone who had no ties with the Maisirian puppets . . . there'll be someone."

I suddenly had a strange idea Lasleigh, Baron Pilfern, might be referring to himself.

Ahead was a long rise, a series of dunes, and on the other side we should sight the village on the Latane's banks.

There was a dark line along the rise, and I thought it

brush or perhaps small trees, then saw my vedettes, coming back at full gallop.

The dark line along the dunes moved, and I realized Tenedos had crossed the Latane and was waiting for us!

There was no panic, though, after the initial surprise, and we marched to a small curling hill and took its high ground for the center of the line. I deployed my army in three wings, sending the left and right out in extended order. My forces appeared slightly larger than Tenedos's, and I hoped I might be able to encircle them if I could convince him to attack my center. To reinforce the center, I put the cavalry on either side, light to the front, heavy in the center.

Yonge's skirmishers were ordered to harry Tenedos's line, but to avoid casualties and fall back through the main positions the minute they were attacked in strength.

Then there was nothing to do but wait and feel the tramp of men's feet shaking the ground as formations were shuffled and arranged, hear the discordance of both armies' bugled signals, and the rattle of drums.

I asked Sinait if there were any spells being cast.

"No," she said. "But the air reeks of sorcery. We'll be ready for them this time."

I hoped she was right but was worried. My scouts should've reported the river crossing, for I'd had them out along the river's east bank for leagues. How'd they missed his crossing? Were we being drawn into a trap?

The ex-emperor's army finally came to a halt, and silence grew between the armies, perhaps a million men on both sides, silence except for occasional shouts and the neighing of horses, very clear in the still, sharp air.

A breeze grew in the near silence, whistling across the desolation between the armies.

One horseman, on a white horse, came out of the

enemy center and cantered toward us. He carried no banner but wore golden clothes.

I recognized him.

Laish Tenedos.

He pulled his horse in, cupped his hands, and his voice boomed:

"I am the Emperor Tenedos! I would speak to General Damastes á Cimabue!"

He lowered his hands and sat motionless. Waiting.

"Well?" I said, turning to my wizards.

"I don't sense anything," Cymea said.

"Nor I," Sinait said.

Again, Tenedos raised his hands.

"General Damastes á Cimabue! Come forth!"

"I surely don't trust him," I said. "But I'm starting to look like a fool."

"Sinait," Cymea said. "Wrap yourself in your cloak, as I'm doing."

"Why?"

"We'll ride out, maybe halfway, with Damastes. Then stop, about halfway between him and the lines. He won't be able to recognize us, cloaked, and shouldn't chance any magic to find out who we are," she said. "Maybe that'll worry him a little and give us a bit of power over him. If he attempts anything against either Damastes or the army, we can respond immediately."

"Good," Sinait said. "Damastes, are you willing to stick your head in the lion's mouth?"

"Do I have a choice?" I said, and tapped my reins on Swift's neck. "It isn't the lion's mouth that worries me," I said, trying to make a tiny jest, "so much as his breath."

The sound of my horse's hooves was very loud as I rode forward. Tenedos sat easily in the saddle, waiting.

The impression I'd had from the Seeing Bowl was confirmed—there was something skewed about his hypnotic stare, and the thought came that his gaze was that of a mad hawk. Then I wondered if all raptors weren't mad, at least from the glazed hatred and arrogance in their eyes.

Tenedos was no longer soft, untrained, but lean, sinewy, almost too thin. He wore gold, with a single circlet around his forehead, much like the crown I'd placed on his head long ago in Nicias. I noticed he favored one arm slightly, and hoped Yonge's arrow wound was unhealed and festering.

"Greetings, General Damastes," he said as I closed. "It's a lovely day for a battle."

I inclined my head. "I greet you, as well, although I doubt if there are any good days for killing. Forgive me for not using a title, but I don't know what that should be."

"Emperor sat well once."

"That was once."

He scowled, and I met his gaze without flinching. His eyes flickered, and he looked away for an instant, then back.

"I must congratulate you on ridding Numantia of its greatest enemy," he said.

I could have made a truthful answer—that greatest enemy was just in front of me, not dead in Urey, but held my silence.

"Interesting," he went on, "we . . . you, I, all Numantia, tried so hard to bring the bastard down, and it cost us everything. Then you succeed with a handful of men and a bit of magic, if the tales I've heard are correct."

I shrugged. "Time, circumstances were right, I guess. And maybe the gods favored me."

"Yes," Tenedos went on. "Saionji howled in glee when

he came back to her, I wager. I wonder what form he'll be allowed next? A worm? A dog?"

"I'm not on speaking terms with gods," I said, "so I wouldn't hazard a guess."

"Damastes, my once-friend," Tenedos said, his voice becoming familiar. "There's no need to speak to me like this, just as there is no need for those two behind you. I would guess they're magicians, but you have nothing to fear from me, not this day."

"There was no need for you to attack my family, either," I said.

"Would you believe that was not done, or even authorized by me, but by one of my ambitious wizards? I promise you I had Gojjam treat him as he treated your people."

I stared at him.

"You don't believe me."

"No," I agreed. "I don't believe you."

"Very well then," and now there was anger in his voice. "I wished to speak to you because I want to strike a bargain."

"There can be no bargain," I said. "Unless you cast that false crown you wear aside and make total surrender. If you do that, I promise . . . and I've yet to break *my* word . . . I'll do my best to make sure you're not executed."

"Now," he said, voice reasonable, "you know I can't do that. I have a million and more, people I've given my word to. But more than that, more important, is Numantia itself. I've vowed my kingdom must be restored to its proper glory and power."

"And you're willing to lay waste to it accomplishing that end?" I said coldly.

"There are two armies on this field," he said. "I could say the same to you."

"And that is why we'll fight," I told him.

"Not necessarily," he said. "Because you've changed the balance with your removal of King Bairan."

I waited.

"I've cast spells from the moment one of those beings I can summon told me of Bairan's murder, then the Maisirians' flight back through Kait toward their own lands.

"Their path is littered with bodies and their loot, and I'm afraid precious few will ever see their homes."

"Not unlike what happened to us in Maisir," I said bitterly.

He gave me a hard look, didn't respond, went on:

"Those that return to Maisir, what will they find? No king, no chamberlain, no ruler, but rather the mad obscenity of chaos, with all those pissant little lordlings we so despised groping for power. Chaos! Anarchy! If Numantians cannot handle anarchy, still less can the Maisirians.

"Now is our chance, now is the time when we must set aside our differences and reunite Numantia immediately. With you and me together again, do you think those idiots Barthou, Scopas, and that general of theirs, Trerice, would stand for long? We must bring peace back to Numantia and make our people content once more, as they were.

"Then we must move into Maisir and bring order to them, the stability those peasants must have.

"Damastes, I'm offering you a kingdom! I want you to rule Maisir and for your line to go down in history as the first proper kings of that barbaric land, from now until the ending of time.

"I know you and know you're the only man who can bring peace and unity to the Maisirians."

"I think you forget something," I said. "We weren't defeated by King Bairan, but by more powerful forces.

King Bairan may be gone, but King Winter and King Peasant still hold the land."

"Pah!" Tenedos said. "We were virgins then, but now we've taken full measure of our enemy, and once a problem is recognized, it can be solved. Put aside those minor quibbles, Damastes! Consider what I'm offering you! Immortality! The greatest of power! Think of what I'm offering Numantia!"

I was shaken for an instant, thinking of the thousands and thousands of leagues that could be mine. I could rule as I chose, if I chose, rule harshly and still be thought a kinder king than any the Maisirians had known. My kingdom, under . . .

"I'd be subservient to you, of course," I temporized.

Tenedos inclined his head. "Technically, yes. Maisir and Numantia must stand together, for there are other kings, other kingdoms beyond known borders that my magic has spied out who have great power and are more evil than any Numantian can imagine. Yes, you'd be under my vassalage, but not in practice, save in the most important areas. You would reign alone, in fact. I'd hardly waste time second-guessing you."

"You certainly wasted no time when I was in Kallio," I reminded him.

"I was in error," he grudged. "I was livid and wasn't thinking. But I've changed, learned from my mistakes."

"Now come, Damastes. Look around. What in this wasteland is worth fighting for? Why couldn't we join together, bring Numantia together, and end this pointless slaughter?

"Things could not return to what they were, at our greatest moment, but be better, be more glorious.

"You don't trust me . . . at least not now. But once

you're in Jarrah, sitting your own throne, you'll realize that was a momentary aberrance. Besides, when there are those thousands of leagues between us, how could trust or not-trust enter into it? I'd hardly send armies across the *suebi* because of some minor disagreement, and I can't see anything worse than that. Remember how many years we ruled . . . yes, I use the word 'we,' for you helped create my policies, my actions, more than anyone besides myself. Why not accept this final recognition, this ultimate honor from me?"

I could feel his will, perhaps his magic, batter at me. I started to say something, stopped, considered, while his eyes burnt. I chose what I was going to say very carefully, was about to speak.

Suddenly his lips thinned, and he flushed with rage.

"Very well," he said, almost shrill. "Very well. You've turned away, turned away from your rightful emperor. So be it.

"Damastes á Cimabue, you've made many mistakes in your life. But this is the worst, for now you've brought complete doom on yourself, and on those fools you lead.

"You will not take my hand, will not accept my offer of peace.

"Then let it be war, total war, until either you or I have been spun back to the Wheel.

"And I promise you this: It shall not be me Saionji takes into her final embrace!"

He kicked his horse into a gallop and thundered back to his own lines.

I rode back to where Sinait and Cymea waited.

"You heard?"

"I did not," Sinait said. "I felt you and the once-emperor would value privacy."

"I have no such honor," Cymea said firmly. "I listened as best I could, and unless you forbid it, Damastes, I'll tell Sinait what happened."

"You have my permission," I said, "and I wish what was said repeated to your Tovieti and the army."

"Good," she said. "I hoped you'd say that, for it gives us strength to know you refused a crown."

Sinait's eyes rounded.

"It wasn't quite that nice," I told her. "With Tenedos I'd be more likely to get seven inches of steel between my ribs than a gold ring on my pate. But come. We've got a battle to fight.

"I've had enough of that wizard and his wordplay."

TWENTY

SAIONJI'S WARRIORS

If it had been my battle for the winning or losing, and I were still Tenedos's first tribune, I would have let the fight come to me. The rebels—my forces—had long lines of communication, longer than Tenedos's, and had slightly greater numbers.

But perhaps his rear, however he'd crossed the Latane so secretly and swiftly, about two leagues wide here, wasn't as secure as I'd thought. So far, none of Kutulu's men, Yonge's skirmishers, nor our magic had been able to report how the feat had been accomplished.

About an hour after the parley, such as it'd been, failed, drums snarled, and Tenedos's army attacked.

There was no subtlety—he began with a frontal attack on my positions. I wasn't surprised, nor did I think Tenedos was careless or incompetent. His magic, whatever it would be, needed blood, and it mattered not whether it was shed by his soldiers or mine.

They came at a walk, breaking into a trot no matter how their warrants shouted, across the open ground and up the slight slope, and our arrow storm met them. Heads down, shields up, they forged ahead. The front rank went down almost to a man, the second came on, was broken, and the third wave trampled their own wounded and dying fellows to get at us.

They closed with my front line, and the battle became a dust cloud, with swirling knots of fighters smashing forward, falling back, milling about, or holding around standards or on a slight rise or even no distinguishable feature at all, swords rising and falling, spears darting, occasionally a spatter of arrows going home.

The second prong of Tenedos's assault came from his right. It went wide, attempting to sweep around my left wing. His cavalry, and I was pleased to note that he had far fewer horsemen than I, covered the gaps in his lines and his flanks.

I sat on that hillock, the highest point of land, trying to keep my damned mouth shut and not tell a domina to guard his right or left or put in his gods-damned reserves and stop holding them for a birthday present. This was the hardest part of battle for me, trying to avoid getting sucked into the little skirmishes, to trust my commanders, and to keep some idea of the situation as horsemen dashed here, formations trotted past there, officers screamed everywhere, and men stumbled out of battle wounded or just fell where they'd been struck.

Sinait saw Tenedos's cavalry on my left go into the trot, trying to flank me.

"This, I think, they'll find interesting," she said, and sprinkled water from a vessel about her. The water smelt strange, as if imbued with unknown perfumes, and fell not as drops, but as colored mist.

All the while, she was murmuring gently, under her breath. When she stopped, I asked what she was doing.

"Watch their horses," she said, half-dreamily.

Tenedos's cavalry was riding hard, jut short of full gallop, and suddenly they veered in confusion. I peered across the battlefield, couldn't make out what'd startled them, then saw the disappearing traces of Sinait's illusion, a wide expanse of water. She'd created a mirage, I suppose you'd call it, except that it'd been real enough to scare the galloping horses, send them veering aside. At speed, it takes little to break a cavalry charge, especially if the horsemen aren't fully trained, which takes years.

The confusion blunted their attack, and I sent a galloper to the skirmishers on my left and a company of archers in reserve, ordered both units to exploit the confusion and attack the cavalry. The bowmen ran hard through our lines, taking only their weapons and leaving their protective stakes, trying to catch up to the skirmishers as they pelted on, intent on killing the enemy and, being skirmishers, looting the corpses. In civil war, ransoms are not generally offered or taken.

I ordered my left wing forward. I was curious to see how they'd do, for they were led by another of the old guard, Captain, now Domina, Pelym, who'd commanded a company of Tenth Hussars and was enraged that I'd made him an infantryman, which he felt was a demotion, no matter the rank. If he did well this day, and lived, he'd be a general, and I wondered if that would shut him up. Probably not. Cavalrymen are only slightly less thickheaded than battering rams.

A swirl of confusion developed, and Tenedos's forces fell back toward the start line. They didn't break but moved in good order.

There were still too many of Tenedos's soldiers held back from battle. So far, this wasn't developing into anything close to the major engagement I'd hoped for, a battle of annihilation that'd knock Tenedos out before the campaign really began.

My center, under Linerges, was holding firm, and reforming as Tenedos's first attack fell away.

Somebody shouted, pointed, and I saw another wave of Tenedos's soldiers attack, again toward my center.

I sent a galloper to my right wing, telling its commander, one Ilkley, a high-ranking Tovieti who'd been one of their spies within the Imperial Army, to move forward cautiously against this new formation, attempting to flank it, but bending his own right flank back in the event Tenedos attacked.

With Sinait, Cymea, Svalbard, and my company of bodyguards under Baron Pilfern, we rode forward. I was trying to determine who the new attackers were.

As they closed, I began to worry, for they wore a common uniform: dark boots, tan breeches and blouse, with black armored back- and breastplates. They wore old-fashioned close-fitting helmets with a nosepiece and ear holes. I wondered where Tenedos had found the money for this outfitting, for they were smart enough to be a king's guard.

The men were commonly armed with a sword and a short stabbing spear. But none carried a shield.

Something more amazing—though these lines of soldiers were very well outfitted, they moved like the rawest recruits, stumbling, waving their weapons about, sometimes tumbling over, taking their fellows with them.

As they came, I heard them chanting, less a battle cry or song than shouted grunts, like a lion's hunting cough.

They slammed into my lines hard, and my soldiers balked a moment in surprise, then struck back. Then the horror began, for as these dark warriors were wounded or killed, they changed, armor melting away, disappearing, as did their arms, and these warriors turned into old men, children, women. A moan of terror came upslope at me.

There was only a moment before panic would strike. I shouted at my aides to get back to the hilltop, at Pilfern to follow me, drew my sword, rose in my stirrups, and bellowed the charge.

There was only a dozen or so yards between us and the lines, so we were barely trotting when we smashed into the struggling mass. I saw one of the warriors in black, drove my sword into his chest, nearly vomited as the face changed into that of a kindly middle-aged shopkeeper, blood pouring from her throat as she fell away, and there was another one, and now I realized they all had the same face, plain, long-faced, not unlikable, with a determined jaw, and I killed this man as well, and he became a boy of ten.

I saw, felt, the battle waver for an instant, and then heard trumpets and from the right flank my Seventeenth struck hard. A sword burned pain across my calf, and I cut the swordsman down, not seeing if it was human or one of these monsters.

They fought badly, but with determination. We drove them back and back, killing as we went. Some of Tenedos's soldiery threw down their weapons, waved white, surrendered, but not these nightmares in black.

Now the battle was fully joined, and what would happen, would happen. All I knew was a mist of blood and my sword moving, flashing, driving into soft flesh, grating against bone, my armored sleeve or shield blocking thrusts, killing, ever killing.

Then there was no one left to kill, and I stood on a field of bodies as Tenedos's army retreated, pulling back steadily, even the few remaining soldiers in black obeying the summons of their trumpets.

I saw the strew of bodies, bodies transmuted into civilians, and knew why Tenedos had rounded up all those villagers. His magic put them through some sea change, turned them into homunculi, I suppose the word would be, and sent them out with one thought—to kill and die for him.

I wanted to collapse, to wash my blood-drenched body, to clean the filth, but couldn't.

I changed horses and called for another attack, and we went forward, slowly, steadily, pushing Tenedos back and back, toward the river, as he'd pushed us months ago.

We crested the hill, and saw the Latane, and I saw how Tenedos had crossed the river. The Latane was spotted with islands here and there, and I remembered passing through this maze years ago, admiring the skill of the ship captain for picking the right passageway.

Bridges now stretched from island to island, and Tenedos's forces retreated to and across them, leaving a rear guard behind to hold us back.

As soon as the last soldier was across, the bridge would vanish, and now I understood the speed of the ex-emperor's crossing. The bridges would have been built beforehand, cut apart, and recreated by his Corps of Wizards at the time of crossing.

Sorcery, again, had carried the day. But this trick would work only once.

But the warriors in black were another matter. I didn't know where this magic had come from—a spell invented by Tenedos, or, perhaps, could this transmutation be allowed by Saionji herself? Was she rewarding her servant, even though he thought himself mightier than the goddess?

I didn't know and doubted if even Cymea and Sinait could investigate successfully.

But I did know one thing.

With this magic Tenedos could change anyone, the most tottering ancient, into a warrior, and the war, which I'd hoped to end easily and soon, had barely begun.

TWENTY-ONE

CYMEA'S RAID

Most of the troops were elated at defeating Tenedos for the first time, although I saw some long faces among the soldiery, worried, like their commanders, about this new evil of Tenedos's.

That night, Yonge, Sinait, Linerges, Jakuns, and Cymea met, but nothing new came beyond this new worry.

"Therefore," Yonge asked, "we do what?"

I thought it was doubly important our army make for Nicias and link up with the Grand Council, not only to augment our forces, but to increase the legitimacy of our cause.

Barthou and Scopas were a negative factor, since they'd been Bairan's lapdogs, but whoever held the capital held Nicias and would be considered by most Numantians to have a legitimate claim to the kingdom.

The back of my brain wondered at all these complexities and longed for the simple, uncomplicated days when whacking someone with a sword was enough to settle the issue.

I decided the army would speed march toward Nicias,

cutting through the edges of the Delta when they reached it, while a specially chosen force would harry Tenedos and try to keep him from either attacking us on the march or somehow beating us to Nicias.

"Interesting," Jakuns said. "Magic against magic."

"Precisely," I said. "Harry him with fire and sorcery, and keep him too busy to follow us."

"So once again," Yonge said, "it'll be fools like my skirmishers who'll get fucked, because they're dumb enough to volunteer because they don't want to be part of the unwashed multitude."

"Precisely," I said. "No guts, no glory, as they say."

"Pah!"

Linerges smiled, a rather evil smile, and whispered something to Yonge, who also smirked in an unsettling way.

"Skirmishers," the Man of the Hills mused. "Plus some of the veteran light infantrymen, perhaps a few of the lads from Khurram. Everyone mule-mounted. We have enough of them. A good wizard?"

"That'll be me," Cymea said.

"And why is that?" bristled Sinait. "Am I too old to go adventuring?"

"Not at all," Cymea said. "You and your wizards set up the protective wards around the army, correct? Who else should administer them? I'm the outsider. And I'll take a couple of sages I know. That'll be enough for what Damastes wants done."

"I vastly admire," I said, "two people bickering about who's going to get to go closer to the heart of danger." I wasn't being *that* sarcastic.

"The only question is," Yonge said, smile growing broader, "who commands this daring expedition?"

"Don't be an asshole," I snapped. "You know the answer."

"We do indeed," Linerges said. "And it isn't you."

"The hells it isn't!" Now I understood the amusement.

"The hells it is," Linerges said with finality. "Nor is it going to be me. Damastes, I know you believe in leading from the front. But gods dammit, now's the time you'll have to start leading, period."

"And what does that mean?" I near-snarled.

"*We're* marching on Nicias," he said patiently. "There's Barthou, Scopas, Trerice waiting. Who do you think they're expecting to meet them? Who do you think will have the most weight? Someone they barely remember, like myself? Or the vaunted first tribune, the slayer of King Bairan?

"And if you give me any answer but the right one, I'll suggest here and now that you've become a little too enamored of being dashing, daring, and all too often too gods-damned close to dead!"

My Cimabuan temper boiled for an instant, and I thought of hitting him, and would have if he'd still been smiling. But his face, and Yonge's, had gone serious. I took a deep breath, then another, then looked at Cymea. Her expression was carefully blank.

"No, Damastes," Linerges went on. "You've got to be at the front of the army, for all the reasons I mentioned. Plus we've got to arrive in Nicias looking like conquerors. If we have to tell those idiots on the Council that you've been eaten by snakes in some swamp somewhere, what do you think that'll look like?

"That's why I said I can't go, much as I'd like to, much as I think I owe our ex-emperor a bit of beard sizzling. This isn't a bunch of happy-go-lucky skirmishers. This is an army. Soon, I hope, to be the only army in Numantia. And you're its gods-damned general, so start generaling!"

He sat down abruptly.

No one has ever said I'm blindingly swift, but I've always been able to face a fact when it slaps me bloody.

"All right," I said, in a distinctly uncivil tone. "I'll lead the march on Nicias."

Yonge waggled his eyebrows.

"And *I'll* have fun," he said. "Myself and the luscious Cymea, eh?" He leered ostentatiously at her.

"But what about your goat?" she said.

"Goat? What goat?"

"Isn't it true that the Men of the Hills carry goats with them for pleasure? I'd hate to interfere with such a warm, tender relationship."

Sinait snickered.

Yonge growled. "I liked you better when you were a demon-worshiping strangler."

One hundred fifty skirmishers and infantrymen were ready to march off two days later, with Cymea and two other magicians, both Tovieti. They moved afoot for ease and because well-trained soldiers can move faster, for longer periods of time, than any mounted force.

The raiding force's departure was covered by a rain-storm and Sinait's magic.

Cymea kissed me; then I watched them move away, irregular lines disappearing into the driving rain, and learned in my guts yet another of war's nastinesses: worry.

Sometimes it's harder for those who stay behind.

The long march began. There was no enemy to worry about, and we marched, through the last of the unworked lands, into the rolling farm country. This was the rice bowl of Numantia, the endless paddies of southern Dara, interspersed with patches of jungle.

Then we reached the Delta. The swampland around us was broken with great rice plantations, small farming villages, and tiny, settled islands, some existing by fishing, some by farming, a few even by ranching. We could have been on a peacetime exercise, except I couldn't remember any war game that involved this many men.

We acquired carriages here and there, paying again with our scrip, and these became ambulances for the sick and the lame.

We weren't often forced into the swamp as we moved, but the rough lanes we moved along weren't much better than mire by the time we'd passed through.

Sinait and her wizards were divided up, some riding forward with the cavalry screen to see if there were any traps laid, the others at the rear, alert for any move from Tenedos. Only a few magical tricks were attempted by his wizards, like a fear wave, an overnight coughing spasm, and unusually voracious fleas, but two could have been natural, and the other cast by someone little more than an apprentice under Gojjam.

I was unsettled and could not figure what the problem was. For a few days, I thought it was worry for Cymea, and certainly that was true.

But there was something else, something dark I felt, and it lay ahead, in Nicias. I thought I was merely fed up with dealing with Barthou and his lot and put my mind's warning aside.

A week and a half later, we were barely a third of the way through the Delta. Late one afternoon, a galloper came up from Linerges, commanding the rear guard, announcing a sorcerer had discovered soldiers coming from behind, coming fast.

I hoped it was Yonge's raiders but didn't know if Tenedos had come after us and so rode back with three gallopers, Sinait, and my bodyguards, ordering the army to keep moving. I found a lovely spot for an ambush—a long straight stretch of road with swamp on one side, fairly thick underbrush for hiding on the other, and curves at either end. I showed Linerges the spot when we reached him, and we laid an ambush.

Perhaps Yonge was right, and I was that invaluable, but I'd be damned if I'd wrap myself in batting. I had Swift tethered beyond the ambush zone, with the other horses, borrowed a bow and arrows, and concealed myself with Linerges.

Silence fell, and there was little sound except for the whispering wind, water noise from the swamp, then chitters and shrills building as the insects and birds regained confidence. A monkey howled, and another echoed its call. Someone tried to hide a cough, buried a yelp as a warrant kicked him, but mostly the soldiers were quiet. Waiting.

After an hour or so, the animal noises broke off, and someone was coming. We readied our weapons, set to spring the trap when the enemy entered the killing zone.

Four, then eight men rounded the curve. They were ragged, clothes ripped, but carried their weapons at full readiness. Ten yards behind these point men came the rest of their squad, as alert as the others, although three or four were bandaged, and one was limping.

The advance party was almost on us when the main group came around the bend.

I recognized Domina Sendraka among the point men,

just as one of his soldiers' heads jerked, and he swept an arm in circles, a silent alarm.

I stood, which wasn't the smartest thing I've ever done, for the alerted soldier almost put an arrow through my weasand before realizing who I was.

"A little careless, Domina," I said. "We could have been the enemy."

Sendraka grinned. "No, you couldn't have, sir, unless you've learned how to fly, for the bastards haven't a boat to float."

"You did well?"

"We hammered the sons of bitches," he said, face in a hard grin.

"Casualties?" I said this as if it wasn't the most important thing in the world to me.

"Four killed, about twenty wounded," he said, and eyed me. "No civilians, all soldiers."

Was I this transparent to everyone?

The main element of the skirmishers had closed on me, and Linerges was breaking up the ambush force. I saw Yonge, Cymea beside him.

"I greet you, General. Seer," I said formally. "Domina Sendraka said you have done well."

"Perhaps a bit better than well," Yonge said. "Would you care to stand here in the road and hear the bloody details, or be a proper general and let us get to a campsite where there'll be wine and soap?"

Cymea was in front of me. "What's the proper procedure . . . oh, the hells with it," she said, and was in my arms. I heard hoots and laughter, ignored them, and kissed her thoroughly.

"Welcome home, love," I whispered.

"Welcome indeed," she said. "I want to rape you."

"I'm rapeable," I said. "Except . . ."

"I know. I stink."

"Well . . ."

We broke apart. Yonge came close.

"You might as well marry her, Cimabuan, for she's impervious to the many charms and virtues of a hillman, and such women are priceless."

Someone had somewhere acquired a marvelous invention and given it to me. It was a two-piece steel ring with four legs that a canvas bathtub fit into, just big enough for me to sit in, and it was one of my great pleasures to fill and splash about in it for a few minutes at the end of the day's march.

I'd also become enough of a sybarite to have a light canvas tent, not much more than a pavilion with sides, in one of the supply wagons and had given up sleeping on the ground unless I had to.

With Cymea's homecoming, I had it erected a bit away from the rest of my headquarters. Svalbard, unbidden, had heated water and filled the tub.

Cymea squealed as if this were the most precious present imaginable, and having been as dirty as she was, I well understood her glee. There was lime-scented soap Svalbard had bought from a farmer, and I left her to soak while I took care of some administrative matters.

Four canvas buckets full of hot water stood outside the tent when I came back, and I lugged them inside.

"And how did you know the water was just getting cold?" she asked.

"I know things like that, because I've been associating with evil wizards," I answered. "Now, if you'll step out for a moment and allow me to recharge this tub?"

I tried not to think about her brown sleekness while I dragged the tub to the tent's mouth, upended it, and filled it again.

"Now, milady," I said, "If you'd be kind enough to get wet, I'd be delighted to scrub you."

"But I've already soaped," she said.

"Done a shoddy job of it, too. I'm a general, so do what I tell you."

"Only if you'll take off your general suit to keep it from getting wet."

"Your wish . . ."

She splashed water while I undressed, tossing my clothes into a camp chair nearby. She stood, and I picked up the soap and began moving it across her body.

"I know what I want," she said, turning, letting me wash the front of her body, lingering over her breasts, stomach, abdomen. "I want to have you on top of me, with your full weight on me, while you're in me. Right over there, on that camp cot, right now, while I'm still wet and slippery."

She stepped out of the bath, went to the cot and lay down, brought her legs up and parted them. I moved atop her, slid my cock into her, buried it full length and lay, as ordered, atop her.

"Now I *am* home," she sighed, lifting her legs around my back. "Now no tricks, no pulling out, no teasing, just move, keep moving, until we both come. That's what I want."

I obeyed, moving within her slowly, deeply, her hands pulling at my back, her lips moving against mine, and I felt the wave building, and she whimpered, her body jerking hard against me, and I went off, and a few seconds later she did, too.

Her body pulsed for long seconds, then went limp.

"You're nice to be in love with," she managed after a while.

"Likewise," I said.

"That was once," she said. "I promised myself, out there with all the killing, I'd get fucked at least three times before doing anything else when I got back."

"Excellent idea," I said. "But there's a banquet of sorts planned, and you're going to have to learn a new skill."

"What's that?"

"Telling war stories."

"Poot on war stories," she said. "I just want to fuck for a while. That's the only skill I need work on right now." She lifted one leg down onto the cot, began moving it back and forth, and her sex moved with her leg, pulling at my cock, and it stiffened again. She slid one hand down, began caressing my balls.

"Once more like we just did," she whispered. "Then you'll need the soap, for I want it in all three places next."

My ardor was at least as strong as hers, for we did manage three times before an aide tapped decorously on the tent's entrance pole and announced the staff was assembled for dinner.

"We had no troubles at all on the march," Cymea began. We'd eaten, cleared our dishes, and those who wished had more wine. The improvised mess we sat in was a series of interconnected tents, rather shaky, but easy to move and to split apart for other purposes. I sipped a spiced orange drink, listening.

"Tenedos's forces were about ten leagues beyond where they'd escaped from us. We found some boats in a village and shuttled across above his positions without being discovered. There were patrols out, but we evaded them."

"You flatlanders," Yonge put in, "should be complimented if someone calls you blind. We slid past them like . . ."

"Like a Bandit of the Hills past warders?" I suggested.

"Carrying a dozen chickens and the warder's daughter," Yonge added. "But this is Cymea's story."

"They had magic out as well, but not much. I suppose Tenedos thought no one would have the temerity to use his own art against him," Cymea continued.

"Yonge decided we wouldn't pull any pinprick raids, as we did against the Maisirians, but hit them as hard as we could with one single attack, then pull out, and not give Tenedos a chance to use his magic against us.

"Tenedos is moving north, because there were rows and rows of boats pulled back from the Latane or into sloughs around his position.

"Each day at dawn, he'd fill the boats with maybe a third or so of his army and let the current carry them north. The rest of the army would march and ride to keep up, and generally they'd join up sometime after nightfall. The next day, the boatmen would be walking, and a third of the others floating. By the way, I noted his officers either rode or were on the boats, and never saw one afoot.

"We followed them for four days, as they moved north, very quickly, as two men with one horse can move faster than two men walking. Yonge said if they were able to hold their speed through the Delta, they'd reach Nicias about the same time our soldiers would.

"I thought the most important thing would be to destroy their boats, but we didn't have enough men. Or so

I thought," she went on. "Then I noticed something. All of the boats looked the same."

There were about sixty men sitting, all high rankers, listening intently to an eighteen-year-old woman, and there were more standing, packed tightly under the canvas. There was only one other woman, Sinait, and she appeared as fascinated as the men.

"Which meant magic had built them.

"I knew how that had been done: One boat would be carefully built, then cut into fragments. All things are part of the whole, so a fairly simple spell would make each fragment into a complete boat.

"What magic can do," Cymea said, "magic can undo. It was Yonge's turn next."

"Eh. There's nothing to tell," Yonge said. "I took a little stroll, did a little whittling, brought Cymea back some woodshavings for her to work on."

"What he's not telling you is he and two other men sneaked into the middle of Tenedos's camp without being seen, cut fragments from a dozen or more of the boats, and brought them back out without notice," Cymea said.

"It took me the rest of the day to make the spell," she went on. "Not because it's complicated, but because it had to be powerful, so I had to keep reciting it over and over, building it, along with my assistants.

"I wish," Cymea said to Sinait, "I'd had some of your people with me, for it would've been a lot easier. At least on my throat.

"Yonge said we should strike that night, but I thought we should wait until the next morning, when we could do the most damage. I had a great fire readied, from the dry driftwood along the banks.

"I didn't sleep that night, but continued building the

spell. I had to take one of my assistants away from the task for a counterspell, to make sure Tenedos didn't sense what was building, for it was becoming most powerful.

"But no response came. Maybe he was arrogant, maybe he was 'looking' in the wrong direction. I don't know.

"Before dawn, we heard Tenedos's camp being bugled awake. I waited until the light came across the river, mist walking low along the water."

There wasn't a sound in the tent.

"It got light enough to see movement," Cymea said. "Their boats were being loaded, and we saw the first ones being poled away from the banks and out of the sloughs they'd landed in, and the current taking them.

"I lit the fire, and it caught at once, the herbs and powders I'd added sending the flames roaring in a great, spinning cylinder. We'd have only a few moments before someone saw this fire, which looked . . . and was . . . completely unnatural.

"Once more, I said the spell and then cast the wood bits from Tenedos's boats into the flames."

Cymea broke off, took a very deep breath, finished the wine in her glass, and refilled it.

"Out of the river, the boats caught fire as well. First sparks, then small flames, which the men tried to beat out, but this fire wasn't of natural origin and could only be extinguished when my fire on the land burnt out.

"The fires raged, and men themselves began burning. Burning or jumping overboard. I don't think many of them could swim. The fires kept burning, and boats were floating away, empty, roaring in flames.

"The river was full of men. Then there were louder screams, echoing down the river, and the water was torn. Crocodiles."

She shuddered, drank more wine.

"The river beasts fed well that morning," Yonge said happily. "And the river, the great Latane, ran with blood. All was crazy, all was havoc.

"So then we attacked them, running into the middle of where their camp had been, where their columns waited for the marching order.

"*Now* there was a slaughter," he went on. "One hundred fifty madmen, against an army of what, a million? Two million? But all was confusion, screaming, no one knew what anyone was doing, what was going on, and we flung the little firesticks we'd used before against their pack animals and wagons. We kept at the run and killed as we went.

"That was where we took our casualties, but we slew far more, ten, a hundred times more than we lost in the minutes we were in the middle of their host.

"We ran out the far side of the enemy camp, laughing like loons," he said. "We stopped long enough for Cymea and the other mages to cast a diversionary spell, then ran on. Cymea said magicians were casting after us, but their strength was broken, their confidence shaken, and so we escaped, running down a farming road in broad daylight with no one, not sorcery, not soldiers, chasing us.

"North of the disaster we found an abandoned ferryboat, a big one, tied to a dock. We piled aboard and pushed off, and the current carried us downstream, through and around the islets, and we used the boat's rudder to steer us through the mire. By the time we were forced to abandon the boat, bits and pieces of our handiwork were floating past us."

"Bodies," Cymea said softly, so we all had to crane to hear her. "I've never seen so many bodies. Bodies . . . and parts of bodies. And the creatures that still fed on them."

She drank her glass dry, stood.

"And that was what we did to Tenedos."

The officers were standing, cheering her and Yonge and the incredible victory.

I wonder how many of them noticed Cymea was crying.

TWENTY-TWO

BETRAYAL IN NICIAS

I t was a fine season as the Time of Dews gave way to
the Time of Births, but the dark foreboding still hung
over me. I'd been fighting almost continuously since I
was eighteen. Twenty years of bloodshed or its threat, and
I was tired.

"So what shall we do when peace comes?" Cymea
asked.

"It's now we? I'm deeply honored," I said, bowing in
my saddle.

"You're about the only option I'm interested in,"
Cymea said. "Play politics with my brothers and sisters? I
don't even know if the Tovieti would be willing to go into
a legitimate government. I'll wager it's hard having to
compromise with your enemies when the best solution
before was just throttling them. For all I know, the Tovieti
will develop a purity problem, go underground once more
and dig out the yellow cords. Although I'll always be a
Tovieti in spirit, I don't think that's for me."

"That's a true blessing," I said. "I can't quite picture
explaining why my partner's a little late coming home—
'had to stop and strangle a couple of the local merchants

she thinks are overcharging her, but won't you have some tea while you're waiting?'"

"What kind of home would we have?" she asked.

"I don't know," I said, leaning over in my saddle, plucking a scarlet flower from a bush and presenting it to her. "I don't know if I want to go back to Cimabue, even though I've blathered on about the joys of being a noble bumpkin."

"And do you . . . we . . . want to live that far away from the swirl of events?"

"Hells yes," I answered quickly. "I've been too much in those moils and toils. But we could live in . . . no, not in, but maybe near a city, and you could keep me posted. Ride back every night and tell the old man what the latest styles and gossips are."

"Poot," Cymea said. "Where I go, you go."

"Something interesting just came," I said. "You know, I never worried about money. Either I had none but had the army, or I had an enormous amount and couldn't spend it all in a lifetime.

"Now?" I fished into my sabertache, took out a bare handful of coins. "I've had these since . . . since when? Since we looted the boat? And that's all the gold I've got to my name."

"Numantia will hardly let someone who's done as much as you have starve."

"You have more faith in people's generosity once the emergency's over, than I. I remember seeing all too many crippled soldiers put out to beg in the streets.

"Maybe," I continued, "maybe I could get a job with Linerges, and we could go on the road, peddling fancies off a cart."

"Poot twice," she said. "But come to think of it, I

doubt if my claims to the Amboina estates in Kallio will be honored, so I guess we're determined on a life of being poor but dishonest.

"If it comes down to that, the hells, let's go across the border and join your friend Bakr. You make being a Negaret sound like fun.

"If you get ambitious once we're Negareting, you could always take over the throne in Jarrah. It sounds like their noblemen will spend more time hitting each other over the head than trying to take care of their country."

"Poot three times," I said. "Fuck a whole group of thrones. Can you see me as King Damastes?"

She looked at me queerly, and I felt a shiver. She changed the subject.

"At least one thing," she said. "So far neither one of us has mentioned marriage."

"You aren't interested?"

"Not unless there's a way of doing it without it becoming *my* wife, like *my* horse, *my* house. I'm not a possession and never will be," she said, a bit fiercely. "As far as I can see, the only purpose marriage has is if somebody's dying, and there's a lot of things to divide up, which it doesn't sound like there'll be for us.

"Or, maybe, if there are children." She bent her head, sniffed at the flower I'd given her. "I think I'd like that," she said, softly.

The cold came hard, as if a winter wind had blasted down the winding road.

"Please, Cymea," I said. "Please don't talk about things like that."

"Why not?"

Emotion washed over me.

"Because . . . and I guess I'm going to sound as if I'm

feeling sorry for myself, and maybe I am, but every time things like children and being happy for very long come up, they get taken away from me."

Her face hardened. "Am I always going to be reminded about that?"

"Oh, for Irisu's sake," I said. "I didn't mean it like that. I wasn't thinking of anything, except that when things start going well for me, my luck always seems to go into the cellar. What's the old soldier's line—if it weren't for bad luck, I wouldn't have any luck at all? Sometimes it seems like that to me."

"Bad luck?" she said. "Ex-First Tribune Damastes á Cimabue, escaped prisoner á Cimabue, General á Cimabue, complaining about his luck?"

"The glory sometimes doesn't compensate," I said.

"You *are* feeling sorry for yourself. Here, lean over and let me kiss you."

I obeyed, feeling somewhat foolish.

"Now, you take care of the outside luck," she said. "I'll handle the inside luck, all right? Your only concern is keeping my insatiable lust satisfied. Otherwise, I might have to go creeping out at night to Yonge's tent."

"His tongue isn't half as long as mine," I said, glad to be onto another topic.

"I wouldn't know," she said. "I found him a bit of a disappointment, when we were raiding. He never made even one suggestive remark, let alone anything else."

"Yonge?" I said, in some amazement. "Nobility from a man who fucked his way through most of the married women in Nicias, fighting a duel with every affair?"

"Not this incarnation," she said. "I'd heard the stories . . . hells, you'd told me some of them. He might as well have been a temple guard. Or I a temple virgin."

"I've heard about those temple virgins," I said, looking lustful. "The subject of many a barracks ballad. What do you know on the subject?"

"I was one, for about a month," she said. "When I was being bounced from place to place."

"You didn't tell me about *that* in your tale."

"Nothing to tell," she said. "Sleep on stone, get up before dawn, go to your cell when it's dark. Pray a lot and eat food a peasant would scorn. Then pray some more. It was so deadly dull I didn't even want to play with myself, although there were a couple of women who offered to take care of that detail for me. I was never so glad to move on in my life . . . other than when I was broken out of prison, back at the beginning."

So it went, idle chatter as the leagues wound past, and the roads grew better, the farms more frequent, and the bridges across the creeks and small rivers more modern, wider and stronger.

The farmers and workers lined the roads now, sometimes cheering us, sometimes just watching curiously. Every now and again one of the few youths among them would follow in our dust until we camped, then enlist, eyes shining for glory and adventure.

Kutulu's spies reported that Tenedos had regrouped and was moving north, again by boat and by land.

But we were far ahead of him.

When we were about six leagues beyond Nicias, a rider came back from the scouts. We'd made contact with the Council's army. I went forward with my command group and saw a smartly turned out troop of cavalry, wearing the gray with red of the Peace Guardians, led by an officer named Cofi, who announced himself, to my great if hidden amusement, as a domina instead of a *shalaka*. Evidently, with the Maisirians back across the border, their ranks were no longer in such high regard in Nicias.

He bade us welcome and said an empty down a league farther would be ideal for our camp, although no one had expected quite this large a formation. He seemed a little upset by that.

He said the citizens of Nicias welcomed the army, and vast amounts of supplies were already on their way to the down to prove their sincerity.

"Good," Linerges murmured. "Always good to keep the troops fattened. Keeps them from looting."

"Isn't there something," Yonge asked, equally quietly, "about feeding a calf while you're thinking about a good recipe for sweetbreads?"

"That too," Linerges said. "I can tell we're coming into the capital with a proper attitude."

"Except for him," Yonge said, indicating me. "He no doubt thinks that all this is sincere and meant only to show the toadies' sudden respect and love."

"I'm not *that* stupid," I snarled. "Now shut up. That damned domina might have better ears than you think."

In the old regular army . . . and I wondered if I was starting to become a frizzled old fart, thinking like that . . . soldiers set up their camp methodically. First the commander would determine which unit went where after riding the land with his subordinates.

Each regiment, company, troop, squadron, whatever, would be marched to its designated area. Warrants would determine the locations of cook tents, horse lines, wagon parks, jakes, then a ranking warrant would take a post, and the soldiers would tell off on him, and the tents, or sleeping positions if the unit was living rough, would be laid out. The men would set to work with canvas, ropes, and mauls, and in an hour, sometimes less, you could look down any row of tents, and the lines holding the canvas taut would be perfectly aligned, like soldiers in formation.

This wasn't quite the style of my army. I rode across the down, decided which unit would go where, and then the units pitched their tents—those that had them—wherever was convenient, with close to the cook fires and far from the shithole preferred.

Since it was wartime, my camps, while somewhat disorderly on the inside, were laid out like a prickly hedgehog. We barricaded the camp: stacked brush, long stakes sharpened on both ends and set in the ground facing outward, entrenchments, or even natural barricades like thorny thickets. Guard posts were set at regular intervals before anything else was done.

No matter how tired, the men always worked hard, for the quicker camp was set, the safer everyone was, and the sooner meals could be cooked and eaten.

I chose a commanding hill for my headquarters, had Cymea's and my tent pitched close behind it, and began digging my jakes while Svalbard tended to the horses and Cymea set up our bed, two camp cots Svalbard had modified to lash together, my field desk, her chest with magical implements, our bathtub, and that was all the furniture we owned.

I'd barely turned a few spadefuls of earth when civilians swarmed into our camp. They must have left Nicias that morning and stayed behind Domina Cofi's horsemen until told it was all right to proceed. They brought fresh vegetables, fish, cooked fowls, cuts of beef, wine, brandy, and often as not, themselves. The only thing I had my provosts refuse was the brandy, and I made sure the wine was evenly shared, so there wouldn't be enough for any man to get drunk on.

The camp was more a feast than a military post, but there wasn't any danger. Or not much, anyway. I'd expected something like this and told my officers to turn a blind eye to most things as long as there wasn't any violence, and the provosts and the poor bastards on sentry-go didn't get careless.

I was about knee-deep in the earth, planning to dig to my waist, since it appeared we'd be in this encampment for a while, bare-chested and sweating, when bugles bellowed, and a galloper announced that Scopas and Trerice, accompanied by a hundred horsemen, had arrived.

I started to clamber out and pull on my jacket when I caught myself and went back to digging. Indeed, when Scopas and Trerice arrived, they both showed surprise, seeing a general actually working, instead of ordering others about, exactly the impression I wished to make. This was an army where everyone worked, everyone fought, and if we went into the field together, that'd be the rule for the Council's army as well.

Scopas wore something that could have been called a military uniform, since it included high boots, breeches, and a high-necked tunic, but his vast chest was so ridiculously laden with golden and silver geegaws I couldn't tell what army he thought he was serving in. Trerice wore, as before, his plain grays and ready weapons, and his eyes were as cold as his sheathed steel.

Scopas greeted me effusively, calling me the hero of the time, one of the greatest generals . . . and warriors . . . Numantia had ever known, and so on and so forth, very definitely playing to the aides still ahorseback behind him, and to any of my soldiers within earshot. If Barthou had done this, I might have laughed, but I noticed Scopas's shrewd eyes looked here, there, as he spoke, assessing the impact of his praise. This calculation and cunning was precisely why I wanted no part of politics.

I climbed out of the hole. "Greetings, Councilor Scopas. And General, as I assume your title is now, Trerice. Might I ask where the honored Barthou is? I assume he survived the somewhat rapid withdrawal your forces made after I saw him last?"

"His duties made it impossible to join us," Scopas said.

Trerice's words, intended to be civil, came out a bit clipped, unsurprising after what I'd just said: "You have surprised us all, General."

"I should hope so," I said, turned to Scopas. "I welcome you to the people's army, Councilor. I wish that I had the words that you do and the ability to compose them as well. But I don't, so that's the best I can do.

"Perhaps you'd join me in the mess, and we'll find a bottle of wine worthy of your attentions. Trerice, I don't recall if you drink."

"Seldom."

"My own habit."

"We'd like to take advantage of your hospitality," Scopas said. "But we must return to Nicias before nightfall.

"There is business, urgent business, that we must discuss. In private, if you wouldn't mind?"

"Perhaps in my tent?"

They followed me inside.

"This," I introduced, "is Cymea. She's one of my advisers and one of my wizards."

They both bowed politely, but it was obvious what they

thought her to really be, considering her beauty. She responded politely, slipped out.

"I assume this area is safe?" Scopas said.

"Against eavesdroppers, I assume you mean," I said. "For there's no one in this camp who wishes you harm. It is. I always have Sinait, my chief wizard, secure my sleeping quarters against any intrusion."

Yonge would have been proud of my increasing ability to lie. Unless everyone was completely asleep, since I'd given no orders to the contrary, Sinait would be setting a Seeing Bowl at this moment, and most likely Kutulu himself would have his ears pressed against the back wall.

Of course I didn't think these two believed me, since they weren't babes, either.

I seated them, offered drinks again, which were refused.

"Your exploits have certainly gone before," Scopas said. "When last we spoke, things were somewhat different."

"They were, indeed," I said. "I was your prisoner. Now I have about a million and a half men, probably another five hundred thousand joining in Kallio or following our tracks north. We've fought Tenedos twice, south of the Delta, once with arms, once with sorcery, and defeated him both times."

"We've heard of the one," Trerice said, "and rumors of the other. But my intelligence suggests neither battle was conclusive."

"No," I said. "But both accomplished far more than when our forces were at Paestum."

Scopas looked pointedly away. Trerice's anger was clear. "Back then . . . we . . . neither side . . . had the experience we have now, and Tenedos was able to strike us in the most vulnerable area," he snapped.

"Good generals do things like that," I agreed, enjoying

Trerice's discomfort. "Now we must make sure he doesn't do it again.

"That is," I said carefully, "if I'm correct in assuming any sort of alliance. Perhaps you wish to continue your old fealty to the Maisirians, in which case I must consider both of you my country's enemies."

"No, no," Scopas said hastily. "That was something we were forced to do, to save what was left of Numantia. But you, thank Irisu, have removed that problem, for which we're all extraordinarily grateful."

Trerice didn't look grateful at all but held his tongue.

"The question then becomes," I said, "what comes next?"

Scopas blinked. "Why . . . we deal with Tenedos in the best way possible."

"To me, that means only one thing," I said. "We completely destroy him."

"Is that a wise position?" Scopas said. "If we leave him . . . and his soldiers . . . no options other than total defeat, won't that make them fight all the harder? Make them willing to destroy all rather than accept defeat?"

"Listen to me, Scopas," I said. "Tenedos already has taken that stance. Do you know what he's doing? He's seizing innocent villagers and using his magic to turn them into warriors. Have you heard about that? Has your vaunted intelligence told you about those soldiers who, when they're cut down, turn back into babes and beldames?"

Scopas was shocked, Trerice tried to hide his surprise.

"We'd heard something about his having significant increases in his forces," the general said uncomfortably, "but . . . no. We hadn't heard the details."

"My staff will brief you, as soon as I authorize it," I said. "Do you see what I mean? There can be no surrender but an unconditional one.

"And when we have seized Tenedos, we must make sure he'll never be able to try to seize power once again."

"You mean kill him? Without a trial?"

"I mean kill him," I said firmly. "Or, if you want it to sound less grim, reunite him with his beloved gods-damned Saionji, if that's more comfortable on your lips. We can have a trial, if it pleases you, after the funeral pyre burns out."

"General Damastes," Scopas said, "I realize, as a soldier you take, must take, a firm position. But—"

"There are no buts," I said. "That is the position we take . . . not just myself, but my entire army. We don't have a motto, but if we did, it'd be *Tenedos or Death*. And death's a lot cleaner than allowing him to take control again of our country, of our souls."

Scopas took a deep breath, Trerice looked grim.

"I see your point," Scopas said. "And perhaps that's what we lack . . . what we have lacked. Perhaps we need to take a firmer stance, and oppose the ex-emperor more directly.

"Perhaps that's your great strength, what you can add to our government."

It was my turn to look noncommittal.

"Here is what we came to ask," Scopas said. "There have been few enough victories to cheer the citizens of Nicias. Would it be possible to have a triumph? A review of your army, as soon as possible. The people want to see the victors of the Latane, which is what they're calling you now. They want to see you, Damastes."

"It would be a simple matter," Trerice said. "This area you're camped in is intended to be only temporary. A larger camp, better drained, with some outbuilding already standing, is being set up for you to the west of Nicias.

Perhaps you remember it from your army days, General. It was the old sporting and review grounds outside the city."

I did remember it and had enjoyed its greens and sweated on its dusty parade fields. It was convenient to the capital, just on the other side of one of the wider branches of the Latane, served by regular ferry services.

I considered, saw no hidden tricks, and recognized another advantage.

"Yes," I said. "We could do that. Perhaps it might do my soldiery some good as well, to see who we're fighting for."

That was about the end of the conversation. But after I'd bidden the two farewell, and they'd ridden away with their retinue, I saw a piece of paper on my field desk that hadn't been there before.

It was in Scopas's careful script that I knew well from my time serving the Rule of Ten:

> *We must speak more of my previous offer as soon as possible. I will make the arrangements.*

"Interestin'," Yonge observed. "Thieves falling out, and all that sort of thing, isn't it?"

There were five besides myself in the tent, Linerges, Yonge, Kutulu, Cymea, and Sinait. Both wizards had cast separate Squares of Silence, to prevent anyone from overhearing.

"Hardly surprising," Sinait said. "Both Barthou and Scopas desperately want to save power for themselves and will align themselves with anyone to keep it."

"It looks to me," Linerges said, "they've got three choices: to try to hang on to what they've got by themselves, which doesn't look possible from here; to link up with Tenedos, which they'd consider, except I don't think he'd give them anything except a sacrificial knife if he wins; or get in bed with you, Damastes."

"They made the offer before," Sinait mused. "What makes them think he'd be interested in taking it this time?"

"Pure desperation," Yonge said flatly.

"I'll agree with that," Linerges said.

I glanced around. Cymea nodded, as did Sinait. Kutulu considered carefully for a time.

"The simplest explanation that Yonge offers is the most likely, in my opinion," he said.

"So we're agreed," I said. "What next?"

"I don't think," Yonge said, "we can ignore Nicias. It's good for victors to show themselves to the people they're going to rule . . . sorry, Damastes, that they're fighting for, since you insist we're all in this madness for the sheer nobility of the deed.

"I did my share of parades and things after I killed Achim Baber Fergana and took Sayana. But are things different here? Are we endangering ourselves by taking part in this banners and bullshit they want?"

"The review?" Linerges thought. "I can't see how. I'll arrange the army so that we can fight back, if we're attacked in the city. We'll keep our weapons ready at hand, and since we haven't been able to afford dress uniforms, wear what we fight in. The citizens will never notice and think it's a thrill they're seeing real warriors equipped for the field.

"We can pull back if there's any sign of danger early; then, if we're hit in the center of the city, make for one of the parks and fight from there. Once we're in that camp on the far side of the city, we're pretty invulnerable."

"What about magic?" I asked.

"All I've been able to sense," Sinait said, "is the most minor of spells. They don't seem to have any great magicians like we do, or Tenedos does. Have you found any signs, Cymea?"

"None," she said. "And we've quizzed our brothers and sisters who've come to this camp."

"I have a few agents in the city," Kutulu said. "And I've read the Tovieti reports. Nothing of significance appears to be happening."

"So it then becomes their play," I said. "We proceed as if that note had never been written, and see what happens next?"

"That," Linerges said, "appears to be the most obvious plan."

"Why don't I like it at all?" I asked.

"Nor do I," Yonge said. "But there appears no other choice."

The night before the review, an idea came.

"Cymea," I began, "I would like you to do something."

"Such as? I'm being suspicious," she said, "because you've got that tentative note in your voice."

"It's very simple," I said. "You're in touch with the Tovieti in the city. I'd like to get a message to them. Please let Jakuns, Himchai, and Jabish know of it as well.

"When the army marches through, ask your brothers and sisters not to cheer too loudly for us, especially not anyone they recognize as one of them."

"Why not?"

"Right now, nobody knows who the Tovieti are in Nicias, correct?"

"I'd guess not," she said. "Or the warders would've arrested or killed them."

"Let's not have the brethren make themselves obvious, then. We're just having a parade, and the war's a long ways from being over. We might need them, need them while they're still underground."

She looked at me thoughtfully. "You're becoming very devious, my love."

"No, I'm not," I said. "Everyone else is already sneaky, and I'm just trying to keep up."

"You show great promise at being a Tovieti," she said. "Would you like a silk cord for your day of birth?"

I was proud of myself, and what Cymea had given me, that I was able to chuckle a little instead of losing my temper.

"Yes," she said. "Yes, I think you've had a good idea. I'll tell Jakuns, and if he and the others agree, we'll arrange for our brothers to just stand and stare when we go traipsing past."

"They don't have to go to *that* extreme," I complained. "A friendly wave or two is quite acceptable."

A delegation of Nicias's tailors came, and Scopas was with them, dressed as they were, except his garments were far finer than any weaver could ever afford. He asked what I now thought of his offer.

"Exactly what form does it now take?" I inquired.

"We want you, as before, to become supreme commander of the armies. Both armies."

"What about Trerice?"

Scopas looked uncomfortable. "If he isn't willing to serve under you, then . . . well, then, he'll have to be replaced."

"What about your other high officers? Drumceat? Taitu?"

"They'll obey our orders."

"Let's discuss something else," I said. "What happens after we defeat the emperor? Who rules Numantia?"

"Then will come your great reward. Barthou and I will create a third Grand Councilor. You. And the three of us will rule and return Numantia to its greatest days."

I thought of asking why everyone talked about "returning" to better days, rather than rising to new greatness, but refrained. I temporized and told him I'd make some sort of a decision after we'd regrouped in our new camp.

Scopas returned to the others, trying to pretend that he was but one of them, evidently thinking everyone would ignore the four hard-eyed men who surrounded him, their hands constantly brushing their swords' hilts. I hoped he had done a better job of appearing a nonentity leaving Nicias than he did here.

As for the tailors' business . . . that gave us a bit of merriment. They'd been appalled to note the shabbiness of my soldiers and their motley attire.

"You propose to outfit all of us?" I inquired. "With only a few days until the Grand Parade? You must have more men and women skilled with the needle and shears than I thought. And I warn you, we don't have great chests of gold."

"Well, no," their leader admitted. "And such a gift, even though you and your men certainly deserve that, nay, deserve to have the finest raiments sewn with golden threads, would bankrupt all of us.

"What we propose is to give each of your men a tunic and breeches like these."

A man stepped out from their midst wearing a rather nattily cut maroon outfit, with slash-cut thigh boots. It wasn't bad looking, but I wondered if its designer had considered what would happen when its wearer attempted to conceal himself in a forest.

"Interesting," I said, neutrally.

"We can have our . . . not our, actually, but ones we have on retainer, or at any rate who've worked for us in the past and hope to work for us in the future . . . magicians duplicate this uniform, and have thousands, perhaps even a million in your hands within two, no, three days."

I looked into the spokesman's eyes. He was terribly sincere and meant the best, and I hated to do it to him.

"Sir," I asked. "Do you know anything of magic?"

"No, well, not a great deal, other than who I can have quickly duplicate a design for my seamstresses, or perhaps fabricate a different pattern of cloth from a sorcerous design . . . but no, not very much, not really."

"When armies go to war," I explained, "each side generally has wizards casting spells to do harm to the other side."

"I knew *that*," he said, a bit indignantly. "I'm not a complete dunce."

"Each side also has wizards casting counterspells, to negate the others' thaumaturgy," I went on.

The tailor looked puzzled.

"What do you think would happen to your finery, of magical origins, when a counterspell intended to cut through all sorcery is cast at an army?"

Someone snickered, and the tailor understood, turned red, and began stammering apologies for taking up my most valuable time. I bowed them out before I gave in to my own laughter.

But the idea of an entire army, suddenly stripped naked in the middle of a battleground, still amuses.

* * *

The Latane River spiders through Nicias, but most of the branches are narrow enough to be bridged. Two are not—the major branch, which most river traffic uses, on the east, which is also where the Imperial Palace lies and where my former mansion, when I was with Marán, was; and one on the city's far west, along a peninsula almost a third of a league wide, a budding business district as the city has expanded.

We rode ferries across the Latane, formed up along the waterfront, and marched forth.

The parade was the strangest I've ever marched in, let alone led. Most parades are either held in peace or at the beginning or end of a war, not in its middle. Very few have an entire army participating, and that meant everyone, from cavalrymen to skirmishers to sutlers to blacksmiths to teamsters to camp followers, for we were leaving nothing behind us on the down. But mostly, I know of very few parades whose leaders were waiting to be attacked.

We were tatterdemalion and ragtag, with only a few of us in any sort of uniform, let alone a common one. Lasleigh, Baron Pilfern of Stowe's fifty cavalrymen were an exception in their green and black, although even their finery was trail worn and shabby.

We marched in formation, but most hadn't had much drill training, so the drums and trumpets may have been sounding one beat, but the marchers were holding to another. Around a million others, to be exact.

Some units marched well, some shambled. They say drill is the mark of a good soldier; yet the skirmishers, easily the most dangerous men in the army or anywhere else I could think of, were the worst of the lot, and the most disreputable looking, even if their clothes were clean, constantly hooting at a pretty woman or boy, asking for drink to be tossed them, and sometimes running out of ranks for a kiss, a drink, or a hasty bite of some viand, then marching on, chewing and laughing.

The crowds cheered, and the bands played, but here and there I saw men and women trying to appear uncaring. But when formations led by men like Jakuns, Jabish, Himchai, Ilkley, or other Tovieti came past, their fellows were hard-pressed to hold their calm.

I'm afraid I noticed too much and too little of the parade, constantly watching here and there, trying to tell if the scattered soldiery we passed were cheering us or waiting for the order to attack.

The parade went on and on, taking almost the entire day to wind west through the streets and across the bridges. Great riverboats waited at the city's end and took us across the river to the open land where our new quarters were.

Nothing had happened out of the ordinary, and I wondered if all these years of chicanery and intrigue had made me into a nervous twitch.

But I forgot about it and went to work setting up the new camp.

The next day, in the middle of more than a million men trying to establish their new homes, a courier came, and said the Grand Councilors were pleased to announce a banquet to personally honor General Damastes á Cimabue, to be held at my convenience. A note was appended in Scopas's handwriting:

Barthou and I are intending this as a small event that might give us a chance to discuss various interesting ideas, so it might be well if you'd only bring enough of

your staff to fulfill ceremony and provide sufficient
security. But let's plan on this in the very near future,
for obvious reasons.

"Now if it were me," Yonge announced, tossing the
note back across the field desk, "I'd bring two regiments of
infantry, and that'd be for the main course alone. I don't
trust these bastards."

"Nor do I," I agreed. "But what do they think the army
will do if they murder me?"

Yonge looked skeptical. "If you think that's what's
holding them back," he said, "you're being your usual
fool. Barthou and Scopas don't know soldiering from shitting and have no idea what the army will do.

"Not that you do, either. Look at what happened when
I killed Achim Baber Fergana. Do you think his army went
mad with fury, tore their hair, and attacked me, wailing
like frenzied loons? Hells no. They couldn't wait to say
how glad they were the rascal was dead, and they, and
their sons, and their sons' sons, and their sons of bitching
sons would be delighted to serve me until the hoolieth
generation.

"If you get yourself killed, most of these troops will
make whatever convenience they can. Some'll desert,
some'll do whatever their officers tell them, some'll try to
join the Peace Guardians or the Army of Numantia or
whatever they now call themselves.

"The only people you can absolutely depend on is us,
your immediate staff, plus morons like Svalbard who don't
know about self-preservation and other romantic fools."

"You've made my day full of cheer."

"Full of realism would be a better way to put it," Yonge
said. "But look, you really shouldn't have anything to

worry about. We have magicians who can see if there's any spells being laid, don't we? We have the Tovieti, who've got their fingers around the neck, I mean on the pulse, of Nicias, right? Including, I assume, some inside Barthou and Scopas's palace. Plus you have the Snake Who Never Sleeps, who's got to have friends among the warders and his usual worms wriggling about with their ears open, if worms have ears.

"Ask all of them if any plot's being plotted, and if no one can say yes, we can go off to dinner with a clear conscience."

"We?"

"Of course, we. I want to see if their food's better than the emperor's, and besides, who'd grudge a meal to the private secretary of the mighty General Damastes á Cimabue? You might need a hand with the dessert.

"Eh? There you have the fruits of my careful thinking. What have I missed?"

"Nothing," I said slowly. "Nothing at all."

There was no plot to be found. Sinait and Cymea agreed there was building menace to the south, but that was from Tenedos, as he made his laborious way toward Nicias. We must work matters out with the Council quickly, so we would be ready when he arrived.

I had Kutulu inquire about Trerice and their army, which was the least of my worries. Their forces were confined to camp, undergoing strenuous training, he told me, somewhat amusedly, so they'd not embarrass the Councilors as they'd done before.

So, although I had many more important things to do, I sent a note back, suggesting we assemble three nights hence.

✳   ✳   ✳

I decided to indulge my peacockry and chose tight boots that came to mid-thigh, made of fantastically tooled leathers of various shades, the predominant color black, a matching hat with a white plume dropping almost to my shoulders, complementing my carefully brushed hair, a silk lace blouse with a frothy scarf, both in white, red trousers that flared above the knee, and a black cloak with red silk lining.

Cymea also wore black—a clinging suit with flaring sleeves and pants legs and high collar. But this seemingly modest description doesn't allow for its wide buttons down the front that she only fastened from below her breasts to her waist. The buttons were ensorcelled and shone with spinning colors echoed in her disc earrings and necklace like a twisted silver rope.

"You'll note my nice, sensible shoes," she said.

"Sensible?" They glittered like silver mail.

"They're without heels," she explained. "Easy to run in."

"Ah."

Cymea wore a suede belt, and from it hung her sheathed wand and a needle-like shortsword.

"I've also got a dagger on the inside of my thigh, so be careful how you grope, sirrah."

I wasn't unarmed either, carrying Yonge's dagger hidden and my plain straight sword in plain sight. Concealed in a small pouch were two of the iron pigs I liked for throwing or hiding in my fist for a bone-shattering strike.

I'd decided to promote Svalbard to captain, and Yonge chose the same rank. Lasleigh's men were the only bodyguard I'd take, and while they wore their finest, they were also fully armed.

I saw Sinait and Linerges talking at length, guessed they were taking other precautions.

Suddenly the thought came—all this worry and scheming was absurd. If I had a brain, I'd simply find an excuse to cancel the banquet.

But since we'd checked everything imaginable, and it was important to get along with our allies, I decided to proceed.

The palace had gone through three name changes within the last twenty years: first the Rule of Ten's Palace; then, massively refurbished, it became the Imperial Palace. Now I noted it was called just the "Palace," which was either tired, realistic, or cynical, depending on what the speaker thought of the current regime's life expectancy.

There were few soldiers guarding the palace, no more than the required honor guard, which made me relax a bit more.

The palace's chamberlain said a meal had been set for my escort, and so Lasleigh and his fifty, some licking their lips at the thought of doing real damage to royal cuisine, were led away.

The rest of us were taken, with babbling escorts and bowing retainers, through the main entrance and announced with trumpets into a great room on the palace's second level. I knew this chamber well, for I'd suffered through many of Tenedos's banquets here, not interested in the overly rich food and bored cross-eyed with the endless speechmaking.

It was a long room, very high-ceilinged, with three swinging doors leading to the kitchens at the rear. Above, on a small balcony about fifteen feet overhead, was a small orchestra, already playing. The banquet room could be enlarged or made smaller with sliding walls. Tonight, it held just one long table toward the rear of the chamber near the kitchens. Around the room were heavy carts with punch bowls, brandy, and wine, and servants swarming around them.

The chamber was already full of the court retinue, all the noblemen in their finery. There was no more than a scattering of wives or consorts, but that was the unfortunate way of Numantia when the event was less social than business.

Barthou and Scopas weren't advertising their ignorance in military costuming this time, but wore nearly identical white robes dressed with red and gold, their breasts covered with flamboyant unknown and therefore meaningless decorations.

They greeted me effusively, were properly polite if a bit condescending to Cymea, and ignored Yonge. I looked about for Svalbard, but he'd vanished. I shrugged, thinking that he, clearly wiser than I, had chosen to go belowstairs with the other soldiery so he wouldn't have to suffer oratory with his beef.

I moved around the room, making small talk and being congratulated for "dealing with" King Bairan, although it was clear none of them had any knowledge of what a bloody business it had been, no doubt believing we met on the field of battle in sparkling armor and hewed mightily at each other until the better man won. If I survived the war, there'd be great paintings about the duel, none of which would suggest how filthy and smelly I was and how brutal the murder from a cloakroom had been.

I was amused to see noblemen blustering and cooing over Cymea. It would have been very funny if she'd suddenly draped a yellow silk cord about her neck and told them about her brethren.

After half an hour or so, we were escorted to our places by servants. I was seated between Barthou and Scopas, Cymea was down the table next to some fairly young baron, who appeared thrilled at his dinner companion, and Yonge was put, as befitted a secretary-aide, somewhere far away, well below the salt.

Naturally, the service was perfect, and the banquet began with a sparkling wine—I was mildly impressed that someone had been coached, and I was given mineral water instead—that accompanied dilled shrimp on cucumber. The next course was another wine and a wild mushroom soup I would've liked better if it hadn't had a float of a sweet-sour wine atop it.

We finished our soup, and the table was cleared. Barthou and Scopas were both making sure I was well entertained, filling my ears with the latest court chatter. I listened politely, not telling them I gave a thin rat's ass about who'd said what to whom and who was sleeping or not sleeping with whom. Most of the names were unfamiliar, anyway. For the past few years I'd been, as the phrase went, "out of town," and hardly following who'd found favor or been exiled by the Grand Councilors.

The wait for the next course grew long, then longer, and diners began looking at the kitchen doors curiously, then a bit angrily. A couple of thumps came from behind them, and I wondered what disaster was occurring, if a cook had gotten drunk and was crashing about, or if the next course had caught on fire, when the center door slammed open.

Domina Cofi stood there, in dress uniform with all his medals, holding naked sword high.

"Traitors! No one move! In the name of the Numantian Army, we who hold the heart of Numantia . . ."

His voice broke off. I was on my feet, sword halfway out.

Cofi's face paled, and the huge room was completely still.

"Guk!" was all that came as blood poured from his mouth. His fingers opened limply, and his sword clattered to the floor. About six inches of reddened steel stuck out the front of his chest.

Svalbard kicked the corpse off his sword, spun through the door, pulled the doors to behind him, and shoulder-blocked one of the serving carts against it.

"The Peace fuckers've attacked!" he shouted. "They've taken the palace!"

Barthou's eyes went wide, and he dashed to a window, peering out. He screeched peculiarly, turned, and there was an arrow through his throat and he sagged down.

Another kitchen door came open, and three soldiers burst through.

"No one move! You're all—"

I was across the room, spitted one, and slashed the other one down as the third gaped, then died under Svalbard's blade. Another drink cart went tumbling to block that door, but the third door was open, and ten or more men ran in.

I had time to glance out a window, down at the court-yard, and saw a roiling mass of fighting men, some in gray, some in the green of Lasleigh's men, others the gray of the Guardians. There were more of Trerice's men than mine, but they clearly hadn't been ready for my well-armed sol-diery and were falling back, Lasleigh pressing them hard.

But there was greater danger close. A man ran at me, was tripped by Cymea, and her short sword went into his back before he could get up. A bruiser almost the size of

Svalbard was grappling with Yonge, swords hilt to hilt, growling as if he were a bear. Yonge got one hand free, grabbed a crystal goblet from the table and shattered it into the brute's face. He screamed, stumbled back, face all blood, and Yonge killed him, went for another target.

The banquet room was an abattoir. A few noblemen were trying to fight back, either with their pathetic ceremonial shortswords or with weapons taken from corpses. More were trying to run anywhere, nowhere, or holding up their hands in surrender. No quarter was being given— I saw a man with his hands up, a woman sheltering behind him, and three soldiers killed them both.

No one had come through the main entrance yet, and I guessed Lasleigh's men in the courtyard were keeping that prong of Trerice's attack at bay.

"Come on," Yonge shouted. "Away from here!"

I reflexively glanced at the window, where my men were fighting and dying.

"Forget them!" Yonge bellowed. "They're doing what they're supposed to! Dying to keep you alive! Out of here, Cimabuan!"

For an instant I didn't know what to do, then remembered the palace's layout.

I yanked a long tablecloth off the table, and crystal and dishware smashed to the floor. I knotted one end of it, ran to just below the balcony, where the orchestra played numbly on, not knowing what else to do.

"Here!" I shouted, and tossed the cloth to the band's leader. He automatically caught it, thought better of involvement, started to drop it.

"Let go of that and I'll kill you!" I shouted, and he began nodding jerkily, holding it close as if it was his newest, dearest possession.

"Tie it to the railing!" He clumsily wrapped it around the railing twice, made a knot, and Yonge swarmed up it before it could pull free.

There were four men coming at me, and I went to one side, letting them block each other. I fought with one for an instant, dropped to my knee, and ran my blade into his thigh. He yelped, hopped away, and I came up into the guts of a second man, my sword burying itself to the hilt. He stumbled sideways and fell, pulling the sword from my hand. The third man drew back for a lash, I stepped into his guard, butted my head into his face, and Yonge's dagger was in my hand, and I cut his throat open. The fourth man jumped back to get fighting room, and Svalbard came in from behind and put his sword into the man's heart.

I pulled my sword out of the corpse, looked for another soldier, saw one struggling with Scopas. Scopas had his hands around the man's throat, strangling him. He may have been soft, but he'd been strong as a young man, and the soldier's face was purpling. The soldier brought both hands up, smashed Scopas's grip, and I was running toward him as the soldier pulled a knife and drove it into the Councilor's chest.

Scopas whimpered like a struck dog, clutched at the knife-handle, collapsed forward in stages, like a suddenly loosened puppet, fell dead, and I killed his murderer.

There were still a handful of soldiers in the room, but they seemed as confused as the nobility.

"Up here," Yonge shouted, and I saw Cymea clamber over the railing and ran across the room, sheathing my sword. Svalbard caught up with me as I began climbing, grabbed my leg, shoved hard, and I went straight up; Yonge caught my free hand and pulled me to safety.

A soldier was running toward Svalbard, sword back for

a cut, and I hurled one of my iron pigs into his face, and his skull smashed and he fell cross a chair.

Svalbard sheathed his sword, pulled himself up the cloth as far as he could, and somehow I muscled him up to the balcony. I had an instant to realize the musicians were still playing, intent on their sheet music, trying to ignore the bloody four amongst them.

"After me," I shouted, and ran to the back of the balcony, through the door, and down a long hall to the servants' area. The palace had been carefully constructed, so that the nobility would seldom have to see the servitors who made their lives not only comfortable but possible, and I hoped that would make our escape easier.

I knew its intricacies well because one concern, long years ago, was whether an assassin could creep in and attack the Emperor Tenedos, and so I'd spent some days wandering the maze with a chamberlain to keep me from getting lost.

We encountered only three soldiers, killed them handily, and wove toward a palace exit, only losing our way twice.

The closer we got to the exit, the more servants we ran into, some with crude weapons ready to fight Trerice's forces, not knowing their masters were dead; others wanting only to flee; still others in complete shock, wandering about, some numbly dusting the same place over and over, others carrying brooms, candles, vases of flowers.

I found the door I wanted, was about to go through it, when Svalbard pushed me back. He unlocked the door, booted it open, and jumped out.

"Clear," he said. "Come on."

We ran out into the late afternoon sunshine. Far along the wall, I saw a detachment of soldiers. They shouted at us to stop, but when we ran they didn't follow.

We came to a boulevard, with carriages and a scattering of soldiers on horseback.

"That one!" I pointed at a closed light carriage with a team of four, and Svalbard had the lead animal by the harness, and Yonge was swarming up to the postilion's seat, yanking the reins away.

I tore the carriage door open, saw a couple in a deep embrace, grabbed the man by his half-unfastened pants, and pulled him bodily out of the carriage. He made noises like a beached fish, and his nearly naked lady began screaming, no doubt thinking she was about to be attacked. Cymea had her by the arm and pulled her out. She stumbled on the doorsill, fell into my arms, and was dumped into the gutter in an ungentlemanly manner.

I jumped in as Yonge whipped the horses into a gallop, and Svalbard leapt onto the running board, and I dragged him inside.

Yonge drove the team hard around a corner, careening through a narrow alley onto another broad street, then slowed the carriage to a trot.

We went through the city toward the outskirts as though we were nothing more than a wealthy couple out for the air. Twice cavalry galloped past, but no one even glanced at the carriage.

I was afraid they'd have the bridges blockaded, but the revolt hadn't gotten that far yet. We abandoned the carriage at the docks and found a boatman to ferry us across the main tributary.

It was a momentary embarrassment that none of us except Svalbard had any gold to pay the man with.

Then we were at the camp's gates, and I shouted for a provost to call the alert.

I'd sold Trerice very short. Obviously he'd been very

aware of Barthou and Scopas's plottings and skillfully set a counterplot in motion.

All three of us, myself, Barthou, and Scopas, had been intended to die. No doubt he'd blame the deaths on some evil noblemen or such and broadcast the wonderful news that once again the Peace Guardians had saved Numantia.

Now he ruled Nicias, and he who held Nicias held Numantia.

I mourned, for a moment, for Lasleigh, Baron Pilfern of Stowe, and hoped he'd been lying about being a virgin and there was a bastard child somewhere to inherit his estates, and hoped Saionji would reward all of them with better lives when she judged them on the Wheel. But there wasn't time for anything more. Later, if peace came, we'd have proper sacrifices for him and his fifty who'd died doing their duty.

But the dead had to give way to the living. There were far more important matters to worry about.

Less than half a time later, things were very much worse.

We'd fortified our camp to prevent the Peace Guardians from attacking across the wide branch of the Latane, and saw Trerice's forces doing the same on their bank. They seized all watercraft up and down the river.

Kutulu's spies reported Trerice had taken over the broadsheets, and they were braying the obvious explanation for what had happened: A cabal of rural barons had plotted to overthrow the Grand Council and install themselves as Numantia's rulers.

This was a good choice of enemies—the ancient barons were mostly absent from Nicias, which always makes an enemy easier to despise; and they had a long tradition of considering themselves not only above the law, but able to write their own on their vast estates, which was fairly close to the truth for many.

The Peace Guardians—the Army of Numantia—had heard of the plot at the last minute and attacked the palace to save the Grand Councilors.

They'd been too late to save Barthou and Scopas, and only I'd escaped the barons. The army had taken terrible revenge against the plotters. Since their treason was obvious, no trials were necessary, and besides, the "righteous wrath of the army" had been aroused, and no prisoners were taken.

There was considerable wonderment about how I'd managed to escape the evil noblemen and why I'd fled Nicias, instead of joining Trerice's forces in restoring order.

A few days later, dark whispers began, and the broadsheets legitimized them slowly. I hadn't escaped; in fact I was the leader of the conspiracy, one of those country land barons myself, and had cravenly abandoned my co-conspirators for the safety of the ragtag rebels.

If it hadn't been for Trerice, a new despot would have taken over Nicias and Numantia, the truly evil Damastes á Cimabue, a monster whose crimes were manifold, from betraying his emperor to the Maisirians; murdering high officials in the Numantian Army, which I assumed meant my killing of Herne in my prison escape; and allying myself with the demon-worshiping Tovieti and the blackest of magicians so that I could seize power and then allow the murderous barons freedom to bring their iron heel down on the country. There was an omission we found interesting: any mention that Trerice, who'd now taken on the title of general of the army, had ever had anything to do with the Maisirian puppet government of Barthou and Scopas.

"Do they think the people of Numantia are complete fools?" I growled.

"That's exactly what they do think," Yonge agreed. "The Maisirians were yesterday, and since more than a few Nicians collaborated, the whole time should be not forgotten but rewritten to become palatable as quickly as possible.

"The swine on the streets will lap this swill up without gagging for even an instant."

"Don't be too sure," Cymea said. "You're a nobleman, Yonge, even if you come from the Hills, so you don't really know what the people think, not in your guts. Don't you think the Tovieti, for instance, will remember?"

"I don't think Trerice cares," Yonge said. "I'll wager he and his officers think the Tovieti are too small a group to worry about. With the 'peepul' behind him, what else does he need?"

"A great deal of luck," Linerges put in. "Because now he's got Tenedos to deal with. Which brings up a good question, Damastes. What are *we* going to do next?"

"I think," I said slowly, "I'm going to forget about Trerice for the moment. Leave him hiding in Nicias. I think we've got to turn south and prepare to meet Tenedos when he comes within range.

"He's by far the more deadly enemy. When we've beaten him, then we worry about Trerice."

"I don't like leaving that bastard in our rear," Linerges worried.

"He won't be," I said. "For we'll have no rear. We'll move as we paraded, taking everything and everyone with us. We'll guard our rear and flanks, assume that once we clear an area, it's the enemy's.

"We'll have to fight a new way, like partisans, and not

measure our success by the amount of land we hold. Our only goal must be the destruction of Tenedos and his army."

But it didn't happen that way.

Twelve days after the revolt, Sinait woke me at midnight. Her magicians had reported great spells being built, and the first had already manifested itself.

By dawn we could see the river near our camp was a frothing maelstrom, worse even than in the Time of Storms, although the sky was quite clear and a soft breeze blew. Nothing smaller than one of the great riverboats could have chanced the tossing waves and swirling currents, and even it would be hard-pressed.

Sinait used the Seeing Bowl and found the storm only roiled this one branch of the river. Elsewhere it was as calm as the skies above it, and the weather was clear. Then something struck at her out of the Bowl, something dark and deadly, and if her assistant hadn't overturned the copper vessel, she might have been killed. Clearly Tenedos had learned how to strike against snoopers, as the demon Thak had almost killed the two of us years ago.

I ordered Sinait to assemble her magicians, Cymea and her staff to help, and try to overcome this water spell, but if she couldn't, to accept it, and broadcast it to all branches of the Latane. Whatever was happening, and I had a fairly good idea what it was, if the river was storm blocked everywhere, we might be able to keep the worst away.

I sent skirmishers south on the fastest horses.

The camp was ready to march or stand off an attack. But nothing came, not mortal, except periodic battlespells of depression and fear, spells broken by Sinait's wizards without trouble.

The skirmishers trickled back late in the day and through the night. Some were wounded, some never returned, all were ragged and torn by hasty flight after coming in contact with far-ranging heavy cavalry patrols.

Their news was the blackest.

Tenedos had used his magic to make us think he was moving north far more slowly than in reality, backing it with small formations pretending to be larger ones, while his main force moved swiftly through the heart of the Delta toward Nicias.

We could do nothing but rage impotently while the ships and boats the Army of Numantia had seized went south to meet Tenedos and carried his army into the city.

The storm disappeared as it'd come after two days, and now our spies and Tovieti inside Nicias were able to report.

Trerice had struck a shameful bargain with Tenedos. He was now first tribune, my old imperial title, as well as general of the army of Nicias, and at his behest and that of "the great nation of Numantia," Laish Tenedos had agreed to form a provisional government.

The emperor's return to the throne was almost complete.

TWENTY-THREE

TENEDOS'S LAST OFFER

The irony was staggering. I'd schemed all this time to get within range of Tenedos and his army, and now he was less than a third of a league away. But neither one could attack the other without some change in the situation: to assault across water is fairly suicidal if you don't have vastly greater forces, surprise, or a foothold on the far shore.

The two options I had were distasteful and self-destructive.

One was to withdraw, hope to further build my forces, harry Tenedos and bring him to battle at another time in a more advantageous place. That wouldn't work, since he held the greater advantage, especially with the canard Trerice had spread about my treason. My soldiers would quickly grow discouraged and slip away or be cut down by sickness or combat until my defeat was foregone.

The other plan was to wait here to be attacked, for Tenedos couldn't ignore the running sore in his nation. But my army required massive supplies, and we'd quickly despoil the countryside. Then Tenedos would strike, probably with great magic in addition to physical force.

There *were* no options.

Therefore, I decided to attack.

I had a few ideas, and the first required my consultation with Sinait and Cymea. Could magic guide a boat on a river? Not very well, not very precisely, compared to a skilled man with oars and a rudder, was the answer. I worded my question more precisely and reminded Cymea of something we'd done, times past.

"Maybe," Cymea said.

"Definitely," Sinait said, more firmly. "You give me the material, far enough distant from the field so my spell has room to build, and we'll do it."

That was enough for me to assemble my advisers and lay out my plan.

"That's damned complicated," Linerges said. "Complicated plans mostly fail."

"True," I agreed. "Do you have a better one?"

He lapsed into thought, while we went on.

"My objection is, it's going to be bloody," Yonge said. "Especially for my skirmishers."

"My network, such as it is, within Nicias will be torn apart," Kutulu said. "And spies don't necessarily make good assassins."

"While a lot of my brothers and sisters can, and have killed, now you're wanting them to become soldiers without any training," Cymea said. "And once they're in the open, they'll have nowhere to run and nothing to do but die."

"You're all three right," I said unhappily. "At best, if it succeeds, it'll be a bloodbath. I like this not at all, because if we fail, it'll be the last chance Numantia has for a generation, probably more.

"You remember Tenedos told me he has plans to make

himself immortal. I don't know if that was braggadocio, but if he's discovered a way to live forever . . . our failure could cause an eternity of darkness, not only in Numantia, but across the world, for his lust for power has no limits."

"What cheerfulness," Yonge said. "At least we won't be alive to see that nightmare."

"If you believe in the gods, as I do," Sinait said, "then you're wrong, and we'll return from the Wheel again and again to live under Tenedos's lash."

"So there isn't any other option," Linerges said. "I can't see one, any more than Damastes. I say we try his plan. But I've an addition."

"Please," I said.

"Once again, you're not going to be part of anything until the final fighting begins."

I glared, and he looked back defiantly.

"This isn't another argument that I should be a studied, aloof general, keeping myself out of harm's way, is it?" I said. "Because if it is, I discard it out of hand."

"No," Linerges said. "You're being thickheaded, for now *is* the time for you to lead, to be clearly in the vanguard of battle. And by the way, I'll be staying here in this camp with you for a time, for exactly the same reason."

"Then why will I . . . we . . . be stewing in our tents, while everybody else is out there doing my bidding, taking all the risks?"

"Because," Linerges said, "Tenedos fears you more than anyone else, as he should. If you're here in this camp, working day and night on a tactic I'll suggest in a moment, and I'm working alongside you, then Tenedos will think the army is doing nothing but what he sees in front of him.

"Sinait's wizards will have less work with camouflaging spells if Tenedos is spending his hours peering at you and not even thinking about Yonge and the others."

This time, I didn't get even slightly angry, for Linerges was right.

"Then we do it?" I asked.

"We do it," Linerges said.

"And the gods help us all," Cymea said.

The truth of Linerges's statement came that night. I dreamed once more, as I had in that prison tower in Nicias, but again I wasn't dreaming, and the seer king stood before me. Cymea tossed uneasily beside me, as if in a nightmare, but didn't wake.

"Again I come to you," he said, and his face was more like a hawk about to swoop than ever before. "You have refused me twice, and there can be but one more time."

I managed, in my dream, to get out of bed.

"I can sustain this spell for only a few more seconds," Tenedos said, "for I've taken an unusual way to reach you, and your magicians will soon snap this slender thread.

"You are now my greatest enemy, Damastes á Cimabue. But you are nothing compared to the powers I now hold, less to the powers I gain daily, and I'll destroy you as a cleaning maid tosses a spider into the fire, without even thinking of it.

"But I choose to offer you mercy, a final mercy.

"If you arrange the surrender of your forces to me, immediately, I'll allow you to live. I'll also grant your life should you be unable to accomplish this, but manage to cross the Latane and give yourself up.

"Of course, there can be no place for you in my court, in my future greatness. You were offered a position before and refused it, and I can never forgive you for that further betrayal. But you'll be allowed a certain amount of money and be escorted to any border you choose and pass into exile.

"I give you my word I shall not pursue you, either with assassins or with magic.

"That is the only offer I am prepared to make."

"What about my soldiers? My officers?" I asked.

"I shall do with them as I wish," he said. "They will no longer be your charges, so you should not concern yourself with them. Some I may allow to serve me in some capacity under arms, others will have to expiate their crimes by serving Numantia in ways I see fit, still others must be punished for their crimes against me."

"I remember," I said slowly, "something you said, years ago and far away, when we encountered a bandit in the frozen Sulem Pass, and can think of no better reply to your kind offer: Fuck you, fuck the whore who called herself your mother, and fuck the father you never knew because he never paid." My voice was as controlled as Tenedos's had been on that long-ago day of ice and death.

Tenedos jolted as if I'd struck him.

"You insolent piece of shit," he said. "How *dare* you?"

I made no reply.

"Very well, Damastes. You've refused me a third time, and now I promise the death I shall give you will bring horror when it's told of a thousand years hence.

"I will not make any more threats, for you know my word is law, and what I say comes always to pass.

"Always!"

The tent was empty, and I was fully awake.

I drank some water and considered the arrogance of the man and realized he'd actually convinced himself by now that every statement he'd made had been realized, forgetting the disaster in Maisir or, closer to home, the lies he'd told me over the years.

The seer king, then the demon king, was now a complete madman.

It was up to me to see he did not become the lunatic king.

The choice was now perfectly clear: either Tenedos or Numantia was to be destroyed.

Surprisingly, I had no trouble falling back to sleep.

I was half-dreaming, and again remembered the prophecy at my birth: "The boy will ride the tiger for a time, and then the tiger will turn on him and savage him."

My mind dimly thought that had come true, and then the other words, of the bearded old man in the mountains, when we were retreating from Maisir, came—that my life would continue far longer than I then thought, and that a color came to him, the yellow of the Tovieti strangling cord.

That, too, had occurred.

So what came next?

Again I remembered the sorcerer's words my mother had repeated, that beyond the tiger were mists, and he could see, could foretell, no more.

Now would begin the Time of Mists.

At dawn, we set our plan in motion. Aides, not knowing what the mission would be, combed through the proven infantry regiments, taking one company from each regiment rather than the usual volunteers, for I needed unit cohesiveness. Most of my sappers were detailed off with these men, along with their tools.

Sinait had devised a subtle cover. A spell was cast around the camp, so any magician using a Seeing Bowl or its equivalent would see things dimly, as if water flowed between him and his target, not completely blocking all magical sight. The seer could make out fuzzy details, enough to keep him content, as if the blocking conjuration wasn't that well cast.

But the spell wasn't consistent, its power ebbing back and forth, like clouds scudding across the sky. It completely blocked, for instance, the detached soldiers as they made a forced march south for two days, long enough to clear them from the closely observed area around our camp. With them went Cymea and a team of her wizards, to maintain a rigidly cast spell to keep Tenedos or Gojjam from seeing them, hard at work in the Delta.

Wooded islands would be logged off, the logs crudely trimmed and dragged to the river's edge, ready for use.

The second part of my plan, the deception, was done in the camp. Work parties went out in all directions with saws, axes, and wagons. Straight trees were cut down, dragged back to camp, and carpenters set to, making great rafts clearly intended for a cross-river assault.

Sinait knew we were observed, for she "smelled" watchers. Tenedos must have been ecstatic that I would do something as stupid as attack him frontally. He would be readying his water spells, monsters, and storms, and Kutulu's spies reported troops moving to the peninsula across from us by night, preparing hidden positions they'd launch counterattacks from once we landed on their shore.

I spent many worthless hours with my staff, riding back and forth downriver from our camp, pretending I was scouting possible invasion routes. We picked some decent-appearing places where the land sloped gradually into the water, had the rafts dragged there, and I had some of my staff prepare a full-scale order. I doubt if any of the unseen watchers realized the officers detailed to this task weren't my best, but the inevitable paper shufflers any army accumulates around its headquarters.

Romances would be bored by all this careful preparation, but without preparation, war becomes nothing else than a barbaric gang-fight—not that it's much more at best.

I had a very sharp, not pleasant set-to with Jakuns, Himchai, and Jabish one evening in my tent.

"We're troubled," Jakuns said, without preamble, "about this plan of yours, or rather how it would involve us Tovieti."

I may have had serious doubts about my strategy, but I certainly wouldn't reveal my hesitations to anyone below my highest advisers. I waited patiently.

"I understand," he went on, "why you're keeping the exact details of your military moves against Tenedos close. We don't have a need to know such things."

"I disagree," Jabish said. "We have every right to know everything, since what you do, General, will not only involve us, but conceivably could cause the obliteration of our order."

"If the Tovieti are destroyed," I said, "so will my army be . . . and I myself will meet you on the Wheel."

"There are those," Himchai said, "who see a somewhat different possibility."

"Which is?" I asked.

"That we do as requested," he went on, "and rise up, as we did once before, under other, less wise leaders. That rising, as you well know, was disastrous to us, and it's taken all this time to regain even a part of our former power."

"What would happen," Jakuns said, "if we rise up, and Tenedos's magic and the Nician warders move against us?"

"They won't be able to," I said, "for we'll be attacking at the same time. They'll be too busy to do anything except be terrified, always looking over their shoulders for the dagger or the yellow cord."

"Suppose," Jakuns said, "for the sake of argument—"

Jabish snorted. Obviously whatever Jakuns was about to suggest she took as utter truth, not a theory. He gave her a harsh glance, spoke on.

"Suppose that the army is a little late in making its attack?" he said. "Suppose that the warders *do* have time to turn on us? What then?"

"Why would we be late . . . although I can't deny that could happen, and we've got to give some latitude to the operation? There's never been a battle that went as planned."

"Suppose," Jabish said, "that your plans are just as Jakuns suggests? Except that you *deliberately* want to hold back for hours or a couple of days to give Tenedos a chance to destroy us?

"Wouldn't it simplify matters for you and for your brothers in nobility after the war if there are no more Tovieti? If there aren't any of us still alive to make you keep your promises about a new day, a day with justice for everyone?"

Now I understood why they'd come. I could have gotten angry, but chose not to.

"Jabish, I'd suggest you ask around about my reputation. I could say that I'm too honorable for that, but I know you believe honor is impossible for anyone in my position. So ask another question of some of the men who have served with me before.

"I'm not that subtle a beast. If I want someone dead, I'm more likely to challenge them to a duel than to put poison in their chalice."

Jabish looked disbelieving, but I saw a trace of a smile on Jakuns's face. Himchai looked, as always, sourly thoughtful.

"But a still better argument just came," I went on. "You reminded me of the Tovieti rising what, fifteen, seventeen years ago? The Emperor Tenedos and I swore we'd obliterated your order then. We'd killed your highest leaders during the rising, destroyed the demon Thak, and then winkled the hidden Tovieti out of every part of society, tried and executed them. Don't get angry, Jabish. That's what happened, and the past is beyond changing.

"I'm not bragging about that. My point is," and I spoke measuredly, hammering each home, "there still are Tovieti! You're strong once more, you've got soldiers in the open serving well with me, your agents are a big part of the skein I'm weaving about Tenedos, your magic and your magicians are used and appreciated. If I wanted you destroyed, why did I ask, back when we paraded through Nicias, for your members to not show wild enthusiasm, for fear of being exposed to the warders or the Peace Guardians? Wouldn't it have been simpler to ask that you all wave flags with your serpents' nest on it, so you'd be ready targets?

"If Tenedos and I couldn't destroy your order seventeen years ago, why should I have the arrogance to think I could now?"

I started to go on, but stopped, poured myself a glass of water, and drained it.

Jabish had her lips pursed, but Himchai was nodding slowly, ponderously.

"There's only one more thing," I said. "If you don't do anything now, if you stand aside from this final battle, what do you think Numantia's gratitude will be, when the war is won, when Tenedos is brought down? A pogrom such as we held years ago is terrible. But it's far worse when the people themselves savage their own.

"You've seen that happen, you've seen what ruin the masses can bring to everyone. How many of your best-laid plans, back then, were ruined because the people lost control, went mad with bloodlust, and all dissolved into chaos?

"And if Tenedos wins? What then? I can tell you truly that he has a terrible fear of your order. He knows you exist, knows you're fighting with me. If he's victorious, don't you think he'll wreak terrible revenge on you, just as he will on me and everyone else who's standing against him?

"I'm sorry. This is one time you can't stay in your hiding places and ride things out."

My argument hadn't been that organized or coherent, I knew. Finally I had brains enough to shut up.

The three looked at each other. I couldn't tell how they signaled their decision, but Jakuns was the first to speak.

"We'll follow your orders," he said.

"Yes," was all Himchai said.

Jabish looked at me harshly, her lips thin. She and I would never be friends.

"We'll fight," she said. "But don't think for a moment of betrayal."

She stalked out of the tent, and the other two followed. Jakuns looked back, shrugged in what might have been slight apology, then the flap fell closed.

The last thing I needed was dissent this close to battle. I gritted my teeth, then started to consider the map I'd been studying.

Not five minutes later, Svalbard tapped at the tent pole.

"Yes?"

"Kutulu to see you."

What now?

"Send him in."

The slight man entered.

"You handled the matter with the Tovieti well."

"You heard?"

"Of course."

"All right," I said, somewhat amused. "How do you eavesdrop in a tent that's got Svalbard in front, damn all in the way of furniture to hide behind, plus half a dozen other sentries all around it making it impossible to approach secretively. Magic?"

"I'm not a wizard," Kutulu said, frowning.

"But you have your methods?"

He nodded, saw me smiling, and his lips bent a little.

"I'm glad you approve of what I did," I said. "Hopefully, the problem is solved, and we can continue worrying about the real enemy. Is there anything else?"

"I was wondering if it would improve the situation if that woman Jabish had an accident."

"Fatal?"

"I can't think of anything else that'd stop her trouble-making."

"It's tempting," I admitted. "But no."

"You're sure."

"I'm sure." I chose my tone carefully, for I didn't want to offend the Snake Who Never Sleeps. "That way is Tenedos's way. Not mine."

Kutulu half rose, then sat back down. His face was even paler than before. He bobbed his head.

"I'm sorry," he said. "You're right to reprove me. I wasn't thinking."

"My friend," I said gently. "I wasn't reproaching you, just reminding you of how I work."

Again a touch of a smile came, and he rose.

"Thank you, Damastes. I, uh, I chose the right man to follow."

Before I could respond, he scurried out. I shook my head. A very strange man, one none of us really knew.

I went back to the map and its simple lines, curves, and colors.

The phony rafts were going together well, and word came from upriver that the logging was also on schedule. More soldiers went south to join them, this time with just their arms, and Linerges and Ilkley went with them, together with a lot of our Tovieti warriors. They'd be the first to see action, and I hoped this would convince Jakuns and the others that I had no intention of deliberately sacrificing the Tovieti.

I also arrived at an emergency plan, a terrible last resort that would be far bloodier than what I'd already foreseen. Then I prayed I would never have to use it.

Command of the camp went to Chuvash, and I set the hour for the battle to begin, the battle that must end the war.

TWENTY-FOUR

ACROSS THE LATANE

A battle always starts at night, even when the actual
fighting doesn't.

First are the sappers, those seldom-honored
laborer-soldiers who make the fortifications, build the
bridges, lay out the roads and then, as frequently as not,
die fighting on them.

I could imagine every part of this battlefield, although it
was far scattered.

Dusk . . .

*Far upriver, the sappers labored, heaving the huge logs
into the river, mooring them to the banks in long lines.*

The wizards, too, haven't slept, craftily building their
spells to unloose at the right moment.

Full dark . . .

*The magicians, here and upriver, cast spells of confusion,
of fear, panic, and doubt. My few master sorcerers attempted
to summon insects and vermin to the enemy lines, although
this is seldom successful.*

Other spells had been cast earlier, spells against rain, so
the Latane's current was very slow, and the river itself low,

even lower than normal at the beginning of the Time of Heat.

There are others who didn't sleep—those who'd been told off for the first wave; those who were about to enter their first battle; and, though they never admit it, their commanders, who pretend calm, confidence.

The assault troops upriver, Yonge's skirmishers and the chosen infantrymen, waded into the water, and pulled themselves onto the logs or tied themselves to a branch, and the sappers pushed the logs out to be taken downriver, toward Nicias, by the current.

I'd become a master of faking it, of lying still and breathing deeply, appearing completely at ease, assured of victory. A few times I'd even deceived myself and had to be wakened at the proper hour.

Not this time, with everything riding on the matter and the battle plan itself ridiculously complex. Without Cymea, who would be among the first to go into action, there wasn't much point in lying sleepless in my tent.

I went there for a couple of hours around midnight, but then returned to the command tent.

One of Kutulu's spies, just across the river from us, in the heart of the enemy's lines, moved past a guard post, around a warehouse, then out on a small dock. He slid down a rope into a small canoe and cast loose. He dipped his paddle slowly, careful to never make a splash, and let the river take him across. He met the challenge of one of my vedettes, was hurried to my headquarters. There was no sign Tenedos had found us out, and the army was on only quarter-alert.

Someone once said there's never been a battle plan that survived the first spear cast, when all deteriorates into confusion, with only the poor foot soldier perhaps knowing what's going on, his task no more than killing the man who stands against him, and then another and another until there's no one left to slaughter or he himself welters in his gore.

The discs Sinait had used to show me Tenedos, back when we were building the army, had been improved. She'd found sometimes a picture could be made out, but more often the magician who carried it might be able to talk into it, and his words understood by all others with the mirrors. The problem would be not only hoping this spell would survive Tenedos's magicians, but that everyone didn't babble at the same time.

The logs were roiled downstream, soldiers clinging to them just as Cymea and I'd lashed our boat to a great log. Here and there, someone slipped off, or a log rolled and men were flung into the water, some managing to swim ashore, others being pulled under, men whose bravery had bade them make foolish claims about their water talents.

But the logs rushed on, hundreds of them, with fifteen or more men on each log.

That afternoon Sinait had a pavilion pitched near the river, just behind a hill to hide her actions from the enemy, and then began digging with a small, ensorcelled trowel. She could have been a somewhat oversize child at play, making tiny ditches for toy boats.

But this was hardly play.

When she'd finished sculpting the mud, she went to the Latane with her guards and ceremoniously filled a bucket, emptied it again, while chanting, then filled other buckets and poured them into the little ditches.

Now, deep in the night, braziers were lit and her magicians began chanting, and strange smells and sparks grew. The muddy water in her ditch appeared to begin flowing, as if it was part of a river with an invisible headwaters and mouth. I blinked, seeing the ground blur and change, until it was a perfect model of the Latane.

Sinait continued chanting, more loudly, still in a language I knew not, went to one end of her ditch, and opened a sack. From it she took minuscule splinters, barely visible to the eye, and carefully set them in the water. These were fragments cut from the logs now carrying soldiers toward Nicias.

The camp around me was silent, dark, but the men in their tents were awake, waiting, arms at hand. When the assault wave secured the peninsula, and the boats the Army of Numantia had assembled, they'd cross as reinforcements, and the battle for Nicias proper would begin.

The current took the bits of wood, washed them very slowly down toward the other end of the ditch.

Now we'd see whether her spell would take, whether she would, as promised, be able to guide these logs down the Latane into the branch on the other side of the peninsula across from us.

Amazingly, the splinters did just that, sliding into the proper channel.

Her chant changed, and they began drifting toward the banks and grounding.

I rode back to the command tent, dismounted, and listened. Nothing for long moments. Had my troops run into some kind of trap and been cut down in awful silence? Then I faintly heard bugles and, across the water, saw torches flare as Tenedos's troops came awake.

Svalbard came out of the tent.

"Sir. The wizards say we're getting something from those mirrors."

I hurried inside. One of Sinait's magicians held up his disc, which was now blank.

"We had them for just a moment, sir. No picture, but a scatter of words. I think it was Angara, who was supposed to be with the lead elements. She said, and I'm repeating exactly, 'ashore . . . by surprise . . . guards . . .' then it cut off."

Another magician yelped. There was a swirling flash on his mirror, then it steadied, and I saw a building in flames, running figures outlined by the fire, and a man's calm voice: "second wing skirmishers ashore, a hundred yards short of where we were supposed to be, but no problem. No enemy waiting, all of our soldiers landed successfully, now moving—"

His words cut off. Three, then four other sorcerers were reporting, and it appeared we'd landed successfully, Tenedos and the Army of Numantia caught in complete surprise.

Yet another bowl lit, and this one showed nothing for a long moment. "Sir," a magician said, "this is one of the ones we gave the Tovieti."

A woman's voice suddenly came: "We're moving into the main streets now. We fired Drumceat's palace, he's definitely dead. We hold Chercherin firm. So far, no response from the dog-emperor's warders. Please hurry with your soldiers."

I told Chuvash to get the troops assembled and sent a message to Sinait congratulating her, telling her to return to headquarters and begin the next stage of the wizard's battle.

Both riverbanks were alive with light as my troops left their tents and moved toward the rafts, and Tenedos's troops swarmed to their fighting positions to repel us.

If all continued well, Tenedos would think the landing on the peninsula was just a feint and pay little heed to it, concentrating on the main thrust to come from over here, where most of the army was concentrated.

But I didn't plan to send them across until the peninsula was secured and there'd be little danger of Tenedos's water magic striking them.

A prickling came, and a wind whispered, then whined, and the Latane grew choppy, and I grinned. Tenedos's magic was at work, keeping us from mounting our invasion. He *had* been fooled.

Now all I could do was pray the assault troops would take the peninsula, start sending the boats across for us while others assaulted across the bridge and established a foothold on the far side. Then the rest of us would ferry across to the peninsula and attack into the city.

An elaborate plan, but one that appeared to be working.

Then things went awry.

A garbled message: "holding strong . . . reinforced bridge . . . can't . . ."

Minutes later, another: "storage yard . . . they've fired . . . both . . . holding . . . building . . . third attack driven back . . . sending in . . ."

At the river, the chop and wind were building. I scanned the far bank, saw movement, away from the river, toward the other side of the peninsula. Tenedos clearly felt his magic controlled the water, and was moving soldiers to the other side of the peninsula to attack my landing force.

Another mirror flashed, its message very clear: "Tenedos's soldiers still hold the bridge, and are attacking across it in strength. We'll mount a counterattack with—"

The message stopped, and the mirror stayed dark.

I grabbed a magician, told him to get down to the pavilion and have Sinait and the others cast a counterspell against the weather magic on the Latane.

It appeared my worst-case plan might have to be set in motion.

Another garbled message came:

"holding . . . they're holding . . . for the love of Irisu, come help us! Linerges cut off, and . . . Come help—"

The voice broke off, and we got a picture. A woman's dead face, eyes glaring, mouth gaping, flashed for an instant, vanished.

Now I had no other option.

"Chuvash!"

"Sir!"

I gave the order I'd been afraid of.

"Get the rafts ready. We're going across."

Now my bluff would have to be played for real. It took half an hour to drag the rafts into the water, and troops clambered aboard, clumsy as the waves pulled at them.

All of the discs had gone dead. Either their enervating spells had run out of energy, or Tenedos had discovered and silenced them.

I'd gone farther upstream, with a special detail of men and women taken from my handful of experienced river boatmen I'd had standing by, and twenty archers chosen from the Seventeenth Ureyan Lancers. If I were to die now, and the odds were excellent, I'd do it with the soldiery I began serving with. I had a bow across my back and two full quivers at my belt.

We were clambering aboard a clumsy river flatboat whose stern was piled with tough rope, which was firmly lashed to other, stronger rope, rope capable of towing a ship, hundreds of yards of it, nearby on the shore.

Chuvash came. "Sir, you can't be thinking of—"

"I'm not thinking, I'm doing," I said. "Take command

of the army and bring them across as best you can, when you can."

He stood helplessly gaping, then was pushed aside as someone rushed me out of the predawn blackness. A dagger was raised, and I had a moment to react, step into the attack, snap up a blocking arm, and then my attacker was knocked sprawling by Svalbard.

The person still held the dagger, and Svalbard's boot came down on her wrist, and I realized it was a woman as she shouted in pain.

The big man dragged her up, and I saw it was Jabish.

"You bastard! You fughpig!" she sobbed. "It's just as I thought . . . you're letting us die, gods damn you! Tenedos has his warders out with soldiers in the city, and they're killing my people . . . killing all of them!"

I thought of explaining, saying my whole gods-damned *army* was dying, but I didn't have the time.

"Chuvash, take her back to the camp, and get her into restraints! We need no more lunatics about on a night like this. Svalbard! Get your ass aboard, and thanks." Then, to the men:

"Push off, and row hard. Let's go get into some trouble over there."

The river pulled at the boat, and we were bobbing, almost sideways, the line unreeling to our stern, dragging at us. The night was wind and spume, and I cursed the gods or perhaps prayed as I felt the storm getting stronger. Sinait's counterspells hadn't taken, and Tenedos would drown me, here in this swirling madness, and at that moment the wind died, although the waves still reared and foamed.

"Row harder," I bellowed, and the men obeyed as the current pulled, trying to tear us downstream to the sea.

There were fires ahead, closer, getting larger, and I could see the far bank. A man beside me coughed apologetically and went down with an arrow in his lungs.

A bow thwacked, and an archer said, satisfaction in his voice, "Got the fucker," and I heard shouts as the enemy saw us.

The boat slammed into the shallows, almost sending me overside, and men tumbled off and pulled heavy mooring lines ashore, found pilings, a beached fishing boat to tie them to. Other men began pulling in the line across the river, and the work got harder and harder as that heavy rope on the other side was dragged into the water toward us.

Men choked, dropped, and other men ran up the bank and drove back a ragged line of attackers, came back and pulled on.

Svalbard and I went on line with the archers. More of Tenedos's men rushed, and we drove them back, and I sent men forward to take the corpses' weapons.

I heard a shout: "We have it!" and saw the end of the cable being dragged out of the river, like some huge snake or worm. It was run up to the bank, looped around a statue of some god I'd never seen before, and the boatmen lashed it firm.

Behind me, across the river, those rafts intended for a deception were being put to use, pushed out, using that rope to help them across, keep them from being swept away. But no more than three or four of the rafts could use the rope at a time, and that sparingly, for fear of snapping it.

More soldiers charged, and others tried to flank us, and we drove some back, forced others to duck for cover. The night was fading, but fire still seared red across the black as the warehouses around us burned, and we choked on the boiling smoke.

My plan was a shambles now, and I should have stayed at my command post and tried to keep what order I could. But I could send no man to die without going there myself.

So I crouched, arrow nocked, stood and whipped an arrow away when I saw a target, ducked as a spear clattered across cobbles toward me, took a blow on my mail as a slung stone bounced off the ground and struck me.

There was cheering, and a raft came out of darkness, and dawn was here, and men were streaming off it, up the bank, and another raft was behind it, coming close. I swore—they were coming too fast, in spite of my orders.

That raft landed its men, and another, and we had two companies' strength on the bank.

I saw a man wearing a captain's sash, didn't know him, told him he was in charge of the beachhead and to get some of those empty rafts back across for more men, and he nodded understanding.

We couldn't hold here, had to move, and I shouted for the charge, slinging my bow. We went forward, running, and we were on the enemy positions, and swords were clanging, thudding into unprotected flesh, men screaming, swearing, dying. A man swung with a flail, and I ducked and slashed his arm to the bone, and there was another one, coming in with a spear. He knew what he was doing, had its butt back, under his arm, and was attacking with short jabs. I parried, parried again, and he struck long, almost getting me in the stomach. I spun, let him go past, slammed him in the face with the pommel of my sword, and then Tenedos's men were retreating.

"Come on! After them!" and there was a soldier pulling at me.

"Sir! The rope's broken!"

I almost slumped in defeat, but couldn't give up. I snarled something at him, ran after my soldiers, into the heart of the enemy. Very well, we were doomed now, but we surely didn't have to admit it.

At least the soldiers we were facing weren't those faceless killers Tenedos had created from innocent civilians. At least, not yet.

Ahead was a knot of officers and warrants, and they had a moment to realize we were their enemies, and we were on them, killing, and running on, leaving a trail of our own wounded, dead, as we went.

Then there was no enemy around, and we were in the middle of the peninsula, among burning, deserted buildings. I pelted to the front of the ragged, panting soldiers.

"To the bridge," I bellowed, and white eyes glared, understanding seeped through, and they followed me toward the shouting and death.

We rounded a corner, saw the lines of Tenedos's men. Barrels, crates, bales of cloth had made barricades here, and others—my soldiers—were across a square.

Soldiers turned, hearing us, thinking we were reinforcements, had seconds to realize who we were before we were among them, hewing, killing, always moving, for if we stopped for an instant we'd be dead, although we were clearly in Saionji's palm, her talons closing about us, less than two hundred men against a thousand, maybe more.

I heard a cheer, and a long ululating call, and men, my men, attacked from behind their hasty ramparts across the square, and all became madness.

Then there was no one else to kill, and I saw Yonge.

"Eh, Cimabuan," he panted. "Your great plan isn't as impressive here as it was on the other side of the river."

"No shit," I replied. "So what do you want to do?"

He shrugged. "Leave a dozen men to hold here, and go back to the bridge. I assume these other fools aren't all there is."

"You assume wrong." I told him of the rafts, and of the line breaking.

"Not good," he said. "But I still think we can have some pleasure as we die."

"All officers, warrants, forward," I shouted.

Three legates, one wounded captain, and a handful of warrants came.

"Form up," I shouted. "With your mates if you still have any."

Yonge glowered. "We're wasting time."

"Shut up," I advised. "This is why bandits like you lose, being sloppy and undisciplined and shit like that. Number off by tens!"

The men obeyed, raggedly.

"All right," I shouted. "Those are your new squads. The man in front's in charge. Back the way you came to the bridge! Don't wait for the order! We'll charge them as soon as we get there!"

Somehow, lungs burning, I managed a dogtrot, and we went down a narrow, curving lane.

"There's a boulevard one street over," Yonge said. "Nice and wide and dangerous. This'll come out in the same place, right at the bridge approach."

A shattered shop was ahead, on a corner, and there was water beyond it. We came into the open, saw more improvised barriers around the bridge, with uniformed men, some uniformed as Peace Guardians, some as motley as we were, Tenedos's men, and we charged.

Archers rose, and spattered shafts, one whispering down my side, and men spun, died, and we fell back.

"Again, gods dammit! We'll break them this time!"

We ran onto the killing ground, not many of us, maybe 150 all told, and once more they drove us back.

This time we left a guard, fell farther back into the alley to regroup. I marveled I hadn't been wounded, then winked at blood trickling down my forehead, and felt a throbbing pain in my thigh. The wound on my head was superficial, the one on my thigh from a blow or perhaps I'd slammed into something. Nothing to worry about.

"What now?" Yonge asked, sounding amused. He was tying up a slashed arm with a torn shirt and had lacerations down one bare leg.

"We do it again," I said grimly.

"You should learn a new way of war than charging down someone's throat," he said. "A man can die that way.

"Sendraka got killed doing that, a couple of hours ago," he added, and heaved a deep breath.

"Get ready!" he shouted, and we heard other shouts, and hurried back to the end of the alley.

Men were pouring down the boulevard from behind us toward Tenedos's position, men by the hundreds, my gods-damned men, coming from nowhere, somehow they'd crossed the river and we shouted with them and charged, and this time we overran the bridgehead.

"Don't stop!" I shouted. "Secure the other side," and officers and warrants recognized me, echoed my command, and we ran onto the bridge, into an arrow storm, men falling on either side, and there was a gray-clad archer in front of me, in middraw, arrow aimed at my chest, eyes widening in panic, and he dropped his weapon as he loosed the string, arrow flipping end over end above me, and my sword was in his throat, letting loose of it as his mate tried to spear me, got Yonge's wedding dagger in his guts.

I pulled the sword free and fought on. Svalbard was dueling three men, and I took one of them off him, and he killed one, then the last before I could recover.

Soldiers streamed past, in a solid wave, and then I saw Kutulu, for the love of Isa, long dagger in each hand, eyes mad as any of us, and I had him by the shoulder.

"What happened! Where'd you and the others come from? I thought the frigging rope went!"

"It did," he said. "But one of the rafts saw it go, and followed it, pulled it on board, and then let themselves be swung toward the other side like a boy on a line! I don't know if anybody used magic to help it.

"Now there's other lines across the river, and the army's coming across, and nothing can stop us!"

"Us? What the hell are you doing here, anyway?" I said.

Kutulu grinned, a wide, happy smile, I think the first time I'd seen him ever look so ecstatic.

"The time for spies is over. I can finally be a soldier!"

He ran after the others.

I saw Linerges limping toward me, flanked by his officers, and then, running toward me, was Cymea. Her wand was in one hand, bloodstained sword in the other.

We were in each other's arms for an instant.

"Gods, but I'm glad you're alive," I managed. "I don't know what I would have done—"

"Quiet," she said hastily. "I don't either. But I love you." She pulled away.

"We've broken through," Linerges said. "Your plan worked."

"Badly," I said. "Bloodily."

"What else is war?" he said.

I looked at the spray of bodies around the bridge's ramparts, so thickly piled I couldn't see the cobblestones they lay on, and shuddered.

Linerges nodded.

"Bad. But now the real slaughter begins," he said. "Now it's time for Tenedos to face the sword."

TWENTY-FIVE

THE FINAL BATTLE

We didn't give Tenedos time to recover, but immediately assaulted across the bridge. With a foothold, other attack teams went down the peninsula and captured other bridges and attacked across them.

The battle became a meat grinder, slow, day by day. I'd send a unit into battle, and hours or days later, a few survivors would shamble out. Now I was no longer Damastes the Fair, or Damastes the Brave, but Damastes the Butcher.

With this scatter of men, I'd reform the unit, using them as cadre, and fill the ranks with the recruits that streamed to our camp, eager for a taste of war. I doubt if many relished that taste once it was swallowed, nor the emetic dose of blood and horror that followed.

Tovieti came to us, and I changed my policy, letting them fight together, with only a few veterans to try to teach them enough to stay alive for the first decisive hours.

A soldier in those terrible days had only two fates: to be killed or wounded. Mostly they went down within their first few hours of combat, but enough survived to become tough veterans who killed without qualms, without mercy, without malice.

The least happy men in my army were the cavalry, for there was no room to maneuver in the rubble-strewn streets, and so I dismounted them and turned them into infantry, their horses stabled behind the lines.

Neither side took many prisoners, not after we saw what the former Peace Guardians did to anyone they captured and, later, deeper into the city, to our Tovieti brethren.

A human soldier of Tenedos might have a very slight chance of survival in our hands. But Tenedos's magical creations, even though we knew they were men, women, children in reality, never surrendered; nor did we make any attempts to capture them. We let them fight to the death.

These clockwork warriors were improving in their fighting ability as the battle went on. They still weren't able to stand up to an experienced soldier, but they were far better than the recruits I shoveled into the front lines. They never seemed to tire, hunger, or need rest.

Sinait tried to create a spell that would break the magic that created them, but without success.

As for Nicias's warders, we saw how they'd kept the city's peace the first time we smelled the stink coming from Tovieti households. Everyone, not just the fighters, had been killed, no doubt under Tenedos's direct orders, and the warders had been creative in the way they slew.

I waited until some warders had surrendered, then turned them over to Tovieti formations and told them to do what they liked. Anyone who believes the enemy is the only one who can torture with imagination has never been in a war. I was disgusted with my allies, with myself for allowing it. But word spread, and after that, we found fewer butchered women and children in houses with the upside-down U symbol.

I expected Tenedos to attack with Great Spells, for certainly the streets of Nicias were drenched with enough blood for Saionji to be cackling in joy, but nothing came. What spells he and his Corps of Wizards sent were mostly turned aside by our wizards.

"You see," Yonge said. "This proves Truth and Right are on our side, and surely Goodness always triumphs. Heh. Heh."

Linerges and I stared, all three of us as shabby as any of our soldiers, then, for the first time in days, found raucous laughter.

The fighting was grim, made worse because each little engagement was much like the previous as we fought from building to building, block to block, street to street. Scouts would dart forward, find an enemy strongpoint. Sometimes . . . not often, but sometimes . . . it was possible to use magic to drive the enemy out, but normally they had to be winkled out by men willing to die, knowing their epitaph— "killed while assaulting the four-story white apartment building at the crossing of Ker and Mamin Streets"— would be their only memorial, unlikely ever to become the subject of a ballad.

My soldiers grew cunning as the battle ground on. Instead of attacking frontally, they'd go to the roofs and rain down spears, arrows, roofbeams, cobbles. Or else they'd go through the walls with battering rams and burst in behind their foes.

The people of Nicias cowered in their basements, in their rooms, surrendered when they could. But mistakes were made, and sometimes an archer would loose at a sound, and a child would go down screaming, a child who'd been running to him for protection.

All of us were stumbling, drained, and men began making mistakes, standing up in a position they knew within range of enemy archers, lighting a fire for cooking at night, running into the open for a better shot, the careless errors of the completely exhausted.

I saw Cymea from time to time, generally when each of us was on the way to another emergency.

I'd brought my headquarters across the river, moving it as we advanced, staying very close to the lines. I had my tent pitched wherever there was room, every now and again getting a chance for a quick wash or an hour's rest, and sometimes she'd be there asleep, and I'd try not to disturb her. Twice we met when awake, and both times made fierce, angry love, reaffirming we were alive and there might be something beyond this death-in-life called war.

We fought by day and night, night combat the most eerie, for Nicias's famed gas still burnt, but sometimes now through cracks in the pavement or setting unexpected fire to a building no one was near.

We fought not just with a soldier's normal weapons, but with fire, putting a building full of stubborn defenders to the torch, filling flasks with cooking oil and stuffing a rag in its mouth, firing the rag and hurling the flaming jar into an enemy position. In low-lying districts the sappers pumped river water into basements still held by the enemy. Or we used earth, entombing entire positions without wasting a man's life entering them.

We'd had no time to build siege engines, but we found some in a storeyard. That gave us a few mangonels and ballistae that cut down our casualties. Others came from an army museum. These had been chosen as much for their beauty in carving and decoration, but once we replaced the leather ties, the ropes, and rotten wood, they worked as efficiently as their stark, younger relatives.

Building by building, street by street, block by block, we fought our way toward the heart of the city.

But by the near-end of the Time of Heat, we still held only a third of Nicias. My army had been decimated, and Tenedos's men fought as stubbornly as before. We hadn't been able to surround the city, and so they were still getting supplies from the north and east.

I needed a master stroke, and remembered a legend.

The troops had been alerted for a general attack and given tiny ensorcelled bits of wood that would become torches when rubbed and three words said over them by anyone. They were warned to expect the unusual, and not panic, not give up hope. I wished I could have put a wizard with each company, to reassure the men, but all magicians would be busy, some casting the counterspell to keep Tenedos from discovering our plan, the rest creating the master spell.

A day before the spell began, thirty-nine—thirteen times three—magicians had begun chanting, over and over again:

"Jacini, Varum,
Listen
And give forth
Shahriya, retreat
Give up
The domain is lost
The domain is lost
For a time
Give up

And ye shall regain
Give up
Your domain
Is not below
Submit
Turn away
Turn away
Kanaltah hwah doy
. . .
Jacini, Varum,
Listen . . ."

On and on, over and over, in a drone that grew louder, though none of the chanters raised their voices; nor did anyone or anything visible add to their ranks.

On the ninth hour, braziers were lit around a multi-circle, strangely lettered figure drawn in black sand, and acolytes fed tiny amounts of herbs into them, dried aloe, barberry, blue vervain, storksbill, anise, comfrey, quaking aspen, others. The braziers fumed and smoked, as if unwilling to burn.

Nine hours after that, as it was growing dark, Sinait, flanked by Cymea and another powerful wizard, all three wearing blue robes in honor of Varum, god of water, each with her own brazier, began their own chant:

"Varum, Jacini
Take the lesser god
Take the lesser god
Take the lesser god
Give him not his name
For a time
For a time

For a time
H'lai vatha p'rek
H'lai
H'lai
Hold him close
Deny his freedom
Deny his birthright
R'wen al' gaf
For a time
For a time
For a debt."

The two drones mingled, wove together, almost musical.

The three wizards' chant grew louder, burying the others. Acolytes handed each of the three a bowl of salt, a bowl of water, a tiny bundle of green wood.

Sinait made measured motions with her twigs, the other two followed with their bowls. At a signal, all three cast water, salt, and green wood onto the braziers. The smoldering fires flared out, and all the other braziers were extinguished at the same moment.

Total silence, total darkness, an anticlimax.

Then, from our lines and from the city, a wailing began, a moaning of complete despair.

The gas fires of Nicias, the fires that had given it the name of City of Lights, were out.

Then the screams began, for legends said if the gods-given flames of Nicias ever went out, Numantia was doomed.

Now all was dark, all was terror, all was hopelessness.

Officers, warrants, most as fearful as any, roared for the torches to be lit, and fire flickered up and down our lines.

I shouted to a squad of buglers, and brass railed against

the night, and my troops went forward. At first they moved slowly, reluctantly, then stronger, faster, as long-held positions fell, their enemies stumbling out, hands high, eyes glaring in panic.

The first wave swept forward as ordered, bypassing resistance. The second and third waves closed with these strong points, mopping up.

We moved far and fast, and I had no alternative but to commit my reserves, and still the advance continued. I sent gallopers to pull the dismounted cavalry out of the lines and march them back to their stables. Now we were fighting in clear streets, unruined buildings, and there was room for the horsemen to fight in.

Suddenly the blackness became gray and I could see, and I sagged, my voice no more than a croak.

But this was triumph. We held more than half of Nicias, and the defenders had pulled back into a tight circle around the center of the city, the palaces of power, the barracks, and the Imperial Palace itself that Tenedos fought from.

Then their lines firmed, and we were stopped cold.

I ordered the offensive halted, and for our lines to be stabilized.

Svalbard brought tea, a hunk of bread, and a large piece of cheese that wasn't too dusty.

I saw Sinait and Cymea hurrying toward me, faces worried, afraid. I drained the tea, cast the food aside, fatigue gone.

"There's a spell being mounted," Sinait said. "A big one. A very big one."

I knew what that spell must be, the greatest of all spells ever cast in Numantia, the same spell Tenedos had indebted his kingdom to learn.

This was the spell to summon the monstrous black

demon that had destroyed Chardin Sher and his castle, the terror Tenedos had later almost loosed on the Maisirians and then on Nicias, the spell I'd broken by clubbing down Tenedos.

Just now Tenedos would be striking a bargain with this demon, a bargain of blood and death. The last time the deal had been struck, millions of Numantians, more Maisirians, had died in payment.

What would be the demon's price this time?

And how far, how long, would Tenedos let the horror rave?

There was only one way to possibly stop the demon.

I expected argument from Linerges about haring off once more, but got none. He looked at me strangely, said something about the long bond being broken, said he'd make a feint wherever I wished to cover me.

Sinait said she should go, but I refused. She'd created and trained my wizards, and I thought she was still a slightly greater sorcerer than Cymea. With great magic being imminent, I wanted Sinait with the army, able to instantly react to whatever happened.

I took Cymea aside, told her what I intended.

"Good," she said. "I would have been angry if you'd gone without me. What are our chances?"

"Perhaps seventy-thirty we'll reach the Palace, forty-sixty we'll be able to get inside, and from there, Saionji holds the dice."

"What a noble speech," she said. "Makes me want to rush right out and die for somebody. I'm getting Jakuns. We've got even more of a score to settle with Tenedos than you."

"No," I said flatly. "In that, you're wrong."

I looked around for Svalbard, saw him coming toward me with Yonge.

"If we're going after Tenedos," the big man said, "I thought Yonge should be along."

Again, there was no argument. Yonge had been with me from the beginning, back in Kait, with the Seer Tenedos.

"Ten of your best skirmishers," I said, and Yonge nodded.

I washed, made sure my sword, my dagger were sharp and easy in their sheaths, took a plate one of my gallopers had loaded from a mess line, gobbled hastily. All I took was my weapons and a canteen. If we were gone more than a day, we would have failed.

Yonge came back with ten men. "I've created a corps of fools," he said proudly. "Every one of these idiots wanted to come, even though I didn't tell them what was up, but only they'd certainly die in the attempt."

The men grinned good-naturedly.

I had Cymea cast a Square of Silence spell, told them the mission. One of the skirmishers spat.

"'At's a good 'un," he growled. "About time t' send that fuckin' demon back to whatever hells he come from.

"Get this fuckin' war over with, so we can go back to tryin' t' live like people again."

We were about to move out when Kutulu trotted up.

"I hear you've business on the other side of the lines."

"How'd you hear that?"

"Don't worry," he failed to explain. "No one else knows but me. And I know the best way to reach the Imperial Palace."

"You've got as much right as anyone to come with us," I said. "Not that I think there's anything other than rope that'd hold you back."

"No," he said seriously, "no, this is repayment of a debt I incurred a very long time ago."

He actually laughed, beaming once more like a child at a birthing-day celebration.

I told Linerges where I wanted the attack mounted after Kutulu showed me on a map his route, which was, indeed, most practical.

Then we set forth to kill the demon king.

Passing through the still-fragmented lines was easy. We made our way east, past piled bodies, burning buildings, and grimy warriors to the Latane River, to the branch that ran down to the Imperial Palace.

We found a boat basin, with half a hundred craft still moored, and I chose a good-sized one, some sort of work boat with a small cabin that looked terribly ramshackle but wouldn't sink too quickly.

We boarded, cast loose, and let the river take us downstream, turning slowly, aimlessly, as if there was no one aboard, no one at the rudder.

The banks of this waterway had been a favorite riding place of mine years ago, under spreading trees and bushes, a parklike strand that ran through Nicias's government district.

It'd been long without maintenance, and trees had been cut down here and there for firewood and other purposes. Bodies, human, animal, floated downstream, lay on the banks, and all about us in the heat was the stink of death.

I could feel the building darkness, oppression, as one feels a thunderstorm before it breaks.

We bumped past a downed bridge that marked our front lines, drifted on into enemy territory as the river widened.

Minutes later, bugles sounded from behind us, and Linerges mounted the covering attack not far distant from where we'd crossed the lines.

I peered out of the cabin, saw the rearing battlements of the Imperial Palace ahead.

I was about to go over the side with two other men and push the boat toward the bank, but Cymea shook her head and moved her wand in peculiar fashion, whispering as she did. The current spun us once more, leisurely, then we drifted into a knot of brush and were trapped, very naturally, very innocently.

No one was watching, and we went over the side in a rush into the water, waded to the shore and crawled up it. A sixth of a league away was the Imperial Palace.

Those who design gardens for palaces, especially those intended for troubled times, are in an interesting trap. The lord who hired them generally wants his fortress to be beautiful, ringed with parks, walks, and genteel surroundings. Yet for every tree planted, every topiary sculpted, every rock garden built, the lord and his underlings' danger grows, for each can give cover to an enemy.

So it was with the Imperial Palace, and I remember well, in the old days, soldiers muttering at how many patrols were required, simply because the emperor wanted beautiful gardens. For an instant, I remembered one of these gardens, a secluded place where Marán, Amiel, and I'd first made love, then cursed my mind for behaving like a drunken monkey.

The sixteen of us slid across the ground silently, like fog moving through trees. There were guards, but we bypassed them, the palace's roofs and blank, staring windows closer and closer.

There were only five or six guards, the identically faced

homunculi, on the bridge across the moat. Drop them without raising the alarm and minutes later, we'd be inside.

The doom feeling was growing stronger, closer. Tenedos must have begun his spell. Now, if Irisu would give us a few more minutes . . .

But he didn't. Or perhaps he wished to, but Saionji begged a boon, laughing in glee, anticipating the tide of souls who'd be coming to her, coming to the Wheel.

Thunder whiplashed twice, though there wasn't a cloud to be seen, and the ground rumbled as if in an earthquake.

Across the Latane, beyond the city, a dark form materialized. It grew and grew until it was taller than the highest building in Nicias, and again thunder lashed as its features took on form, horrible V-mouth open, fangs dripping venom. Four arms extended, and the demon looked up at the skies as it had done before, but more terrible now, for this was day, not storm-tossed night, and bayed defiance to the gods and triumph at being reborn.

Then it glided forward, toward the city, and one of the skirmishers whimpered, and I had to force control, for I wanted to pray, run screaming, or even worship the dark horror to save my soul from its embrace.

But I pushed weakness away, and shouted, "Come on," and half, then all the skirmishers were rushing the palace as the demon came across the Latane.

One guard tore his gaze away from the nightmare, saw us, and shouted a warning.

Then we were on them, and the guards went down, and we ran across the bridge, through open gates into a courtyard.

"Up here," I pointed, toward where Tenedos's private apartments had been when he was emperor, just as twenty or more guards, more of Tenedos's monstrosities, stormed out of the doorway toward us, paying no mind to the stalking doom beyond, good soldiers doing their duty to death.

"We'll hold them here," Yonge said, and I nodded. "On them," he called, charging forward.

"Follow me," I shouted, and Cymea, Jakuns, Kutulu, Svalbard, and I went up the long flight. We rounded a landing, a servitor came toward me, clumsily waving a long two-handed sword, and I clubbed him aside with my sword pommel and pushed him over the railing.

We pelted down a long corridor, to more stairs, started up them. I heard a shrill cry, saw Cymea go down. Something bounced away from her body, and I never saw whoever had loosed the sling, and my heart snapped, and I had to go to her.

But I couldn't, couldn't hold her in her dying moments, if she even still lived, and ran on, the last of life dying within me as I raged, wanting only to drag Tenedos down into death with me, for everything now had come to an end.

We came to a barred door, and Svalbard put his shoulder to it, but rage gave me power beyond any man's, and the panels smashed aside under my boot heel.

We were in the open now, a bridge across a courtyard far below, Yonge and his men still holding back the homunculi, the palace gardens, and Nicias beyond. We slid to a halt, as the monster came ashore, and I heard the sough of his breathing even at this distance, if breathing it was.

He smashed his fist, backhand, in an idle blow, and the huge Ministry of War building broke apart as if it was made of a child's blocks, and the demon roared savage glee, and glass around us shattered.

The demon's foot lashed out, smashing buildings along the waterfront, perhaps one the mansion Marán and I had shared.

The horror screamed its joy; then its howl stopped.

Another apparition was building, to the west, within Nicias. Brown mists swirled, became solid, and a warrior was born. It was a woman, wearing brown armor and helm, with a red shield. She was armed with a stabbing spear. I knew the face, and it was that of Seer Devra Sinait.

Fearlessly the figure advanced on the demon, although it was only two-thirds its size, and the nightmare roared and closed. He swept out with his arms, and the spear flashed, and the demon screeched agony, and ichor poured from its arm. Again the spear darted, but this time the monster brushed it aside and struck with a taloned claw, past the warrior's shield, and the warrior stumbled back, something reddish, like watered blood, floating through the air.

Again the warrior struck, this time to the body of the demon, and again he howled in pain. But as he did, he had the spear in two hands, yanking it, and the warrior, toward him, then the demon had her by the neck, pulling her toward those terrible fangs.

The warrior screamed as the creature tore her throat open, convulsed. The demon lifted her body, and hurled it from him, baying like a lion over his prey, and I knew, far away across the city, Seer Devra Sinait had died, trying to save her country.

I broke from my daze and ran to the doors at the end of the bridge, Jakuns beside me, and jerked the door open. An arrow flashed, took him in the stomach, and he fell, writhing, lay silent, and now there were only three of us, as Kutulu threw one of the iron pigs he, too, favored into the archer's face, stabbed him in the guts as he went down, and we ran up a long, curving ramp, and there were high doors at its end.

On the other side would be the imperial apartments, elaborate, lavish, and I slammed the doors open, and they boomed as loud as the screaming of the demon as he ravened through Nicias.

The rooms were different, had changed. The walls were warped, twisted, as if seen in a distorted mirror, furniture bent in strange ways, as if it'd melted.

The air itself swam, as if through heat distortion.

"Welcome," Tenedos's voice came softly. "Welcome to death, Damastes."

He stood before me, not as I'd seen him recently, but young, vibrant, clad in the armor of twenty years ago, a sword in his hand.

"Your man will not bother us," he said, and I heard a sigh and Svalbard crumpled beside me. Kutulu stood on the other side, motionless, paralyzed.

"I'm hardly a romantic," he said. "But I wanted the pleasure of killing you myself, in the flesh. My magic is committed to helping my friend finish the task I should have had him do years ago, when I was still emperor.

"To destroy Nicias, so that I can rebuild it, and its people, in the form and image I desire.

"Yes, yes indeed.

"This is the end, Damastes, the end for you, but my cord, the line of *my* life runs on forever now."

I broke his spell, jump-lunged, and my sword cut nothingness, and Tenedos was standing five feet to the side. He flicked a lunge, I parried it, felt steel against my blade, felt an instant of hope this wasn't an apparition, but was real, and could be hurt, could be killed.

"Now my empire will be eternal, as shall I," he mocked. "There is no hope of stopping that, no way of denying me my true destiny.

"Once I worshiped Saionji, but then I learned I could be greater than she, for who has sent more souls to the Wheel than I? What are gods, but demons who've managed to be worshiped and taken great strength from that adulation?

"Isn't it true that all of those we call gods, Umar, Irisu, Saionji, the others, were once men who became demons and then gods?

"Now I'll be one with them, greater than they, for I know what I want, know that everything that exists is one, and all that matters is power, for with power you control fire, water, earth, air, war, even love.

"Now come, Damastes," he said, relish in his tones. "Come and try to save your world from me."

I paced toward him, and his image flickered, and four of him stood in front of me, as if I were looking in mirrors.

He thrust, and Kutulu came alive, diving forward, taking the thrust and the blade flickered in, out of his body, and the slight man fell, lay motionless.

Tenedos looked down at his corpse, curled a lip.

"A better warder than warrior," he said. "And in the end, no more than an unfaithful servant, punished as he deserved.

"Now, Damastes, fight us . . . fight me, for which of us is real, which is illusion?" he mocked. I lunged at one, he jumped aside, and I felt pain in my side, saw steel flick away.

"A pinprick," he mocked, and I lunged at one Tenedos, sidestepped and slashed at another. Again one of the images cut at me, and I parried, felt steel, struck quickly in a stop-thrust, and the point of my sword drew blood across the image's forearm.

"Good," Tenedos gritted. "I forgot what a swordsman you are. So let me give myself greater advantage."

Again the images flickered, and now there were nine.

"Unfair, Damastes? Why don't you complain? Say something. Pray, call to your gods if you wish. Perhaps they'll intercede."

He laughed, and his laughter echoed, then stopped suddenly.

"Enough playing," he said impatiently. "Enough jesting. My creation calls for guidance on what to destroy, and I have no more time for you.

"Fare thee well, Damastes á Cimabue. Go to your doom and hope Saionji grants you another life before I am ready to conquer her kingdom as well."

His eyes slitted, and he was about to lunge.

I back-leaped, and his concentration was broken.

"You don't die easily," he said, and shuffled toward me, the careful stepping of a trained fencer.

His muscles tensed, and then, from behind me, a woman's voice came:

"Lyrn, dav, maheel, nast
F'ren, lenp aswara ast
G'let!
Now, Damastes! Strike now!"

The room around me changed, was suddenly just a room, the swirling air stilled, and there was only one figure in front of me.

For a moment he didn't realize what had happened, then I cut at him and he pulled back, shouting in pain as blood crimsoned his side.

Tenedos struck as I recovered, hit nothing but air, and

I lunged, my sword going into his shoulder. He ducked then, swung his blade at my legs, and his sword tip nicked at me below the knee.

He came up, driving hard in a full lunge, but I wasn't there, but to his side, hard in my own thrust, and it took him in his side, opposite his heart, and my blade came out half a span on his other side.

His body contorted, his face turned to me, wizened in pain, hatred, and fear, and he opened his mouth to curse me, but nothing came, and he sagged.

I pulled my sword out, and he fell.

I heard a scream, but more than a scream, a howl of defeat, of the very fabric of this world being torn, and the ground shook under my feet. Or perhaps my mind told me that was what should happen when the greatest of all wizards dies.

Tenedos lay on his side, completely still, but I was not sure, kicked him over on his back, drew Yonge's dagger and drove it up under his rib cage, into his heart.

His eyes were empty, gone, but I remembered how he'd been reported dead once. Without his head, there could be no doubts.

But the air thickened around me before I could strike, and I heard the whirring of wings, and I stepped back.

I'm not sure I believe in gods anymore, at least not in the form we worship them in.

But what I saw was very real. Hanging in the air, for just a moment, was a woman's face and shoulders, hair wild and uncombed, eyes glaring in abandon. I couldn't see her bare breasts, but she wore a necklace, a necklace of skulls.

Perhaps it was a hallucination, perhaps not.

Then Saionji's image vanished.

The body of Laish Tenedos lay motionless. This time I knew he was gone, that there would be no returning, and I need take no further precautions.

I saw Cymea crouched in the doorway. She got up slowly, rubbing her stomach.

"That gods-damned rock knocked the wind out of me. It took a while to get my breath back."

Before she finished I was holding her, wanting to crush her close, but forcing gentleness, cautious of bruised ribs, feeling life come back to me.

I held her, listening. The city was almost silent outside. The awful destruction, the smashing and roar of the demon was gone.

The creature must have vanished when his master died, when he realized the bargain he'd struck would never be fulfilled. I hope Tenedos's death destroyed him as well, but know not what rules the lives of demons.

Cymea said she could stand, and so I knelt over Svalbard. His eyes opened slowly, then snapped wide, and he rolled to his feet, grabbing for the sword beside him. Then he saw Tenedos's body.

"Oh," was all he said and sheathed his blade.

I looked at Kutulu's body. The strange smile he'd carried in the last days was still on his face. I hope it was there because Saionji had granted him the gift of knowing his onetime master had finally met doom.

Cymea and I walked outside, onto the bridge. Below us, in the courtyard, three men in motley attire, my skirmishers, rested on their swords, the other men I'd brought lying dead or wounded around them. The monstrous guards they'd fought had vanished, and there were bodies of men, women, children scattered on the paving stones. Another of Tenedos's evils had vanished with his death.

One of the men was Yonge. He saw me, shouted up.

"Cimabuan! I think it is over!"

It *was* over.

The blood-drenched reign of the seer king, the demon king, was finally ended.

TWENTY-SIX

PERHAPS A BEGINNING

B ut nothing ever ends neatly, except in the romances.
Most of Tenedos's army surrendered or just
fled, discarding their uniforms as they did, trying to
submerge themselves back into the people. There were still
some stubborn soldiers who fought on, and they had to be
winkled out and slain.

Gojjam, Tenedos's wizard, was never seen again, and we
have hopes he died with his master or was taken by the
demon.

Trerice hid for some days, then tried to flee by night,
although where he planned to go is unknown. He made it
to one of the ferry landings on the Latane, hoping to take
a boat across the next day. Probably he discarded his uniform for some disguise.

But someone recognized him, for when the sun came
up, his body was sprawled on the bathing steps, naked except for the yellow silk cord that had strangled him.

As for the rest of us:

We implored Linerges to stay on as general of the
armies, but he refused, saying his shops needed him, and
he needed his wife, Gulana, and so the quiet man who'd

served his country well gave it up and went back to the country town he'd come from.

Sinait had, indeed, died fighting the demon, and great were her funeral ceremonies, and the pyre could be seen for leagues around, and long will her memory be celebrated.

There was another, sadder funeral, for Kutulu, the Snake Who Never Slept. The pyre was small, and the ceremony held in a small death ground not far from the palace. In contrast to the thousands at Sinait's funeral there were, besides a priest, only four people present: Cymea, myself, and Bridei dKeu, a beautiful, if a trifle vapid society woman who'd an affair with Kutulu that lasted for perhaps a night, perhaps longer. No one knows.

The last mourner was a rather plain woman, simply dressed, neither rich nor poor, her age impossible to tell. She stood to one side while the priest chanted, face still and calm. She remained until the pyre's last ember burnt out, then left, without speaking to anyone. Who she was—wife, lover, sister, possibly even mother to Kutulu—no one knows, and so the little man took his last mystery with him to the Wheel.

Cymea and I will be wed within the month, and she swears she's pregnant and has decided the babe will be named Devra if it's a girl; or, as I promised myself years ago, Athelny if it's a boy, after the commander of my Red Lancers who died so bravely in Maisir.

There are other problems, though.

My country is in ruins. Numantia has known little but death and ruin since Tenedos and I came back from Kait. It'll take a generation or longer for the torn land to come back, and even then there will be whole districts barren and empty.

At least we finally have peace, and there are seed and

water, and the seers predict a mild winter and gentle spring.

Numantia *will* recover.

Cymea and other wizards managed to reignite Nicias's gas supply, so once again it's the City of Lights, Numantia still exists, so another legend goes down into the dust.

There are great problems.

The first is the Tovieti. No one knows what they'll do, whether they'll remain above ground and help put their country back together in return for a share in the power; or slip away, back into darkness, back into murder and robbery, back into the old thinking that only they deserve to rule, and there can be no compromise.

But even that isn't the most pressing issue.

The worst dilemma is Numantia's government.

Simply, there is none, and nothing presents itself.

No one wants to return to the vacillations of the Rule of Ten or the corruption of the Grand Council.

Perhaps each town, each city, each state, should nominate worthy leaders, men, and why not women as well, commoners as well as noblemen, who could somehow remain responsible to the people who chose them to rule and not become bloody tyrants.

I don't know how such a government might be formed, nor does anyone else, not even the Tovieti.

There appears to be one popular choice:

To name me as king of Numantia.

I shudder at the thought, at the idea. I've seen what happens to men when they take the throne, when gold circles their brow.

There are worse things than the vacillating, incompetent Rule of Ten.

There's the oppression of monarchs, the evil they willingly fall, leap joyously into.

I remember King Bairan of Maisir and how little he cared for his people, both great and small. I remember how he permitted the Dalriada, nothing more than the slavery of women under a fancy name. I remember how he ordered me to murder my friend and servant, Karjan, a man who'd done him no wrong, merely to test a spell, other obscene crimes his predecessors wreaked on the people of Maisir.

I remember Laish Tenedos, once my closest friend, a man who wished to rule wisely and well, a man I served proudly. How long did it take for him to change, or did he actually change at all? Was his benevolence before I crowned him a pretense, and the mad demon within always within? Was that what drove him to the throne, instead of letting him become a quiet, prosperous island sorcerer?

I can't believe I was a complete fool to believe in him, nor that everyone around me was equally taken in. But still . . .

No. I cannot be a king.

Who, then, *will* rule my beloved Numantia?

Who'll be willing to try to solve our many problems?

These big problems are obvious, but there're others that grate at me. Lynton Barda, if she lives, is still a whore, and her family, who served the country well, still in poverty's depths. The bandits on the roads, but also the wandering men, some ex-soldiers, looking for they know not what; villagers like Gunett and her people, although they're far more fortunate than some I remember, having at least a good leader.

What of all these people who have come into my mind, as clearly, sharply as if I'd just left their company, people I knew years ago, people I saw this day, people I knew well, strangers glimpsed in passing? Who shall rule them?

I remember my family motto:

We Hold True.

But no one has the right to ask me to wear the crown. I've given enough to my country. All I want is to be left alone, perhaps in Cimabue, perhaps in Nicias, perhaps as a rover, a wandering Negaret, across the border in Maisir. Cymea had said she'd like such a life.

Late this afternoon, Yonge came and said a delegation of the highest surviving noblemen of Numantia had assembled in Nicias.

Tomorrow, he said, they will call on me and insist I be crowned king.

Yonge thinks it's very funny.

I talked until midnight with Cymea, then let her go to bed and came, alone, to this great chapel in the palace, where kings and other rulers of Numantia beyond memory have prayed to the gods.

I, too, have prayed.

But no answer has come, not from Irisu, not from Saionji, not from Cimabue's wise monkey god Vachan, not from my family's own godling, Tanis.

The dark reaches of the chapel send back only the rustling of my clothes, my breath, my footsteps as I pace back and forth.

And the question remains:

What now, Damastes á Cimabue?

THE SEER KING

Chris Bunch

An epic fantasy tale of empire, power
and magic begins.

Numantia is a dying empire, the frontier ruled by
outlaws, the provinces by rebels, the citizens by
discontent. Ancient forces of dark magic grow
everywhere, ignored by the Empire's rulers. For
two people it is a time of immense possibility
and infinite danger.

Hotheaded young cavalry officer Damastes and the
wizard Tenedos were supposed to die in a mountain
ambush. But their enemies underestimated the amazing
powers of the seer and the bravery of the soldier. And
the friendship that forms between them will
change history itself.

As Tenedos and Damastes begin to outwit usurpers and
necromancers, word spreads that theirs is a path of
destiny. For Damastes, it will lead to glory, and the
love of a beautiful, troubled countess. For Tenedos, it
points to unimaginable heights of ambition. And for
Numantia, it shows the way to a renaissance . . . in
service to the Goddess of Death.

'Slam-bang excitement, lusty action and military
magic . . . fast-paced and ferocious'
JULIAN MAY

**Look out for THE DEMON KING,
the second book in this magnificent fantasy series**

Available from Orbit

THE EMPIRE STONE
Chris Bunch

A new fantasy epic from the author of
THE SEER KING, THE DEMON KING and
THE WARRIOR KING.

According to legend, the Empire Stone was larger than
a fist and could light a man's path in the dark of the
moon. Fashioned by gods – or maybe demons – it
could give power and riches to anyone who held it. But
it was lost when the city of Thyone was destroyed, and
now its secrets lay buried in the past.

The Year of the Eagle has begun badly for Peirol of the
Moorlands. He'd fallen in with Koosh Begee and his
gang of tricksters. He'd fallen to gambling. And he'd
lost. Heavily in debt to Begee, Peirol is forced to
travel to the ruined city of Thyone on a
perilous mission . . .

And so begins an incredible adventure, full of danger,
mystery and magic, which will take Peirol across
oceans and kingdoms in search of his destiny.